beginnings

a Blood Angel novel
by Nina Soden

This is a work of fiction. All of the characters, organizations, businesses, and events portrayed in this novel are either products of the author's imagination or are used fictitiously.

ISBN: 978-0-9858853-1-1 (paperback)

http://www.ninasoden.wordpress.com

Editors: Ula Manzo, PhD., and Nicole Smith

Front Cover Design by: Julie Csizmadia

DEDICATION

For my beautiful children, Sydney and Ethan, who inspire and amaze me every day.

ACKNOWLEDGEMENTS

I want to acknowledge my wonderful friends and family who never let me give up. Your encouragement throughout this process and your constant love and support have been a true gift. Thank you for reading and re-reading my multiple drafts with smiles on your faces, and encouragement in your constructive criticism. I appreciate your kindness, generosity, creativity, and honest feedback. I could not have completed this book without each of you. Thank you, thank you, thank you: Nicole Smith, Clara Tapaninen, Britney Malone, Gena Rawdon, Kim Holmes, and of course Ula Manzo my patient and wonderful editor.

A special thank you to Ula Manzo, for your excellent, sometimes frustrating, yet thorough proofreading and editing skills. I hope to work with you again in the future.

1

The blaring alarm could have raised the dead, but Alee didn't even flinch. It was the pounding on her bedroom door that finally jolted her back to life. "Aleerah, wake up. You have to leave in twenty minutes." It was her mother. It wasn't the mother she had known and loved all her life—no, this was the mother she had never even known to be in existence until a few weeks ago—until the man she had always called Daddy—the man she had known as her father—died—suddenly—and way too early in life.

She rolled over, turned off the alarm, and struggled out of bed. *What to wear?* It was the first day of school, and Alee was once again the new girl. The new girl in her senior year at the school she had attended the previous year. Something about that just didn't seem right. She had already reinvented herself once. Why should she have to do it again? Oh yeah, because her life had been turned upside down. She was now the actual birth daughter of a vampire and a witch, who were happy to have her back in the family. Besides that, everyone she had ever known in her life thought she was dead—had, in fact, attended her funeral. Yeah, that's as good a reason as any.

Kyle and Alee had gone over the plan a thousand times with her new—real—parents, Eric and Loraline, in these past two weeks, but Alee still wasn't sure if she was going to be able to pull it off. Pretending not to know anyone was going to be hard, but keeping herself from running up to her best friend Dani, and telling her everything, and apologizing for lying to her—*that* was going to be the real test. Alee would see Kyle every day, and it was going to suck not being a couple at school, but at least she knew that would change in a few weeks. They just had to play the game, making everyone believe their relationship was just beginning. It might even be fun to play the role of a brand new couple in a fun new relationship: flirting, passing notes and having their first date all over again—especially since they never really had a "first date."

The bathroom was thick with steam, and yet the air was cold on her exposed skin as she stepped out of the shower wrapped in a plush warm towel. Her bathroom was huge, with marble countertops, a glass sink, and a natural stone floor and shower. Her closet door was just to the left of her shower, and inside was a wardrobe that made the local department store she was used to shopping in look like a thrift shop. After the dad who had raised her died, there was a large bank account left to her in the will. Since she was also supposedly dead, the money went to the beneficiary, Edith Wenham. Apparently, the Wenhams had been paying her parents to take care of her since she was just a baby. Being the stubborn people her parents had been, they had refused to keep the money. Instead, they had put it into an account for Alee. Even in the event that Alee didn't live long enough to use the money herself, they didn't want to have anything to do with it. They didn't want to take charity from "witches." Now it was Alee's, and she was having fun.

Her new life was going to take some getting used to, not that she minded this part of it. Not entirely anyway.

Her new parents hadn't had time to put together all of the paperwork for her new life. Everything had just happened too quickly. They had promised, though, to have a driver's license for her within the month. Without a license, or even a car to call her own anymore, Alee would have to ride to school with her cousin Phoebe. Phoebe had just gotten her driver's license a few months before, but drove as if she had been driving for years. Phoebe sped around corners without even pretending to brake, while Alee gripped the edges of her seat and just concentrated on breathing without throwing up, rather than looking out the windows at the view.

"Take it easy, I know what I'm doing." Phoebe's lips curled up in a wicked smirk and the fact that she was looking at Alee, instead of at the car they were quickly gaining on, didn't really put Alee's mind at ease.

Alee just nodded, gripping the edge of the seat even tighter, "Yeah—I can tell. Just get me there without killing me—please."

Phoebe just laughed, but after one more quick right turn she slowed to a crawl. Atlanta High School was just ahead on the right, and she pulled into the parking lot and eased up to the walking path that led to the main entrance to let Alee out.

"You're not parking?"

"Nah, you have new student orientation—I have another hour before I have to be in class. But don't worry, I'll be back. You made me miss coffee this morning having to be here so early." She started to drive off as Alee was shutting the door, but then only five feet up slammed on the breaks causing the tires to squeal as they came to a stop. Phoebe lowered the window and yelled after Alee, who had already started up the path. "Hey, Aleerah, you want any?"

This was the first really nice thing Phoebe had done since Alee had arrived at The Black Onyx a few weeks ago. "Really?"

"Sure." Phoebe nodded, "I mean, we're cousins right? I guess that means we're on the same side—kind of like—friends."

"Yeah—thanks—just a—." No point finishing, since Phoebe was already driving away.

Phoebe called back, "I know how you like it. No worries—go have fun with the new kids. Don't forget to play nice." She was out of the parking lot and around the corner so fast it was almost as if she had never been there.

Alee stood there on the curb looking out at the sad, barren parking lot, took a deep breath, and then turned toward the admissions building.

Looking around the main office Alee realized just how strange this year was starting out to be. She had been in the school office lots of times over the past two years, and even a few times during her sophomore year when her parents had home schooled her. Now she was one of five new students sitting quietly, waiting for Principal Davis to get in. Gregory Davis, or Principal Greg as he liked students to call him, wasn't your typical principal. That is to say, he didn't walk around the school scolding students and rushing them off to class. He actually seemed to care about the students, their interests, and their futures. He was a good looking man for his age, which Alee figured must be around forty-seven or forty-eight, because he had the same distinguished salt and pepper hair that her father David—the man who raised her—had had.

The school secretary, Ms. Thatcher, an older woman in her early fifties, was sitting at the front desk sifting through stacks of papers and distributing them into the teachers' mailboxes along the back wall behind her station when the phone rang. "Hello. Yes, Mr. Davis, they're all here." She looked out and smiled at the five students sitting in the wobbly hard plastic chairs on the other side of her office countertop. Ms. Thatcher had always been nice to Alee, and having her there on her first morning was somehow making her feel a little better about everything. "Yes sir. OK sir. I'll take care of it." She went into the principal's office. "All right, I'll see you later this morning."

Later this morning? OK, so Principal Greg wasn't going to show up for new student orientation. That wasn't the worst news Alee could have gotten. She preferred Ms. Thatcher anyway.

There was a section of the front office countertop that could be lifted to allow people to walk in and out of the back office area—the kind you might find in a cheap backwoods bar —but this one wasn't covered with beer bottle rings, cigarette burns, or chunks of chewing gum. This one was spotless and fully functional. Atlanta High was pretty old, and a lot of it was falling apart, but, every year, money was put into renovating and re-furnishing one area or another. The renovations had started just four years ago, the summer before Alee's freshman year, and the first area to benefit was the main office. The school administration said that a prospective parent's first impression of the school was the front office. Half a million dollars had gone into beautifying and revitalizing the lobby, the front desk, the school counselor's office, and of course the principal's office. Where the money had come from no one really knew, and the school board wasn't saying.

The second section of the school to be renovated was the gym. It used to be just one big room, not much different than one of the classrooms, except that it was larger, and had basketball hoops at either end. There were no bleachers, no locker rooms—nothing even remotely fancy. The new gymnasium, or "stadium," as a lot of the kids like to call it, was a completely different building. It was back behind the main school facility, and it not only had separate locker rooms for boys and girls, but separate locker rooms for the different team sports: basketball, football, and even baseball. Not to mention the state of the art weight room and exercise facility. Everyone in town was still wondering why a small town like Atlanta would need such a high-tech facility.

Ms. Thatcher came out of the principal's office with a stack of bright blue and orange school-emblem files, and raised the lift-up portion of the countertop. A smile brightened her face as she spoke. "These are your class schedules, locker assignments, school map, and some other information about our campus." Yes, she called it a campus. It made sense, seeing how different it was now from the old facility, which had been a single small building. The new campus consisted of: the Classroom Building, which housed all the academic classes, the library, the cafeteria, and the school offices; the new state of the art Huskies Stadium that was used for sports activities and gym classes; and the new Creative Arts Building that was for drama, music, and art classes. "But, we'll get to the paperwork later." Ms. Thatcher smiled. "First, shall we take a walk?" She acted almost giddy, which seemed out of place for someone her age.

Alee just nodded, keeping in line with the behavior of the other students sitting with her. Not a single one had said a word since she came in, and she wasn't sure she should be the first one to start the cycle of conversation. As a small child she had been overly outgoing, but as she got older she had become more of a silent observer. She was curious to know what grades they were in, but figured she would find out soon enough. Although she wasn't really a "new" kid on the block, no one else knew that, and it might be nice to have some friends right off the starting block.

"All right then, shall we begin the tour?" Ms. Thatcher was nodding and walking out the office door as she spoke. Alee imagined, from her bubbly behavior that Ms. Thatcher had probably been a cheerleader back in her high school days—that is if they even had cheerleaders back then.

Great, a tour, Alee thought as they all got up to follow Ms. Thatcher out of the office. She rolled her eyes toward the other students and a couple of them chuckled, but one—a dark-haired slender young boy—just stared at her. He didn't smile—he didn't even blink. She had noticed him looking at her a couple of times before while they were sitting in the lobby listening to Ms. Thatcher's phone conversation. Now it was more obvious, seeing as he didn't look away when their eyes met this time, as he had before, but somehow Alee wasn't uncomfortable, like she normally would have been. Instead, she felt almost intrigued by the intensity of his gaze. She wanted to know what he was thinking, but would have to settle for just knowing he was most likely thinking about her.

"This hallway houses all of the seniors' lockers. Let me see, how many seniors do we have here?" Alee raised her hand, looking around at the other students, noticing that the dark-haired boy raised his hand too. "Wonderful, and what is your name young lady?" Ms. Thatcher asked her.

"It's Aleerah."

"Aleerah, such a pretty name. All right then, the senior lockers will be down this hall." The dark-haired boy just nodded in acknowledgement. He had moved behind Alee and was standing just inches away from her.

"My name's Jathan by the way." He whispered it into Alee's ear.

Hmmm, interesting name—Jathan. She turned to meet his eyes, but he had already backed away.

Ms. Thatcher scanned her notes, "Let's see, the rest of you are sophomores—your lockers will be this way." She moved quickly for someone of her age. Looking back over her shoulder, she called, "Come along. Follow me."

Jathan hung back watching as the rest of the group moved down the hall. Alee looked back a couple of times but he just stood there. When they turned the corner toward the library, he was finally out of view. She wondered what he was doing—why he had decided to ditch the tour—and just how much trouble he might get in. *Oh well, not my problem,* she decided.

The library was the next big renovation that they had done after the Huskies Stadium.

It had been completed the summer before her junior year, and it was amazing. For a lot of high school students a school library isn't really a place they care to go, but Alee had never been like a lot of other high school students. She loved to learn. From the time she started school she was always a straight "A" student. When she first learned about the plans to renovate the old library she had sent a letter to the school board with a few suggestions, and when she started her junior year she was pleased to see that they had actually incorporated all of them into the design. Even though she couldn't prove that it was her influence that got the changes made, she was still secretly proud of herself.

The first of her recommendations had been wireless internet and multiple computer stations throughout the library. Next she had asked for quiet study rooms. They incorporated five soundproof glass rooms along the back wall, each with privacy blinds, comfortable seating, a conference room style table and chairs for group project work, and a computer station. Alee's last major recommendation had been to replace the ancient card catalog file with a computerized system. Now there were two dedicated computers near the front entrance for that purpose alone. They had also added a small coffee café, to which Alee had quickly become addicted.

"This is the library. I'm sure you'll all want to spend a good amount of your time here." The brunette girl standing on Ms. Thatcher's right was snickering, but as Ms. Thatcher pushed open the door to the library her mouth closed, and the snickering ceased.

"Wow." The girl gaped as she walked in circles, around and around, looking at the computers, hardwood floors, beautifully crafted study desks, green glass lamps, leather covered seats, and rows upon rows of shelves filled with books. Then she noticed the coffee café. "It's beautiful! What time does it open?"

Ms. Thatcher just smiled, "Not until after first period. Now, as I said—" Ms. Thatcher scanned through her papers. "—Miss Wilkins, I'm sure you'll all want to spend a good amount of your time here. We have found that a lot of the students find it very relaxing between classes, or even during their lunch hour. Here at Atlanta High we participate in altered scheduling, allowing for longer rest periods between classes. You'll find we aren't the typical high school." She led them back out the door and into the hallway, stopping briefly once they were all out. "Now—do we have everyone?" She seemed to be looking back into the library.

"I'm sorry." Alee interrupted, "I just need to run back to the bathroom for a minute. I think we passed it back down the hall, right?" Why Alee felt she needed to distract Ms. Thatcher from the fact that Jathan was gone, or to stall until he got back, she didn't know.

"That is correct."

"I'll only be a minute." Where he had gone off to wasn't really any of her business anyway, and just as the words started to tumble out of her mouth she was wondering why she even cared. She didn't know him. What did it matter to her if he skipped out on the tour, or if he got in trouble because of it for that matter.

The older woman smiled at her, "Thank you Aleerah—" She glanced down at her list. "—Aleerah—Wenham." Her eyes narrowed as she looked back up at Alee. She held her gaze a few seconds longer than what was comfortable for Alee before she turned to look down the hall. "Since you seem so eager to run off, I'm sure you wouldn't mind just meeting back up with us down the next corridor and out back. We're heading to the Creative Arts Building, and I know you wouldn't want the others to have to miss part of the tour." She turned and, before Alee had a chance to say anything, was headed down the hall with the other three students following fast behind.

The Creative Arts Building had been the most recent renovation. It had been started during the end of Alee's junior year, and completed this past summer. Alee was actually excited about seeing it. She and Dani had often talked about wanting to try out for a school play together, but her parents never would have let her. Now, with a brand new Broadway style facility, she finally would be free to try, but without her best friend to share it with, there didn't really seem to be much of a point.

"Great, just great." It was to herself, since no one else was around to hear her, but as Alee turned the corner she slammed right into Jathan's chest.

"Whoa, where's the fire?" Jathan's voice was deeper than she had expected, kind of rough, but still pleasant to the ear. *Where's the fire.* She had a flashback to the previous year when she had been waiting at her locker for Kyle. When she was finally giving up and heading off to class she ran right into him. He had said the same thing. *It's just a figure of speech*, she reminded herself.

"Where did you run off to?" Not wanting to sound startled, Alee tried for casual but didn't really succeed.

Jathan just went around her and off down the hall, not even looking back. "I had things to do. Where were you going?"

"I was—the bathroom."

"No you weren't. You were coming to find me." Alee stood there staring until he finally stopped walking and turned to face her. "So, are you coming? Then he gave her just about the most charming smile she had ever seen. His bright white, perfectly straight teeth were a dramatic contrast to his dark black hair and his deep, chocolate brown eyes.

Alee froze. When she finally found her voice, it was small and frail, no more than a whisper, "Yeah." But she still didn't move, and his eyes hadn't left hers.

Eyebrows lifted, Jathan held a hand out to her. "Then come on." *That smile again—wow.* Alee took his hand without thinking, and five steps down the hall she realized that his hand was still wrapped around hers. It felt warm and comforting. Something inside of her didn't want to let go of him, but she forced herself to pull away. She felt him turn toward her, but she didn't look at him, and he didn't say a word. She somehow sensed that one corner of his mouth turned up faintly in the slightest of smirks.

At the end of the back hallway Alee pushed open the door that led outside to the brand new Creative Arts Building. "They went this way."

"So, how do you know where everything is already?"

"I used to—I read the map on the office wall." She corrected herself before blurting out that she wasn't really a new student. Lying about reading the map just made her look like a complete dork. She could feel the judgment in the way he studied her.

But he just said, "OK—."

Judgment, judgment, judgment!

"Let's just go." She stood there holding the door open waiting for him to exit, but finally just walked out and let him catch the door before it shut in front of him. The outside of the Arts Building looked just like the Main Classroom Building except that it was one story instead of two. They had used the same colonial revival style of architecture on the Arts Building that had been used so many years ago when the high school was first built. The cast stone detailing of the entryway and the tall stone pillars framing the entrance at the top of the stairs matched those of the older building perfectly. If Alee hadn't known that one of the buildings was new, she would have thought that they had been built at the same time. That is, until they walked in and realized that everything in the new building smelled clean and rich and, well—*new*.

"—for you creative students." Ms. Thatcher was just finishing her tour of the building when she looked up to see them coming in. "Well, I'm so glad you could join us again."

There was a hint of sarcasm in her voice that Alee had never heard before. Usually Ms. Thatcher was so sweet, but now she seemed watchful—even critical. She led the students back out the main entrance, gesturing toward the gymnasium. "Your gym classes will be over there." Then, as she scanned the group, she added, "Though I doubt that any of you will be participating in sports. So we'll just make our way back to the office." They all just looked at each other in amazement at the blatantly obvious way she had just judged them.

"Actually I'm a swimmer." *Where did that come from?* She had no intention of joining the swim team or any other team for that matter, but the way Ms. Thatcher had just assumed, even judged them all by their looks, Alee knew she couldn't just not say anything.

Ms. Thatcher stopped and turned quickly to face Alee eye to eye. "Are you now? Well then Miss. Wenham, I'm sure you will be happy to know that the pool is just as impressive as the amphitheater." Then, as she turned back around and continued walking she added, "Oh wait—you missed that part of the tour." Everyone looked at Alee, who just smiled and shrugged her shoulders, all the while wondering what she had done to piss off such a sweet old woman.

Jathan continued to eye her, as if looking to see something he might have missed the first time. "A swimmer—really?"

"Don't sound so surprised," Alee hissed under her breath, then rolled her eyes, and headed off to catch up with the rest of the students. "I run too!" she called back over her shoulder.

"Yes, yes fine," Ms. Thatcher responded, as if she really didn't care.

"No, I wasn't talking to—oh never mind." She turned back to glare at Jathan, but he just smiled.

When they had finally made it back to the office, Ms. Thatcher thanked them all again for making it in so early, handed out their student folders, and set them loose to find their lockers and locate their morning classes. Glancing at the clock on the office wall, Alee realized that she still had about ten minutes before the majority of the students would begin to arrive. She wasn't worried about finding her classes—she already knew the school like the back of her hand. What she really wanted to know was where her locker was and how close it was to Kyle's and Dani's.

After finding her locker, practicing the combination a few times, and committing it to memory, she tossed the new-student folder on the shelf, folded her class schedule, and shoved it into her back pocket. Before she could even close the locker door, Phoebe was standing right behind her, coffee in hand. "Your drink." She handed her a brand new travel mug with a lid and a drinking spout.

"Wow, thanks. I could get used to this, but you know you could have just gotten the regular paper cup." Then she took a sip of the coffee, only to find that it wasn't coffee at all. Not quite ready for what she tasted, Alee gagged on the thick red liquid that began to drip down her chin as she desperately tried to wipe it off with the back of her hand. She coughed, trying to catch her breath, as Phoebe handed her a napkin. She hurriedly cleaned off her lips and hand while scanning the hallway to see if anyone was close enough to notice. Luckily no one was around.

Her eyes flashed with anger as she turned to Phoebe. "What were you thinking?"

Phoebe raised her hands up, as if surrendering, and whispered back, "I just thought you might need it. I was only trying to help." She smiled an innocent little smile. "I figured your first day of school—might be stressful, and—."

Alee cut her off. "It's fine. Thank you. I'm sure you meant well. I was just expecting coffee. I wasn't expecting—well, this." Holding up the cup she smiled, and they actually shared a laugh. Phoebe held up her own cup, actual coffee, and knocked it up against Alee's. "Cheers."

Alee tipped back her mug and drank the "red syrup," as she liked to think of it, as quickly as it would come out. Then she turned, opened her locker, and placed the mug in the back of the locker on the top shelf. It wasn't as if she could really throw a cup of blood into the school garbage can. "Thanks."

Phoebe was smiling even more now. "Any time."

2

Alee had settled down in a large leather reading chair in the back corner of the library, already engrossed in a book called *Light vs. Dark* that she had found on one of the shelves, when she heard the warning bell go off and the hurried footsteps as students headed toward their morning classes. She slid the book back into its place on the shelf, planning to come back and check it out later, when the librarian made it in.

Without the book to distract her, her thoughts returned to the moment when Jathan had taken her hand in his, his warm smile, his—. "Excuse me." She barely heard the words, but moved out of the way just the same. Looking around, she realized that the hallways were starting to empty as students found their way to their classrooms up and down the hall.

Alee knew that by now Kyle was somewhere on campus. It wasn't just because it was almost time for classes to begin. Ever since she had bitten Kyle she had moments when she could sense him, almost feel that he was near. It didn't happen all the time, but when it did it was like nothing she had ever felt. Right now, she could almost smell his presence. Knowing that he had arrived made her wonder if Dani was here yet, and how she was doing since the funeral. Alee had forced herself to stay away from everyone, not wanting to seem suspicious, but being back at school she couldn't help wanting to be around her old friends.

Of course Damian was also at the top of the list of people she wanted to see. She worried, though, whether the connection they had shared would still be there. She worried even more that it wouldn't. She worried that it may have been lost the day she "died." As if the thought of her death would have caused him to shut her out, without his even realizing it. Or maybe the shock of her death had had no effect on him at all. Alee wasn't sure which reality would be harder for her to handle. If the connection were still there, would he realize who she really was? Could he? So many questions were knotted up inside her that she started to feel sick.

She must have looked just as bad as she had started to feel, because a small crowd had gathered around her, and one of the teachers had placed her hand on Alee's shoulder, "Are you all right dear?"

"Tell them you're fine and come with me." It was Jathan, and he had put his arm around her waist and was leading her down the hall toward her first class.

"I'm fine, thank you," Alee called back over her shoulder to the teacher and the lookie-loos who had gathered. However, she was still wobbly on her feet, even with Jathan's help.

"We have first period AP English Literature together. I hope I don't have to carry you all semester." His smirk became that gleaming white smile again, and she felt anger building as she pushed away to walk on her own.

They were all alone in the hallway, and she was feeling a little steadier on her feet. "I can walk by myself, and you don't need to be ordering me around, telling me what to say."

Jathan just raised his hands. "I was only trying to help."

"How do you know my class schedule anyway?" Alee eyed him. Apparently he was going to be someone she would have to keep track of.

Jathan just grinned. "I told you I had things to take care of." He turned and walked into the classroom they had been standing in front of. When she glanced at the room number she realized that it was in fact her morning literature class.

The final bell rang just as she was taking her seat, one row to the right and two seats ahead of Jathan. She could just spot him out of the corner of her eye, and could feel him observing her the entire class period. The teacher talked on and on about the writing assignments they would have to complete during the course, when the tests would be, and what her expectations were for what they would learn and walk away with by the end of the semester. It was your typical start-of-the-year teacher lecture, and Alee had a feeling she would be hearing a few more throughout the day.

Alee had zoned out halfway through class, which was completely unlike her usual attentive school behavior. But for some reason she just couldn't seem to focus this morning. The small hairs on the back of her neck stood up when Jathan's hand lightly brushed hers as he dropped a folded piece of paper onto her desk in front of her. She suddenly realized that the bell had already rung. Half of the class was already out in the hall, and the rest were out of their seats headed toward the door. She palmed the note without her teacher seeing it, gathered her things, and followed the crowd through the door and down the hall. Jathan was nowhere to be seen, but she clutched the note tightly in her fist.

Glancing at her schedule she realized that her next class was AP Calculus. *AP Calculus—really?* It wasn't that she was bad at math—she was actually really good at it—she just didn't like it all that much. She definitely didn't like it enough to want to take an AP Calculus class.

When she was finally settled into a seat at the front of the class, Alee hurriedly unfolded the note she had been holding in a death grip. *The literature class syllabus? What was the point of that?* She rolled her eyes and folded it back up. Holding it between her fingertips and the desk, she flicked it with the index finger of her other hand. It flew across the gap between the front row of desks and the teacher's desk and landed directly in the center of the wastebasket.

"Wow. Nice basket." Alee turned to see Kyle walking in and her heart skipped a beat, and the rest of the world seemed to melt away. He had seen her miraculous paper flicking three-pointer from the doorway. She couldn't help but smile as he held out a hand to her, "Hi. I'm Chucky. Wanna play?" She glared playfully at him, stifling a laugh. "Oh. Sorry, I'm Kyle. Movie quotes are kinda my thing." Then he looked around the room before continuing. "You must be new. What's your name?" His hand was warm around hers and his thumb caressed the outside of her hand as he held it. He was playing his part perfectly.

"Ale—Aleerah." She was trying not to giggle, but what she really wanted to do was jump into his arms and press her lips to his.

When Kyle pulled his hand away, the cool air conditioning of the room reminded her of where she was. "Well, Aleerah, it's nice to meet you, and if you need anything—I'll be around." Then, with a wink, he passed her and slid into the seat directly behind her.

She smiled delightedly, failing in her attempt to hide it.

Her right wrist started to heat up, almost as if she had wrapped a heating pad around it. Hesitantly, she pulled the sleeve of her shirt up just enough to reveal an edge of the tattoo that magically wrapped itself around her wrist. Can you even call it a tattoo if it isn't created with needle and ink? I guess it doesn't really matter. The black ink of the pentagram was once again glowing like polished silver, and moving just under her skin like a rivulet of liquid metal through the vines that wound themselves around her arm. Alee quickly covered it back up and glanced back at Kyle, who had just been looking at his own wrist with a puzzled expression. She worried that Kyle was getting freaked out, but he put her mind at ease with a quick little smile.

For the rest of the class, Alee tried desperately to focus on every word the teacher said. She jotted down notes on the class syllabus while the teacher talked, just too busy her hand, and keep from looking at the tattoo again. When the bell finally rang, she walked out with Kyle not too far behind, but in the hallway she saw Jathan standing just across the hall, leaning up against the front of a row of lockers, clearly waiting for her.

Jathan caught up with her as soon as she started up the hallway, "Next stop, Advanced Art. We'll finally get a chance to see the inside of the Arts Building." He pulled her through the crowd toward the back door as she glanced over her shoulder at Kyle, who just watched as she maneuvered her way off into the crowded hallway without him. She whispered a silent *"I'm sorry—."* before rounding the corner and disappearing from view.

"What are you doing?" she snapped at Jathan. Who do you think you are, just dragging me away? And what do you mean Advanced Art?" She pulled her arm away from him to search her pockets for her class schedule. Other students were slowing down to watch them, moving aside a little to give them space as they passed.

"Try your other pocket," Jathan said smugly.

When she pulled a tightly folded paper out of that pocket unfolded it to find her schedule, he just smiled. "Did you find what you needed?"

She quickly scanned the paper and, sure enough, he was right. "How did you—. Oh never mind." It was right there on the paper—Advanced Art. "Why am I—? I'm not even—." But then it dawned on her. Alee wasn't artistic, but her parents wouldn't know that because they didn't really know her. Besides, she wasn't Alee anymore.

"What's wrong?" Jathan was just looking at her like she had just escaped from a mental ward.

She just shook her head, still looking down at the paper gripped tightly in her hands. "Nothing—nothing. So you're in Advanced Art too?"

"Does a bear shit in the woods?" They stood there in silence. "Yes. Yes. I'm in art too."

"Hmmm, I wouldn't have taken you for an artist."

"There are many things you have yet to learn about me." That was an understatement, but the way he said it seemed almost to imply that they *hadn't* just met each other that morning—but that couldn't be. She surely would have remembered those brown eyes—that bright smile—that dark wavy hair. Then he winked and took her hand again. "Don't worry, you have time to get to know me." He was smiling, but something in his voice didn't sound as happy as he was acting. "Now, come on, we're going to be late."

After the hour-long lecture, Alee was surprised to find that Advanced Art didn't seem like it was going to be all that bad. Besides it was nice knowing she would get a little fresh air between her second and third period classes. Lunch was right after Art, and she managed to break away from Jathan, explaining that she already had plans for lunch with her cousin. "Hmmm, a cousin huh?" he seemed intrigued. "Well, no worries. I have plans myself." As he left her without any objection, she couldn't help feeling that it wasn't going to be the last time she saw him that day. If she was being honest with herself, she was kind of intrigued by the idea that she would be seeing more of him.

Alee wasn't excited about lunch. This had been a time when she and her friends got together, talked, and just hung out. The idea of sitting with her cousin Phoebe, no matter how cool she had been that morning, just didn't seem nearly as fun as being with Kyle, Dani, Damian, Victoria, and Tyler. Thinking of Tyler made her wonder if he and Dani were still dating. She knew they had broken up midway through summer vacation, when he had gone off on a family trip and Dani had turned into the overly needy girlfriend from afar. But then again, with their on-again off-again relationship, who knew how long that had lasted.

Sure enough, as she inched along in the lunch line, scanning the tables in the large cafeteria, Alee saw them. They were sitting at their usual table at the back of the room. Dani was sitting as close to Tyler as the cafeteria seats would allow without actually being in his lap, and smiling up at him longingly. Damian and Victoria had their backs to her, but as Alee moved further into the room she noticed Damian's reaction. He stiffened, sitting straight up, and even turned around to scan the room, but his glance only briefly registered her face before moving on. He obviously, and luckily, didn't realize who she really was. Kyle was sitting across from Damian and talking his ear off like he always did. She couldn't tell what he was saying, but she assumed it had to do with a movie he watched recently, a new band he had discovered, or something less likely like his class schedule.

Alee longed to join her friends, but knew it would only seem weird— an unwelcome intrusion. She had been easily accepted into the group only a year ago, but that was with Dani's praise and introductions. Now she would just be the crazy new girl. It wasn't the right thing to do, at least not yet.

"Hey, Aleerah, over here." Phoebe was waving at her from a table along the side wall.

Weaving in and out of the tables, Alee made her way to the seat next to Phoebe, who quickly introduced her to the other two girls sitting with her. Molly was slightly overweight with a round face and shoulder length curly hair that she had dyed black. Kim was tall and slender with long hair also dyed black. They both wore black nail polish and dark red lipstick just like Phoebe. Only somehow it worked on Phoebe, on Molly and Kim it just looked—awkward—or pathetic. Alee hadn't really decided which just yet.

"This is Aleerah—." The girls just stared at her like they were confused, or maybe offended by the intruder at their table. "Be nice girls, she's my cousin. Besides, she's a senior. Sit down and join us, Aleerah."

The four of them sat there for a while in an awkward silence, eating their lunch. Alee privately wished she were somewhere else. She could see her friends, only six tables away, and she wondered what they were talking about as they quietly whispered together. They seemed almost somber today. She wondered if it had anything to do with her absence, but there was no way to know. She'd have to remember to ask Kyle about it later. After a few minutes she caught Kyle's attention, and his beautiful green eyes caught hers, and sparkled like emeralds. He smiled and nodded, but Dani quickly pulled his attention back to the group with a dirty look. Alee imagined her friend scolding him for checking out another girl—protecting her best friend's honor. It was actually nice to think that Dani still cared enough to keep him in line.

"—Hello—Earth to Aleerah!" Molly was waving her hand in front of Alee's face and snapping her fingers. "Wow Phoebe, your cousin sure does know how to zone out."

"What? I'm sorry—I was just thinking. What did you say?"

Molly sighed. She obviously didn't like having to repeat herself. "We were just wondering how you like Atlanta so far. Phoebe was saying you're a senior. It must suck having to transfer to a new school in your senior year."

You have no idea. "Yeah, it does." They were just looking at her. It was obviously not the answer they had been expecting. "But, so far—the people here seem pretty cool." Alee smiled, and it seemed to put a crack in their hard shells. With any luck she would break through.

"So, where'd you move from?"

Crap! Alee had no idea what to say. With all the prep over the last two weeks no one had thought to give her a backstory. Her parents hadn't even bothered to tell her what classes she was going to be taking, let alone what made-up past she was supposed to tell people.

Thankfully, Phoebe didn't miss a beat, "California. She's from California." She didn't sound like she was making it up—just stating a fact.

Both Molly and Kim were wide-eyed, "Really? You're not even from Michigan? That is so cool." Kim's voice was softer than Alee expected. "Do you miss it? I would totally miss it. The ocean, the weather, I mean—wow. Do you miss it?"

"Um, no—not really." *How am I supposed to miss a place I've never actually been?* Alee was having a hard time focusing on the conversation because she kept noticing Kyle and the others glancing her way. He even pointed to her at one point. *What can he possibly be telling them?* She started feeling nervous. She knew how important it was that her identity be kept secret no matter how hard that was. *Kyle wouldn't say anything, would he? Of course not, what are you thinking?* She tried to brush the idea out of her mind. She knew it was ridiculous.

The girls kept talking, but eventually they stopped asking Alee any questions, and before she knew it the lunch bell was ringing. When she looked up, she and Phoebe were the only ones left at the table and the cafeteria was already half empty.

"Well, Molly was right; you do know how to zone out." Phoebe was just looking at her. "Are you OK?"

"Oh God, did they leave?" Alee had a sinking feeling she had made a bad first impression on Phoebe's friends. "I'm so sorry."

"Don't worry about it. They'll get used to you. I just told them you're more homesick than you'll admit, and that you're missing an old boyfriend. Besides, I'm sure this is a lot to handle on your first day." Phoebe seemed so much friendlier and way more understanding than she had any time before.

"Thanks."

"So, are you OK?" Phoebe sounded honestly concerned.

~ Nina Soden ~

Alee just shook her head. What she really wanted right then was to sit down and cry, but she had to be stronger than that. Only three more classes to go and she would be able to go home and figure everything out. "I'll be fine." She said the words, but even she didn't believe them. She was starting to wonder if she should have just skipped senior year altogether.

Phoebe reached into her purse and pulled out an unmarked pill bottle, and slipped it into Alee's hand. "Here, take these—for—clarity."

"How did you—?"

Phoebe had helped her with the 'coffee' that morning and now this? It was as if she knew what Alee needed better than Alee knew herself. "Your mom was worried. No one really knows what you're going through, or how this whole change is going to affect you. She just thought you might need a little help, but she didn't want to seem too pushy."

Alee stared down at the pill bottle in her hand, rolled it around a few times, and looked back up into Phoebe's eyes. "Thank you, and—I promise—I'm OK." Even as she spoke the words, Alee opened the bottle and popped one of the small liquid-filled pills into her mouth. It melted instantly, and a rush of heat went through her. "Wow, how can one little pill do so much more than the—coffee—this morning?"

"You really don't know?" Phoebe stared at her with narrowed eyes.

"Know what?"

"It's your father's—you know." Phoebe was whispering so quietly Alee had to lean in to hear her. "This morning, that was just, well, animal. Your dad says human is better, but that for real power and control you need—."

"Vampire!"

"Shhhh. You can't talk about that. Not here." Standing up quickly, Phoebe put her arm through Alee's and guided her toward the front of the cafeteria where students were emptying their lunch trays and chatting with friends before making their way to their afternoon classes. "We should get going—before we're late."

Alee felt more at ease. Maybe it was Phoebe's kindness, or maybe it was just the pill. Whatever the reason, Alee was glad, because she had actually been looking forward to her next class, Advanced Placement Psychology. She had always been intrigued by what makes people behave the way they do—by the different types of mental illnesses, and whether or not they were in fact illnesses at all, or just different ways of being—different ways of thinking.

As soon as the girls exited the cafeteria doors and stepped into the hallway Alee stopped. There was no one in front of her and nothing blocking her way, but she felt as if she had just walked face first into a brick wall. The air was suddenly thick. The sounds of students passing by seemed miles away in the distance. Her ears started to ring and she cupped her hands over them to drown out the sound.

"Alllleeeerrrrahhh" It was Phoebe's voice. "Arrrrrrrrre yooooooouuuuu oookaaaayyyy?" but Alee couldn't really make out what she was saying.

"What is that smell?" She slurred her words as she spoke, and began to feel as if the room was spinning around her.

Not knowing what to do, Phoebe tried to hold her up, but with little success. Alee was getting sick for the second time today, which was not really the best start to a new school year.

Alee shook her head to try and focus. Suddenly the spinning stopped and she was able to focus on something other than the sweet smell that had filled the air around her. She could hear voices coming from down the hall so clearly it was like she was standing right next to them. "I just need a band aid, it's nothing really. I'll see the nurse and it will be fine." Victoria pushed past her in the direction of the main office and the sweet scent washed over Alee, almost knocking her down again, "What are you looking at, freak?" As soon as Victoria turned the corner the overwhelmingly exotic smell was gone.

Now it was Kyle's voice that Alee heard as clearly as if he were standing next to her. "I don't know what you're talking about, Danielle." He sounded mad. *Is he arguing—with Dani?* But Alee couldn't tell about what, or why. She stood up and pulled away from Phoebe, assuring her that she had her balance back.

"Aleerah, are you OK?"

Alee was conflicted, wanting to follow after Victoria and that sweet alluring scent, but also needing to find out why Dani and Kyle were arguing. There was no way to do either with Phoebe following her around. "Yeah, I'm fine." She said the words, but they didn't sound very convincing. "Really, it's just a little headache, and I am pretty sure it will be gone in a few minutes." She smiled half-heartedly, but the smile didn't make it to her eyes. She shook the pills in front of her to reiterate her point, but Phoebe didn't look convinced either. "Sorry for the scare, but I'm good."

"OK, well if you need—" But, before she could finish her sentence Alee was down the hall and out of sight. "—me—." Phoebe just turned back around and made her way to class. "Whatever."

Alee stood with her back against the wall and listened to the conversation just around the corner. She was right—it had been Kyle and Dani—and it sounded like they were in fact fighting.

"Don't tell me you don't know what I'm talking about, Kyle." Dani was mad, but about what Alee didn't know.

"I don't," Kyle said flatly.

One of them slammed a locker door shut and the crash echoed through the hall, but there was no way Alee was going to look around the corner to find out which one of them had done it. "Really? So, you're telling me you weren't being all flirty-flirty with the new girl in the cafeteria?" *OK, so it had probably been Dan who had slammed the locker door shut.*

Kyle didn't say a word.

"No answer? Big surprise. At least you could pick someone other than the new freak-in-the making." Alee's mouth fell open at the sound of her best friend calling her a freak. Even though Dani didn't know who she was, it still hurt.

Kyle didn't get upset very easily, so when Alee heard anger in his voice as he answered Dani, Alee was both surprised and flattered. "What did you say? You don't even know her."

Dani snapped right back, "Neither do you Kyle; but I do know that freak, Phoebe, and her little followers. I'm sure there's not much time before she's converted the new girl into a member of her cult."

"You don't know what you're talking about Dani." A moment later Kyle turned the corner and just moments before he passed Alee in the hallway she lifted a folder up in front of her face in an attempt to hide.

"Kyle!" Dani was running after him.

Alee was surprised when Kyle actually stopped, but he didn't turn around to face Dani, "What. What else would you like to say, Dani? What else am I doing wrong?"

"Alee's grave isn't even cold yet." There were tears in her voice, but Dani was trying to be strong as she spoke to him. "Don't you even care?"

Alee just stood there hiding behind her open folder, pretending to be reading, and trying not to be noticed. She wanted to inch away, find a hiding place; but she couldn't, not without calling attention to herself. She was trapped.

"Come here." Kyle's voice had changed. Alee knew that tone well, and she could picture him pulling Dani into his arms, and wrapping her in a warm hug. His hugs were the best. "Of course I care. You know I care." Dani's cries were muffled by Kyle's shirt as she cried into his chest.

Alee felt like crying herself. She had to hold herself back because what she wanted to do was run up to them and to tell Dani everything.

"I'm so sorry Dani. You know I love—" Alee lowered the folder and caught Kyle's attention as he stood with his arms around her best friend not ten feet away. "—loved Alee, but she's gone, and nothing is going to bring her back." The words seemed so final as they crossed Kyle's lips. Alee gasped, trying not to break down. "She wouldn't want us to stop living our lives. You know that." He wrapped his arm around Dani's waist, and led her down the hall, "Come on. We should get to class."

With her back still against the wall, Alee slid down to the floor and sat there in stunned silence for what felt like a lifetime. She had known this was going to be hard, but this was unbearable.

When she finally opened her eyes, it wasn't the rush of students pushing their way out of the classrooms around her, or even the slamming of locker doors echoing throughout the building, that caught her attention. It was a soft hand on her shoulder, and a fluid, almost musical voice, that eased her awake, "So this is where you spent fourth period. I never—." His voice trailed off.

What? Oh my God, I feel asleep.

How had Jathan even known where she was, and why did he care so much if she made it to her classes, or if she decided to skip them all?

Jathan held out his hand to help her up, and she took it without a word. "I'll walk you to class, but you'll have to somehow manage without me for the next hour." Alee was confused, but Jathan must have mistaken her look of confusion for disappointment because he quickly explained, trying to comfort her. "Don't worry; we'll see each other again in P.E."

Alee had no idea what he was talking about. "P.E.?"

"You know, physical education—" Although Jathan was charming, handsome, and all around intriguing, he also had a very sarcastic side to him that would soon grow on Alee. "—also known as gym class—the easy A. How's that for a great class to skip at the end of the day? Want to?" At that she actually smiled. Without even checking her class schedule, Alee let him lead her hand in hand through the busy hallways, not bothering to really pay much attention to everything happening around them.

"So, what were you doing hanging out in the hallway all alone anyway?"

Alee blushed, "I don't really know. Just tired I guess."

Jathan raised his eyebrows, almost surprised at her lack of excuses. "Have any good dreams?"

She just shrugged. She vaguely remembered being alone with Kyle in her dream at one point, but waking up to

Jathan made her question who it was she had actually been dreaming about. Was it really Kyle?

Jathan had a charm about him, and when he smiled it was as if her mind was slipping away. "You're here," he said.

"Where?" She couldn't take her eyes off of his, and she wasn't so sure she really wanted to just yet.

Jathan just chuckled, "U.S. Government." He pointed toward the classroom door, and Alee realized that class was about to begin. "Go, you don't want to be late." Then, with his hand on her lower back, he gently guided her into the classroom, and when she turned around to watch him go he was nowhere to be seen. It was as if he had just vanished.

Government class went by at a snail's pace as she watched the second hand slowly tick its way around the clock over and over again. When the bell finally rang, Alee felt a flash of excitement at the idea of gym class.

She rushed out the back door and into the open courtyard that connected the three campus buildings. For most students, seniors especially, gym class was seen as a blow-off class, just like Jathan had suggested. For Alee, who all her life had been told she wasn't allowed to participate, and was given doctor's note after doctor's note to be excused from all physical activities, gym class was an exciting new opportunity, and she planned to have fun.

The teacher had everyone find a seat on the bleachers, and the second she started to climb she noticed Kyle sitting three rows from the top and there was no question that he had noticed her too. Sitting on the very top row, only a few feet to Kyle's right, was Jathan—smiling and waving for her to come up and sit with him.

Awkward! Alee wasn't really sure what to do. Not wanting to upset Kyle, or lead Jathan on, she decided to take a seat in the second row, trying hard not to look up again at either of them.

Coach Jenson talked for the better half of the hour going over his class rules, the required gym uniform, and what he expected of each and every student in his class. At the end of his rather long and very boring speech, he announced a pop quiz, which got everyone's attention. He began distributing a one-page handout while instructing everyone to fill it out and leave it in the basket just outside his office door on the far side of the gym. Before he left them to complete their task, he gave them the freedom to leave early for the day as soon as they had finished.

Other than the line at the top of the page for their name, there was only one item on the paper: What are your physical/athletic goals?

Alee just sat there, drawing a blank. It was the first time she actually didn't know how to answer an essay question. She had no goals when it came to gym class: who did—its gym class, not a job application, not a college admissions application, not even a New Year's resolution for that matter. She couldn't help but think how absurd the question was, and wondered if Coach Jenson knew it too. Was he really serious about this, or was it a joke?

She wasn't the last student to finish, but after staring at the paper for about three minutes and seeing other students busily filling out the empty white space on their papers, she decided to take the question seriously and really try to answer it honestly,

I've never really thought much about my goals when it comes to athletics, or exercise for that matter. I've never struggled with my weight, but I've also never been a star athlete. I don't wake up in the morning and feel the urge to lift weights or join an aerobics class, but I don't hate the idea of the benefits those things might bring either.

Over this past summer, I discovered that I can swim. I don't mean I jumped in the pool and taught myself to doggy paddle back to safety. It's more like I've always been able to swim, but I recently learned that holding my breath under water for long periods of time isn't all that challenging to me. I also recently found myself enjoying long runs out on the paths through the woods behind my house, but I don't really consider myself a runner either.

I guess if I had to pick a goal for myself over the course of this class, I would have to say, confidence. With every new thing I try, and especially those I succeed at, I get a little more confident in who I am, and what I am capable of. I like the feeling of knowing there are things in life that we can control, but I also like knowing that some things, well, you just have to try and see before you know if you will succeed at them or not. That's what this class is for me, a way to try new things, and hopefully learn from them. Maybe I can even build a little more confidence along the way.

Alee didn't know whether or not the answer to her essay was what her teacher was looking for, but it didn't really matter. She was satisfied, and even a little proud of herself and what she had written.

As she made her way out of class, she realized how hungry she had gotten without even noticing. Considering that she hadn't really touched her lunch, it shouldn't have been much of a surprise. But it was, and she was worried. It seemed more and more, over the last few weeks, that the foods she used to love just didn't really satisfy her hunger anyway. Then she remembered the pills that were still in her locker, and she headed straight there.

The last person in the world she expected to find waiting for her there was Dani, but sure enough, there she was, just like old times. But it wasn't like old times, and Alee knew it. She knew it by the cold look in Dani's eye—by the stiff way she stood there instead of comfortably leaning on the locker. She knew it before Dani even said a word.

"What's your name?" It wasn't the warm hug from her best friend that Alee had wanted—needed. At least her friend was talking to her, even if Dani didn't actually know it herself.

"It's Aleeeeerrah." She almost blew it, and had to elongate her name preventing herself from almost saying Alee. She took a deep breath. It wouldn't have been the first time that day that she had almost messed up, but she hoped it would be the last. "It's Aleerah. What's yours?"

Dani just stood there, staring at her through narrow eyes. Alee knew that look well; after eleven years of being best friends with someone you get to know their quirks, and this one told Alee that Dani wasn't altogether comfortable or happy about being there. Someone had put her up to it, and Alee had a good suspicion as to who it had been. "Danielle, but my friends call me Dani."

"Did you need something, Dani?"

Dani snapped back more quickly than Alee had ever heard her do, "I said my *friends* call me Dani. You can call me Danielle." Alee was shocked. Dani had never been the blunt or boorish type, but clearly she was in no mood to mess around.

Alee put her hands up, yielding. "I'm sorry. I didn't mean to offend you. Let's start over, did you need something, Danielle?"

"No—. Well, yeah, a friend told me I should say hi. He said you're new to the area and that you seem kind of cool."

Alee tried to hide a smile, but she had never been very good at that in her "past" life and it didn't seem she was much better at it now either. "Well, I *am* new, so—I don't know many people. Can I ask who it was?"

Just then the hairs on the back of her neck stood at attention, her heart started to speed up in her chest, and she felt a tickle in her throat as the burning got worse, Kyle was close by, and his scent had been easier to handle earlier in the day when she had already fed, but it had been hours since she had eaten, and he smelled—delicious. Not that she would ever feed on him. She loved him, but to have him so close when she felt this way was devilishly exciting.

Alee had grown accustomed to hearing the heartbeats of everyone around her—a form of training her father had come up with. It just seemed like a game to her. She would close her eyes and focus in on the different heartbeats and see if she could guess how many people were in the room with her. She was always right. She was even getting pretty good at distinguishing among heartbeats. She could tell Kyle's apart from her cousin's—she could hear the difference between her mother's and her grandmother's. She found it fun and challenging—like a mystery. However, being at school and surrounded by so many people she had found it hard to focus on anything, let alone pick out just one or two heartbeats from the crowd. She was surprised that Kyle had been able to get as close as he had several times that day without her sensing him first.

Maybe it was because the hallway was almost empty, or maybe it was because she was thirsty. Who knows, but as he got closer, she could feel her own heartbeat speeding up—racing. She quickly opened her locker, trying not to be rude, and grabbed her pills from the top shelf. She popped one in her mouth and when she turned back to Dani, she was more relaxed than she must have seemed previously.

"What was that?"

"What?" Alee asked, realizing that Dani had seen her take pills so often in her previous life that it might have reminded her of, well—her.

"What did you just take?" Dani was trying to see around Alee and into her locker, but Alee quickly, yet casually, closed it behind her.

"Oh, that's nothing, just some vitamins."

"Hey Dani, I see you've met Aleerah." Kyle nodded to Dani then gently patted Alee on the shoulder in passing, like you would an acquaintance who was engaged in conversation with someone else. Her shoulder warmed at his touch, and he paused for a moment. "How was your first day, Aleerah?" Kyle made everything seem so easy, but Alee wondered whether deep down this had all been as hard for him as it had been for her all day.

With a coy smile, Alee blushed ever so slightly. "Interesting, I guess."

Kyle rested his arm on Dani's shoulder, as if she was his own personal walking stick, but she didn't bat his arm away. She actually looked as if she kind of liked his weight on her shoulder. Alee didn't want to, but she actually started to feel a little jealous watching him look down at her friend. He was almost a full head taller than Dani. "You almost ready to go?" he asked her. "I need to stop somewhere and get some

Excedrin. My head has been throbbing since last period started."

"I'm ready. I just have to grab something out of my locker," Dani said. "I'll be right back." "Oh, Tyler said he'd meet us out at your truck after class." She turned to walk away, but before leaving, she looked back at Alee and smiled. "Well, it was nice meeting you Aleerah. Maybe I'll see you around some time."

"Why don't you join us?" Alee knew what Kyle was doing: trying to speed up the process of bringing the old gang back together. Dani didn't seem to like the idea very much, though.

"What?" Her voice kind of cracked awkwardly as she stopped in her tracks and spit the question at him. "No. Kyle, I'm sure Aleerah has other plans already. Besides, I doubt she would even want to hang out with a bunch of people she doesn't even know. She'd be like the fifth wheel and all." Dani was staring right at Alee as if trying to tell her to back off without just coming right out and saying it.

Kyle's eyes narrowed, and Alee could see the gears turning in his head before the words even came out of his mouth. "Actually, there are already five of us, so she would kind of balance us out don't you think?" Before he even finished, a smirk had already started to form. However, Dani had stopped paying attention and was already half way down the hall. His voice just a whisper now, he leaned in close to Alee, their shoulders barely touching, but she could feel his breath on her cheek as he spoke, "Sorry about that."

Alee just shook her head. What was she supposed to say? There was nothing to say.

"How are you holding up?" Given the situation, you would think that was a completely unnecessary question, but when Alee looked into Kyle's eye she knew he just really wanted her to know he was there for her, no matter what.

To say the least, Alee's day had not really gone as planned, and from what she could tell there was little hope of that changing any time soon. She didn't want to burden him with her worries now though. "I'm fine. I think I just need to eat."

He quickly clasped his hands over his neck with a laugh and the biggest smile she had seen in a long time, then said, "Not me I hope." Kyle had a way of just making everything bad slip away and Alee couldn't help but laugh with him. He quickly looked around. They were the only ones standing in the hall, so he leaned in and kissed her softly on the forehead. "Go home. I'll be there later tonight. I need to talk to you about something, OK?" He looked at her with those eyes that told her he wanted to talk about something more important than whatever his Physical Education goals paper had been about, and she was, unexplainably, a little worried. "And don't worry about Dani; she'll come around eventually." Then he was off down the hall in the same direction that Dani had disappeared. "Hey, Danielle—" Kyle's voice echoed through the senior hall as he called out to her, "—you coming or what?" Then he was gone, disappearing around the corner.

Alee stood there debating about what to do next, but she knew she really only had one option: meeting her cousin at her car and heading home for the night. The problem was she really didn't want to go home, at least not yet.

Just before school started, a new rule had been issued: students were allowed have cell phones at school as long as they didn't use them during class. The change came about after two freshmen girls had gone missing in the middle of the school day. After weeks of searching with no luck, the parents had decided to petition the school board to allow students to carry phones. They argued that if their daughters had had their phones they could have called for help if they were in trouble. Everyone just figured the girls ran away, but the principal approved the rule anyway.

Luckily for Alee, her cell phone just happened to be in her pocket. Phoebe's number was already preloaded when her mother gave her the phone a few days ago, but then again, so were the numbers for just about every member of the Wenham family, half of whom she didn't even know, and the other half she probably would never call.

She dialed Phoebe, who picked up on the first ring. "Where are you?" She wasn't too happy about being left to wait in the school parking lot.

"Wow. No hello? No hi—how was your first day?" She waited but Phoebe didn't respond. Apparently Alee's attempt to lighten the mood wasn't really working. Phoebe just huffed on the other end of the line.

"OK." Alee gave up. "Never mind. Listen, I have to take care of a few things, so—."

"No, I was instructed to bring you to school, and take you straight home after."

"But—."

Alee couldn't even get a sentence out before Phoebe jumped right in again. "No buts. Sorry, Aleerah. If you want time to yourself that's fine, but you'll have to do it at home with everyone else. I don't make the rules, but I sure as hell am not going to break them just so you—."

"Phoebe, please. I just need a few hours to—." She was pleading now, something she hated to do, but Alee couldn't see any other way to make her cousin listen. It was no use. She could feel Phoebe's mood getting worse as the seconds passed. "Never mind, I'll be right out." She hung up the phone with a sigh, and slid it into her back pocket. She didn't need anything from her locker, she already had her purse, and all of her teachers had decided to forgo homework on the first day, so she just gave in to defeat and headed for the nearest exit.

Phoebe was waiting impatiently when Alee walked up. "The last bell rang fifteen minutes ago. What took you so long?"

What the hell? Who do you think you are, my babysitter? "Just ran into someone I used to know is all." She hoped she sounded casual, but Phoebe had a way of knowing the things you were trying to hide. Phoebe seemed to know how to read people—maybe even hear their thoughts. Alee wasn't completely sure, but she had known what Alee needed that morning, even before she knew herself. It was cool in a way, but Alee suspected that it might also mean she couldn't really hide things from her. In her other life, Alee had discovered that she and Damian could communicate telepathically, but it seemed that Phoebe's powers only worked one way. She didn't let others into her mind, even if she felt it was perfectly fine for her to roam around in theirs.

"I'm not your babysitter, Aleerah—."

OK, so yeah, hearing your thoughts is most likely a yes.

"Why are you looking at me like that?" Phoebe snapped.

"Do you—I mean, can you—?"

"What? Spit it out."

"Can you hear what I'm thinking?"

Phoebe burst into laughter. "Are you serious? No, I can't hear your thoughts. I'm a witch, not a psychic."

"I just thought—never mind."

"Aleerah, you're not that hard to figure out. You're kind of like an open book. Your mother just made me promise to get you straight home after school. I had a feeling you wouldn't be happy about it. I know you've been feeling stuck or tied down at home, I know I would be. But your parents really are just trying to do what's best for you. Come on, let's get going." With that, Phoebe slid in behind the wheel, and started the car. She was trying to find something to listen to on the radio when Alee finally sat down and buckled her seatbelt. However, they didn't get far. Just as Phoebe was about to pull out of the parking lot, a tall, slender student with dark black hair stepped in front of the car and Phoebe slammed on the brakes, throwing Alee forward and then back into the seat as her seatbelt locked into place.

Alee looked up, and was eye to eye with Jathan. He looked just as shocked as she was, but he recovered much faster than either Phoebe or Alee did. Before either one of the girls could respond, he was gone—off into the tree line just beyond the road.

"Did you see a—? What the hell was that?" Phoebe sounded honestly freaked out and she put the car in park as she turned to Alee. Alee could hear her own heart pounding in her chest. It sounded like someone using a sledgehammer to break through a locked door. Alee looked at Phoebe, who was gripping the steering wheel so tightly her knuckles were turning white.

Alee didn't know what she could do, if anything, but she wasn't the type of girl to just sit around when something went wrong. She had to do something, and with the way Jathan had moved she knew that her window of opportunity was quickly closing. She had to act fast. "Phoebe, look at me." Phoebe did as she was told, and Alee looked deep into her eyes. Apparently Alee was channeling Kyle because she had to fight the urge to say, *"These aren't the droids you're looking for,"* and instead, softly whispered, "Go home, everything is fine. I'll be right behind you." Alee's pupils expanded and contracted like it was the most natural thing in the world, and as quickly as that Phoebe was slowly shifting the gear to drive and Alee was out of the car and into the woods.

Stopping briefly at the tree line, Alee turned to watch as Phoebe pulled the car out of the parking lot and headed home as if nothing had happened. Alee ran swiftly into the woods—heart pounding, mind racing. She didn't know where Jathan had gone, or what she would do if she found him.

She approached the dense center of the forest—the trees surrounding her like guards standing tall to protect her from an unknown enemy. She stood silent—waiting, listening. She could feel the warm summer wind against her skin and it sent a chill down her spine. She could smell the fresh scent of wildflowers lingering in the air from the open field just beyond the tree line. She sensed danger approaching, but couldn't see it. Then, without warning, she heard him rushing toward her. A gust of wind brushed her cheek, and Jathan appeared before her as if he had materialized out of nothing at all. Tall, dark, handsome—he stood in the distance, shaded by the cover of the trees above and surrounded by a soft mist of ominous fog.

Jathan moved with a grace Alee had never seen, and in seconds he was there, only inches away. He reached up and gently rubbed his thumb along her jaw. Without thinking, she leaned into him and their lips met for less than a second before he turned away and rested his cheek upon hers. The warmth of his breath was almost overwhelming as he leaned in close to her ear. "You don't need to be afraid—not of me." Pulling back he looked deep into her eyes, "Oh how I have missed your kiss."

"What? We've never—."

"Wake up." It was no more than a whisper, but her eyes flew open and the seatbelt tightened around her as her whole body jerked awake. Her breathing was labored and her chest hurt as if a heavy weight had been laid upon it.

"Wow, you must have been tired. You were out before we even left the school." Phoebe didn't seem surprised, or even all that concerned.

"What? Where are we?" But even as she asked the question she knew. They were just pulling into the parking lot of The Black Onyx, her new home. "Oh—." Alee didn't even try to hide her disappointment. Something about being in the woods, something calling to her, danger, mystery, freedom—

being with Jathan. She couldn't shake the feeling that it had actually happened. That it wasn't just a dream.

Phoebe parked the car and hopped out, leaving a pile of books and papers on the floor in the back seat. "Must have been some dream. You didn't even stir when your phone rang." Alee quickly reached for the cell phone in her back pocket, but it wasn't there. "Looking for this?" Phoebe held her hand up, revealing Alee's small pink phone, and then quickly tossed it back into her purse. "Kyle said he'll be by around seven. I told him tonight wasn't really good, and that you'd see him tomorrow at school."

Anger boiled up inside of her, and if Phoebe hadn't been on the other side of the car, Alee probably would have attacked. "What? Why would you do that? You had no right!"

Her answer was just as cryptic as everything else Phoebe did. "I told you, your mother said to bring you straight home. She has something planned." Then she nodded toward the front of the building. Alee turned to look where Phoebe was gesturing and saw Loraline standing in the open doorway dressed in a long flowing white gown. Behind her stood five generations of Wenham woman, all dressed in similar style dresses made of lace, silk, and ribbon. They were beautiful. Standing there, Alee could almost feel the power that they possessed right then, gathered together.

This was the first time she had seen so many of her coven family members together at one time. As she stood there, she noticed a warm glow of light that seemed to envelop them. The longer she stared at it, the more the light seemed to actually vibrate with life. Hues of every shade of the rainbow   greens, blues, oranges, yellows   glistened and sparkled before her. It was the most incredible thing she had ever seen. When she turned to Phoebe for an explanation,

Alee was astonished to see that a soft purple haze shimmered about her cousin. Alee reached out with timid hands, searching the air, but couldn't feel anything as her fingers seemed to move through the light. "It's so—wow. What is it?"

Phoebe must not have seen anything, because she backed away from Alee's probing hands. But then Phoebe snatched Alee's hand out of the air and turned her wrist up to reveal Alee's tattoo. *What the hell? Phoebe thought.* Alee's tattoo was glowing in Phoebe's hand.

Why is it doing that? Alee wondered.

Phoebe pulled away, only to realize that her own tattoo was also glowing softly—something it had never done before. But it quickly faded when she let go of Alee's wrist.

"I don't know why it does that," Alee said, answering the question as if Phoebe had asked it out loud.

"What? I didn't say—." Phoebe turned and ran up the walk to join the others, rubbing her wrist. Alee just stood there next to the car watching in shock, not sure what to do.

"Phoebe?" Alee called uncertainly, but her cousin didn't turn back to answer. Phoebe went straight to her mother, Jacinda, who quickly examined the tattoo on her daughter's wrist. But there was nothing wrong with it, and no one had a clue as to why it had been glowing.

Alee slowly followed.

Inside, Loraline handed Alee a large black box, a little bigger than a gift box you might wrap a shirt or sweater in. When she opened the lid, Alee couldn't help but smile at the white silk sundress that lay inside. "It's beautiful, but why?"

Loraline's smile was soft like a mother's should be, but wise far beyond her years. "Tonight is a time to celebrate—a time for family." Her eyes sparkled as she spoke. "We will welcome in the new moon together tonight, as a family, for the first time." She pulled the dress out of the box and held it up in front of Alee. "This was my ceremonial gown when I came of age. I think it will look beautiful on you." She brushed the hair out of Alee's eyes with a light sweep of her fingertips. "I do hope you like it." Alee could only nod. "Good. There are sandwiches and a vegetable tray laid out in the kitchen. Go grab something to eat and get dressed. We'll meet out back this evening at six o'clock. Phoebe and Petra will help you get ready."

Everything was happening so quickly. When they got to her room, the girls helped her into her dress and changed into their own dresses as well. Ribbons were braided into her hair and even around her bare feet and ankles to replace her shoes. Somehow, through this process, Alee started to feel calm, still, and almost serene.

There was a hushed knock at the door, just before Eric stepped into the room. Eric was Alee's father—her biological father—and the reason, as far as Alee could tell, that she had struggled with illness for her entire life. She didn't blame him though. It wasn't his fault that he was a vampire. It wasn't his fault that he fell in love with a mortal woman. It wasn't even his fault that she was born. Who would have guessed that all that was even possible? Certainly not Alee, but then again, until a few weeks ago, she thought of vampires and witches only as fictional characters in novels and movies.

"Girls, may I have a moment alone with Aleerah please?" Eric was, in every sense of the word, enchanting—from his piercing eyes to his alluring voice, from his chiseled build to his lightning speed. It was hard to say no to him, and she could clearly see why her mother, Loraline, had fallen for him in the first place, and what had kept her hanging on even after so many years of being apart. Petra and Phoebe nodded, and disappeared into the hall. "You—you look beautiful."

Alee could feel the heat rise in her cheeks and knew that she was blushing at the compliment. "I can see your mother in you."

Eric approached her with caution, not wanting to startle her. In his hands he held two items out to her. One was a black velvet bag with a soft red drawstring ribbon holding it closed. The other was a small wooden box she knew well. She had had it since childhood, and knew that it was filled with birthday cards she had been receiving since she was six years old. Seeing it now made her heart skip a beat. "It was you—but how?"

"After I lost you and your mother, I was in a very bad place in my life. I did things I'm not very proud of. But I never stopped searching for you. Then it happened, I knew it was you from the moment I laid eyes on you." Eric paused and turned away.

"Then why—?"

After a deep calming breath, Eric continued his story. "I wasn't able to take care of you. After everything that had happened I didn't have the self-control to keep you safe. Martha seemed like a very caring woman, and I could tell she loved you very much. I knew that in the Moyer's home you would be safe, so I decided to keep my distance, at least until you were older, and I was more stable. I visited often, watching you sleep."

"That was you!" Alee remembered the feeling she would often get lying in bed, like someone was standing in the shadows of her room. But whenever she turned on the lights, no one was there.

"Yes, it was me. I was there." Eric took another step closer. "You have to understand Aleerah, I wanted nothing more than to be a part of your life, but I didn't know how. You were sick, and they took care of you. If I had known that all you really needed was blood I would have stepped in sooner, but I didn't know that. I thought—." He took a deep breath before continuing. "I watched through the window as you celebrated your sixth birthday and I could see how happy your parents made you. I left the gift on your balcony so that maybe someday you would know that I loved you as much as they did." He turned his face away for a moment.

It all made sense to her now—like the pieces of a puzzle falling into place. Of course it hadn't been her parents leaving those special birthday gifts for her every year. It had been Eric all along—year after year. "But why these gifts? Why crystals?"

"I hoped that you would be blessed with your mother's gifts, and that one day, when you came of age, the crystals and gems I left you would help you find your way home."

Alee took the box and traced the rose engraved on the top with the tip of her finger, as she had done so many times before. "What does it mean, the rose?"

"You've seen your mother's tattoo?"

"Yes, it's a pentagram like mine, with a rose—oh." It made sense now. Why she hadn't put the two together weeks ago when she first saw Loraline's tattoo, she didn't know.

"It's called a b—."

"Blood rose." She said, finishing his sentence.

"Yes. It is a very delicate and very robust flower all at once. Much like your mother and you." Eric gently ran his hand down the side of Alee's cheek. "They are rare—very rare in fact, which is one of the reasons they are seen as a highly treasured gift among our kind."

Our kind. Her eyes went to his with a flash of red. She didn't mean any disrespect, and she blushed from embarrassment—shame—when she realized what she had done, but she still didn't really see herself as one of "his kind" as he had so plainly put it. She wasn't really ready to accept that side of herself just yet, even if she did admittedly partake in the "red syrup" as she called it.

"You will find, Aleerah, that *who* you are has very little to do with *what* you are." Eric's demeanor was always so calm and reserved. Maybe, after over seven hundred years of living, if you can call it living, you gain a little more perspective on what is really important—you learn to choose your battles.

What could she say to that? Not much. Alee lowered her eyes to avoid Eric's serious gaze. "I'm sorry. I didn't mean it," she said.

He didn't want her to apologize. He didn't want her to feel regret for showing her feelings. He especially didn't want her to feel shame for who and what she was. "Have you ever noticed that flowers don't live as long around you as they do around others?"

She thought about it for a few seconds. "I, um—. Yeah I guess I don't really have a green thumb, if that's what you mean, but I never really thought about it." *Where is he going with this?* Alee thought to herself.

"Vampires' bodies crave life because it is the one thing they don't fully control. Although we are not dead, our hearts do still beat, but we are not fully alive either. At least not in the same manner that humans are alive. And because we are connected more closely to the earth, and to nature, our bodies will try to feed on any life that is around us. Therefore, most flowers cannot survive the touch of a full-blooded vampire—at least not for long."

"What do you mean? They die, just being around—."

"No, but the touch of a vampire will slowly drain them of life. You see, flowers are seen as the bloodline of nature." He made his way to the dresser at the other end of the room where a beautiful bouquet of fresh flowers had been placed just a day ago. Reaching out his hand, he selected a single flower, being careful not to touch the others around it, and pulled it slowly out of the vase. "As we live beyond death, we, and living flowers, cannot both survive together." The flower slowly wilted and dried in his hand. Crisp and weak, the petals began to fall one by one to the floor at his feet.

Alee gaped. "But, that doesn't—. They don't—. I mean—that has never happened to me."

"No, it wouldn't. Not yet. However, the life of flowers such as these—" He gestured back to the vase, careful not to touch another of the blooms. "—is, and always has been, shorter in your care than it would have been in the care of a mere human. It may not have been noticeable, because it would have just seemed natural to you. You said it yourself, you don't have a green thumb."

"Are you saying that vampires can actually feed off of flowers?"

"No, not feed. It's more just a draining of life that we don't gain anything from. No power. No energy. No relief from our hunger."

"Then, why would a rose be a treasured gift among vampires? How could it even be given as a gift if it would die almost instantly in your hand?" She hadn't lost sight of her original focus—to figure out what the blood rose on her box and Loraline's tattoo meant. However, they seemed to be taking the long way to get to the answer.

Eric shook his head. "Not just a rose. A blood rose. Like I said, they are very rare, and just as vampires live off of the blood of humans, blood roses live off the life of other flowers. They attack through the root systems of other plants, and feed until the other flowers around them wither and die. A vampire's touch has no effect on the life of the blood rose, or its beauty."

Alee just stood still, taking it all in—fitting it all together.

"Open the bag." Eric broke the silence first.

Alee untied the red ribbon, and poured the contents into her hand. It was every crystal—every stone. He had gone back to her old house and salvaged the things that meant so much to her. Her eyes filled with tears, and she fell into his arms. "Thank you." It wasn't much, but it said everything she was feeling. Eric wrapped his arms around her, not holding back this time. He held her close to his heart. He had been longing to hold his baby girl ever since that night, so long ago, when she had slipped out of his life. But hadn't wanted to rush her.

With her ear to his chest, Alee's crying slowed, and finally stopped. The silence of her father's chest was deafening. "Wow." It was one thing to be told about vampires, and maybe it wasn't even so hard to believe in the possibility, but to hear firsthand the silence where the beating heart should be—that made it all real.

Alee had hunted, killed, and drained numerous animals over the past few weeks. She had tasted the blood on her tongue and craved it, longing for the strength she felt after she fed. She had even learned to control the thirst that had been growing since that first kiss she shared with Kyle when she had tasted his blood, ever so slightly, for the very first time. But, it wasn't until that moment, standing here in Eric's arms, that everything truly sank in.

Softly, pulling away, she turned to face him. "I can't hear anything, but you said—."

"Listen again. It's there. Only it's much weaker and slower." Alee pressed her ear against Eric's chest, and listened for at least twenty seconds, until she heard a single thump. It was softer than normal, almost unrecognizable.

"My heart still beats normally though, Why?"

"Your heart will continue to beat as it does today until the day you've completed your change." Eric's answer was so simple, yet Alee didn't feel satisfied.

She probed for more, feeling in her gut that Eric wasn't telling her everything. "And, then? What happens then? You say vampires aren't dead, but can I die?"

Eric took a deep breath, more as a way to postpone answering her question than anything else, seeing as vampires don't really need to breathe, let alone take such labored breaths. Breathing is more of a habit than a necessity for vampires, as well as a way to more easily blend into society. "Yes, you can die, if your body rejects the change, or if you are injured badly enough. Although vampires aren't dead, it doesn't mean that they cannot die. It is just harder, and so until your body has accepted the change—." He looked away. "Before your body has changed enough to heal on its own, at some point the part of you that is still mortal will not—die— but will cease to exist. It is hard to know what will happen at that time, no dhampir has ever lived that long. However, legend states that if you complete the change like other vampires do, you will—" He started to get choked on his words, "—in a way, be reborn."

A thousand possibilities went through Alee's mind: vampire, zombie, walking dead. "You mean I'll—." Scenes from her favorite horror films flashed before her—arms reaching out of freshly packed graves, corpses springing to life on the autopsy table. None of the possibilities seemed as intriguing at that moment when anything was possible so much more so than they had been on the television screen that portrayed make-believe and fantasy.

Eric's face hardened, "You would be what you are today, a vampire and a witch. The only difference is that you would have the same vulnerabilities and strengths that I have—that all full-blood vampires have. You would be immortal, but you would—." He turned away again, speechless.

Alee almost lost her footing, feeling lightheaded—a sensation that had been happening more and more frequently, and she moved to the edge of her bed to sit down. The thought of dying didn't scare her. She had grown used to that idea as a young child who had been in and out of hospitals since birth, but the thought of walking the earth for all eternity—that was a different story, and she wasn't sure how she felt about it. Now, to have Eric here with her, obviously speechless, what could possibly be worse than what he had already told her?

"I would, what?" Desperation was welling up inside of her, and every second felt like an eternity.

When Eric finally turned to face her, all the hopelessness she had been feeling melted away. His face was soft and comforting once again. He spoke plainly, stating the facts simply. He knew it wasn't going to be easy, but he was there for her. "You would stop aging, like I have."

"OK." Alee couldn't really understand why that had concerned him so much.

"Aleerah, you don't understand the gravity of how that will affect your life. Time would stop for you, but continue for those around you." Eric sat down beside her on the bed, and gently held her hand. "The hardest part about living this life is watching those you love grow old without you. Watching those you love as they live, and as they die.

Saying goodbye doesn't get easier with age or experience."
Alee could see in his eyes that it truly was the hardest part, at
least for him. She had never even considered that kind of
possibility.

So there it was—the catch. You get to live forever, but
those you love do not. She would have to watch Kyle grow
old and one day die. She would live a thousand lives, never
really able to connect to people, because she would always
know that they would die while she lived on. Everything
seemed so final now, but somewhere in the back of her mind
she was already accepting her fate. At least in this reality, as
unreal as it seemed, she had a family, and although she knew
that someday they would die she didn't think it would be any
time soon.

Alee stood up and with a crooked little smile. "Wow,
you sure do know how to lighten the mood don't you Dad?"
Then she spun around in her new white dress. "How do I
look?"

He was a little shocked by her sudden dismissal of
what he was saying, but to hear her call him Dad—that was a
step closer to the relationship he had been hoping for all these
years. "Beautiful. I think you're ready."

The clock on her bedside table said five fifty-three as
Eric led her out of the room and into the darkness.

4

In the field down the hill behind The Black Onyx, there was a large stone-lined fire-pit, but as of yet no fire was burning. All of the Wenham woman were there, gathered together. All eyes turned to Alee and her father as they walked down the path, and a hush filled the air. Eric led Alee straight to Loraline, who he leaned in to kiss softly on the lips. He turned to Alee and smiled. "Go and have fun, but after the Celebration is over the real fun begins." His smile turned playfully wicked and then he laughed out loud. He seemed happier than she had ever seen him, almost younger, and she was honestly pleased for him.

Playfully, as if she had known him all her life, Loraline smacked him on the shoulder. "Hush now."

"What. You know it's true." Then as an aside to Alee, "There is nothing like hunting under the new moon." Eric headed back up to the shop, waving over his shoulder. "I'll see you ladies later." He had a grin on his face like he knew something they didn't—his own private little secret. It hadn't taken long for Eric to slip back into his old life. He knew the woods behind the Black Onyx well, from the many years he spent hunting there. He was comfortable among Loraline's family and felt at times like it was a perfect fit. It was times like these that made him remember how hard it had been when he and Loraline had first announced how they felt about each other. Had her family only accepted their relationship, things would have been so different. He never could understand how they could be perfectly fine having him around to protect them, but they couldn't bear the thought of him becoming a part of their family.

The word "witch" had always left a bad taste in Alee's mouth. It wasn't the idea of witchcraft, but the preconceived notion of what a witch represented: evil, dark magic, human sacrifices, and even Satanic worship. Alee knew it was silly to believe such myths, but having been brought up in a fairly religious family, the ideas that those things might actually be real was a little scary. She had dabbled with her girlfriends in potions, spells, and other such things, but at the time it was just for fun. They had never taken it further than what they were comfortable with. The only thing she ever really believed in were the powers of her crystals, but even that had more to do with nature and healing then with witchcraft. It was kind of like the difference between weed and cocaine. Somehow weed seems safe, like less of a drug because it's all natural without any manmade chemicals mixed in.

Witches, in Alee's mind, had always been the stereotypical old hags with the big black moles on their noses and the long black gowns blowing in the wind behind them as they flew on their old wooden brooms. So basically, she imagined the Halloween version of a witch

Over the past few weeks, Alee had already begun to regret all of the negative feelings she had had about witchcraft over the years. Seeing all of these amazing women standing there together was lovely. The rainbow of colors she had seen earlier was still there, flowing all around them as if they were standing in the middle of a magical river. Individual colors followed each woman as if each woman's aura were somehow connected to her. Where one woman stood by another, the colors mixed, forming different shades as the women moved around, mingling together.

Loraline and Alee stood off to the side as Alee took it all in. For Loraline, seeing everything through Alee's eyes was like seeing it all for the first time again. When Alee finally turned to Loraline, she saw a brilliant emerald green glow radiating around her mother. It was mesmerizing, and almost musical.

Loraline was smiling as she watched Alee's wonder and amazement. "What are you looking at? Tell me what it is you see?" Alee could hear her voice, but Loraline sounded miles away.

"I don't know."

"Can you describe it to me?"

Alee reached out to touch the air around Loraline's face, but unlike Phoebe, Loraline didn't move away. As Alee ran her fingers through the green light it almost moved with her, mirroring her movement and wrapping itself around her hand before pulling away as she retracted. "It's like—you're bathed in beautiful green light." But, even as she said it, she knew those words didn't do justice to what she saw before her. "All of you—every shade of every color it's—."

Loraline took a deep breath and let it out with a sigh of bliss. When Alee looked up, the others had joined them and were standing close together in a half circle around them watching, waiting. Their delight was apparent—like children's joy on Christmas morning—spreading throughout the group. Alee's talents, as witches call them, were beginning to show themselves, and although she herself didn't understand them, those around her did. It was obvious, already, that she was going to be very special and ultimately very powerful, given the proper instruction and time to learn.

Edith Wenham, Alee's great great grandmother, moved to the center of the gathering. Alee noticed that she was the only one enveloped in a soft white glow, and unlike everyone else's her light seemed to stay only with her without clinging to others around her when she got closer to them. In awe, Alee had to ask what seemed to her to be the obvious question, "Are you an angel?"

"She has your gift, Granny Edith. She sees the auras." Loraline was thrilled at this new revelation and filled with deep wonderment. "My Aleerah has the gift of a seer."

"Does she now?" Edith took Alee's hand in hers and led her to one of the sixteen small meditation blankets that had been placed in a circle around the fire pit. One by one, each of the women took her place on one of the mats that had been placed around the fire-pit, but Alee could not take her eyes off of the soft white light that was illuminating her grandmother. "For generations, the Wenham women have been gifted, powerful witches. Those around you, and you yourself, are no exception. In time you will learn to perfect your talents—to control your gifts."

What gifts? What talents? Alee had never felt all that special, and to think that she might have anything that could possibly qualify as a gift or a talent was more than a little thrilling.

Edith was wise, and like a natural teacher, she led her great great granddaughter to the answers that were already in Alee's mind, though not yet in her awareness. "A seer, your mother called you. This means you have an open eye. We shall see in time how open. Auras are only the beginning of what a true seer is able to see." Alee had heard of auras before, but had never imagined them to be as beautiful as the currents of colors she was seeing this night. She wanted to know everything, learn everything possible that she could about them, but right now was not the time, or the place. "And this—." Edith ran her coarse, old fingers over the tattoo on Alee's wrist "Such a mystery. Well, I'm sure there is so much more to come."

They were gathered to welcome in the new moon. Alee had no idea what the new moon was, let alone what it meant to welcome it, or why you even would. The ritual was simple. From a small bag, Edith brought out five candles in deep holders and arranged these in perfectly sized niches around the base of the fire-pit. Then she withdrew a number of smaller round white "moon candles" in clear glass globes. She placed one of these candles on each of the women's mats. She began the ceremony, welcoming each element into the circle by lighting a candle for it. She withdrew the first candle holder from its niche, and gazed at it intently as she chanted in a strong, unaccented monotone, "The evening breeze holds me in her arms and I too welcome the wind into our circle." A flame sprang up within the candle holder, and she replaced it in its niche. Alee's hair ruffled around her face as the wind began to pick up. "The stream of life brings new beginnings and I too welcome the water into our circle." The second candle came alive, and Alee felt moisture, like a fog, around her, but as she glanced around the circle it didn't seem like anyone else had noticed the change. *Maybe they're just used to it, or maybe I'm just crazy,* she thought to herself.

"The warm dancing flames guide our way and I too welcome the fire into our circle." The third candle lit, and Alee felt warm inside. Small beads of perspiration began to form along her hairline, and she quietly wiped them away with the back of her hand.

"Are you all right dear?" Loraline whispered. Alee could feel her quiet, watchful concern, but, unsure of her voice, Alee only nodded.

"The dirt below our feet feeds new life and I too welcome the earth into our circle." As the fourth candle began to flicker, Alee caught scents of fresh mown grass, and blooming flowers.

What is this? Alee thought to herself. Again she scanned the faces of the women around her, but still no one else seemed to be fazed by anything that was happening.

"With the power of wind water fire and earth I welcome the goddesses into our circle." Alee shivered, and took a deep breath of anticipation.

Edith stepped out of the circle and stopped at her own empty mat beside Alee's. She lifted her small moon candle and gazed at it until it began to glow, then placed it into the fire-pit. Loraline picked up her moon candle, which came to life in her hands. She lifted it to her grandmother, who turned and placed it in the fire-pit. Each woman, one by one around the circle, did the same. As each moon candle was lit, and placed, the women chanted, "I welcome the moon and the changes she brings. I let go of who I am for the woman I am becoming."

Finally, it was Alee's turn. She lifted her moon candle as she chanted, and, as Edith took the globe from Alee's hands the candle flickered into life. When Edith placed the final glowing candle amongst the others, the affirmation was complete. The moon candle flames began to swell and join one another, reaching above the rim of the fire pit, reaching four feet above the rim—much higher than even that many candles of that size should burn—in a solitary blaze that revealed the women's faces, their intent expressions.

It started quietly at first, with a single voice "Fire burns and fire turns. So shall she let us see." Alee didn't recognize the dark-haired girl on the other side of the fire-pit who started the chant. The others joined in quickly, everyone speaking in unison. "Fire burns and fire turns. So shall she let us see." Alee couldn't help but joint in as well.

The brilliant yellow, blue, and white flames now blazed high above their heads, rolling and swirling, rotating and growing above them into a sphere of light. Then, without warning, the flames burst overhead, erupting into tiny specks of glowing dust that seemed to drift away into the sky, disappear, and disintegrate into nothingness. The circle of women now sat, surrounded by the darkness, and, as if choreographed, a glimmer of light appeared just above the horizon of treetops. Within moments the light was transformed into a rising moon—the largest, most awe inspiring and mysterious moon of all: the black moon—the new moon. The phenomenon only lasted for a brief instant—before the thin crescent of bright moonlight began to form around the edge of the giant black moon—but Alee felt blessed by the goddesses to have been there that night to see it, and to have shared it with these astonishing women.

The heat of the fire had practically liquefied the candles in their glass globes, but Alee still picked hers up. She wanted a way to hold on to the memory of that evening. As everyone around her slowly made their way back up the hill and into the house, she remained, staring into the moonlit night.

There had been so many times in her childhood when Alee had found herself wondering if there were more to life, bigger things out there than just what you see day to day. She no longer wondered. She knew, and she realized that knowing doesn't always make it easier to accept, or less scary. Sometimes knowing actually makes it harder to look into the darkness, harder to open the door when you don't know what is inside. But—Alee wasn't afraid.

It had been a while since everyone had gone inside, and Alee was enjoying the peace and quiet—listening to the sounds of the night, focusing on everything and nothing at all—when she felt a sudden chill. It wasn't the cool night air, or even the whispers of the wind in the trees that had startled her. It was knowing, without a doubt, that she wasn't alone. She was on her feet in seconds, scanning the tree line when she saw what looked like a person moving among the trees. Her first thought was of Jathan, and she watched carefully as the shadowy figure hovered near the cover of the tree line, disappearing each time it got to close to the trees. Now there seemed to be two figures, but who—*what*—they were, she didn't know.

Alee crouched down, hidden by the shadow of the hill behind her, and stopped focusing on looking, and focused on *listening*. She knew the sound of her own heartbeat well, but in the distance she could hear two additional, and distinctly different heartbeats. One was slow and soft, the other was so rapid that it sounded frantic. She was used to hunting: after doing it a couple of times it had become almost natural. Eric had told her that it was in her blood, and that it was only natural that she should be good at it.

Against her better judgment and her extensive knowledge from old horror movies—about what always happens when you follow strange noises into dark places— she started moving slowly in the direction of the heartbeats. Once she reached the cover of the trees, she moved rapidly toward the location where she had seen the thing, or things, moving in the shadows. She used the trees for cover, and the softness of the forest earth absorbed the sound of twigs breaking beneath her feet as she ran.

She was practically flying through the forest—ducking under low hanging branches, and leaping over fallen trees—when out of nowhere, she was pummeled and thrown to the ground. Her fangs came out effortlessly as she found and gripped the throat of her attacker—purely by instinct, as if she had been doing it all her life. She had managed to sink her teeth in, but only briefly, not long enough to release enough venom to sedate her attacker before an intense pain ripped through her leg. She broke free, rolled to the side, and leapt to her feet. Not five feet away stood a large black and brown wolf with chocolate brown eyes. Glancing down at her leg, Alee realized that the wolf had bitten her. The long skirt of her dress was absorbing the blood that drained from the exposed wound on her thigh.

The wolf was poised to attack again, and just as it pushed off into its leap, a snowy white wolf flew past Alee from behind, meeting the black and brown in mid-air and forcing it to the ground. For a moment Alee stood in shock, watching the wolves battle. Then, as reality dawned, she turned to run away. She was losing blood quickly though, and her injured leg was weak. She stumbled and fell, hitting her head on the edge of an old tree stump.

Before she blacked out, Alee saw the back of the white wolf as it stood ready to attack again—not her, but the black and brown wolf—and the darker wolf turned and ran, the white wolf in chase close behind. She watched them grow smaller and less defined, until finally they were gone, and she was surrounded by nothing but darkness.

Eric was already headed out to the field to find Alee when he was struck by a sudden premonition that she was in trouble. He had been excited to take her on their first new moon hunt, but now all he could think of was the need to protect her. She was part of him. His blood flowed through her veins—which meant that he was able to feel her emotions, both good and bad.

It didn't take him long to pick up her trail. He followed it to the edge of the trees and, instantly, the scent of her blood surrounded him. He dashed at full speed into the woods, his senses guiding him flawlessly. When he found her, she was limp and lifeless. Her heartbeat was deathly shallow. It was all too familiar, and he could see that she had lost a lot of blood. He knew that he didn't have much time to stop the bleeding. "Aleerah? Aleerah, wake up!" he begged. Being only a half-breed, Alee didn't heal at the same speed as other vampires. The wound on her leg could be fatal if not treated right away.

Eric had flashbacks of the night he had found Loraline lying on their bedroom floor, covered in her own blood. He remembered how frantically he had tried to stop the bleeding, before he was knocked unconscious from behind. He had been too distraught to notice that there was someone else in the room. He wasn't going to make the same mistake now, and he scanned the darkness around them.

He hadn't been able to help Loraline, but he knew what must be done for his daughter, here in these dark woods. Yet *knowing* didn't make it any easier. How would Alee react to having drunk his blood straight from the vein? He couldn't know that, but he knew that this was the only thing that could save her.

With his fangs exposed, he bit into the flesh on the inside of his wrist. Blood started to trickle out slowly at first, but soon it poured freely. With his other hand, he opened Alee's mouth and then placed his wrist above it, allowing the blood to drip in, and watching carefully he made sure that she didn't choke.

The minutes dragged on as he waited for the blood to take effect. Just as he started to think that he had been too late once again, she gasped, pulled his arm toward her mouth, and bit down on his wrist. She was still so new, and didn't yet have control over the thirst during feedings. It was one thing to stop a craving before it took over, but trying to stop feeding when your body needed it as badly as hers did was completely different, and almost impossible for such a young vampire.

Eric managed to pull his arm away and regain Alee's focus. She realized what was happening and—stunned— pulled herself to a sitting position, backing up to the nearest tree with her arms wrapped tightly around her legs. "I'm so sorry." She couldn't bring herself to look him in the eyes.

"It's OK. I'm all right," he assured her. And it was true. The wound on his wrist had already closed, and what looked like a small red scratch was already beginning to fade.

Still staring at his wrist in shock, Alee asked, "How?"

"It could be a combination of things—your saliva, my age—."

"What do you mean?" Alee asked uncertainly.

"You're young, and not fully changed, but you may already have the saliva of a vampire. When you feed, two things happen, first, as you bite down you release a venom that acts as a sedative to calm your—prey. Then, when you're done feeding, your saliva will help to heal the wounds, leaving little trace of what you have done." He lifted his wrist again for her to see, as if he were participating in grade school show and tell. "Besides, I am a vampire, and we heal faster than humans. The older we are the faster we heal, and, well, I'm not young." Eric chuckled.

"How—old—?" She looked up at him as Eric slowly unwrapped her arms so that he could examine the wound on her leg.

"In human years I would be—" he thought for a moment "—just over seven hundred years old." Alee was speechless. Eric looked back down at her leg. "How's it feeling now?" There were still traces of teeth marks where she had been bitten, but the bleeding had stopped, and the wound was already scabbing over.

"I think it's OK." She ran her hand over the scabs cautiously.

When Eric lifted her to her feet, Alee was surprised to find that she was actually able to walk with only a little pain. Other than the rather large bump on her head and the throbbing headache, she felt all right. However, her once beautiful gown was now torn apart and covered in mud, grass stains, and blood. She started to feel sick. *What the hell just happened?* She thought to herself, but something completely different came out of her mouth. "I think I'm going to vomit."

"Just try to breathe." Eric sat her back down on the cool ground. Kneeling next to her, he rubbed her back. Within a few minutes the nausea faded. "Are you ready to try walking again?" Alee nodded, but she didn't move to get up, at least not right away.

"How long will it take?"

Her question came out of nowhere, so Eric's obvious confusion was understandable. "How long will what take?"

Alee had picked up a small stick from the ground in front of her, and was fiddling with it. "How long will it take before I can control my cravings? You don't seem to eat as much as I need to, and I haven't seen you take the pills either—."

"No, I don't. I don't need them, I never have. Besides that wasn't an option when I was a new vampire." He sat down in front of her. "Your body is still alive, fully alive. You understand that right?" Alee nodded. "In order to sustain that life, you have to eat regularly—not only blood, but food as well. However, when you can't get blood, the pills are the next best thing. Think of them as vitamins."

"The next best thing? They're made of blood right?" Eric nodded "Animal blood?"

"No."

"Human?"

"Not exactly."

"Vampire blood?" Alee saw the answer in his eyes before he had a chance to say it out loud. "Your blood?"

"Yes."

"Phoebe told me, but I didn't know if it was true or not. I thought she might be, I don't know, messing with me." Eric shook his head.

"Why? Why not animal? You said animal blood is just as good as human blood."

"Animal blood is—." Eric struggled to find the right words. "It will do. However, it isn't the same as human blood, and it doesn't even come close to that of a lycanthrope, although I find their blood to be too sweet. But vampire blood is in a whole other class, and shouldn't be taken lightly."

"What does that even mean?"

"Vampires only share blood for two reasons. The first is with others of their bloodline, as you are to me. My blood will help you heal more so than any other blood. It will also help you through your transformation, and assist you in the development of your powers. You will most likely have many of the same powers that I do, but, since you are a dhampir, I really don't know what you will be capable of."

"I won't have to take them, after I—."

"No. You also won't need to feed more than once or twice a week. Well, after you get through the initial newborn phase." *Newborn phase?* She wanted to know what that meant, and by the look on his face, he knew what she was thinking. "Don't worry. You won't have to go through it alone. Your mother and I will be there with you, when that time comes."

"Is it hard?"

"It isn't easy, but as long as you get the blood you need while your body is changing, you'll be fine. Besides, I have a feeling that what you're going through now will only make that part of the change easier when it does happen. You will already be used to some of the cravings you will feel then." Alee wanted to know more, but was too afraid to ask. "Now, let's get you back inside."

"What about our hunt?" Alee asked him apologetically.

"Not tonight. There will be many more to come. I promise." They stood up and made their way back through the woods, following the ridgeline. They could have run the distance in less than a minute, but instead they took their time, walking in a comfortable silence for a while, and then Alee remembered something.

"Wait, you said there are two reasons a vampire shares blood. What is the second?"

"Oh, yes. The second is, well, it's more of a private act between—"

"Between?"

"—lovers. Between lovers."

"Oh." Even under the glow of the moon Alee was sure she was blushing.

"Yes, 'oh.' Now, let's get you inside. I'm sure you need your rest, and I—well, I think I need a drink." Eric and Alee hurried into the house, taking the back steps two at a time, neither one wanting to make eye contact.

Finally home, all Alee wanted to do was take a hot shower, crawl into bed, forget that the last hour of her life ever happened, and sleep. Unfortunately, that wasn't in the cards for her.

When they walked through the back door into the kitchen, Loraline was waiting with her arms crossed over her chest, and a look on her face that would have scared a ghost. "What happened to her? What did you do?" Loraline was angry, and all of it was directed at Eric.

"You're over-reacting—she's fine." He spoke too soon. At his side, Alee began to slowly drift off, fainting into his arms. "OK, maybe not fine now, but she was, and she will be."

Loraline didn't have to say anything. The glare in her eyes told him exactly what she was thinking.

"I promise." Eric hated to be in the hot seat. "Besides, this isn't my fault. We didn't even have a chance to hunt. She was worse off than this when I found her." That wasn't helping his case, as far as he could tell. "What I mean is that she had lost a lot of blood, but I helped her. If I hadn't found her. Never mind." He gave up and lay Alee down on the kitchen table, while Loraline called down the hall to her sister, who—surprisingly—was still there, long after everyone else had gone home.

In minutes, Jacinda and Loraline were working in silent harmony. Loraline smoothed a dark salve over the bite on Alee's leg and wrapped a warm towel around it while Jacinda worked on the welt on the back of Alee's head.

Eric watched as the women worked. They were alike in so many ways—graceful, beautiful, talented. And yet Loraline, with her hunger for excitement and her zest for life, was almost more like Eric than she was like her own sister. Maybe that was what had drawn him to Loraline so many years ago; maybe it was what had drawn him to her family long before she was born. "You are so beautiful." There had always been something special about the Wenham women, and Loraline's generation was no different than those of the past hundred years.

"What are you babbling about?" Jacinda snapped. "If you aren't going to help you might as well go in the other room."

"Jacinda, leave him be," said Loraline. She was still diligently wrapping Alee's leg, but found herself looking at Eric, a hint of a smile beginning to curl her lips. "I love you too," she mouthed in a whisper so quiet he could only read her lips.

Finally, when they had done all they could do, Eric carried Alee to her room and lay her down on her bed. Loraline had followed and, moving across the room to the one small window, she placed a large purple stone on the windowsill. It was as smooth as ice and parts of it were almost translucent. "What is that?" Eric asked.

"Amethyst—" When she looked back at him, he melted. "—for protection."

"I—." Eric started to speak but she cut him off.

"You mean well, I know, but even you can't be with her a hundred percent of the time. She is still a child of the daylight, and although you are old, and you last well into the morning hours most days, you are useless by high noon." Eric just nodded. Though he would like to say otherwise, he knew better. Besides, if placing the stone on the windowsill made

Loraline happy then it made Eric happy too. She turned back, placed her hands over the stone, and said a quiet incantation before she left the room. Eric couldn't make out the words, but the soothing sound of her quiet voice repeating the calming incantation put Eric's mind at ease.

5

It was still dark outside when a soft tapping at her window woke Alee up. Not remembering going to bed, she was a little disoriented. The last thing she remembered was walking into the kitchen of The Black Onyx after being attacked in the woods out back, and that wasn't a pleasant memory. She wasn't quite awake, but she could feel that her throat was already beginning to burn. She reached down and opened the door to her bedside table, which was actually a small refrigerator designed to look like a wooden end table. She pulled out a small sports bottle, and popped open the top, tipping it back to drink. Instantly, the burning stopped and she heard the tapping again. Realizing where it was coming from, she slowly got out of bed. She turned her bedside lamp on and cautiously crossed to the window as she slipped on her robe, tying it tightly around her waist. Eric had put her to bed in the torn and tattered dress, not wanting to wake her. Her leg was swathed in bandages, but from what she could tell, it felt much better than it had just hours before.

When she pulled the curtain back, Alee's heart almost stopped and she had to bite her lips to keep from screaming. Quickly, she released the curtain, letting it fall back across the window. She dropped to the floor, pressing her back hard against the wall. *Oh my God. How does he know where I live?* It had been Jathan standing there outside her window, staring blankly into her eyes, when she had pulled back the curtain.

"Hey, open up." Tap-tap-tap—he wasn't going away.

"How do you know where I live?" Alee asked frantically.

"What are you talking about? Alee—rah, it's me, Kyle. Are you OK?" *Kyle? It couldn't have been Kyle. I know who I saw. It was—.* She slowly pulled herself up, and took a deep breath before pulling the curtain back again. There, before her, was no one other than Kyle. When she glanced back at the clock next to her bed, she realized it was only one o'clock in the morning. "What are you doing here?" If she hadn't already started pulling up the window to let him in he might have thought she wasn't happy to see him, but she was. The window stuck a little, but with one final push she got it all the way up. She didn't notice the purple amethyst stone falling out onto the ground.

"I told you I needed to talk to you. What was all that? Are you all right?" His eyes were sad, but he tried to half fake a smile for her sake. Kyle knew he should have talked to her weeks ago about what had happened after her "funeral." He didn't want Alee to find out about Damian's little confession of love from someone other than him. For that matter, there was also the fact that Damian was even able to speak, Kyle didn't know how she was going to take the news and, what was worse, he still didn't know how to tell her, but he knew he had to before she passed him in the hallway at school chatting away.

"I'm fine. You just startled me a little." Already a million thoughts of what he might want to talk to her about were going through her mind—most of which had to do with Dani—and none of which were good. She knew it had to be important to make him come all the way out to The Black Onyx so late at night. She walked over to the little tea table in her room, gesturing for him to join her. "So, what's up?" She was hoping that she sounded casual, relaxed, and maybe even a little indifferent, but Kyle knew her better than that.

He was just standing there, inside the window. "I, um—can I at least have a hug?" Kyle wasn't normally the emotional type, but something inside him felt like if she found out about Damian then he might lose her, and the thought of losing her broke his heart. Alee and Damian had always had a special sort of bond, and even though they would never admit it, Kyle wasn't blind. He knew that there was more to their relationship than just a friendship. At least there was the potential to be more. Kyle was afraid that if Alee found out how Damian really felt about her, if she didn't already know, it just might be enough to push that relationship past the friendship phase. Never mind the fact that Damian believed that Alee was dead, and Alee was now Aleerah, with a whole new look and a whole new family. OK, maybe he was worried about nothing—it's not like she could just come right out and tell Damian who she really was, but Kyle just couldn't push away his worries.

Alee quickly crossed back to him and fell into his arms. "I missed you." They stood there wrapped in each other's arms for a while. Alee's head fit perfectly under Kyle's chin, with her cheek against his chest, and his lips resting on her forehead. She could hear the steady thumping of his heart, and the sound was like music in her ears. Comforting. Steady. Strong.

"I missed you more." His voice was a whisper, but when he softly raised her chin with his finger and their eyes met she knew he loved her more than life itself. She could see it in his eyes. She realized she loved him just as much and that there was nothing in the world he could tell her that could change that.

Kyle started by kissing her softly on her forehead, then once on each cheek, and a quick peck on the tip of her nose. Alee waited for his soft warm lips to reach hers, but they never did. When she finally opened her eyes she realized that Kyle's emerald green eyes were unusually dim and hazy. A layer of tears was threatening to pour out if he even blinked. He didn't have to say a word and Alee could already feel all the pain he was bottling up inside. "What is it?" She searched his face for a hint—a clue—a sign. Anything that might tell her what was wrong. "Talk to me please."

He led her to the edge of the bed, and sat down next to her. He needed time to think, but there wasn't any. *Why didn't I wait till morning*, he scolded himself.

"I should have told you before, and I'm sorry I didn't." His throat felt dry, almost like it was closing in around itself. "But I didn't want you to find out from anyone else."

Suddenly a stabbing pain pierced through Alee's heart, and she knew exactly what he was trying to say. She had seen it written all over Dani's face. Her biggest fears realized. "Its Dani isn't it?" She stood up, almost tripping to get away from him. It explained the territorial way Dani had reacted earlier that day when she thought Kyle had been flirting. She wasn't looking out for her dead best friend; she was looking out for herself. Number one! No wonder she didn't mind him leaning on her in the hallway—everything was starting to come together and Alee could feel the anger and pain building inside of her. She was fighting to see which emotion would win.

"What?" Kyle didn't understand.

Pacing the room, holding back the tears, Alee was trying to make sense of everything. "Oh my God. You and Dani. Why didn't I see it before?" She was having trouble breathing. "I should have known. I think I did know. I think I just didn't want to see it. Oh my God—." She grabbed the pill bottle off of the dresser and quickly poured out not one, not two, but three pills and tossed them into her mouth, swallowing hard, almost gagging on the wax outer-coating.

When he finally realized what Alee was going on about, Kyle almost started laughing. He quickly stopped himself, though, realizing that she was not in a joking mood. "What? You honestly think—God no! Danielle and I are nothing more than friends." He stressed her name, using her full name and not her nickname. "You know that. Please tell me you know that!"

"Then why—? Why were you leaning on her today? You never used to do that. That's a thing. That's a thing a guy does with his girlfriend—not with his dead girlfriend's old best friend. Who? Who does that?" When she realized how silly and jealous she sounded, Alee finally just sat on the bed with her head in her hands.

Kyle pulled her in and held her close. "Are you jealous?" She could practically hear him smiling. He was actually enjoying it.

"Shut up." His chest muffled her voice.

With a chuckle, he teased, "You *are* jealous—because you looooove me?" He dragged out the word 'love,' sounding like a bad Sandra Bullock impersonation from one of Alee's favorite movies, Miss Congeniality.

"No!" Alee was trying to be serious, but couldn't help but laugh.

"Hmmm, you want to kiss me, you want to love me." Alee just sat there, wrapped in Kyle's arms. Then his tone became serious. "I love you too, Aleerah." Alee was the first girl he had ever said 'I love you' to, and he meant for her to be the last. There wasn't anything he wouldn't do for her, and right then he realized that if she loved him half as much as he loved her then there was no reason he shouldn't tell her about Damian. He pulled away and looking her in the eye. He planned to just say it. What could it hurt? "It's not Dani. It's Damian. He—."

Alee's eyes widened as if Kyle had just told her that her bedroom was on fire. Panic struck her heart and fear distorted her vision. "What happened?"

"Nothing happened. It's just that he—."

"What!" She was getting impatient and he was taking way too long.

"Well, a few weeks ago, at your funeral—." He wanted to tell her, he did, but seeing Alee's reaction to just hearing Damian's name, to the very thought that something might be wrong with him—. Kyle had been so sure of Alee's feelings for him just a moment ago, but now he was almost having doubts.

"Just tell me what happened!" she shouted.

"He can speak." It came out so quickly he didn't have time to think. Alee fell silent, and Kyle wasn't about to say another word. He waited while she processed what he had told her. For about a minute, they just sat there and she listened to the sound of their hearts beating in unison.

And then—. "So, he's OK?"

"Yes."

"What did he say?"

Kyle's heart began to speed up and Alee could sense that he was afraid. She took his hand in hers and, looking deep into his eyes, she asked him again. "Kyle, what did he say?" She held him in a trance, her pupils seemed to be the size of quarters, and he was lost inside them.

"He said that he loves you. He said that it wasn't fair that I got to be with you, and that he lost you before he even had a chance to tell you he loved you." A single tear rolled down his cheek, and Alee softly kissed it away.

She took a deep breath before closing her eyes and breaking the trance. If she had done it right, Kyle wouldn't remember a thing. Not really knowing how she felt about Damian's confession, she thought it was best not to push the issue any more with Kyle. Besides, she wasn't Alee anymore, not the Alee that Damian loved. More importantly, she was with Kyle and she was happy.

"He said—." She could see the fear in Kyle's eyes as he came out of the trance and back into reality in the exact moment he had left.

She smiled and squeezed his hand in hers. "You know what, never mind, it's not really important what he said. I'm just happy he can talk." Her eyes were filling with tears and she had to turn away, wiping them with her sleeve. "His mother must be so excited, and Victoria—I can't even imagine her reaction." When she turned back, Kyle had relaxed a little. "And, he's OK. He really is OK, right?"

"Yeah, he's fine, I guess." Kyle was confused, but thankful. "Listen, I just didn't want you to find out from someone else. I know how close you guys were and I thought you should know."

Kissing him softly on the lips, she held in all of her emotions, except for the love she felt for Kyle. "Thank you."

Looking back at the clock she saw that it was already close to two in the morning. "Can you stay?"

"I don't think that would be a good idea. Your dad is cool and all, but he doesn't seem like the type who would want your boyfriend staying over unless it was completely necessary. Besides, he's probably out in the hall listening in anyway. Does he even sleep?"

"Of course he sleeps, I think. I mean, yeah, just maybe more like in the daytime. I don't know. I actually really don't know."

Kyle straightened up. He had said what he came to say, for the most part, and he felt good about where they stood. "Well, on that note, I should get going; but I'll see you at school in the morning, OK?"

Alee was disappointed by Kyle's short visit. She had wanted to tell him all about the new moon ceremony, and what had happened afterwards—at least what she could remember about that 'afterwards' part. Part of her, though, just needed to be alone to think everything through—knowing what she now knew. She swung her robe over the foot of the bed, hoping Kyle might tuck her back in before he left. She only got as far as sitting on the bed before he realized that she was hurt.

"What happened to you? What are you wearing?"

The once so lovely white silk and lace gown now looked more like an old torn up rag. Kyle eyed the torn dress while he caressed her bandaged leg that had also been hidden beneath her long robe.

"It's my mom's—*was* my mom's. I was going to tell you. We did this really cool candle ceremony thing under the new moon—." He was just staring at her now, and she started to realize how creepy it must sound to him. She imagined what he must be thinking, picturing all of them under the moon dancing and singing or something, but of course it hadn't been at all like that. "What? Please don't look at me that way. It wasn't weird or anything, I swear."

Kyle just shook his head. "I'm not looking at you any way. I'm sure it was really interesting. It's just that—."

Alee could hear the doubt in his voice, but didn't want to acknowledge it. She couldn't. This was her new life, and she was willing to accept it. If he was going to accept her then he had to accept every part of her, including the fact that she was a witch.

"What happened?" It was the torn dress and the bandage already soaked through with blood that had his attention. The dress hadn't covered much before the attack, and now, with it torn up the way it was, it barely hung on her body, let alone provided any sort of cover.

"Oh, um—. After the ceremony I decided to stay outside for a while, by myself. I ended up taking a walk in the woods out back." Kyle groaned. The mere fact that she had gone off into the woods, alone, was enough to make his head spin. "I know, it was stupid, please don't say it." She looked down at her feet, not wanting to see the disappointed look on his face, and plunged on. "As I was walking and, out of nowhere, I was attacked—"

"Attacked? Attacked by whom?" Kyle almost shouted it. He was standing and ready to fight whoever had hurt her.

"Not whom." Alee laughed at his proper use of the word whom instead of who. "*What!*" Alee could tell he didn't understand, and she really didn't want to explain, but she knew that if they were going to last then she had to be open with him—about everything. "I think it was a wolf, well, two wolves actually, but one of them didn't hurt me. It almost—. I don't know, maybe protected me?! It was kinda weird."

He didn't know what to say. Instead he just lay down next her in bed, and pulled her close. "Maybe I can stay—just one night. What would it hurt?" Then he softly kissed her on the lips, and she closed her eyes, settling into the warmth of his arms. She lay there listening to the brisk beat of his heart as it gradually slowed down until finally he was sound asleep. Thoughts of Damian and Kyle ran through her mind and she had never felt more confused. She loved Kyle with every ounce of her being and yet she couldn't deny the connection she had with Damian. She eventually drifted off to sleep, with silent tears drying on her cheeks.

Damian slammed the door behind him as he and Victoria ran into the house. He was breathing heavily, and his heart was pounding. Victoria smacked him on the back of the head as he passed her. "What the hell Damian, why did you stop me back there?"

"We were going there to gather information, Victoria, not to start an all-out attack on them." Damian wasn't in the mood to mess around, or fight. He had spent the last couple of weeks of summer doing his research, trying to learn as much as he could about the Wenham clan, and in particular about the infamous vampire, Ermanes, son of Chalkeau, who had supposedly been associated with the Wenhams for years. There was little in the history books about the family name Chalkeau, and nothing of Ermanes. He had to rely only on what he could find out about the Wenhams themselves, which was more than he could have expected, but so far hadn't led to evidence that Ermanes was still around.

"It wasn't an attack on all of them you idiot, and taking out one little witch wouldn't have hurt." Damian was surprised to hear what sounded like disappointment in his sister's voice at the thought of missing the chance to kill a witch. He stared at her, wondering if she was feeling the same way he had felt so many times over the years—just wanting to run out and kill anyone or everyone, to try and bring back his father. But this was different. That girl had nothing to do with their father's death, even if her family *were* connected in some way to the man who killed him. She was no older than Damian, and there was no way to connect her to their father's death. He wasn't going to allow his sister to punish an innocent for the crimes of her relatives, at least not without good reason—and being a witch wasn't a good enough reason.

Their mother, Karen, had come into the room carrying a tray with three cups of hot chocolate. "Victoria, I am shocked at you." She set down the drinks, and stood before her children, looking stronger and more in control than they remembered seeing her in all of the past years. "Have you ever known me to be a vengeful person?" Victoria shook her head in silence. "Then you should know better than to think that hurting anyone, even a witch, would be acceptable."

"You weren't there. You don't know. What they did with the fire, it was—." Victoria was defending her actions, but the tremble in her voice made it clear that even she didn't believe what she was about to say. "Besides, she came after us first—and the way she moved—I've never seen anyone move that fast." It was true that Alee had been running in their direction through the woods at not altogether human speeds, but it was because she was trying to figure out who or what they were. She wasn't in attack mode, and Victoria knew it.

Karen's eyes went straight to her daughter's. "Sit." Victoria sat, almost mechanically. Then, turning to Damian,

Karen's eyes softened. "Damian, please sit down." He joined his sister on the couch as his mother paced the room trying to find the right words to explain how she was feeling. "I have spent these last twelve years since your father's death worrying about what would happen when you two found out who you really are. What you are." She finally joined them, sitting in the chair nearest the fireplace in their small living room. "Maybe I should have told you years ago, before you found out on your own. Maybe it would have made all of this easier, but your father and I had promised not to say anything until you were old enough to understand, and with him gone—" A single tear rolled down her cheek. "—I guess I just put it off longer than I should have. I guess I was just hoping that maybe you would never have to find out. It was stupid to think that way, I know. No matter where I took you, there would always be vampires. It was only a matter of time before your bodies started to react to the call."

Damian opened his mouth, but before he could speak, his mother continued. "What you have already been able to teach yourselves, and the few things I was able to show you in the woods, are not enough to survive. Not if you are going to live as shape shifters. You will need to learn the traditions and the laws of our kind. You will need to accept that there are some things you must never do." She was looking at Victoria with a burning power behind her light brown eyes. "The most important of which is that you never, *ever*, kill a protected member of the Underground. Not without cause, and not unless you are prepared for the consequences. Do you understand me?"

"Yes mother." But when her mother released her gaze and Victoria turned to Damian it was clear she had no idea what her mother was talking about. She whispered so her mother couldn't hear her. "Underground? What is she talking about?"

"Seriously Victoria?" Damian snorted back. "The secret society grandma—." He was cut off, but he could see that now Victoria was remembering the conversation they had had with their grandparents.

"Now, who wants cocoa?" Mrs. Ward had a way of turning her mood around on a dime, and, although she had seemed so serious, all of a sudden her smile lit up her face and the mood in the whole room lifted.

Damian took a cup of the steaming hot cocoa, and sat back in his seat before taking his first sip. "Mom, can I ask you something?" His voice was hesitant and almost cracked from nerves.

"Of course, you know you can ask me anything."

It was something he had been wondering since that morning in the woods when she had come to them in her mountain lion form. "Did Dad know?"

"Did your father know what, sweetheart?" She knew many things, but how to read minds was not one of them. She wasn't even aware that Damian and Victoria were able to communicate telepathically. Her parents had made her commit to a life without shape-shifting at such an early age that she had never created that bond with her family, her pack. Although she and her husband were as close as two people can be, without the pack bond, telepathic communication was something they had never mastered.

"Did he know about you—about what you are?" He realized after he said it that the question had come out wrong, almost demeaning, as if she were something unworthy. He had not meant to sound rude, or to offend her in any way, but his father's journal had left out the fact that their mother had been a shape shifter—or at least that she had made her first transformation. Damian merely wanted to know if their father knew she was able to shift. He was not trying to imply that she had kept her identity as a shape shifter a secret from him.

She stood up slowly, gazing down at her son. "What I am? What *am* I, Damian?"

"No, I just mean—dad's journal—. You're not—. It doesn't—."

"Wow, way to stick your foot in your mouth Damian." Victoria had just been sitting there sipping her hot cocoa, but she perked up now, eager to see just how badly her brother was able to mess up. Besides, it took the spotlight off of what she had done and made him the bad guy.

Karen just laughed as she left the living room, making her way into the kitchen. They could hear her opening a cabinet, moving things around, and closing it again before coming back to sit down again. She was smiling again. "I'm only kidding sweetheart. Yes, Damian your father knew. He was actually the one who helped me learn." She was holding an old cookbook that Damian and Victoria had seen her reading a thousand times but had never really paid any attention to. It was a cookbook, after all—how exciting could it be?!

"The reason your father left my identity out of his journal was because of my parents. Your grandparents would not have approved of our lifestyle. Many years ago, they made the choice to live as mere humans. They gave up their powers of transformation, or at least bound them. I was too young to be on my own, and was still living in their home; therefore, they forced me to do the same." When she opened the book, Damian and Victoria noticed a small envelope taped to the inside cover. Karen gently pulled it off and opened it. "They had my powers bound as a young girl, and your father's just before we got married." She tipped the envelope and into her hand fell a ring. It was silver, and looked like a rope with no end and no beginning. She held it up for them to see, being careful not to let it slip onto her finger, although the urge was great—they could see that in her eyes.

"That's your—." Victoria reached out to touch it, but Karen quickly palmed the ring and slid it back into the envelope.

"My wedding band, yes." She held the envelope tightly, as if she were afraid to let it go.

"But what about the ring you're wearing?" Damian's eyes were fixed on the ring on her left hand. The one he had played with as a child, sitting on her lap turning it round and round. The one he had never, in all his life, seen her take off, even to wash the dishes. It was identical, in every way, to the ring she was holding before them now, at least from what he could tell.

"Your great grandfather, Virgil Cummings, had this ring made for me when I was very young." She shook the envelope with a look of sadness and disgust on her face. "I wore it for almost twelve years, but then your father asked me to marry him, and I knew that with him I wanted to live a different life." She put the envelope back in the book and pressed down on the tape, securing it to the inside cover once again.

"We had plans, your father and I." Her eyes filled with tears as she spoke of her late husband. "He knew how my family felt about shifters, even though their ancestors had lived as shifters for all the previous generations. When James asked my father for my hand in marriage, it meant accepting the destiny my family had chosen for us. He knew, though, that his promise was in word only, and not in belief or action. The first thing he did after your grandfather gave him his blessing was to take our rings to an old friend of his, to have them duplicated." She held out her hand for them to see. "This ring is identical in every way, except for the curse that was placed on my original ring and your father's. This ring, and the one your father wore, protected us from the wrath of my father, but gave us the freedom to be who we were."

He knew the answer, but Damian needed to ask the question anyway. "Where is dad's ring now?"

"He was buried with his real ring, the duplicate one that symbolized our love, but the ring forged by my ancestors—that one is locked away. It's safe with so many other things of your father's—." She hadn't thought about their rings in years, and she hadn't made the connection until that moment. She had locked the ring up in the chest in the attic to keep it safe—to keep Damian safe—and it hadn't even dawned on her that, when she found the twins in the woods with their father's journal, it meant that they must have been in the chest. She hadn't made the connection that they may have also found the ring. "Damian, do you have your father's ring?" She knew Victoria wouldn't have wanted it. It wasn't that their father's death hadn't affected Victoria; it was just that Damian, having been right there in the room the night his father was murdered, had been much more deeply affected. Damian had been searching his whole life for ways to get closer to the father he had lost. Victoria, on the other hand, had coped by staying away from everything that reminded her, even the slightest bit, of her father.

"No." It was no more than a whisper.

"Damian, look at me." He did, and his eyes welled up with tears. "Do you have your father's ring?"

Holding up his hands to show his empty fingers, he shook his head. It wasn't a lie. He didn't have it anymore. On their way back from their grandparent's house, he had made

Victoria stop the car on a bridge that crossed over a rather wide and rapidly flowing river. He had stood there for about a half hour, fighting the urge to break down, and then he threw the ring as hard as he could out into the middle of the river. It had landed with just a small splash—and it was gone forever. He didn't regret tossing the ring into the water, but as he stood looking at the spot where it had landed, he did feel guilty for having taken it in the first place, without his mother's permission. It hadn't been his place, or his right, to take what didn't belong to him, and definitely not to get rid of it like he had, even if it was cursed. "No—but, I did. I'm sorry."

"It was cursed. You can't really blame him for getting rid of it." Victoria was defending him? She usually loved to watch him squirm when he got in trouble, and now she was defending him. She was also making it clear that she had been involved; at least enough to know what had happened to the ring.

Everything started to click in Karen's mind, and although she knew that her children understood some things, having read her husband's journal, there were still so many things they shouldn't have known. "When did you get rid of it?" She was looking at Victoria, but it was clear she expected Damian to answer. She sat there waiting patiently while he thought through his words very carefully.

"It was a couple weeks ago."

"And, how did you know the ring was cursed?" She had him, and she knew it. She had never told them about the ring. Not until tonight. And, since James had never written about it in his journal, to protect himself and his wife, there was no way Damian or Victoria should have known. There were only two other people, aside from her own family, who would have known, who could have told them.

With his eyes closed, he decided that there was no other way out of this, except the truth. "We went to see Grandma Margie and Grandpa Phil." Karen took a deep breath in and just as she was about to speak he stopped her. "Before you say it, please hear me out. We didn't know what else to do. We were afraid and confused. Victoria had been living with this all on her own, not understanding what was happening. My body and mind felt like they were fighting. We needed answers, and we didn't know where else to go."

"Why didn't you come to me?" Karen stopped herself, and changed course. "Don't answer that. I never should have kept this from you—any of this."

Victoria sat forward on the couch and put her empty mug on the coffee table in front of her. "Then why did you? Is it really what dad would have wanted?"

"I don't know. I don't know what your father would have wanted had he been here. I do know that he wouldn't have wanted you to find out from someone else. But he would have been proud of you both for going to your grandparents to find the answers. He would have been proud that you cared enough to know. Your father was a very strong man, with very strong beliefs. Hiding who he was and lying about it to his family was the hardest thing he ever did."

"Why did he have to hide it from Grandma and Grandpa? They had no problem with him living his life as a shape shifter. They do it." Damian's mind drifted back to the beautiful golden retriever that had met them as they walked up the path to their grandparent's house. Knowing now what he did, the thought of having such a peaceful life seemed so amazing to him.

Karen just nodded her head. "You're right. You're absolutely right. They had no problem with it. They wanted us to live our lives as shifters, but I wasn't willing to just walk away from my family so easily. Your father was the one who finally decided that we could do both, but in order to protect ourselves he decided that we must never reveal what we were doing—to anyone." She wiped away the tears that had started to wet her cheeks. "He died with his parents still believing he had thrown his gift away. That's why I never went to see them after his funeral. I couldn't face them. I couldn't face the fact that they would blame me—that they might hate me for how they felt their son had turned out."

Damian hated to see his mother sad, and honestly believed that there had to be another answer. "But, they wouldn't hate you. You know that, you must. They loved you."

Karen wiped her eyes will a napkin from the table and sat back in her chair sipping her hot cocoa. She shifted the conversation away from herself and back to them. "Now, explain what you were doing this evening."

Damian and Victoria just sat there in silence for a few minutes, looking back and forth. Neither one wanted to speak up first. "You mentioned a young witch. Who is she?"

"Just a new girl from school, she's staying at The Black Onyx with the Wenham family. She's a cousin from California or something."

Karen's eyes got wide, yet narrowed, all at the same time. "How do you know about The Black Onyx?" No one said anything. "Victoria, how do you know about The Black Onyx?"

"Humph" Victoria huffed and pouted at her mother's accusation. "Why does it always have to be me?"

"Just answer my question Victoria!"

"Mom, it's not a big deal, really. I've only been there once—with Danielle and Alee, we were just—."

"You are never to go to that shop again. Do you understand me?" Victoria nodded her head yes, but that didn't stop her mother from reiterating her point. "Never, Victoria! That's not a suggestion. It's an order! If I find out you've disobeyed me, you won't be seeing that girl Danielle again. She's always been something of a bad influence on you."

"Are you kidding?" Damian couldn't help blurting, "Dani, a bad influence on anyone, is ridiculous, but Victoria can take care of herself. Dani is more of a follower than anything else."

"Although I appreciate your opinions Damian, I didn't ask for them. The Black Onyx is dangerous and I expect you both to stay away. Have I made myself clear?"

"Yes."

"Why? Why isn't it safe?" Victoria asked, "It's just a shop."

"They're witches Victoria, and they have ways of knowing what you are," her mother answered. "Besides, that particular family—." Karen looked down into her empty mug. "They have power here in Atlanta. You don't want to get on their radar, let alone their bad side."

The tension was thick and everyone seemed a little on edge, and although it was getting late Damian still had a question that he was hoping his mom would be willing to answer. "Mom, you mentioned the Underground—Grandma Margie told us a little about it, but not much. What is it exactly?"

She took a deep breath, gathering her thoughts. "It's kind of like a club—or a secret society."

"You mean like the Mason's, Skull and Bones, or the Illuminati, like from that movie?" Victoria often thought of things in terms of pop culture or popular songs and movies.

"No—maybe. It's hard to explain. The Underground is a society of, well—beings that most people wouldn't even believe existed." Her tongue was tied, but she didn't know what else to say. Karen didn't want to scare her children, but she also didn't want to keep them in the dark any longer and, right now—they just looked so confused, like puppies the first time they open their eyes.

"OK, the Underground is literally that—under the ground! It's not a very original name, but it wasn't meant to impress." She went to take a sip of her hot cocoa before remembering it was already empty. She set the empty mug back down on the table. "It's been around in cities all over the United States as well as other countries for hundreds, if not thousands, of years. As you can tell by the architecture, Atlanta is a pretty old town, and back when the original settlers built the city there were quite a few who were protected members of the Underground. Those who weren't, well, you could say they were sort of like pets. The Founders selected this area because they felt it would be a safe place to begin an open society. It would be a place where members of the Underground could not only live comfortably as their real selves in seclusion, as they had for so many years, but where they could also start to establish lives and families above ground, as normal members of society."

Slightly disgusted, Victoria spoke as if she had just been told they were moving her room to the cellar. "You're telling me there are people living in the sewers beneath Atlanta? That's disgusting."

"That is not at all what I said." Karen rolled her eyes at her daughter.

"How do you become a member?" Damian wasn't as concerned about the where, as he was the how and why, of the Underground.

"You don't become a member, it isn't as simple as that. You either are a member or you aren't. However, even if you're born a member you aren't born with all the rights that membership entails. Those come with age. There are a lot of politics that govern who is and who isn't a full member."

"Then who is and who isn't?" It was getting later and later, but Damian was feeling more alert and eager as the night went on.

She looked at her son, who desperately wanted to understand, but didn't know where to begin. She had already told them so much more than she had wanted to, and she didn't really have much experience with the Underground. Except for the annual Founders' Celebration and, of course, the stories her parents and grandparents had told her as a child, there was little more she could have shared. "The Underground is much like any society or organization I suppose. But, instead of being divided by upper, middle and lower class in terms of money, the division lies with power. Today, witches are seen as the elite group, and are ranked among themselves based on the purity of each coven's family line. They help maintain order among the others. But—even more powerful than witches, are the night walkers."

"You mean vampires. Right?" Damian's eyes burned with rage. To think that vampires were accepted disgusted him more than anything, but to think that they were seen as better than shape shifters in the hierarchy of this society was even worse. "You're telling me that blood-sucking, murdering vampires are seen as the leaders within the Underground? Above us? Above the shape shifters, whose sole purpose is to protect society?"

"It isn't as simple as that Damian. At this time, shape shifters are not welcome in the Underground. We aren't members, but it hasn't always been that way. There was a time when our kind ruled the Underground. We were seen as the protectors of not only unsuspecting humans, but protectors of the Underground as well."

Still angry, his voice was almost a growl. "Then what changed?"

"The same thing that happens in politics around the world, the balance of power shifted. Vampires became more powerful, and they multiplied at a much faster rate than we ever could. Our race started dying out as theirs only continued to grow. Eventually, they pushed us out completely. That is, except for those who remain as pets or servants to those in power. The only reason the witches were able to maintain their position was because many of the covens signed contracts, promising allegiance to vampire clans, for guaranteed protection."

"So that's it, vampires and witches became more powerful and now we're out?"

"Think of it like this. Society votes in a Republican president. He's in charge for a while and screws things up. Then society votes in a Democrat. After a few years he screws things up, and everything changes again. The Underground is political, just like every other society. This isn't the first time in history that there has been a shift in the powers, and it won't be the last. The previous shift was over a hundred years ago, when our brothers and sisters seized control." Karen got quiet and took a sip of her cocoa as she stared down at the table.

"And?"

"And—we were not so merciful either. Power can make people do things they would never imagine possible. The shifters of that time brutally mutilated the dream walkers because they saw them as a threat, much in the same way that the vampires later did to us. I suppose it was karma."

"What is a dream walker?" To Victoria dream walker sounded mysterious.

"From what my great grandmother once told me, they are a very intoxicating, powerful, and exotic male race, similar to sirens. They lure you, not through song like the sirens do, but through your fantasies—your dreams—your daydreams. They are said to be extremely attractive, and to have the power to make people do things they wouldn't normally do. They love to cause confusion in the minds and hearts of their prey." She started laughing at the thought. Karen wasn't so sure she really believed in dream walkers, but the legend was still one she had heard many times as a child. "The last known dream walker in the northern states died during the Underground shift in power, and sirens have become almost extinct in these parts. Who knows, maybe they're just fantasy anyway."

Damian and Victoria were on the edges of their seats, waiting to hear more. "Vampires, witches, dream walkers, sirens—does the list keep going?"

Karen nodded, unsure how much her children were really ready to hear. "There are other races that still remain, although their numbers are said to be low and continuing to drop."

Damian remained silent, just listening. However, the idea of other races intrigued Victoria. "What other races?"

"Fairies for one—."

Victoria laughed out loud at the thought of tiny little winged fairies fluttering about. "Fairies? Seriously? You mean like Tinker Bell?"

"No, Dear, not like Tinker Bell. Fairies are actually not at all like modern day fairy tales would have children believe. They are mischievous creatures, of human size, and can in fact be very vicious. Most are not to be trusted." She had gotten up and crossed the room to search a bookshelf.

"Have you ever seen one?"

"I have, but it was a long time ago." She found the book, a black hardback sketchpad, and pulled it down for them to see. On page after page there were exquisite sketches of delicate-winged fairies, both male and female.

"They're beautiful, did you draw these?" Victoria was holding the book in her lap in awe of the remarkably lifelike drawings inside.

"I did, but that was a lifetime ago."

"How can such a beautiful creature be vicious?" Victoria was awed by the striking beauty of her mother's art. Each page was more fascinating than the one before, and there was a drawing of a very handsome man with dark black and silver wings. His arms held a woman close to his chest. You couldn't see her face, but she clung to him as if she didn't want to let go, and his wings were wrapped around them both. "They look so in love. Who are they?"

"They were." Karen stared down at the drawing as if remembering.

"You knew them?"

"Yes and no. I didn't know their names. I only knew of them, but I was just a child back then. They used to meet in the park, and I would watch them while I played."

"They met out in the open?" Damian asked. "He felt that comfortable spreading his wings like that for everyone to see?"

"It wasn't like that. It was always in the middle of the night. Besides, things were a little different back then. There were protections in place, spells that had been set in order to keep the humans from noticing certain things. Then, after some changes in the Underground, after certain groups were kicked out of the Underground, the Founders had the protection spells deactivated. They thought it would make everyone a little more mindful of what they did in public." Karen shook her head then turned that page to another drawing. "None of that matters any more. It was a long time ago. Besides, things aren't always what they appear to be." Karen took the book and, flipping through it to the back, held out another picture for her daughter to see. It was of a fairy, much like those in the beginning; only this one had harsh black heavy wings. It was standing over what looked like the body of a child, a small boy. There was blood pouring out of the child's throat, covering the ground in a pool all around him. The fairy's image was mostly hidden by the shade of a tree. All that could be seen were the blackened wings, long claws dripping with blood, and a bright white smile. "Not all fairies are evil, but those who are—." She stopped. There was no need to continue. The picture said it all.

"If those things—" Damian pointed down to the open book. "—still hold a place in the Underground, why not us? What could we possibly have done that would make us worse than someone who would attack and kill a child?" His mother didn't answer. "How do you get to the Underground?"

"No, Damian. That is a question I will not answer. It is way too dangerous, and I won't have my son—" She glanced over toward Victoria. "—or my daughter, risking their lives just because things aren't always fair in the world."

He was angry. "Don't you care? Don't you think it's about time we—?"

"Yes, I care. I have thought about little else since your father died. But there is nothing I can do. I am only one woman, and a mother at that, who has to put her children's safety first. Of course I think it's about time that things change. Our time will come, I'm sure of it. But it isn't today, and it won't happen at the hands of two teenagers and their worn out mother. When it is time, there will be a sign, but sadly I doubt it will be in my lifetime." It had been a long night, and the sun was going to be coming up in less than two hours. The weight of the world seemed to be resting on their shoulders and all three of them looked as if they could fall asleep right there in the living room. "Besides, it's late and the night has ears of its own. You never know who might be listening. I've already said too much. You two should get some sleep. Go to bed, you have to wake up for school in less than three hours."

"But—."

"No buts, Damian. We can talk about this some more another time. Until then, please just leave it alone." Karen knew her son well enough to know that he wasn't going to leave it at that, but for the moment there was nothing more she could do.

Both Damian and Victoria slowly dragged themselves up the stairs and off to bed. Karen, however, didn't move. She waited until she heard their bedroom doors shut, and then she quickly grabbed the phone off the coffee table and dialed. After about seven long rings, she finally heard his voice on the other end of the line. "Hello?" She could tell by his slow response that she had woken him from sleep, but she didn't care.

"It's Karen! They know, and, just like their father, I don't think they're going to let it go." She waited and listened. "I understand. I'll see you soon." She hung up the phone then pulled a blanket off of the back of her chair and covered herself up. She stared at the glowing embers in the fireplace as she thought about her husband, and all the memories they never got to make together. She finally drifted off to sleep, with tears moistening her face, just before dawn.

~ Beginnings ~

She slept soundly until the front door slammed shut as
Damian and Victoria raced out to the car later that morning.

7

Kyle whispered into Alee's ear, "I love you," and kissed her cheek one last time before slipping out of her bedroom window, the same way he had gotten in the night before.

Having woken up in Kyle's arms, Alee had all but forgotten about Damian. She was practically floating on air as she danced her way through her morning routine of showering, dressing, and doing her hair before going to the kitchen for breakfast. Alee was startled to find almost everyone there, and even more surprised to find that everyone there was waiting for her.

"Do you have something you would like to tell us young lady?" It was Edith, Alee's great great grandmother, and although Alee had grown used to her over the past few weeks, this morning there was something about the way she spoke that made the hairs on the back of Alee's neck stand up. It was almost like a cat when it sensed danger around the corner; or the way an animal somehow knows, instinctively, that bad weather is coming. Seeing Edith that morning reminded Alee of the breathtaking white glow, that the woman had been enveloped in the night before—an aura, Edith had called it. When she focused, Alee could see glimpses of it still. Alee made a mental note to do some research on auras later, when she found some time to herself—*if* she found time to herself.

Standing there stunned, Alee just stared back at everyone, not really knowing what to say. *How do they even know he stayed the night? Why do they even care? It's not like we did anything.* "Um, no?"

"Granny, please, let me handle this." Elizabeth—Loraline's mother and Alee's grandmother—was a little more rational than Edith was, and it appeared, from Alee's outside perspective, that Elizabeth just might be the next in line to take control of the family once Granny Edith passes away—that is, if the old lady ever did. When Elizabeth turned toward Alee, her eyes were soft and her voice was almost sweet as she crooned, "Aleerah dear, are you feeling OK?"

"Yes. A little sore, but I'm fine."

"Good. Would you mind telling us what happened last night, after the ceremony?"

Oh thank God—they don't know about Kyle. She let out a breath she hadn't even known she was holding. She shook her head, because Alee didn't really know what had happened the night before. She remembered the wolves and the pain as the brown wolf's teeth tore into her leg, but other than that she wasn't really sure what had drawn her to them, or brought them to her for that matter. "I'm not really sure. I was out back—just watching the moon, and then—." She thought for a while, trying to remember what it was that pulled her attention from the moon out into the woods. "I don't know, I guess I felt like someone was watching me."

The mood shifted in the room as Elizabeth moved closer, handing Alee a coffee cup, and guiding her to sit with them at the table. "Could you see who it was?"

"Not exactly."

"What did you see?"

"I don't know. It's silly really, but I thought I saw someone I know from school standing out in the woods, but that's crazy, right?" She slowly sipped from her drink. *Red syrup, red syrup, red syrup,* she thought as she swallowed the thick warm liquid. "I mean it's crazy. It wasn't even a person; it was a wolf, two wolves actually."

"Why would you think someone from school was out in the woods?" Elizabeth seemed calm, but the thought that someone could have followed Alee home from school was very disturbing.

"I don't know, day-dreaming, I guess." Alee could feel her cheeks getting warm. "I mean, not 'day-dreaming' day-dreaming. Not like fantasizing or anything. There is just this guy—."

"Kyle?" Edith snapped with a disapproving tone.

"No!" Alee returned the attitude. "Not Kyle. This guy is, I don't know, kind of weird I guess. But he just keeps showing up. It wasn't him, anyway. Like I said, it was two wolves. After I went out into the woods and got closer—I'm not really sure what happened."

"Wow, everyone's here this morning, huh?" Eric said, as he and Loraline walked into the kitchen, more as an observation than a question.

"Of course we are." Edith stood as she spoke, watching Eric closely with narrowed eyes. "What would you expect when there has been an attack on our family?"

"Well, considering past experience I guess I assumed—."

"Eric, please." Loraline stopped him. "They're here to help. Granny, I'm sorry. Of course you would come." Then, turning to Elizabeth and William, Loraline crossed the room. "Mom. Dad. Thank you for coming. I know it's early, but—."

"Not at all, we've been up for hours. Besides, we want to know as much as possible about what happened to Aleerah last night. We need to know everything before Eric is down for the day."

"I won't be going down today. I have things to take care of."

Elizabeth glared at Eric. "You know you can't stay up all day without—"

"I know what I must do; you don't have to explain it to me like I'm a child, Elizabeth." Eric scolded.

"Then you—?"

"Yes, I have fed."

"Should I even ask?"

"Mother!"

"No, Loraline. If he is to stay in my home then I have the right to know!"

"This is my home now mother, and no you don't have the right to know. But, if it's that important to you then I will answer your questions." She took a step closer to her mother closing the gap both physically and mentally. "He fed, and yes, I was a willing donor! Is that enough, or do you want all the gory details?"

"That is enough Loraline." William's voice was like a cool breeze rolling through the room and calming the tension that had built among them all. "Elizabeth, they are married. You have no right to interfere."

"But—."

"No." Elizabeth just stood there staring into her husband's deep blue eyes. He was normally very passive, not interfering when it came to matters of the coven, but when it involved his daughters he was and always would be their protectors. "Now, Eric, let us hear what happened last night so that we can focus on what is really important today." He nodded to his son-in-law to continue as he pulled Elizabeth toward him and wrapped his arms around her waist.

"She was attacked, by two wolves." Eric mirrored William's movement and closed the space between him and Loraline, pulling her closer to his side.

"I know you say they were wolves, but are you really sure? Did you find them?" Loraline asked.

Eric just shook his head. "They were wolves, of that I am sure. But, no, I didn't find them. I tracked them back into town. Their pattern was too rational to be wild wolves."

"Are you thinking—?" It was William who asked.

"Yes." They shared a look that Alee didn't understand, but before she had a chance to ask what they meant Eric had moved on. "I don't know for sure, but they smelled—different. It has been a long time, but anything is possible, I suppose. But they must have either known their way here, or they followed her."

"Followed me? Why? From where?" Alee was naturally alarmed at the idea.

"I'm not sure, but don't worry, we'll find out." Eric opened the fridge, leaned in, and grabbed a black sports bottle from the top shelf. It was the kind of sports bottle you would take to the gym to work out, but Alee knew he wasn't drinking Gatorade. Crossing the kitchen, Eric went directly to William, who was standing next to the microwave. Elizabeth pulled away, still obviously too upset and cross to sit at the kitchen table. Eric popped the bottle in the microwave for a quick twenty seconds. "Dad, if they were following her they'll most likely be back. Can you—."

"You don't even have to ask, son." William finished off his coffee then went to the door. "Jacinda, call Tom. Tell him to meet me outside my house in twenty minutes." Jacinda nodded, and then pulled her cell phone out of her pocket to dial her husband. "We'll make sure everything is set up. You just make sure she makes it to and from school safely. I doubt they'll try anything while she's there—the high school is too populated.

"I was thinking the same thing." Eric's calm disposition easily camouflaged his restlessness, but Alee could tell that he was still concerned. With the rest of the group it was easy to detect their restlessness: a quickening of the heartbeats, shallow breaths, even an increase in perspiration that she could smell from almost a quarter of a mile away now—literally. With Eric, though, it was harder. A vampire's heartbeat is much harder to hear. Breathing isn't a requirement—simply something they do out of habit and to blend in—and finally, a fact that truly pleased Alee, vampires don't sweat! That meant that Alee had to rely on body language. She had always had an instinct when it came to reading people, and after a few weeks around Eric, she realized that whenever he was upset or nervous he clenched his jaw. The muscles in his jaw would tighten and release over and over and more quickly the more angry or nervous he became. It was his 'tell,' and Alee guessed that it would probably make him a pretty bad poker player.

Before leaving, William looked back at Eric who was still standing by the microwave. "Son, try to get some rest today. I know you say you don't need it, but we'll need you at your strongest tonight if they do decide to come back."

Just as William was leaving, Phoebe walked into the kitchen with Petra, her older sister, slowly following behind. "Mom, tell Petra that I can drive Aleerah and me to school."

"What is the problem now?" Jacinda asked.

"Petra said—."

"I said that I would take the girls to school today, because I need to use the car." She was swinging the key ring around the index finger of her left hand while adjusting the strap of a messenger bag that was hung across her chest. "But we need to head out soon if I'm going to get them there on time." She poured herself a quick coffee, black, and headed back out the door.

"Wait!" Jacinda stopped her. "What is so important that you have to take the car instead of the tunnels?"

"Jacinda!" Loraline snapped.

"I'm sorry. I wasn't thinking." Jacinda turned to her daughter. "Of course take the car. Just make sure you're there on time to pick them up after school."

"You know I will." Petra called over her shoulder as she walked out, not wasting any time waiting for anyone else to object. She was in the car with the engine running before Alee could even think to call shotgun.

"This is so not fair." Phoebe mumbled to herself as she made her own coffee, then grabbed a black sports bottle from the refrigerator. Tossing the sports bottle to Alee, Phoebe headed toward the door. "No time to heat it up this morning. Sorry." It would be Alee's second of the morning, if you counted the small cup Elizabeth had given her, but after yesterday she figured it couldn't hurt to fill up, and she took it with a smile.

Once in the car, Petra quickly turned to look at the girls directly. Her long black hair flowed around her face, reminding Alee of a lion's mane. Petra was beautiful, and yet she seemed so powerful that she was almost intimidating—or maybe it was her beauty that intimidated Alee. "Neither of you are to leave campus today, and make sure you are ready to go right after school. I have some things to take care of today, but I'll pick you up at the main entrance right after the bell." She caught Alee's eye in the rear-view mirror, and shot her a look that could have killed if that were possible. "Don't make me come find you."

"Got it." What else could she have said?

For the rest of the ride, Alee sat there wondering what her aunt had meant by Petra taking the tunnels, and what Petra could possibly have to do. Petra was dressed in camouflage pants, a tight black top, and black high heel boots. She took the militant tough girl look to a whole new level, with her added sex appeal. Secretly, Alee wished she possessed even half the confidence that Petra had.

When they finally made it to school, Alee spotted Eric across the street on the far side of the parking lot, and realized that he had followed them the entire way. She already knew about the increased speed that vampires come by naturally—she herself had firsthand experience—but seeing him standing there, not even a little winded, was still weird. She lifted her hand to give a small wave in his direction, but he had already vanished into the tree line.

"You going to stand there all day or do you want to head in with me?" Phoebe was waiting patiently with her bag slung over her shoulder, sipping her coffee.

When Alee looked back, she realized that Petra was already gone. She hadn't even noticed her leave. "Sure. Yeah, I'm coming." She half smiled then headed up the walk with Phoebe. "Hey, what is it that Petra does all day anyway?"

Phoebe didn't even glance back. "What do you mean?"

"I don't know. Does she work? She said she had things to do, but I mean—did you see how she was dressed?

What could she have been doing?" Alee was almost whispering.

Phoebe turned back, and stopped only inches in front of Alee. "It's hard to explain, but Petra works for the Founders." Before Alee could ask, Phoebe stopped her. "Don't ask me who or what they are, I'm not the one to explain it. Just know that because of Petra's rare talents she's moving up rather quickly in the ranks of Atlanta's Underground. Rumor has it that she could be the first new witch to take a seat on the Council since—. You know what, we should go. It's getting late."

"But—."

"No buts, let's go."

"Um—could you be any more cryptic?" Phoebe didn't respond. "OK, well at least tell me what her talent is." Alee's interest was sparked and a million ideas went through her mind—stories and 'facts' about witches based on horror movies or television shows that she had watched growing up. Not a single one seemed realistic, but then again so many things that had happened lately didn't seem realistic. There was no way to know for sure what Petra's talent could possibly be without someone just telling her, so why not ask?

Phoebe just turned and continued walking toward the school, rambling on about her classes and which teachers she was dreading.

Alee couldn't really pay attention, because the sound of his voice came into her head, gradually becoming clearer. *"I don't know how to explain it. Something just seems wrong about the way Alee died."* He sounded muffled and far away, but Alee would know Damian's voice anywhere. Alee was confused. She had always been the only one he communicated with telepathically, and although Kyle had told her that Damian was able to talk again, somehow she knew that he wasn't just around the corner talking out loud to a friend. There was a different way of hearing things when someone was speaking telepathically. The idea that he would be talking to someone else in that private and intimate way that they had discovered somehow felt wrong. But the worst part was that he was talking about her, and she didn't even know who he was talking to.

"What's the matter?" Phoebe asked, looking concerned, when she saw Alee standing staring off to the side of the building. Phoebe didn't particularly like being ignored, but that wasn't the reason she had stopped talking. "Aleerah, what's wrong? Do you need your pills already?"

Alee just shook her head, and started walking again. But, the voices didn't stop. *"We have more important things to think about than Alee. Besides, she's gone and you haven't felt right about her death since the funeral. But you haven't been able to find any evidence that anything was wrong either."* It was Victoria and she sounded just the same as always—bossy, and in charge. There was a hint of sadness, maybe, or loss, when she mentioned that Alee was gone. Or at least, that was what Alee was choosing to believe.

"Except the closed casket!"

"Damian, she was a child. Her mother didn't want to see her like that. It isn't unusual to have a closed casket at a funeral. Her dad's was closed too."

"He was in a car accident. Of course he had a closed casket."

"OK, well we need to focus on the shop. Besides, I thought you wanted to start with Em-in-en Chalk-er-us or whatever his name was."

"It's Ermanes Chalkeus, not whatever the hell you said. And, I get that we have to focus on the shop, and even that you don't think it appeared at all odd that she didn't

*have an open casket at the funeral, but come on V. Her
mother hasn't changed a single thing in her bedroom. That
can't be normal. It's like she is just waiting for her to come
home or something."*

*"It's only been a couple of weeks D. Her mother is
grieving! Not only did she lose her husband, she lost her only
daughter too. I get that she was important to you. She was
my friend too, remember? But it's been weeks—she's gone—
and you have to try to move on."*

A million things ran through Alee's mind all at once.
*How does Victoria—? When did she learn to—? Who's
Ermanes Chalkeus?* Alee made a mental note to try and
remember the name for later.

"—then he said we'd have a test this week. God, I
wish I was the one who graduated last year and Petra was the
one still stuck here for two more years."

"What? Oh, yeah, right, tests—suck. Anyway, I'll
catch up with you later OK? I have to take care of something
before first period." She didn't give Phoebe time to react,
knowing that she would have objected, or at least forced Alee
to take her with her. She quickly darted off around a corner
and headed to the back of the school. She wasn't sure where
they were, but she needed to hear more, if possible.

'She wasn't just important Victoria, I loved her.'

'Oh God.' Alee's heart started to pound. It was as if
she had run straight into a wall, but it didn't stop her. It only
slowed her down. She couldn't breathe. It is one thing to
know someone loves you, but it is a completely different
thing to hear that person say it. She felt like she was moving
through a thick cloud of fog, unable to speed up. For just a
second, she remembered having that same feeling the night
she found out about her father's death. Then suddenly,

everything came pouring back into focus, and she was running, toward—something.

"Did you hear that?" Damian was panicked.

"Hear what?" Victoria didn't seem to notice anything but, at that moment, Alee came running around the corner and ran right into Victoria, knocking her and her books down to the ground. "Hey, watch where you're going freak!"

"Um, I'm sorry." Alee looked from Victoria to Damian, trying not to think about anything in particular. She knew he had heard her, and that somehow, their connection hadn't been severed like she had thought, but maybe he didn't know it yet. *La la la la la.* She sang in her head trying to distract herself as she backed away. She realized she was going to need to learn to block her thoughts, if that was even possible. But, more importantly, she needed to get out of there as quickly as she could.

"Just go, freak!" Victoria snapped at Alee, and pushed herself off the ground.

"I'm not a freak." Alee snapped back without thinking. Luckily, Victoria wasn't fully standing yet, and Damian stepped between them.

"Just leave her alone V. She didn't do anything wrong." When he turned back to see if Alee was OK, she was already gone, and he helped his sister gather up her books.

Alee slipped through one of the building's side doors and merged with the crowd of students in the hallways. She got her books from her locker and headed toward first period, English Literature. She was surprised, and somewhat relieved, to see that Jathan wasn't there. Class went by uneventfully—the next couple of weeks would be fairly easy, seeing as she had already read the first two assigned literary works. Writing the necessary reports wouldn't be hard at all. The bell rang, and she was out the door before anyone else, heading down the hall with fevered anticipation. Kyle was in her second period, and ever since their goodbye kiss earlier that morning she had been longing to see him again.

Alee sat in the front row in the same seat she had sat in the day before. She was a creature of habit. She waited patiently for Kyle to arrive, watching the door eagerly any time someone came in. But he never came. The minute hand on the clock above the teacher's desk slowly made its circuit, and with each passing minute she felt more and more alone. This time when the bell rang she didn't jump out of her seat to rush off to her next class. Instead, she slowly gathered her things and reluctantly joined the stream of students in the hallway. Pulling her cell phone out of her pocket, she sent a quick text to Kyle, 'You weren't in class. Everything OK?' but he never texted back, which wasn't like him at all.

She got to art class just as the bell was ringing and found a stool behind a blank canvas and paint setup near the door. She couldn't see the other students who were sitting at easels that had been placed more or less in a circle, but the teacher stood tall on top of a platform in the center of the class, and Alee could see her easily over the easel. Mrs. Massey was one of those teachers who made you wonder why she had become a teacher in the first place. She was a very talented artist and probably could have done something creative with her life if she had left Atlanta. However, she was born and raised in Atlanta, and after college she returned to work at the high school. She had only been teaching for about two years, and although all the students loved her, she already seemed bored with doing the same thing over and over each day. Alee figured she would be burned out long before she was able to retire.

"OK class, today we're going to see what's in your souls." Mrs. Massey pulled a piece of yellow silk out of her pocket and waved it in the air in front of her. "There is a blindfold draped on each of your easels. Please put it on at this time."

Alee couldn't see anyone else, but as she pulled her blindfold off her easel, she could hear the others doing the same thing while grumbling and moaning in protest and disapproval. She tied the piece of silk around her eyes and realized that it felt cool and relaxing, but that it didn't completely block out all of the light or the images in front of her. She wondered if she should ask for a darker material but, as if hearing her thoughts, Mrs. Massey quickly answered her. "Don't try to completely obscure your sight. Some light will still come through. This exercise is designed to force you to feel what you're painting by using your senses other than sight. Instead of trying to paint the perfect picture, allow it to paint itself." Her footsteps indicated that Mrs. Massey was moving around the room, but Alee couldn't tell exactly where she was, until she starting talking right behind her. "You may begin at any time." Alee jumped, startled, but Mrs. Massey's calming hand was instantly on her shoulder.

From across the room, she heard other students mumbling back and forth when, finally, someone asked what they all had been thinking, "What are we supposed to paint?"

"Whatever you feel, just don't try to control it. Let it just come from within."

"Can you believe this? It's weird right?" Jathan was whispering right in her ear.

"Um, yeah weird." *Jathan is here? He must have been sitting right beside me the whole time. Where was he first period?* Alee could feel her heart start to race, and without realizing it, she had started to paint. She remembered seeing paintbrushes on the easel tray next to the paint cups, but instead of using them her hands were covered with paint, and they were moving across the canvas as if they had a mind of their own. In the distance, she could hear Mrs. Massey talking to the other students, but she didn't have the time or the energy to try to hear what she was saying. She was beginning to feel tired when suddenly she heard the door slam shut.

When she pulled off the blindfold she was shocked to find herself alone in the room. Apparently, the bell had rung, and everyone had already gone off to lunch without taking two seconds to let her know. But more shocking than that was the painting in front of her. It was no longer a lonely blank canvas. It was covered in a mixture of black and blood red everywhere, except in the center and along what looked like thin cracks stretching out to the edges, as if the central bright white and blue light were trying to escape. The more she looked at it, the more the image came into focus. The edges of the canvas framed the outline of a single blood rose blooming outward from the light in the center. It was stunning, but there was no one to share it with.

"It's beautiful."

She spun around on her stool, hands still covered in paint, and found herself face to face with Jathan. She hadn't even heard him come up behind her, which suddenly struck her as odd. "What *are* you—?" The words came out before she could stop herself. She had gotten so skilled at sensing people around her that it sort of scared her that she couldn't do it with him. She even knew when her father was about to come into the room, and he was the stealthiest person she had ever met. But, Jathan, he was just a guy, and a high school guy at that. He was nothing special, as far as she knew. So the idea that he could sneak up on her so easily really bothered her.

Eyes wide, he actually appeared offended at her snappy remark. "What does that mean?"

Alee clasped her paint-covered hand over her mouth, mortified when she realized what she had said. She knew it was a stupid thing on so many levels. First off, he was just a guy, one she had been thinking about way too much lately, but he also didn't need to be thinking anything was off about her. She had to keep a low profile, and at the rate she was going he was sure to start suspecting something about her, or at the very least start thinking maybe she was a little off in the head. Either way it wasn't something she wanted.

"I'm sorry, I didn't mean that. It's just that you scared me. You're a little stealthy you know? The way you sneak up on people. I mean, I thought I was alone in here." And, she was rambling. Something she always tended to do around guys, especially guys she kind of liked, or at least was attracted to. But, this was Jathan, not Kyle—. *What is wrong with me? Just shut up already!*

"I didn't mean to sneak up on you, but your picture—." He spun her around, so Alee was facing her own painting, and her back was to his chest. "—it's amazing. Almost like a—."

"—rose." They said it at the exact same time. Her heart was racing as she turned to face him. They were only inches apart and she could feel the burning beginning in her throat.

He brushed the hair away from her eyes and, as his fingertips brushed across her cheek, Alee could feel a warm current running through her body. It didn't hurt, but it tingled, as if every atom, every molecule, was coming alive all at once. She wanted to taste him, or at the very least to kiss him. It was hard to restrain herself, but she managed somehow. Jathan leaned forward, rubbing his body against hers as he grabbed a towel off of her easel, and softly began cleaning the paint off of her hands, and then her face.

Alee didn't move as Jathan dropped the towel to the floor and ran his fingers down her check, along her neck, then down her arm until her hand settled snuggly in his own. "It's almost as if it's on fire." He leaned in closer, and pressed his lips to hers. Instead of pulling away, Alee wrapped her arms around his neck and pressed her body harder against his. She could feel his body reacting to her touch, and she wanted more of it.

"Oh, God," she moaned softly, her lips still pressed to his. Then her eyes opened wide. *What did I just say? Oh my God.* Realizing what was happening, yet not really understanding it, Alee pulled herself away from him, bumping into her stool and knocking her painting off of the easel. She picked up her things, and ran out the door. "What did I do? I—I have to go."

Jathan didn't leave. "Oh sweet Aleerah. How I miss your kiss already." He picked up her painting, set it back on her easel, then walked out of the classroom. He didn't say a thing, but the smile on his face was worth a thousand words.

Meanwhile, as Alee ran out of the Arts building into the courtyard, she ran right into Damian, literally a repeat of what had happened earlier that morning with Victoria. Only this time it was she who ended up on the ground with her books scattered around her. "I'm so sorry. I didn't see you coming," he said hastily. She didn't realize who she had run into until that moment, and she finally looked up, rubbing her head, to find Damian standing there with his hand held out to help her up. "It's you again. We need to stop meeting like this." His voice was just like she had imagined it, deep, clear, and as smooth as chocolate. The words flowed out of his mouth effortlessly, without hesitation.

Alee was so overcome with emotion, hearing him speak and looking into his beautiful grey eyes again, that she started to cry. "Oh my God, I'm so sorry." Damian looked around for help. "Did I hurt you?" Alee didn't say a word, just shook her head frantically, trying not to think. She wanted to grab him in her arms and tell him how much she had missed him. That she loved him too. That she wasn't really dead. But she couldn't. Instead she gathered her things and took the books that he had already picked up out of his hands and ran off in the direction of her locker.

The day had become too much for her and for the second time in only two days she was starting to wonder if coming back to school so soon had been a bad idea. They had reinvented her life with a new identity and everything. Why couldn't they just say she had already graduated from a high school out in California? She was starting to think that maybe this wasn't something she could handle after all.

Alee headed for the front office, stopping first at the library to check out the book she had found, *Light vs. Dark*. She hoped it might have information about auras. She was certain The Black Onyx would have everything she needed but she also wasn't a hundred percent comfortable just looking around there yet. Although *technically* it was her home, it still didn't feel like home yet. She wasn't sure how much she was really allowed to do, or what she was and wasn't supposed to touch.

When she finally made it to the office she was greeted with an under the breath groan by Ms. Thatcher. "Yes, Ms. Wenham, what can I do for you?"

"Um—." Alee lost her train of thought as a sweet scent filled the office around her.

"What is it?" Ms. Thatcher asked. "You look, hungry."

"No. No, I just—I don't feel very well. I think I need to go home."

Ms. Thatcher looked her up and down, and rolled her eyes as she pulled a hall slip from the desk drawer. "Have your parents sign this and bring it back in the morning. Otherwise, your absences will count against your grades in your afternoon classes." She practically tossed the paper at Alee before turning around and busying herself with stacks of papers on the back table. Oddly, just before the door closed behind her, Alee thought she heard Ms. Thatcher mumble, "Feel better Alee——."

Did she? Her mind was racing a million miles a minute. *No, she couldn't have.* She turned back to look through the office window, but Ms. Thatcher wasn't even looking in her direction. She was busy stacking papers and stuffing envelopes. Alee just shook her head, and headed for the parking lot.

Of course, she didn't have a car there, having given hers up when she supposedly died. She was still trying to figure out how she was going to get another one without a driver's license in her name, besides a car was a lot of money and she wasn't sure she wanted to spend her money on just any car. She wasn't comfortable asking Eric and Loraline for the money yet, even though she knew that Eric, having been around for hundreds of years, had plenty to give. She would just have to wait, and actually, not having a car wasn't really an issue, she remembered. It would take her just as much time to get home driving as it would on foot. Being part vampire had its perks. She slung her bag over her shoulder, and headed into the tree line across the parking lot. Once she was out of sight—she took off.

The day had started off so perfectly that Alee wasn't altogether sure how it had gotten so messed up. Between Kyle, Damian, and now Jathan, Alee was an extremely confused ball of hormones. All she knew for sure was that she couldn't tell Kyle about Jathan, and that she had no idea how to deal with Damian. Alee was positive that she needed to find a way to break the connection she had with Damian, but first she wanted to figure out what he and Victoria were talking about and who, or what, Ermanes Chalkeus was. When she made it home, she sneaked into the family library without anyone noticing, but none of the books she found made any references to an Ermanes Chalkeus, only to an Eric Chalkeus. *Eric, as in, my father?* She thought to herself. Then Edith walked into the room.

"Aleerah?" Alee's great grandmother seemed more frail than usual, and her voice was shaking. "What are you doing dear? Shouldn't you still be at school?"

"I'm just—I wasn't feeling well."

"Hmmm. You seem fine." Edith gave her a thoughtful look, but she didn't seem entirely upset. "What are you looking for?" She gestured toward the pile of books scattered around Alee on the table.

"I was just looking—I wanted to learn more about auras." It wasn't a complete lie. She had intended to look that up too, she just hadn't quite gotten to that yet.

"And what have you learned so far?"

Alee scanned the books around her. "I—um—." Nothing was jumping out at her.

"It's OK to say it. You don't have to hide what you know, not from me." She moved closer, and started to sift through the books laid out on the table. "I am fully aware that I am sick." Alee had never been good at covering her emotions and clearly this was no exception.

"You mean the white light?" Alee asked, remembering the beautiful white glow that had surrounded only Edith.

"Don't look so sad, dying is just another part of life."

"Dying? What—Why?" It wasn't an act. Alee was truly surprised, and concerned. Although Edith was old, and seemingly fragile, Alee never would have suspected she was dying.

Edith quickly realized that it wasn't auras Alee had been studying. "Child, are you keeping something from me?" Her eyes burned into Alee's.

"No." Alee said firmly, yet still not really believably.

"What color was my aura?"

"It was white, like an angel," Alee said.

"Well then, if you had read even the basics on auras you would know that as death gets closer the color drains from your aura leaving only a warm white glow." Then, picking up a large book from the table and snapping it shut, she stared into Alee's eyes. "I do not recommend lying to me again." She put the book down, turned toward a bookshelf on the back wall, and held her hand up in front of her. "Reveal!" With that single word, the book she desired slid itself off of the shelf and floated through the air to land softly in her waiting hands.

"Wow." Alee was speechless.

"Here!" Edith held the book out for Alee to take.

"What is it?"

"Let it guide you." Then, gesturing down at the other books on the table, she grabbed the library book, *Light vs. Dark,* and tucked it under her arm. "These others will only mislead you."

"I have to return that—."

Edith didn't let her finish. "The book will get back to the school, don't worry. It contains nothing of use to you. Start here." She tapped on the cover of the book she had just handed her. "When you're done I'll give you another. There is much for you to learn." Then, turning to leave, Edith left the room without looking back.

After Edith left the room Alee turned the old leather-bound book over in her hands to read the cover, *Dhampir* was all it said. After putting all of the other books away she sank into the chair in the corner and began to read. Within minutes, she was so engrossed in the book she had completely forgotten the real reason she had gone to the library, which was to find out who, or what, Ermanes Chalkeus was. There were no windows in the room, and Alee had no idea how long she had been there reading when her cousin Phoebe poked her head in the door. "Hey, dinner's almost ready." Then, as an afterthought just before leaving. "Oh yeah, by the way, it was so not cool leaving school without letting me know. I had to deal with Petra questioning me for like a half hour while we waited for you in the parking lot. Believe me when I say that she isn't happy with you right now."

Alee didn't even look up when she answered. "Sorry." She meant it, but she was so engrossed in the book that she didn't even realize she was talking at first. Then, a second later, she called out to stop Phoebe from leaving. "Phoebe, wait!" She closed the book and tossed it on the seat as she bolted to the door.

"Yeah?"

"Um—. I was wondering—where do you live?" She almost felt stupid asking, but The Black Onyx wasn't a very large place, and she knew it wasn't possible that Phoebe and her family lived there, let alone the rest of the Wenham family. "I mean, you're always here, but you don't live here, right?"

Phoebe almost started to laugh, but stopped herself. "No, I don't. I was wondering how long it would take you to ask that. You've been around for a few weeks now. I guess kind of thought you would have asked sooner."

Now she felt really stupid, but Phoebe still hadn't answered the question. "So, where do you live?"

Phoebe sat down and Alee followed suit. "Our family owns a little over a hundred acres of land. This is only one of the five houses we have here on the property. There are more in town. Your mom owns The Black Onyx, although my mom helps her run it. Petra and I pretty much grew up here."

"Who lives in the other houses?"

"One is empty and off limits, I'm not really sure why. It's just been that way since before we were even born. I think Granny Estelle used to live there, but no one ever talks about it. Granny Edith and Granny Estelle live in the main house. Granny Elizabeth and Grandpa William live in the house just up the road from here, and that just leaves my mom and dad's place." Alee was just staring at Phoebe. "We have more houses in town where Granny Elizabeth's sister, Elaine, and her family live. She has two daughters who are about the same ages as our moms, but they're not married. Then of course, Great Granny Estelle's sister Ellen and her family still live in town, but we don't see them very often."

"Um—. Why not?" Alee had had no idea the Wenham family was so big.

"I don't really know. Just conflicting ideas about how the family should be run I guess. A few years before I was born Ellen, along with her husband and their daughter, broke ties with Granny Edith. I've only seen them a couple of times over the years. We actually have a cousin named Luvena. She's only a couple of years older than you but—." She swallowed hard, stopping herself.

"But what?" Alee asked.

"Nothing." Phoebe shook her head. "It's overwhelming, I know. We have a pretty big family, but you'll get to know who everyone is eventually. You need to just give it time." Then she was up and heading for the door. "Come on, dinner's gotta be ready by now."

Alee followed this time, but still wanted to know more. "But, why is everyone always here then—I mean if they—."

"The Black Onyx has pretty much everything we need in terms of, well everything: crystals, herbs, oils. Plus we keep the family library here. It's just easier to have it all together. When they decided to build on to the house and open a shop the decision was made that this would be the place to keep it all."

As they headed down the hall, Alee was still a little confused, and hesitated to ask, but figured, what the heck, she must look like a complete idiot already, so why not. "So, if you don't live here, how is it everyone always seems to be in the house somewhere? And why is it the only time I ever see your car outside is in the morning before school?"

"Aleerah, give it time. You don't have to have all of your questions answered at once." And that was the end of the conversation. Alee was still confused, but it was clear that she wasn't being let in on all the family secrets in one day.

Damian had exhausted all of his resources at home, in the public library, at town hall, and even at school, trying to find out anything about the Wenham family and the mysterious Ermanes, son of Chalkeus. Damian's father, James, had kept extensive surveillance logs on both families, but there was nothing in these that Damian really thought was relevant or useful.

When he visited the Town Hall Records Department, he was amazed at the wealth of information they had available for public review. A little old woman with shiny white hair greeted him in the lobby. "Hello Dear, I'm Anna Voss. What can I help you with today?"

"Um—. I just need to look up some information for a school project."

"You'll need to come in the back then." She pushed a button under the counter and a loud buzzing sound filled the room. "Just pull the door and come on back."

After he pulled the door open Ms. Voss stepped into the hallway with him and led him into the back room where row upon row of filing cabinets filled what appeared to be an old warehouse. "Wow—where should I start?"

"Everything is alphabetical. What is your school project about?" Her voice was shaky, and as she walked the tapping of her wooden cane tapped a rhythmic pattern on the cement floor. "Your family history maybe? Or perhaps information about your ancestors?" When Damian didn't answer her she stopped walking and turned back to face him. "What exactly are you looking for dear?"

"Um—. No, not my family. I'm doing a paper for school. It's um—I'm looking for information on a family by the last name of Chalkeus. If you have it."

The tapping stopped and she turned to face him. Her eyes narrowed, yet lit up with curiosity at the same time. She looked him over and her hunched back straightened until they were eye to eye. She was much taller than he had first thought. "Ah, and what is your name dear?"

"Damian—."

"And, your last name?" She was inquisitive, as if life had just given her a new riddle to solve.

He swallowed hard. The mood had changed suddenly without warning, and he wasn't sure whether he should be concerned or not. "Ward."

A smile stretched across her face, and she turned again and led him down a long row of filing cabinets to the back wall and gestured toward a large metal door. It was the kind of door you would expect to see on a vault at a bank— not in an old run-down records department building, at the far corner of the room. Her voice softened. "I think the information you seek is in there, but of course if you're not ready you may find some *very helpful* information here—." With an emphasis on 'very helpful' she nodded to the file cabinets in the back row. "—along this back wall." Then she turned and tap-tapped her way slowly back through the room and out the door to the front office. Before disappearing, she called over her shoulder, "We close early on Saturdays. You'll only have a couple of hours." Then under her breath, "That is if you choose to leave at all."

What does that mean? Damian wondered as he watched her leave, shutting the door behind her. For a few moments, Damian just stood there, alone, surrounded by the archives of Atlanta—all of the town's secrets—family histories, birth records, and death records. All the records were there, at his disposal, but where to begin, he wasn't really sure. He pulled on the first drawer in the back row, but it was locked. It was old, and he probably could have managed to get it open if he really tried, but he decided to move on, not paying it much attention.

He started trying the other drawers along the back wall, and every one that he tried was locked. "What the hell? How is this supposed to help me?" They were all labeled with dates, instead of letter codes—like, the drawers that were closer to the front of the room had been. 1700-1750, 1750-1800, 1800-1850, and the dates continued. He walked along, pulling one locked drawer handle after another, until he came to a set of drawers labeled 1950-2000. He pulled and it opened, much to his surprise. He didn't really know what he was looking for, but quickly, almost instinctively, he started sifting through the files until the name *Ward, James* landed under his fingertips. He didn't move—he couldn't even breathe for the longest time. Finally, he pulled the file out and, looking briefly over his shoulder, he opened the cover.

Inside the file, he found what looked like crime scene photos of the night his father was killed, along with the coroner's report, a copy of the police report, and article after article that had been printed in the local paper for weeks after his death. Flashbacks from that night poured into his memory, and Damian tried desperately to push them away, knowing full well that his dreams would be filled with nightmares that night.

In the back of the file, stapled to the inside of the file, was an envelope. Opening it, he found an old leather band, with an infinity symbol burned into the center and the word 'Guardian' on either side of the symbol. "Infinity?" he asked out loud, to no one but himself. He held the band in his hand for quite some time trying to remember if he had ever seen his father wearing it, but he couldn't recall. There was a rusty snap on the end, but he got it undone with little effort. He put it around his left wrist and, although it was a little loose, he liked the way it felt. The leather was old and had been worn so much that it was soft to the touch.

Damian slid the file back into its place in the drawer, and realized it wasn't the only one labeled with his father's name. There were at least half a dozen files, all of which were stuffed so full they were tearing at the creases. Pulling one of the files out at random, he found copies of his parents' marriage license along with his and Victoria's birth certificates. When he reached to the very back of the drawer and pulled out the last file, he was shocked to find a picture of his father at the age of sixteen or seventeen stapled to a letter on what looked like Atlanta Town Hall letterhead. The paper was torn in half so only the top portion of the letter remained, and the ink was smudged and faded, making parts of the letter completely indistinguishable.

Dear James M. Ward:
As a valued young member within the Atlanta society,
and a blood born member of the Underground, your

presence is requested at the induction ceremony at
this year's annual Founders' Day Celebration on—.
We will be celebrating one hundred and five years,
and are asking all founding families to—.

Damian had no idea what a Founders' Day
Celebration was, or even who the founders of Atlanta were,
but to see his father's name as someone of importance struck
him as slightly odd, after the way his mother had described
the different levels of society within the Underground. He
folded the letter and slid it back in the file, but instead of
putting the file back into the drawer he grabbed all of the
other files out and swiftly stashed them into the backpack he
had slung over his shoulder.

After closing the drawer and moving on, he tried a
few more drawers, but they were all locked. He made his way
down the row to the large metal door in the corner. Why the
old lady had directed him to yet another door made Damian a
little nervous—a little unsure—but he had come this far, so
what could it hurt?

It took all of his strength but, pulling hard, Damian
was finally able to get the door open. The hinges were old,
and the creaking sound reminded him of an old *Tales from
the Crypt* movie he had seen when he was a kid. Behind the
door was a steep wooden staircase leading down at least two
stories. It wasn't at all what he had expected to find—not that
he really knew what he had expected, other than maybe
another room of filing cabinets. He took the steps slowly, not
sure how old or how safe they were. It was dark, but a single
light bulb hung about half way down the staircase, swinging
slightly from the slight movement of air as the door closed
with a solid thump that made him suddenly feel more than
ever aware that he was alone.

Damian reached the bottom of the staircase to find—
yet another door. "Oh come on. Really?" He asked
sarcastically to himself. This one was larger than the average
door, and was made of solid wood. In the dim light, Damian
could vaguely make out what looked like another infinity
symbol carved into the center of the door. "Oh—." He
squinted at the leather band around his wrist, and then back at
the door, and realization hit him. He knew, somehow, that
this had to be the entrance —to —the Underground.

Damian turned to look back up the long flight of
stairs. He wondered for a moment whether he should continue
or turn back, but it was only a brief moment, and then he
pulled open the second door. It opened much more easily than
he had expected, and what he found on the other side was like
nothing he could have imagined. It was a tunnel, stretching
farther than he could see, and—it was filled with people, and
activity. The walls and ceiling were adorned with large white
subway tile, and the walkways were made of stone. It was
extremely clean for an underground—whatever it was. He
could see booths selling food, drinks, and even cell phones—
anything you might want. There were even restaurants and
shops, as if it were some kind of underground mall—only
much darker and, admittedly, a little creepy. Slowly it
dawned on him that this wasn't just a tunnel. It was an entire
system of tunnels. About every fifty feet was a doorway that
didn't lead into a shop, or other small room. Above these
doorways were signs telling where each of these tunnels led.
Turning back, to look up to the top of the door he had just
come through, Damian saw that the sign clearly read "Atlanta
Town Hall Records."

People were slowing down as they passed him,
examining him with squinted, piercing eyes, and looking
pointedly at the leather bracelet he wore. He tried not to

appear frightened, but he sensed that the beads of sweat forming around his hairline were giving him away. Damian stayed close to the wall, walking slowly and watching everyone around him, making sure not to make eye contact for too long. The one thing he noticed right away was that the symbol on the leather band that he was wearing was *everywhere*. It was not only carved into every door, but everyone around him was wearing it in some form. Some had charms on necklaces. One woman even had it tattooed along the side of her neck. He didn't see a single person, though, wearing a leather band similar to his.

Damian began to be aware of footsteps behind him that were matched to the same rhythm as his own as if following him. Not wanting to look back, but too afraid not to, he glanced over his shoulder and realized that there was a tall thin man walking about fifteen feet behind him, keeping pace with him. Damian sped up, hoping that it was just his overactive imagination playing tricks on him. But it wasn't. The mysterious man sped up as well—clearly, in fact, following him.

Damian quickly turned down the next corridor, which was somewhat narrower than the one he had been in, and there were fewer shops and storefronts. The farther he went, the faster his heart raced. The overhead lights were flickering on and off, and the doorways he passed were darkened. Darkened, but maybe not empty. Looking more closely into one of these doorways, he saw what seemed to be beady eyes glaring at him. Stopping short, he looked from doorway to doorway and in every one that he could see into there was a pair of the same beady eyes. The threat of whatever was hiding in those shadows seemed even worse than whatever the approaching man could possibly do to him. Slowly, Damian started to back up, and just as he turned to run he bumped right into the tall slender man. The man was all in black, and grinned down at Damian with sharp, almost animalistic fangs. Damian screamed, and bolted around him, running as fast as he could. The man just stood there and laughed, calling out. "Run little puppy—run as fast as you can, or you'll be my dinner tonight!" The sound of that voice echoed behind Damian as he ran through the hallway and back to the main tunnel turning back toward the town hall doorway.

He walked much more quickly now, for what felt like an hour, but was probably just minutes, before he slowed down and looked around, realizing that he wasn't all that sure how to get back. He kept his head down to avoid all eye contact, which made it hard to keep track of landmarks. Out of the corner of his eye he spotted a young woman, maybe a year or two older than himself, who he was sure he recognized from somewhere. Hoping to ask her for directions, he sped up to follow her. She turned, seeming to intentionally lead him down a long hallway that had no shops or doorways for over fifty yards, though there were quite a few people going in both directions, and the hallway was well lit. When he finally got close enough to realize who she was he wished he could just vanish. It was Petra, Phoebe Wenham's older sister. Damian pressed his back against the wall and turned away, hoping she wouldn't see him there hidden away behind by the passing people.

Petra was wearing black heels, a skin-tight black shirt, and what looked like military issue pants. "Wow, she makes tough look hot." If Damian had been thinking clearly when he first saw her, he would have realized that she didn't really look like someone he needed to be messing with. She went through a door just ahead of him, and he quickly ran ahead to see where she had gone. "Atlanta Hospital," he read aloud.

The hospital in Atlanta was not much more than a clinic. Atlanta wasn't the kind of place you wanted to be if you had anything seriously wrong with you. In those cases you were guaranteed to be driving for at least an hour, or taking the high-speed ambulance ride to the hospital in Grayling.

"Oh my God, these tunnels are under the whole city," he thought to himself. He turned and made his way back around the corner in search of another door leading to somewhere, anywhere he would recognize. Finally, he found a door leading to the Java Jolt, the hot new coffee shop that had just opened up the year before, and he pulled the door open and ran up the stairs. Without thinking, he burst through the door and flew into what looked like the storage room of the Java Jolt. The shelves were filled with all kinds of supplies, from paper coffee cups and plastic lids to large bags of coffee beans and industrial coffee makers. The smell of coffee surrounded him, and he heard the distant sounds of people talking in the front of the shop.

Damian was sweating, and his clothes were all disheveled from running, but he hastily pulled himself together as best he could. He ran his fingers through his hair, straightened his shirt, and slid out the door into the back hallway by the bathrooms. He looked like any other customer as he made his way to the counter and ordered a large soy chai latte. It was a drink Alee had gotten him hooked on when the shop first opened up. "Damian, seriously, try it. It tastes like Christmas," Alee had said excitedly.

Damian hadn't had the heart to come back since Alee had passed away. Something about being here, without her, just didn't feel right to him. He found a seat in the corner, away from anyone else, pulled his cell phone out of his back pocket, and quickly dialed his sister's number.

"What the hell, Damian, you were supposed to be back over an hour ago. I don't have all day to—." Victoria chimed in as soon as she answered, without even saying hello.

Damian didn't let Victoria finish. He was used to her lectures and knew full well that when it really got down to it she was never actually mad at him. "Well, hello to you too. Don't you even want to know what I found?" He could tell that he had piqued her interest because she fell silent, listening patiently on the other end. Playing with her, he didn't say a word.

"Damian?" She paused, waiting for him to answer. "Damian, are you still there?" He could hear the panic in her voice now.

"Beep. Beep. Beep." Damian mocked a busy signal sound as if he had hung up the phone.

"God, you're such a jerk."

Damian just laughed. Even though he was still pretty freaked out, it felt good to laugh, to pick on his sister, and to just feel alive again after feeling so alone for so long. "OK, I'm sorry. Anyway, can you pick me up? I'm at the Java Jolt."

"What?" She was obviously confused. "Where's your car?"

"Its downtown." Damian wasn't really in the mood to explain his adventures to his sister while sitting there drinking his latte, surrounded by an eclectic gathering of locals. Besides, he wasn't sure what he knew or who knew what about the town anymore.

"But, I thought you went to the—."

"It's a long story." The owner of the shop came around the counter and was walking from table to table, greeting people as he moved through the room. Damian could see out of the corner of his eye that the tall dark-haired man was keeping a close watch in Damian's direction. "Can you just pick me up? I promise to tell you everything when I see you." Damian was practically whispering into the phone, but the urgency came through loud and clear.

"Yeah, OK. I'll be there in twenty, but you better be there when I get there."

"Don't worry, I'm not going anywhere." As he hung up the phone and slipped it back into his pocket, he looked up to find the shop manager standing directly in front of him, on the opposite side of the table.

"How's your drink?"

Looking down at the table, then back up at the older man, Damian cleared his throat as he searched for his voice. "Um—. It's great, thanks."

The owner of the coffee shop extended his hand in Damian's direction. "My name's Jonathan Sanders, but most people just call me Sanders. Welcome to the Java Jolt."

Damian took his hand, hoping his own wasn't too clammy. "Thanks, but I've actually been here before."

Sanders looked him up and down for a minute, not letting go of his hand, but instead turned it until the inside of Damian's wrist was exposed, revealing the leather band. "Yes, that's right. You're Karen's boy. You used to come in here with a cute little redhead." Then, letting go of his hand, he scanned the rest of the shop as if he thought he might have missed someone. "Where is she today?"

Damian almost chocked on his latte. "She's—she um—she passed away." His eyes filled with tears and he fought hard to hold them back.

"Oh. Well, I'm sorry to hear that." Sanders rested his heavy hand on Damian's shoulder and gave him a little comforting squeeze. "If you need anything—I'm here for all

of our—members." He gave a little nod, gesturing down at
Damian's wrist band, and then subtly lifting his shirt sleeve
just high enough for Damian to notice the word Guardian
tattooed on the inside of his wrist. "You may want to be
careful about displaying that so openly. I'm not sure where
you got it, but you need to be careful." Damian didn't know
what to say, but Sanders didn't really give him the chance to
reply before he headed back to the counter and went back to
work as if nothing had happened.

Damian pulled the sleeves of his shirt down around
his wrists, sipped his latte, and let thoughts of Alee fill his
head until he heard Victoria, laying on the horn of her car in
the parking lot. Looking out the window, he saw her. She was
waving impatiently, trying to get his attention. Damian
hurried out to the car and climbed into the passenger seat,
tossing his backpack on the floorboard at his feet. Before he
had a chance to buckle his seatbelt, Victoria was speeding out
of the parking lot.

"Spill it! What happened?"

"You couldn't just have called me? Or texted? You
had to honk the horn and cause a scene?"

"Fine. Sorry. Now talk!"

Damian sat back and took a deep breath. He didn't
know where to start and he wasn't in the mood anymore
anyway. "Can you just take me to get my car please?" A
single tear ran down his cheek. Although she desperately
wanted to know what had happened, she dropped it.

"You OK?" Victoria knew her brother well enough
not to push him when he was like that. She didn't want to
take the chance of losing him to his depression again, after
just getting him back.

"Yeah, just thinking about—Alee." He turned away
from his sister. "Sorry."

"Don't apologize. It's OK." She kept her eyes on the road and they drove in silence, taking the long way through the back roads. Just as they were pulling into the parking lot of the empty Atlanta Records Building, she turned to him. "I'm sorry if I get on you about Alee. I know it's going to take time for you to get through this. I miss her too you know. So, I'm here for you if you need me."

"I know, but thanks for saying it." Damian got out shutting the door behind him, and made his way back to his car.

Alee was sitting in third period art class listening to Mrs. Massey explain their next assignment, a sculpture based on their deepest fears. Right then, Alee's biggest fear was Jathan, but she didn't think making a sculpture of him was going to help.

Alee watched the clock slowly tick by as she counted the seconds before lunchtime. Jathan had been particularly social that day, even more than his normal meeting her at the end of her classes and walking her to the next one. He wouldn't stop looking at her and whispering in her ear from the seat next to her. Earlier that morning, during English Literature, he had whispered, "Meet me after second period. I want to talk to you before art class." He didn't say what about or where to meet. But, Alee already knew that he would be standing outside of her second period class, like he was every day, waiting patiently for her to come out.

Alee wasn't sure how Kyle felt about Jathan. He never actually acknowledged him, or the odd ways he seemed to sweep in and steal her away from him. Alee assumed that

Kyle was jealous, but she didn't want to deal with it, or *know* how to deal with it, so she just pretended that everything was normal. Besides, Kyle wasn't ready to be the 'public couple' that Alee wanted, so there was very little he could do to stop her from hanging out with Jathan. Admittedly, it wasn't that Kyle didn't want to tell everyone about Alee, it was just that he didn't think it was the right time. His opinion may have had something to do with the fact that Alee's father, Eric, had pulled him aside and threatened, in a very 'gentle' way, not to do anything that might expose her true identity. And, being that Eric was not only a father with the 'I'll kill you if you hurt my daughter' act down to a tee, but also a vampire with the 'I can literally suck the life right out of you in seconds' act down to a tee, Kyle didn't really want to tempt his fate.

After second period, Jathan was outside the door waiting, just as Alee knew he would be. They started walking toward art class, and as soon as they made it out into the courtyard, Jathan pulled her off the path to the side of the building, where no one else would be able to see them easily. He had a way of making her feel like everything was perfectly normal and nothing was out of place, but this time, instead of his usual smooth, relaxed demeanor, he seemed all awkward and nervous. It sent up a red flag in Alee's mind, and she quickly made an excuse to leave and get to class early. "Um, Jathan—I need to hurry and get to class. I forgot to clean my brushes yesterday after class. Mrs. Massey is going to kill me." Something inside of her just knew that he was about to say something she either didn't want or wasn't ready to hear, and she didn't want to be put into that situation. In the worst case scenario, Jathan was about to profess his undying love for her, or maybe he was just going to ask her out on a date. In any variation on this theme, she was afraid that part of her might actually want it to happen. The thing was, she liked Jathan—just not as much as she liked Kyle, — and she didn't want to hurt Jathan's feeling if she didn't have to. Or maybe she didn't want to have to face the fact that turning him down wasn't something she really wanted to do. Either way, between her feelings for Kyle and her feelings for Damian, Alee didn't really need to add any more uncertainty in her life.

She had just left Jathan standing there, as she smiled and said, "But we can talk later. I really just need to get them cleaned before class. You understand, right?" She didn't wait for an answer as she turned and walked quickly through the courtyard and into the Arts Building.

Now she was sitting in class listening to Mrs. Massey and thinking about Jathan, and she knew that when the bell rang Jathan was going to try to get her alone again. She needed to think of a plan to get out of class before him, or to distract him in a way he might not suspect. Two minutes before the bell rang, she approached Mrs. Massey's desk, and whispered something in her ear. Mrs. Massey proceeded to pull a pad of hall passes out of her desk, wrote a short note, then handed it to Alee, who quickly gathered her things, and headed out of class like she had an important meeting to get to. In all honesty, Alee had used the oldest female trick in the book. She had told her teacher that her period had just started and she needed to run to the bathroom. It worked like a charm, as it always did. With male teachers you could actually get out of a full class period just by mentioning the word "pad," or "tampon."

After stopping off at the bathroom, because, ironically, she actually did have to go, she went directly to the school library. She had a standing lunch date with Kyle every day in one of the study rooms. It was the one time of her day that she looked forward to. They both brought their lunches, instead of going to the cafeteria, and no matter what, Kyle showed up, books in hand. They set up the room like they were studying—kind of like camouflage for their relationship—but Alee longed for the day when they could actually eat together in the cafeteria like a normal couple, not having to hide. She didn't like the idea of being anyone's secret, and the fact was she didn't understand why they had to hide for so long. How long did Kyle have to mourn anyway?

About fifteen minutes into their lunch hour, the door to the study room opened. A wide-eyed Damian stood there, just staring down at them. "Kyle." He nodded his head in some strange manly greeting ritual.

"Damian." Kyle returned the gesture.

Damian looked as if just being there was hard for him, but he didn't leave. "What's going on?"

OK, so it was more than weird, to say the least. Alee sat there, trying her best to think of nothing, but everyone knows that when you try to think of nothing, everything pops into your mind. Damian gave her a puzzled look when she suddenly realized that she had been thinking of pink elephants for about ten seconds. After that she tried hard to just act normal.

"Not much, just studying." Kyle gestured to all the books laid out on the table in front of them. "Aleerah is helping me with calculus. I hate math."

"Right—. So, you two want to get lunch together or what?" Alee and Kyle didn't know what to say. They just sat there stunned. "Dude," Damian said, "you try to put on the tough guy act, but everyone knows you're an honor roll student with a B average in math. So drop the studying act and come to lunch."

They weren't really sure what had sparked the sudden invitation, but Kyle started gathering up his books and Alee did the same, although a bit more hesitantly. "I'll meet you guys in the cafeteria." Damian headed out without looking back.

Lunch was awkward. It didn't feel at all like old times, like Alee had naively hoped it would. But, they were there, all of her old friends and her, and they seemed to at least be making an effort to accept her. Where did you live before you moved here? Where are you living? So you're cousins with Phoebe and Petra? Who does your hair? Why did you move here? The flood of questions came, one after the other, with no end in sight. But she answered them all, just happy to finally be back at the table. Besides, it gave her something to think of besides old times.

By the end of the day Alee was tired, and yet oddly exhilarated. She had been hoping to get some time alone with Kyle that evening, and when he asked her out to dinner, on a real date, she was so happy she leapt into his arms and kissed him for the first time in public. "Separate, you two. No PDA in the hallways." Alee and Kyle jumped as Ms. Thatcher passed by.

"Sorry Ms. Thatcher," Kyle said, turning to watch her go.

"Hmmm. Just don't do it again, Mr. Fields." Then, noticing Alee standing next to him, "Miss. Wenham, you ought to know better. You know the rules."

"Yes ma'am, I'm sorry."

Alee called her mom to let her know she wouldn't be riding home with Phoebe, but not to worry, that she was just going to dinner with Kyle, and that they would be home shortly after that. She was thankful she was able to leave a message, instead of talking directly to her. She wasn't really sure how Loraline would react, especially since they still hadn't found the wolves that had attacked her a couple of weeks before.

Dinner was great. They went to the Pizza Pit, a small pizza place downtown, and then to the local soft serve ice cream shop for dessert. When they got back to The Black Onyx, Alee asked Kyle to take a walk with her on the trail through the back woods. It wasn't dark out yet, and she figured her mom and dad wouldn't be looking for her, at least for a couple more hours. "Are you sure it's safe?" Kyle asked.

"I think its fine. Besides, Eric has been patrolling the woods just about every night since I was attacked. There hasn't been any sign of the wolves." Then, batting her eyelashes at him, she just smiled, "Please?"

"I can never say no to you. OK, let's go."

They had made it just far enough into the woods to be out of sight of anyone who might be passing by on the road when Alee turned to Kyle, holding his hands in hers. She was small standing next to him, and had to bend her neck all the way back to look up into his eyes.

"Hey." Her eyes were sparkling as she whispered.

"Hey yourself."

"Kiss me."

Kyle didn't hesitate. Pulling her even closer to him and squeezing her tightly around the waist, their lips touched, softly at first, but after only seconds her lips parted and she took his upper lip in. He tasted like sweet honey, and she wanted so much more. Neither Kyle nor Alee noticed when her fangs exposed themselves, just slightly, breaking the skin of his upper lip. But the instant his blood touched her tongue it was like an explosion throughout her body, as all of her senses were awakened. A soft moan escaped Kyle's lips "Yes," he whispered, and she continued to drink.

Their kiss, passionate and sensual, lasted longer than she had planned. It was the cool breeze that finally pulled them reluctantly apart.

Kyle smiled down into her sky blue eyes. "Wow. I can get used to that."

She smiled up at him, and gently wiped the remaining drop of blood off his lip. "Sorry."

"Don't apologize, I liked it."

"Come on." Alee took his hand and led him farther down the path, walking at first, then a light jog, until finally they were running. Alee was giggling like a little girl, and Kyle was dodging tree branches as they flew at his face.

"Wait—wait! You have to slow down for a minute." He was tired, breathing heavily, but still smiling with pure excitement.

They slowed to a stop and Alee turned around and pulled him close. "Can't keep up?" She raised her eyebrows and blew him a little kiss.

Kyle never was one to pass up a challenge, especially from a girl who was small enough for him to carry on his shoulders. "What? You think I—? Oh, it's so on!" He grabbed her hand and took off running again.

They were running as fast as he could for another quarter of a mile, and then, suddenly, without any effort at all, their speed began to increase. It wasn't possible for Kyle, a mere human, to be running that fast, but somehow he was. After almost two miles in less than eight minutes they stopped, tumbling onto the ground. Kyle was breathing heavily, but Alee wasn't even the slightest bit winded.

"Holy crap, that was—." He sat there shaking his head, unsure of what had just happened. "That was—was that—you?"

Their tattoos had started to glow sometime during that last two-mile stretch, and now the small vines that had circled Alee's wrist almost fully covered her right forearm. Instead of freaking out like she half expected Kyle to do, he didn't move. He ran his hand along her arm, and traced the vines with his fingertips. "Why do you think it does that? Do you think it—?" Then, all of a sudden it seemed to sink in. "Did this somehow make that happen?" He nodded toward where they had just come from.

"I um—I don't really know, but do you trust me?" She was shaking.

He gently lifted her chin until he could see her beautiful blue eyes, and then he softly kissed her forehead. "You know I do. Hey, are you cold? You're shivering like crazy."

"I'm fine, really. Come on, follow me." She led him down another hill into a small valley surrounded by trees. "I've been practicing every night, and, well, I want to show you something." Alee walked a few feet away, closed her eyes, and began chanting again and again, in an even, mechanical voice, "Goddess of the seven winds, keepers of the distant powers, create the wind for all to see and I shall in nature set you free."

Kyle just stood there, eyes wide, watching, as the leaves on the ground began to rise around her. Trees swayed in the wind almost as if they were dancing, and the sky darkened with clouds. A clap of thunder jolted her out of her trance. The instant she stopped chanting and opened her eyes the clouds drifted away, the winds died down, and the leaves floated back to their resting place on the ground at her feet.

"That was amazing."

A smile spread across Alee's face and she crossed back to him and took his hand. "You think so? Do it with me."

"But, I'm not—."

"Don't worry." She held his wrist, her hand covering his tattoo. She focused hard, and his tattoo began to glow. Then, with a quick little smirk, she extended her left arm, palm up to the sky, and began the chant all over again, this time *yelling* it to the sky with fierce authority. "Goddess of the seven winds keepers of the distant powers combine our strengths and use our energy. Create the wind for all to see and we shall in nature set you free!" Another crack of thunder, louder than the first, shook the ground beneath their feet, and a sharp stabbing pain pierced Kyle's wrist, but the pain quickly passed, and they were being drenched by a sudden downpour of rain.

Now it was Kyle who was shaking, scared, energized, and amazed all at the same time, in a way he had never felt before. "How did you do that? I mean, you did do that, right?"

"Not just me—we did it."

"But, I'm not a—"

"I'm not really sure how it works, but somehow I—I used your energy and combined it with mine. I should be able to do it with anyone's, I think, to make myself more—powerful." She swallowed hard. "At least that's my best guess." She stood there watching him, waiting for him to turn and run, but he never did. "I don't really get how it works, but I'm stronger—with you."

The real question, the one he really wanted to ask, was harder still.

"How did you learn that?"

"Um, practice." She noticed that Kyle was still holding his wrist. "Did I hurt you?"

Kyle just shook his head and grabbed her, pulling her close to his chest. "You are—amazing. You scare me sometimes, but in a good way."

"I scare you?"

"You make me love you, and that scares me." It was a whisper, but she heard him clearly. Alee kissed him with such force there was nothing he could do but kiss her back. Arching her back she pressed her body as close to his as she could. He backed her up against the trunk of a nearby tree, never once releasing her, only holding on even tighter.

As if her body depended on his for survival, she could hear their hearts beating in unison and felt his body coming alive, growing firmer beneath his already tight jeans. She knew he needed her too.

They stayed like that, lips locked under the cover of the tree, until the clouds parted, and the sun broke through above them. She wanted more of him, but drenched from head to toe in the woods wasn't really the romantic setting she was hoping to have for their first time. Reluctantly, they pried themselves apart. "I'm glad I scare you."

"Me too."

Dripping wet, they made their way back through the woods. They walked this time, enjoying every second they had to spend together. "So, have you told Eric and Loraline?"

Neither Kyle nor Alee referred to them as her parents, aside from the occasional slip of the tongue on Alee's part. She was getting a little more comfortable with the idea of this new family, but at those rare times when her comfort level got so high that she managed to call them mom or dad she would feel a flood of guilt. She had been meaning to stop by her old house to check in on her mom, Martha, but she couldn't bring herself to do it. The thought of seeing her again and not being able to run into her arms killed her over and over again. Granny Edith had worked some kind of spell that helped Martha forget, or at least not care so much, but Alee didn't think it had worked as well as it was supposed to. It was like a magical Xanax, but the prescription wasn't strong enough to do much more than dull the pain.

"You mean, have I told them about the practice and stuff?"

"No, I mean have you told them that I love you." Alee stared at him. "Of *course* I mean about the practice. About everything you showed me. Do they know?"

"No, and I'm not sure I'm going to, at least not yet. I still don't really understand it all."

"You seem pretty comfortable to me."

"Yeah, well, I'm trying. But they haven't been all that eager to teach me. I mean they're trying, I guess. It's just that I feel like they are walking on eggshells around me when it comes to magic. Like they think I'm going to break if they show me too much at one time. But—."

After a few minutes of silence, Kyle gently nudged her with his elbow then pulled her close holding her in the middle of the path. "But what?"

"But, things just keep happening and I want to understand them, but I don't" She tried to pull away and start walking again but he just held her.

"Like what?" Alee turned away, shuffling her feet beneath her. "Talk to me, please. I'm here for you and I want to know. I want to be a part of this."

"I know you do and that means so much to me. It's just that I'm confused and I can't—never mind, you're right." Alee smiled up at him, trying to look more relaxed, but the weight of everything—Kyle, Damian, Jathan, Martha, and even her new family and powers—seemed to be getting worse. "I was in the library back at The Black Onyx one night last week. I was doing a little research when Granny Edith came in." She turned away from Kyle just a little, trying to find her words. "I don't think she likes me." She blurted out.

"What? Why would you say that?"

"I don't know. I just—. It's the way she watches me, like she's just waiting for me to do something wrong."

"You mean the same way every adult looks at teenagers?" Kyle said as the corner of his lips curled to a smile.

"Yeah, I guess. It just feels different. Maybe you can't understand because everyone likes you, but it's almost like she's trying to figure me out, or figure out what I am, maybe."

He lifted her chin so that she was looking up at him. "You are an amazing woman, a pretty powerful witch from what I can tell, probably the next gold medalist in the hundred yard dash, and someday you will be a very strong vampire. So, all in all you're like a superhero. What more is there to figure out?"

Alee just smiled and her checks flushed pink. "You think I'm like a superhero?"

"I know you are." She kissed him again, only this time it was softer, gentler. She trembled under his touch and he pulled her close.

"Everything's going to be OK." He whispered in her ear and she almost believed him.

"Granny Edith gave me a book—all about—me!" When she looked up into his bright eyes, she saw that they were wide with curiosity and intrigue.

"Really?"

"Well not just me—dhampirs in general, and I guess that means me. I mean, I'm the only surviving one, right? At least that's what they say. I don't know—. Anyway I've been doing a lot of reading, and I kind of maybe snagged one of the family spell books to practice on my own at night, so with those two books and my Book of Shadows—well, Loraline's Book of Shadows—let's just say there's a lot that I've been learning." Kyle knew that Alee had been practicing, that much she had told him, but the fact that she had "borrowed" a family spell book, started to make him wonder what she had been practicing exactly. Alee could tell he didn't like it before the sentence even finished coming out of her mouth. "I mean, it's really no big deal. I wasn't even sure this would work today."

"So what did you think would happen?"

"I don't know—nothing maybe." Kyle could see in her eyes that that wasn't exactly true. "I guess I thought it might work, but I had no idea how well. Honestly!"

"Why? What made you think it would work?" Kyle wasn't scared. It was hard to scare him, and more than anything he was intrigued by everything Alee did, from the way she walked to the sound of her voice, and now to this newfound sense of adventure that the old Alee hadn't had.

"This." She turned his wrist over so that he was looking down at his own tattoo. "You weren't tattooed. You weren't branded. You shouldn't have this, but somehow, you do. I think it's because of me, because of our connection."

"Do you remember that first time my tattoo did that glowing thing? I'm not even sure what to call it. I guess it kind of—came alive." Kyle just nodded his head. "Well I couldn't sleep that night, and I kind of went snooping through the Wenham's library, trying to find anything that could explain what had happened."

"OK—." He was beginning to get excited now, because it was obvious that she had learned something pretty interesting. "What did you find?" He did wonder, though, why she hadn't shared the information with him sooner. "Why didn't you tell me any of this before?"

"I didn't tell you because I still don't really understand it yet. This is all still so weird to me, and I—I didn't want to scare you." Alee looked down at the ground, and shuffled her feet. It was something instinctive that she had done all of her life whenever she got nervous. Kyle knew it well, and he quickly moved to grab her hand, and brushed the hair out of her eyes with his other hand.

"Hey, it's OK. I'm not going anywhere. You're not going to scare me away." His voice was calming, and Alee automatically wondered what she could possibly have done in life to deserve such an amazing guy.

She pulled him just off the trail and found a dry place to sit under a large oak tree. "There was this book, or a journal, rather. It had to be either Eric's or Loraline's because there was an entry all about Loraline's pregnancy. Then there were about four or five pages of random notes about the powers that they thought their baby could potentially be born with, being half vampire and half witch. It didn't refer to a dhampir directly, but—." Alee quickly looked around, as if she was afraid someone might be watching, or worse— listening to their conversation.

She continued, but this time in a whisper. "Well, it wasn't until Granny Edith gave me the book on dhampirs that I put two and two together. A lot of the same powers were listed in both the book and the journal. However, the journal said that power sharing, or the transfer of one's energy or powers is rare but definitely possible given their bloodline. When I got the book from Granny Edith the first thing I did was look up power sharing. I couldn't find anything, but it did talk about feeding off of other sources of power. It mentioned that after a vampire has fed off of a witch he is able to utilize the witch's powers for a short time. I guess the power a witch possesses has something to do with their bloodline. I don't really know." There was an awkward silence as they both imagined Alee feeding. "Anyway, because I'm already a witch, and a—vampire, I assumed that maybe feeding would just make my powers stronger. I don't really know what would happen if I fed on another witch." She started to blush. "OK, that sounds bad, the feeding part. But it got me to thinking—.

"The book also talked about how some witches are able to pull energy from nature, by calling on the five goddesses: wind, water, earth, fire, and the spirit. So, I was thinking that if it worked with nature then why not people. Every time we touch I get this surge of energy, like a small shock. I just figured it was because I like you. I mean, I've never felt like that with anyone else." OK, that was a lie. Alee had the same reaction whenever Jathan touched her, only he didn't have the marks to show it.

"But you don't think that now?"

"No. I mean, I still feel that way. But I kept reading and witches believe that everything living has an energy source. That includes plants, trees, animals, people— everything. I started working on spells that used nature to pull energy. The thing was, I kept coming back to the idea that if I could pull energy from—some*one* else—it would work better. And, if I could manage that—why couldn't I share energy and power too. I was trying to hone my skills before telling anyone. Hone my skills? God that sounds corny. Anyway, I figured that if you were here, maybe—." Alee was started to think that she really was sounding crazy, that maybe it was all too outrageous to be real. She had to try it one more time. She turned to him, smiling like a child about to do something devious.

"Come on, try to keep up, but don't try too hard. Just let your body follow your mind, and let your mind go blank." She took off running with him, with Kyle keeping pace beside her, and holding her hand as they went. Sure enough, it wasn't long until it was as if he had all the abilities of her vampire speed. He was running just as fast, just as fluidly, and just as comfortably as she was.

When they rounded the corner near the end of the path they burst into the open field behind The Black Onyx, and crossed the clearing in seconds. Standing just outside the back door of The Black Onyx, Kyle turned to her in awe. "So— when I'm with you—?"

"I can share my powers with you." She answered with a smile. "Yeah, I think so."

"But, I'm not—."

"I know."

"That's so cool." They stood there for a while, just basking in the 'what if' moment of it all, when he swallowed hard and turned away.

"What are you thinking?"

"Nothing, it's just that—. Well, all this stuff is really cool, and amazing, but it's nothing if I can't—."

"If you can't—." Alee said, hoping he would finish his thought.

"I guess what I'd really like is to see you again."

Alee laughed. "What are you talking about? I'm not going anywhere."

"No. That's not what I mean. I know it's not possible, but I wish I could see you again, the way you used to look. The Alee I fell in love with." She understood instantly what he was saying. Although she would never have admitted it to anyone else, she too missed the old her. She had actually learned a spell to dissolve the masking spell that had been put on her, but she only used it at night, alone in her room, and she always made sure she undid it before anyone else saw her.

She looked around to make sure no one was watching and, waving her hand in front of her face, she whispered a quiet incantation. "All I ask is to lift my mask. Reveal the 'me' I wish to see." She could see in his eyes that it had worked.

Kyle ran his fingers through her long auburn curls. His hand on her cheek, he leaned in for a kiss, but before their lips touched, the backdoor opened and Eric was standing there with his arms crossed, and a very disapproving look on his face. "Aleerah! What are you doing?!" Eric's booming voice echoed in her ears, and in seconds her father had grabbed both Alee and Kyle by the arms and yanked them inside. The door slammed shut behind them and they slouched into the kitchen seats.

She had never seen Eric so angry. His eyes were as red as fire, and with his fangs exposed he lunged at Kyle, grabbing him out of the seat and thrusting him against the wall. "What did I tell you about keeping her identity a secret? Your careless behavior has not only put her life at risk, but all of her family's as well, not to mention your pitiful existence."

"STOP!" Alee wasn't usually the type to yell, but she also wasn't the type to let someone treat someone she loved in such a brutal way. "He didn't do anything wrong. It was me, OK. *I* chose to do it, and I will face whatever consequences there might be. I'm not afraid. What is the big deal anyway?" She waved her hand in front of her face whispering to herself. "See, it's fixed. Is that what you wanted? Is that better? Is this the daughter you'd rather have?" She spit the question at him accusingly.

Eric dropped Kyle to the floor as if he were nothing but a sack of garbage, and crossed the room to face his daughter eye to eye. "You really think you're ready to face the world? You have no idea what's out there, let alone who might be after you, and no, it isn't better. I don't want you to have to hide yourself, but I also don't want you to get yourself killed. So, it is what it is!"

"What's after me? You're always so cryptic. What is that? Why don't you ever just say what's on your mind instead of talking around everything?"

"You're a dhampir, Aleerah! Only weeks after you were born your mother was attacked and almost killed. Has it not occurred to you that they were looking for you? If they had found you before I got there, I don't know what would have happened to you. Without knowing who was after you, I can't keep you safe, not a hundred percent. That is why no one can know who or what you really are. Why do you think your mother and I didn't return to Atlanta after we found out we were pregnant? Sure, having family around might have made things easier on your mother, but we weren't willing to risk your life, not then and not now."

"Then teach me more than just about hunting. More than just the mindless potions and spells everyone is throwing my way. Teach me the histories. Teach me about the dangers, or for God's sake just let me live my life." A sudden calm washed over them, and Alee could see the change on Eric's face. He was no longer angry, but almost seemed impressed. It wasn't at all what Alee had expected. "How do you expect me to survive if you're not willing to teach me? You are forcing me to do this on my own, and honestly I think I'm doing a damn good job." She wasn't yelling any more, but she wasn't ready to back down either.

She had made a good point, and Kyle opened his mouth only slightly to back her up, but before he got a sound out Eric silenced him with a glance. "OK. You're right. I do owe you that much. But, it isn't going to be easy, and if you're going to really learn you will have to give up some of the more normal pleasures in your life." His eyes went straight to Kyle. It wasn't hard for Alee to decode the not so hidden meaning behind Eric's words.

"You mean give up Kyle? No, that's not part of the deal. He is with me every step of the way. I want him to learn too." Eric started to shake his head, but Alee wouldn't allow it. "You don't get to make this decision Dad." She practically spit the title at him, and it wasn't loving or endearing in any way. "I have already given up everything, and besides, I'm stronger with him by my side. I can't explain why or how I know, I just know that I am. I won't do this without him. And, he has already been touched by the goddesses. So, you need to find a way to get over it." She stormed out of the kitchen pulling Kyle behind her. She didn't stop until they were in her bedroom with the door locked behind them.

10

Alee stood with her back to the door trying to calm herself down. Her hands were shaking and the rapid beating of her heart almost stopped her breath. She had snapped! She had never blown up at anyone like that before, and to stand up not only to her father, but to a vampire who could literally crush her if he wanted to, was more than she had ever expected to do.

"Alee, what if he's right?"

"What?" Kyle had gotten her attention, and although her heart was still racing she wasn't focused on it any more. "Kyle what are you saying?"

"I don't know." He didn't know what to say. "Nothing, it's just—what if Eric's right? What if the best thing for you right now is not to be with me? Maybe I'm putting you—."

"You don't want to be with me anymore?" She sounded crushed, but her burning red eyes gave a different impression.

"Of course I do but, more importantly, I want you safe. What if I am preventing you from learning what you need—from becoming who you really are?"

"Is this not proof that we belong together?" She lifted her sleeve and then his, throwing their tattoos in his face. "Why would you have been marked if you weren't supposed to be with me? Why would the goddesses have blessed you?" Alee was beginning to feel confused and distressed, and needed time to think. She pushed him out the door. "Just go!" With her back against the door she slid to the ground crying into her hands.

"Aleerah, don't do this. Please. I didn't mean it like that." Kyle just stood on the other side of the wall, his ear pressed hard against the door trying to hear her. "Alee?!" he cried, hoping she was listening.

"Just go away. I don't want to see you right now." She ran through the room gathering things into her backpack, then went to the window, slid it open, and climbed out into the night. The sun had gone down since they had come inside, and it was easy to escape back into the woods without anyone noticing.

Loraline found Kyle sitting outside Alee's door about a half hour later. He had been crying, but didn't really care who saw him that way. The one thing being with Alee had done was to make him care less about how other people saw him, and more about how she saw him. "Kyle?" Loraline was nurturing by nature. She crouched down next to him, and put her hand on his shoulder. "Kyle, I'm sorry about Eric. He shouldn't have talked to you that way. He didn't—."

"I—it's f—fine."

"Then, what's wrong?"

"Alee—rah, she—she won't let me in. When Eric said she should give me up—I—I thought maybe I was holding her back. She thinks that I don't want her, that I agree with him." Kyle shook his head, and the tears began to flood down his face. "That's not what I meant at all. I don't want to lose her. I love her. I love her more than anything, and now she won't even answer me."

Loraline's expression went from consoling to concern in seconds. She stood up, looking from Kyle to the door, before trying the knob, but it was locked. "Aleerah, open the door sweetheart. Aleerah, it's your mother, please open the door." She knocked, but there was no answer. Holding the doorknob in her left hand she pressed her right hand on the doorframe and closed her eyes. Kyle could hear her mumbling something under her breath then there was a soft click as the gears within the lock shifted. She quickly turned the knob and rushed into the empty room. The curtains billowing in the wind from the open window let in a cool draft.

Loraline turned to Kyle with the grace of a dancer, but the determination of a fighter. "How long has she been gone?" Kyle didn't move—he said nothing. "Kyle, how long has it been since you talked to her?"

"Thirty minutes maybe. I don't know." He was in a daze. It hadn't sunk in that she was actually gone.

Loraline ran passed him and went out the bedroom door. She was screaming as she ran down the hall. "Eric, Jacinda, Tom—." As she turned into the library she found her mother Elizabeth, her grandmother Estelle, and her great grandmother Edith huddled close in front of a fire talking quietly. "Aleerah is gone." She was out of breath, but still something inside of her pushed her to keep going. She grabbed a folded map from one of the bookshelves along with a large crystal that hung on a silver chain from one of the sconces. She didn't have to tell anyone what to do, they all just knew intuitively. It was as if they had been through this a hundred times. Who knows, maybe they had.

Elizabeth spread the map across the coffee table as Edith and Estelle gathered candles and began lighting them at the edges. When Jacinda came in she quickly stood at the opposite end of the map across from Loraline. Together they chanted, holding the crystal above the map. "Let the crystal point the way. Show us the location of Aleerah this day." Over and over they repeated the incantation. The crystal, hanging on the silver chain, began to circle above the map as if it had a mind of its own.

Kyle, sleepy eyed and still not quite grasping what had happened, made his way into the room, and stood between Eric and Tom, Jacinda's husband, watching from the back wall.

Nothing was happening—the crystal just circled the map. "Maybe we aren't meant to find the girl." Edith hissed.

"Granny!" Jacinda and Loraline gasped at the same time.

"I'm only saying we have had nothing but trouble since—."

"Edith, stop!" Eric said in a loud and definitive voice.

"What's going on? What are they doing?" Kyle asked, and Eric noticed him for the first time since he had entered the room.

Eric just looked at him with fire in his eyes. It was Kyle's fault that his little girl was off, God only knows where. It was Tom who finally spoke up. "They're scrying, for Aleerah."

"What does that mean?" Kyle asked.

'It's kind of like witchcraft GPS." Tom said.

Then Eric interrupted. "It means they're trying to find her. If it hadn't been for your careless—."

"I know where Alee is," Kyle said quietly and simply.

The room went silent, and all eyes were on Kyle. Even Jacinda and Loraline stopped what they were doing and turned their focus in his direction.

"What do you mean you know where she is?" Loraline was at his side in seconds. "Kyle, if you know where she is, you have to tell me. She could be hurt. She could be in trouble."

"I didn't mean for her to go. I only meant—I'm sorry." Kyle turned to Eric, knowing that he might decide to just kill him right there for hurting his daughter, but praying that he would realize that everything he had done was because he loved her so much. "There is only one place Alee—I mean Aleerah—feels safe. I mean, really truly safe. It's been a while, but she's a creature of habit. If she's really upset, and I know she is, she'd want to be home."

Loraline jumped in, not really hearing beyond the words that Kyle was saying. "But, this is her home. Why isn't she—?" Then it sank in. "Oh no. Martha's." Turning to her husband she grabbed his arm and squeezed. "You have to get her out before Martha realizes who she is."

Eric was halfway out the door when Kyle stopped him. "No. I should go."

Eric and Loraline exchanged looks and she was about to tell him that Eric would handle it, but Edith stepped in before she could say anything. "Yes. It's for the best, if we must bring the girl back Kyle should be the one to get her, but he should take Eric with him." Then she turned to Eric. "For protection only, you are not to interfere." She coughed as she spoke, all but pushing Kyle out the door. "Go now, child. If you are to help her, then you haven't much time."

11

The drive to the Moyer house only took about twenty minutes, but it was the longest twenty minutes that Kyle had ever spent in a car. He could feel Eric's eyes on him the entire time, and wondered if he would have time to grab the silver-tipped stake from beneath his seat, as insurance in case Eric made any sudden moves. He was betting not, and rethinking the hiding place for the weapon for the future. That is if he made it through this night alive.

"Can I ask you something?" Eric asked, still watching Kyle's every move.

"Umm—." Kyle wasn't sure he wanted to know the question. "Sure."

"How did you know where Aleerah went?"

"Are you kidding me? How could you not know?" Kyle was baffled by the thought that Eric was supposed to be this all-powerful vampire, whose daughter had drunk his own blood and consumed it daily, for months, via the little red pills, and yet he didn't know how to find her.

Eric's already intense eyes were burning with disgust now, instead of anger. "Excuse me?"

"Well, for starters, you're her father. She already told me that you used to watch her sleep at night. How did you not know how safe she felt when she was living with the Moyers? And, secondly you're a vampire, and Alee is—."

"Aleerah!"

"Right, Aleerah. She's your daughter. She has been taking pills for the last however many months that have been made from your blood, I assume." Eric didn't deny it. "And, she drank your blood straight from the vein to heal her leg, right?"

"That is correct."

"Then why didn't you know where she went? Why couldn't you sense her? Aleerah has, once or twice, drunk of—. Anyway, my point is, she knows when I'm around. I would think as old as you are your abilities to sense her would be better. What is the point of being a vampire if your special vamp-senses aren't working?"

"Hmmf," Eric scoffed. "My vamp-senses are working just fine. Aleerah is just different. I can sense her— sometimes. But, she has the ability to—block me at times. I'm not sure how, but I assume it has something to do with her wiccan abilities."

They drove in silence for the next couple of minutes before Eric spoke up. "You must be careful how much blood you allow her to take."

"Excuse me? I'm not sure it is any of your—." Eric was surprised at this turn in the conversation.

"It is for your safety that I tell you. She is still young and doesn't understand yet what it could do to you. If she were to lose control and take too much the worst-case scenario would not be your death. Death would be a blessing in comparison."

"What does that mean?"

"It means death is far better than the shell of a person you would become. You have read Dracula?"

"Of course."

"The brides of Dracula—they did not merely love him. They were obsessed with him. When a vampire takes too much at one time, he can take the soul of his victim. They lose all sense of self, and live only for their master. They become no more than a slave, happy to serve, and willing to do anything—questionable or not."

The air grew thick around them, and Kyle watched the road with unbreakable concentration. He couldn't think about that now. He focused only on driving, and what he was going to say to Martha when they got to the Moyer's house.

"Just tell her you wanted to check to see how she was doing."

"What?"

"Mrs. Moyer. She'll ask you why you're there. Just tell her you wanted to make sure she was OK."

"Yeah, OK." Kyle parked his truck by the curb outside the Moyer's house. "Did you—"

"No, I didn't read your mind. It's just what I would have been thinking about if I were in your shoes." Nodding toward the house. "We're here. You should go." But before Kyle could leave Eric stopped him. "Kyle, about the other conversation, I'm sorry. I should have waited, but you did need to know."

"Yeah, thanks."

It was already one in the morning when he pulled up to the Moyer's house. He hadn't been there since the afternoon of Alee's funeral and it felt a little weird to be back now after so much time had passed. When he walked up the path, the front door opened before he could even reach out his hand to knock. He half expected to see Alee there with her flowing red curls and her bright blue eyes, but it wasn't Alee. Instead, Damian stood in the doorway with both Martha, Alee's mother, and Victoria sitting on the couch just behind him in the living room.

"Kyle, what are you doing here?" Damian had clearly caught Kyle off guard, just as Kyle had obviously caught Damian by surprise. "Dude, what are you doing here?"

"I just. I couldn't sleep. I couldn't stop thinking about Alee." Kyle looked back at his truck, but Eric wasn't sitting in the passenger seat any more. He hadn't heard him get out, but then again, more often than not, Eric came and went without anyone ever knowing—just another bonus of being all superhuman and stealthy. "Is Mrs. Moyer here?" Kyle asked, pretending as if he hadn't already seen her sitting on the couch. "I'd really like to see her if she is."

Damian stepped aside and let Kyle pass, as he stepped out onto the porch, scanning up and down the street for a few seconds and sniffing at the night air around him, before following Kyle back into the house. "You do realize what time it is right?"

"Yeah, I know. I'm sorry I just—." Then stopping dead in his tracks he turned to face Damian. "Why are you here anyway?"

"Support. That's what friends do." Damian oozed with sarcasm and disdain. "You would know that if you were around more. Where have you been these days? You're like a ghost, man."

Kyle had been spending his lunch hour with Alee, a.k.a. Aleerah, hidden in a study room in the back of the library, and although Damian already knew it, he wanted

Kyle to say it out loud, in front of Alee's mother. The library was the only place Kyle and Alee could find where no one seemed to bother them, at least most of the time. Not that the library wasn't being used, it was actually busier than most places on campus, but it seemed that no one noticed or cared about anything except the computer stations and the coffee shop. Danielle had made it clear that she didn't really want to have anything to do with Aleerah, but Kyle wasn't willing to give her up. So their only option was to stay in hiding, aside from the occasional and very unexpected lunch invites from Damian, at least until everyone had accepted them as a couple.

"I've been around. Maybe if you guys were a little more open to hanging out with new people I'd be around more," Kyle said.

"That's right, you're still hanging out with your little freak of a girlfriend Alice or Alisha or something." Damian was disdainful.

"Her name is Aleerah, but you already know that. Actually, I think you'd really like her if you got to know her better." No one noticed as Martha sat up in her seat at the mention of Aleerah's name. They were too busy arguing to pay attention to anyone else.

"I invited you guys to have lunch with us," Damian said.

"Yeah you did, and then you grilled her like she was on trial the whole time. You really think she wanted to come back for a second round?" She actually had. It was Kyle who felt too uncomfortable. He didn't want to put Alee or himself through that again. Crossing the room, Kyle nodded to Victoria and then turned his full attention to Alee's mom. "I'm sorry to stop by so late, Mrs. Moyer. I just wanted to make sure you were all right, and to say that I'm sorry I haven't been around more."

Martha sat back in her seat, pulling her blanket up around her. "That's all right dear." Martha spoke so softly that Kyle had to strain to hear her. "It's hard with Alee being sick, but I'm sure she'll be glad to see you again."

Damian motioned for Kyle to follow him into the kitchen, and Victoria followed.

Kyle didn't get it. "Wait, what did she say?"

Victoria explained. "She's just confused. She's been this way off and on since the funeral. She has good days, and then there are days like today where she swears Alee is still here. She says she hears her walking around upstairs in her room. Damian and I check in on her once or twice a week." Victoria's voice was trembling. "She doesn't have anyone else."

Kyle had never seen Victoria so accommodating and helpful. "You miss her don't you?"

For the first time since the funeral Kyle actually believed that Victoria had been affected by Alee's death. "We all do," Victoria said, and a single tear ran down her check. "Damian, we should get going."

But Damian just stared at her, and sent a mental message to his sister. *'It's not time. I need to see more. What if Martha is right this time? What if she really is here?'*

'Damian, we need to go. We have never found anything in all the times we have checked, why should tonight be any different? We can come back later.'

Victoria turned to Mrs. Moyer and hugged her goodbye. "We'll come back in a few days and see you, I promise. You can tell us some more stories next time." Victoria closed an old photo album that was sitting on the coffee table, and slid it into a drawer in the end table next to the couch. "It's late. You should try and get some sleep." Martha only nodded, staring down at the table where the book had been. Victoria turned to her brother, but she didn't have to say anything. He was already saying his goodbyes to Mrs. Moyer. Victoria turned to Kyle. "Goodnight Kyle."

"Yeah, goodnight."

Damian, like a guy, awkwardly held out his hand to Mrs. Moyer. "I hope you feel better soon. We'll stop—."

Mrs. Moyer became suddenly alert. She got up from the couch with newfound energy and grasped Damian's hand in hers. She lifted his wrist and examined the leather band he was wearing. "Why do you have this?" Her words were direct, demanding, and not even the slightest bit confused or unsure.

"I um—."

"Where. Did. You. Get. It."

"I—V?" Victoria turned away from Kyle, finally noticing the panic in her brother's voice.

"Damian," the newly energized Mrs. Moyer demanded, "I want to know."

He pulled his arm out of Martha's grasp and headed straight for the door. "I gotta go."

"You're one of them!" She followed him to the door and shouted after him, "Get out! Get out of my house! It was you who ruined my life and now you choose to come here in sheep's clothing, pretending to care—pretending that you didn't kill my baby!"

Damian was confused, ashamed, and scared. Victoria quickly grabbed his arm and pulled him down the steps and across the lawn. "Damian? What was she talking about?" Her voice faded as the door shut behind them.

Kyle hadn't gotten a good look at what Mrs. Moyer had been going on about, and other than the fact that Damian was wearing a leather bracelet that seemed a little unusual, Kyle hadn't seen anything else really out of the ordinary. He turned back toward Martha, and sat down on the couch next to where she had already repositioned herself. "Mrs. Moyer, are you OK?"

"Yes, of course dear. Would you like something to eat? Can I get you anything to drink?"

"No, I'm fine. I was wondering—would you mind if I go up—."

"Not at all, I think Alee would like that." It was as if her mood had changed on a dime. Just moments ago so alert, now Martha seemed like she was once again unaware of where she was and what was happening around her. She just sat there, and as he crossed to the stairs he saw that she was closing her eyes, and resting her head against the back of the couch. Martha was asleep and softly snoring before Kyle even made it to the top of the stairs. If he was lucky she would stay that way until he and Alee were both long gone.

He opened the door to Alee's bedroom, trying to make as little noise as possible, but as soon as he flipped the light switch up and the lights came alive his heart sank in his chest. He had never actually been in her room before, but it looked exactly the way she had described it. What struck him as odd, and a little eerie, was the way it felt—like it was only yesterday that he had been on the phone with her and she had run out. Her bed was still unmade, her phone was lying on the floor by the window where she had dropped it that night so long ago, and even her laundry was piled up on the edge of her bed. He stood in the doorway for a couple of minutes before he heard it—a quiet whimper, a sniffle. He crossed straight to the closet door.

He knew in his heart that he had been right about her returning home, but it didn't make it any easier seeing her there curled up in a ball, lying on a pile of her old clothes on the closet floor. She was holding a small white stuffed lamb that she had had as a baby, and her eyes were swollen and red from crying. The instant he picked her up she melted into his arms.

It wasn't hard to get her downstairs and into the truck with the state that her mother was in, but Kyle couldn't imagine just taking Alee away from everything she had ever known without bringing some of her past life along. He got her settled in the car, and then ran back up and packed a small bag with some of her favorite outfits, her CD collection, her favorite book—*To Kill a Mockingbird*—her favorite perfume, and the family picture she had kept on her dresser since she was a little girl. He tossed the bag in the bed of his truck and opened the driver's side door, only to find Alee sitting there ready to drive.

"You OK?" He asked hesitantly.

"Yeah." There were still tears in her eyes, but Kyle could see that she had come out of the daze she had been in when he had found her there in the closet.

"You know I'm not going anywhere right?"

At that she smiled. "I know."

He climbed in on the passenger side, and slid over to sit right next to her. They held hands the whole way back to The Black Onyx, not saying a word.

12

Alee spent the next few weeks totally immersed in witchcraft. When she wasn't at school she was either with her mother, her aunt, or her cousins, trying to develop her abilities and learn as much about the Wenham family as she could. Spells, potions, and rituals were just the beginning. It seemed that her little talk with her father had paid off, because everyone seemed much more eager to help teach her.

She enjoyed incantations and spells as much as any other budding witch would. However, during the new moon ritual she had been intrigued by the way her grandmother had called on the elements of wind, fire, water and earth. Years ago, Alee had called on the elements, just playing around with spells, when Dani was first going through her wiccan phase. *If Dani only knew!* Alee often thought to herself.

Having felt the real power behind the elements when her grandmother called on them, Alee couldn't help but want to learn more. She worked with Granny Edith to learn about auras, and questioned her relentlessly about the elements and how to call upon them, and when you should and shouldn't.

"You have to show me. I really think it's something I would be good at. Please?"

"Child, calling the elements isn't something you just do for fun. You have to know what you're doing, and I can't teach it to you overnight. It takes years of practice."

Alee didn't stop just because her grandmother told her to. She couldn't, it wasn't in her nature. Through lots of reading and private practice time she found that it was less time consuming and way more exciting to just pull her strength and energy from the elements. Besides—wind, fire, water, and earth never got tired like Kyle did when she pulled energy from him. Then, when she learned that the fifth element, spirit, could tie all the elements together, she swore to herself that no matter how many potions and talismans her family taught her to make, she would make connecting with the elements her primary focus. Her mother had told her that every witch has a specialty and Alee believed she had found hers.

Alee spent her evenings with Eric, her vampire father. Not only did Eric teach her how to hunt, but he also helped her with some of the more advanced vampire powers, such as voice tricks—also called mind control—that vampires can use to control a human's thoughts. Using only the power of the voice, a vampire could change a human's memory, or divert their focus. A vampire could also weave shadows to create opaque walls for self-concealment, and call animals and control their actions.

Eric made sure to point out that not every vampire could master every power. He explained that most vampires were only able to master one power completely, but could often achieve a low level of ability in other areas. "Being of my line, you will most likely have the most skills in mind control, like me and those that came before me."

"Right." Alee had already had some experience with mind control. But when she had used it on Martha the night of her father's death, or on Kyle the night he told her that Damian could talk, she hadn't really thought of it as "mind control."

"Most vampires can do it. It's usually used for simple things—like making someone forget when you have fed from them, or putting in their mind that it was their idea in the first place."

"Of course, I mean it makes sense. It's not like it hurts anyone, right?"

"Alee, are you OK?" Eric asked watching her as she shuffled her feet across the grass.

"Yeah, I'm fine. It's fine. Mind control isn't a bad thing. It's not evil."

"No, it's not. Vampires are just like any other culture. We do what we have to do to survive. That's how it has been for thousands of years." Eric paced between the trees just beyond the field behind The Black Onyx. "You don't have to try and pretend like you haven't already used this gift before. You—."

"I haven't! I wouldn't!"

"And yet you have."

"No!"

"With Kyle—."

Alee had a flashback of sitting on her bed, asking Kyle what Damian had said when he finally spoke for the first time. She remembered how scared Kyle had been, and how easy it had been to ease that pain and fear, and get him to tell her the truth. "How do you—."

"Kyle loves you. He would do anything you asked of him. But when you showed up at The Black Onyx that first night, it was obvious that you had fed off of him, and yet he had no idea."

"Oh." Alee didn't remember much about that night, but she had never forgotten the taste of Kyle's blood on her lips.

Eric was watching her closely. Watching as she remembered that night. "Drinking Kyle's blood, that wasn't the time you had remembered, was it?"

"No." She looked away. "I didn't mean to."

"I know you didn't, and that is how it normally starts. Your grandmother has said that your gifts are strong, something I have known since the first time I saw you, but they have only recently begun to show themselves. It is your responsibility to learn what you can and begin to control your cravings and your powers."

Aleerah knew Eric was right. She had already experimented with mind control, but she hadn't called it that, and it wasn't just the one time that Eric had suspected. On the night that her father died, she had not only fed from Kyle, she had also calmed her mother down enough to put her to sleep.

Unfortunately for Kyle, after Eric explained more of the details of mind control, Alee found it a little too easy. She had a lot of fun practicing on him, and he often found himself waking from a trance having little or no memory of what he had just done.

Knowing that her connection with Damian could possibly lead to issues at school, Alee started experimenting with reverse mind control. In theory it was a way of building metaphysical walls around herself in order to prevent other psychics from peering in. Alee knew that in order to maintain her anonymity she had to find a way to break her connection with Damian, or at least a way to protect herself from it. Alee's great grandmother Estelle was the talisman expert of the family. So, without sharing too much information, Alee asked Granny Estelle to make a talisman of protection. "I need one that will help me focus more, and keep my thoughts to myself. You know, just something to—well—block everyone else out."

"Everyone else?"

"Everything—. I mean something to block out everything else. You know, to help me focus."

"To help you focus. All right, I think I have just the thing." Estelle soaked a soft wooden rune in a potion of different natural herbs and oils, and created a talisman for Alee to carry with her that would give her the inner strength to focus and block her mind from all unwanted thoughts or invasions.

Weaving shadows was more difficult for Alee, and caused her more stress than she thought was necessary. "I can't do it. This is ridiculous, they're just shadows. They aren't tangible objects. You can't hold a shadow in your hand. They're just shadows." She said as she kicked the tree next to her.

"Stop stomping around and pay attention." Eric said as he pulled her away from the tree. "You aren't going to learn anything if you act like a child."

"You've had hundreds of years to learn this stuff. How can you expect me to learn it all in just a few days?"

"I don't. You're the one who said you were ready, are you not?!" Alee hated to admit it, but Eric was right. She *had* said that she was ready to learn.

"Fine, show me again." Alee watched as Eric scanned the ground around them.

"Stand over there." He was pointing to a small clearing where the trees were not blocking out the sun. Moving into the light, Alee's shadow stretched out before her. "You see your shadow?" She nodded, watching as it moved with her. "Now, don't move." Eric's eyes were mere slits as he focused on nothing but her shadow. With his arms stretched out before him, and his hands open as if he was ready to catch something heavy he whispered, "Come to me—come to me." Alee watched as her shadow slowly inched away from her, moving closer and closer to where Eric stood. He didn't have to bend down to take possession of the shadow; he simply had to command it. "Come to me." His voice echoed, bouncing off the trees around him. The shadow rose, floated, drifted toward Eric, and landed softly in his hands. Quickly he began to pull and stretch at its sides. As if it were a living breathing entity, the shadow pulled away from him, fighting at first, and then gave in to his wishes. In moments Eric was gone, completely hidden behind the shadow. Alee circled the spot where Eric was standing, but there was no sign of him. No sign that anyone was or had been standing there. The shadow merely reflected the world around it giving the impression that nothing stood in her way.

"Where did you—?"

"I'm here!" As he lifted the shadow off of him and dropped it back to the ground, Eric reappeared just where he had always been. "You see, once you learn to control them you can move completely undetected."

"Wow."

"Don't get me wrong, it doesn't always work. If you're in the presence of another vampire they will know, or if you are around a shape shifter they will still be able to smell you. They might not see you, but they'll know you're there. So, it is best, in those situations to use magic. There are spells your mother and your grandmothers can teach you for that."

"But, it's so cool."

"Exactly what I thought you might say. So, I expect you to practice, both the shadow weaving and whatever spells your mother asks you to do. Do you understand?" Eric was looking at her with the eyes of a teacher, or guidance counselor, trying to get their students on the right track.

"I will, I promise." Now that Alee knew how cool weaving shadows could be, having seen it first hand, she was determined to at least try. You never know when you might need to find a quick hiding place. If nothing else, it could be a great party trick.

"This won't be as easy as bending someone's mind. Mind tricks are my specialty and therefore should come easily to you as well. It took me centuries to learn how to weave shadows."

"I know."

"You'll have to practice." He stressed again.

"Yes, I know. You don't have to keep telling me. I promise, I'm listening."

"Good."

When Eric brought up the idea of animal calling Alee wasn't all that excited. She had never had pets, was never all that excited about going to the zoo, and never had the desire to ride horses. The idea of communicating with animals all seemed a little too 'Doctor Doolittle' or 'Snow White' fairytale for her, especially when she was more into hunting them down and drinking their blood-red syrup. Animal calling just sounded like more of a parlor trick than a gift, and a bad one at that. "Give me a break." She had blurted, all too disrespectfully, when Eric first told her.

"Excuse me?"

"I'm sorry. It's just—well, communicating with animals, really? What's the point?" Alee didn't expect a real answer, but that didn't stop Eric from launching into an all-out Vampire 101 lecture.

"For years vampires have had to fight for their own survival. Humans fear the thought of us, without any true knowledge of our existence. All they know is what has been made up in literary works, and, although some of the stories come very close to the truth, others are extremely outrageous. Animals are the only ones, other than members of our own society, who can recognize us for who we are—what we are. Animals have, throughout history, helped aid in our survival. Their instincts rival even our own. Even the smallest ability in this area can mean life or death in a fight, but for those vampires lucky enough, powerful enough, to have an animal to call their own, that animal becomes their eyes in the daylight. If the connection is strong enough, the animal may even become the vampire's protector, always by their side." Eric was leading Alee through the path behind The Black Onyx with only the moon's light to guide them.

"What do you mean 'an animal to call their own'?"

"Some vampires with exceeding power have the ability to form a bond with an animal. It ties them together, much like the bond that can be formed between a vampire and a human servant."

"Excuse me, did you just say human servant?"

"It's a turn of phrase, an expression." He turned away, scanning the trees above them. "As I was saying, the bond allows the two to communicate and to protect each other."

"Humph."

"Believe me it is a relationship of mutual benefit."

"I'm sure it is." Alee scoffed.

"Do you see that owl up there?" He pointed to a tall tree in the distance, and Alee searched the tree line, nodding when she spotted the owl. Eric held his arm out to his side and focused on the owl in the distance, silently calling out to it.

Alee stumbled back into a tree limb behind her as the whooshing sound of the owl's wings cooled the air around her, and it landed softly on Eric's arm. The owl perched tall, with its wings tucked tightly behind it, and Eric leaned in close and whispered something Alee couldn't hear. Then, without warning, the owl pushed off and flew high into the sky above them.

"What did you say?"

"Just watch." Eric nodded to the owl. Alee watched as it slowly circled around for a while then quickly swooped down into the trees. Eric smiled, and pulled Alee behind him so that his body was blocking hers. He pointed off to their right. It was just a slight movement at first, but it quickly increased in intensity as the deer moved toward them. Not one, not two, but six large deer were barreling through the woods toward Alee and Eric. "Take your pick!" Then he was off, after the largest in the herd, with Alee quick behind him chasing after her own prize.

After they had finished feeding Alee followed him back toward The Black Onyx. "So, how did you do it? What did you say? Was that your owl, your animal to call?"

"No, it's not my owl, and I don't have an animal to call. It's not about what you say Aleerah. It's about learning to get into the animal's mind and controlling their thoughts. It's not unlike mind control with humans. Humans may be a little easier to manipulate since they don't often think for themselves, but animals live on free will. No one controls them, and their minds are often very guarded. However, once you have mastered the art of getting into their thoughts, there is nothing you cannot make them do, at least temporarily. Long term servitude requires a bonding."

"Does it work on all animals?"

"I suppose, but I have always found it easiest with birds, owls in particular. Probably because they are nocturnal, like vampires."

"What about shape shifters?" Alee asked, curiously.

"I have been told that shape shifters are much like any other animal, though maybe a bit more stubborn. I have never known of a vampire who actually had a shape shifter as their animal to call, or even possessed the ability to temporarily control them, but it is said that once tamed, they make wonderful pets!" Eric spit the words. "If you can stand the smell, that is."

Alee watched as Eric's jaw clenched tightly shut and every muscle in his body stiffened. "The smell?"

"It's distinct, too sweet for my tastes. Pungent." He shook himself, as if clearing the scent from his memory. "You wouldn't recognize it yet, but once it's pointed out to you, you will have no problem picking a shifter out of a crowd."

Alee didn't know what to say to that. Instead, they continued walking in silence. "That was pretty cool though." Her lip curled up at Eric, and he put his arm around her shoulder as they walked.

She practiced diligently. With the help of her father she was able to summon small birds within only a week. She felt, as she knew she would, like Snow White, in the movie when the little animals started following her through the forest. It was weird and wonderful all at the same time. She took on more reading, and found a book in the family library that went into more detail about the connection between a vampire and their animal to call—comparing it once again to that of the vampire and human servant relationship. Although she hated the idea, the more she read the more she started to understand the possibilities and the benefits of such powerful metaphysical relationships.

Her hope, although she would never admit it to Eric, was to develop her powers enough to allow her to call upon larger animals, and eventually lycanthropes—if she ever met one. Although Eric had explained that it was possible in theory, he also stressed that lycanthropes are very dangerous, and that the detriments of trying and failing far outweighed the benefits of succeeding. Alee didn't agree, and was determined to try.

Kyle was right there by her side for the majority of her training, and behind closed doors Alee practiced power sharing with him whenever they got a chance. Grandma Edith wasn't very happy about him being around all the time. "I just don't understand why she is so attached to that boy."

"Mother," Estelle whispered, patting Edith's hand. "You've seen his mark. Clearly the goddesses have touched him for a reason. We don't have to understand what their plan is; we only have to accept that they have a plan."

"I don't like it when you use my own words against me." Edith was very traditional, and although she couldn't deny that the goddesses had in fact given Kyle the mark of protection, she still wasn't convinced that he was a positive addition in her granddaughter's life. She secretly hoped that he was merely a fling, a phase that she would eventually grow out of.

Edith's opinion of Kyle and of her granddaughter changed, however, just a few weeks later.

Every month the Wenham coven, like so many others, honored the goddesses with their new moon ritual. The ritual is different from coven to coven, but the Wenhams' never changed, and they were always led by Edith, the crone—the elder or leader—of the coven. Nevertheless, Alee had been studying different new moon rituals, and had asked Edith, Estelle, and of course her mother for their permission to allow her to help cast a circle for their next ritual. "What do you know of casting a circle?" Edith had scoffed.

"Only what I've read—."

"Then you know nothing." Edith cut her off.

"—and what I've experienced. Although I was not raised as a witch, nor did I study witchcraft until joining your family, I dabbled, but that doesn't really count. It's just that— some things—just seem to come naturally—to me." Alee continued, not completely unfazed by Edith's interruption. "Thanks to my father, I've been collecting crystals and stones since I was six. At first they were just pretty rocks, but after a while I began studying them and utilizing the powers they have for healing, calming, and strength. I didn't have you to teach me, but I learned anyway. Even without knowing it witchcraft has been a part of my life. I may not have thought of myself as a witch, but why would I? That wasn't part of the world I lived in." She turned to Estelle. "When you first told me I was a witch, what did I do?"

"Nothing."

"Did I question you?" Estelle shook her head. "Did I tell you witches weren't real?" Estelle shook her head again. "I've never thought of myself as a witch, and magic never seemed practical to me, but that doesn't mean that somewhere deep down I didn't believe it. I was raised in a religious family. Magic was something your dad pretended to do with a coin behind your ear. It wasn't something you did with candles, potions and spells." She finally turned to her mother. "I called on the four elements—."

"Five." Edith corrected her.

"No, I was only fourteen, and I had crystals to represent only four of the elements, and besides, I didn't know what I was doing at the time. I called on Earth, Wind, Fire, and Rain to help heal the pain of my disease."

"What happened?" Loraline asked.

"Before my mother—." At the mention of Alee's mother, the woman who raised her, a flash of pain crossed Loraline's face. "Um, Martha—." Alee corrected herself. "Before Martha interrupted me there was thunder, lightning, rain—and wind." Everyone watched with anticipation. "I don't know if I caused it, at least I wasn't sure at the time. But, I've practiced since then, a lot, recently. All I'm asking is that you let me try. What can it hurt?"

Reluctantly, and with a lot of persuasion from Loraline, Edith conceded to Alee's wishes and gave her the blessing to cast the coven's circle. "Fine, but I will be there to take over if it isn't done properly, or if something goes wrong."

"Of course" Alee blurted out a little too excitedly. "But everything will be fine. I promise." Alee ran off down the hall to her room to prepare.

That month, the new moon ritual was like no other the Wenhams had ever experienced. Alee didn't just include the women. She also asked her father Eric, her Grandfather William, and her Uncle Tom to be a part of the circle. Men had never been a part of the ceremony before, let alone men without a wiccan bloodline. However, what surprised everyone the most was when Kyle joined them just before the ceremony began.

Instead of using the fire-pit they usually used, Alee gathered everyone in a circle in the center of the field out behind The Black Onyx. All the men stood respectfully to the right of their wives—or girlfriend, in Kyle's case. Once again, as she scanned the gathering of beautiful Wenham women, Alee could see the flow of their colorful auras all around them. What she most noticed, and thought was most interesting, was that the auras of her grandmother Elizabeth, her aunt Jacinda, and her mother Loraline seemed to not only cling to them, but also to wrap themselves around their husbands, almost hugging them protectively. She wondered if hers did the same to Kyle, but she couldn't see her own aura, and she wasn't even sure she had one.

Instead of pouring a ring of sand or salt around the circle to bind it, Alee stepped into the circle and, standing directly in front of Kyle, she lit a smudge stick. It was made of dried desert sage and cedar needles bundled together and tied tightly with hemp rope. The smell, even before it was lit, was earthy and beautiful.

Alee's hands were trembling, but not enough for anyone but Kyle to notice. When she looked up into his bright green eyes he winked at her and whispered, "It's not brave if you're not scared." She knew it had to be a movie quote, but she couldn't place it and she didn't really care. It gave her the strength to continue and she knew that was exactly Kyle's point. Alee smiled and nodded, and began to recite the purification prayer she had memorized.

"I invoke the goddess within to clear our minds, bodies, and spirits." She chanted clearly, mechanically, as she moved around the circle, leaving an intoxicating path of smoke behind her. "Push out all that is negative leaving only the clear and open channels within us. Goddess be our guide this night and all nights to come." She was halfway around the circle, and staring into the soft tender eyes of her parents, Loraline and Eric. Loraline nodded her approval, and Alee continued to repeat the prayer. "I invoke the goddess within to clear our minds bodies and spirits. Push out all that is negative leaving only the clear and open channels within us." She stood before Edith, but couldn't see her—she only recognized her by the white aura that had thickened around her, enveloping her in its radiant beautiful light. "Goddess be our guide this night and all nights to come." She had completed the circle, and once again stood before Kyle. He smiled and nodded, and she turned and went to the center of the circle, and spoke to the coven. "We invoke the goddess within not because we think ourselves gods, but because she lives and breathes within each of us. We cleanse our minds, bodies, and spirits of all evil, all that is negative because she deserves a place of peace and light." Alee put out the smudge stick and placed it on a small wooden table she had used to mark the center of the circle. She picked up the tall white candle that had been their only source of light, aside from the moon and stars above, since they had come out to the field. She went to William, her grandfather, and she called. "Air, you are the wind that pushes us along our path. You encourage us through hard times. I welcome you to our circle." William held out the yellow candle she had given him earlier, and as she lit it she felt a soft breeze caress them both and sweep around the circle.

Alee turned to her right, moving with the ease of the wind, and stopped in front of Eric. He held out his red candle and she called, "Fire, you strengthen us when we feel we have been defeated. I welcome you to our circle." She lit the red candle and felt the flush of her cheeks as the air around them instantly warmed.

Again Alee turned to her right, and moved to stand before Tom, her uncle, who held out his blue candle. "Water, you cleanse and clean us. You give life to the earth and nourishment to our bodies. I welcome you to our circle." When Alee lit the blue candle she noticed Tom take a deep breath in as the scent of ocean salt water tickled their noses. He held back a laugh of excitement, but couldn't stifle the smile that crossed his face. Alee smiled back and she knew he approved.

The final element was earth, and Alee made her way eagerly to stand before Kyle. He held out his green candle. "Earth, you give life, food, and shelter to all living things. From you we were born and to you we will one day return. I welcome you to our circle."

"You know how they make it through each and every day?" Kyle whispered, and Alee just smiled and shook her head. "They believe."

Alee bit her lip and muffled a giggle. "'Rango'? Really?"

"It seemed to fit." He cocked his head to the side and winked at her.

Alee shook her head and turned back toward the center of the circle. She placed the white candle back on the small table alongside the smudge stick, and picked up the one remaining item—a simple purple pillar candle. She lit the candle and held it up as she called, "Spirit you are our conscience. You help guide our choices to good rather than evil. I welcome you to our circle." The presence of spirit was subtle. It wasn't external like wind, fire, water, and earth, but instead was an overall calming of everyone around her, and a joy that seemed to lift Alee up. Floating on that happiness, Alee made her way to her great great grandmother Edith. "Thank you, Granny. The circle is yours." Edith stood gazing into Alee's eyes, awe and envy both evident. "When you have completed the ceremony I would like to close the circle for you."

Edith nodded. "Of course." As she stepped into the circle, Edith watched Alee move to take her place once again next to Kyle.

Edith's ceremony didn't take long, and Alee closed the circle—thanking each of the elements separately and extinguishing their candles.

After everyone had dispersed and only Alee and Kyle remained, gathering the candles and carrying the table back into the house, Edith stood silently watching.

"Aleerah, can I speak with you dear?" Edith called after Kyle had gone into the house.

"Of course."

"You did…" she paused for a moment, trying to find the right word, "good tonight."

"Thank you." Alee said, not knowing where her grandmother was going.

"We'll need to work on your fire spells. You shouldn't need to light the candles yourself during a circle."

"Um, okay."

"That is all, you can go back inside. I will finish cleaning up." Edith turned away picking up the remaining items with Alee watching, not really sure if she should leave or stay.

A few days after the new moon ceremony Edith pulled Alee aside once again. "Aleerah, I need to speak with you please."

"Um, alright. Is everything OK?"

"I wanted to talk to you about Kyle. It seems that he—."

"Before you say anything, please hear me out. I know you don't like him, or don't trust him. I'm not really sure why, but he's good to me. He's good *for* me, and I won't give him up." Alee was pleading and demanding all in the same breath, and Edith hadn't even told her why she wanted to talk to her yet.

"That's fine."

Hesitantly, she asked, "It is?"

"I can see that he means a great deal to you, and I have decided not to stand in your way. I just think there may be more to your relationship than you might know. The goddesses have touched him for a reason. Have you thought about that?"

"I have, and—." Alee didn't really know what to say. *I think they sent him to me to feed off of his energy like a vampire only without the blood sucking, although, that might be nice too.* Nope, she couldn't say that.

"Aleerah, what are you thinking about?" Edith was looking deep into Alee's eyes, searching for an answer that even Alee hadn't found yet.

"I don't know." She shook her head, that wasn't really true. "I mean, I don't know for sure, but I think I know."

"You think you know what?"

"Remember that book you gave me at the beginning of the school year, the one about dhampirs?"

"Yes. What about it?"

"Let's just say, I've been doing my homework. I get that everything anyone knows about dhampirs is all theory, because none have ever lived as long as I have, but whoever wrote that book kinda knew what they were talking about."

"In what way?"

"Powers. I have powers. Not like Loraline, and not just like you—you know, the whole aura thing. Which, by the way, you still need to explain the whole dying thing to me. But, it isn't just the speed and mind trick stuff that I get from Eric either. I'm not really sure how to explain it, but it's like I can have all that, and whatever else I want."

"Whatever else you want?"

"I mean, I can't walk through walls, which would be totally cool. But I can basically borrow any power I want as long as I know someone who has it. Or I can supersize my own powers by borrowing energy from someone else, like—" Alee stared down at her shoes and shuffled her feet. "—like say, Kyle, for instance."

"Kyle? But, he isn't a witch."

"Right. That's my point."

Edith was visibly confused—and intrigued. "What do you mean that is your point? Child, stop speaking in tongues."

"I'm not speaking in tongues. I just don't know how to say it any other way." Alee tried again. "I can borrow energy—from anyone, even the elements. You saw me the other week calling the elements. I can use the power of the elements, or I can use the power of anyone around me, as long as I have physical contact with them. At least I think that's how it works. And Kyle is no different. He has life, and life is power in its own right."

Edith looked less pleased by the news than Alee had hoped. In fact, Edith looked downright concerned. "Why don't you show me what you mean?"

"Show you?"

"Yes, I think that would be best. Power sharing is a very rare gift indeed. In fact I don't think there is anyone in the Wenham line who can do it. Can you demonstrate it for me?"

"Um, of course." Estelle had been teaching Alee some basic spell writing and casting for weeks, so Alee choose a basic fire spell. It was nothing more than lighting the flame of a candle. She easily lit a candle on the mantle on the other side of the room.

Edith nodded, "That's good. You are mastering the basics quite nicely. However, you should know, I don't like fire spells to be used in the house."

"That's nothing." Kyle had been watching from the other side of the room, trying to give Alee and her grandmother some space.

"Kyle!" Alee snapped.

"What?! I was just saying that you can do so much more than just light a—"

"No, that's not helping."

"Sorry."

"No, I'm sorry. It's fine." She took a deep breath. "Can you help me for a second? Granny Edith would like a demonstration."

"I thought you'd never ask." He swooped in, wrapping his arm around Alee's waist and pulling her in close for a quick kiss on the cheek.

Alee giggled in his arms and spun around pressing her lips to his. Her tension melted away at his touch.

"Ahem—." Edith cleared her throat, and Alee spun back around, still wrapped in Kyle's arms.

"Sorry Granny." Alee started to pull away, but Kyle made no move to accommodate.

Although Edith spoke to Alee, her eyes stayed focused on Kyle. "You were saying?"

"Yeah, right, I think it would be easier to show you." Alee stood hand in hand with Kyle and focused on the far side of the room where the fireplace stood dark and the mantle was covered in candles of every size. The candle she had just lit was the one bright spot. "What once was cold shall no longer be. Fire burn and be set free!" One by one the candles began to burn—slowly at first, and then two and three at a time. "What once was cold shall no longer be. Fire burn and be set free!" There was a crackling, and then a pop, and the logs in the fireplace exploded into flames. "What once was cold shall no longer—"

Edith noticed that the tattoo on Kyle's wrist was glowing like liquid silver under his skin. "That's enough." She cut Alee off mid-sentence. "There is no need to burn the house down."

"Sorry."

"Don't be." Then, for the first time she actually addressed Kyle directly, "Does it hurt? What she does to you?"

He realized that he was rubbing his wrist, and stopped, almost as if he were ashamed. "Sometimes, I guess, but not always. It can be uncomfortable, but it's also exhilarating."

"Is it what you want?" Both Edith and Alee watched Kyle waiting for his answer.

"If it means I can be with Aleerah, then yes."

"Fine, you will continue to accompany her in her training, but if I feel you are getting in the way I will end it. Do you understand?" Kyle nodded

"Granny you—."

"Yes I can." She corrected Alee before the objection was raised. "I am the crone of this family, for however long I have, and that means that I alone will decide how long we shall entertain this experiment between you and young Kyle. Am I understood?"

"Yes Granny."

"Good. Then for now you may practice only while either your mother or I are present. If something were to happen I want one of us to be there to help."

Alee and Kyle had already been practicing in private for a few weeks, but she wasn't about to tell Granny Edith that. Training was often tiring, leaving Kyle with very little energy for days, so they only did it a couple of times a week.

Through the now-supervised training and practice, and with a lot of hard work, Alee continued to refine her ability to use Kyle's energy—and even the energy and powers of others around her. From there it didn't take long before she was starting to share her own powers as well. Eventually, she was able to transfer enough of her own power to Kyle that he was able to perform minor spells on his own. This was particularly impressive because Kyle had no wiccan ancestors. The idea that a mere mortal human could sustain such power and utilize it, even for short periods of time, had never been thought possible. Edith was sure that, given the chance, Aleerah would be able to increase her abilities of power sharing, and she encouraged the practice no matter how physically and mentally hard it became.

There wasn't another witch in the Wenham line who was able to power share, and the fact that Aleerah had developed the ability so quickly, and at such a young age, spread throughout the wiccan community and the Underground like wildfire.

A few days later, Alee came home from school to find Loraline and Eric sitting at the kitchen table, eagerly awaiting her arrival. Alee entered the kitchen quietly, not wanting to interrupt their conversation. "What's going on?" The shop was empty, and there was no sign of anyone other than the three of them in the house, and considering the fact that there were always at least three or four other family members wandering around at any given time, it was kind of weird.

"Come join us." Loraline scooted over, opening the seat closest to the door for Alee to sit down.

"You've received a telegram today," Eric said, and sure enough, there in front of him was a shiny silver envelope with her name written in calligraphy across the front. It was held closed with a red wax seal. The emblem stamped in the middle of the wax was the familiar infinity symbol.

"You know that's just a letter, right? I mean no one uses telegrams anymore."

"Apologies, am I showing my age?"

"Just a little," Alee smiled. "So, who's it from?" She didn't pick it up, or even try to touch it.

Loraline nervously glanced at Eric, looking for answers, or maybe just for support. "It's from the Founders." Her lips were quivering. Alee couldn't tell if she was happy, nervous, or scared as she squeezed Eric's hand tightly in hers. "It's an invitation. Every October Atlanta's Founders have a

Celebration honoring the city and its valued members. This year, you've been invited."

Eric slid the envelope across the table, and Alee slowly picked it up, turning it around and around in her hand. It was still sealed, and yet they knew what it was.

"How do they even know about me? I thought we were keeping a low profile."

Eric took a deep breath before answering—not, of course, that he needed the breath. "We could not keep you a secret any longer. Your powers have been growing so quickly that it would be impossible to think that no one would find out. So, your mother and I spoke to the other Founders a few weeks ago."

"Then, why the invitation? Why now?"

"We don't know. They didn't include your father in the discussions. We can only hope it is because of your accomplishments in such a short time. But—." Loraline was staring up at him in anticipation.

"But, what?"

"But, the Founders are not entirely happy with your mother and me. They feel that our decision to move away, and then our decision to keep you a secret for so many years is a sign of betrayal. They want to meet you, to see what we have been hiding. To see if you are in fact a threat."

"A threat? Me?"

"We know it sounds absurd," Loraline blurted out, "but you have to understand where they're coming from. They don't know you like we do. All they know are the centuries-old theories that people have put together about what *might* happen if a child was born of a vampire and a human, let alone a vampire and a witch. You're the real thing, and they're scared."

"Scared of me?"

"Yes."

"What do I have to do?"

"We will all help you prepare for the ceremony; you have plenty of time. Besides, you won't be alone. We will be there by your side." Eric reached out and took her hand. Alee instantly looked up, into his piercing blue eyes. "You should know that it is a great honor to be invited to the Celebration, but you mustn't mention it to anyone outside of this family. Do you understand?"

"Yes sir."

"And, Aleerah—The Founders' Celebration is no place for a human." His eyes burned into hers like a laser finding its target. "Kyle must not attend." She opened her mouth just slightly to object, but Eric was quicker. "These are not my rules. They are the rules of the Founders together. It is for his protection, and that of our family. Do you understand?" Alee nodded her head silently.

Nothing more was said, but preparations began within days. Alee still didn't understand what the Founders' Celebration was, but she knew it was important—to her family if nothing else. All the time and money that her mother and aunt were putting into the preparation and their gowns was getting to be more than Alee could handle. She knew that she should be enjoying the pampering, but she was more focused on the idea that she was the cause of someone's fear than the fact that her parents were treating her like a princess getting ready for a ball.

14

Victoria wasn't particularly crafty or skilled in any artistic sense of the word, unless you counted putting together the perfect outfit. However, she did have a keen ability to get what she wanted in life. It was her plan to utilize that particular ability for her own personal benefit. Although her plan seemed far-fetched and risky to Damian, Victoria didn't care. Once she set her mind to something there was little that could make her change it, and Damian knew that.

After Damian had explained to her, in full step-by-step, play-by-play detail, at least ten times, what had happened during his visit to the Atlanta Town Hall Records, and how he ended up at the Java Jolt, Victoria was convinced that the answers they needed were there. Well, there, as in, the Underground, where she believed, with good reason, that Damian had been that day.

Victoria assumed that the leather bracelet was what had protected him while he was there, having no way to know that the bracelet was actually the one thing that got him noticed, and almost got him killed—that, and of course, his heartbeat.

She took multiple photos of the bracelet, and blew them up so all the little details could be seen clearly. The high school had a wood shop, a metal shop, and all other kinds of art classes, so finding someone capable wasn't going to be hard, but picking the right person might be. She took the photos to the metal shop teacher with a sob story about how she remembered her father wearing the bracelet all the time when she was a little girl. She explained that after her father died, the bracelet had been lost, and for years she had been trying to find it. It was very sentimental to her and her brother, and her hope was to have a replica made for her brother's birthday. She hoped that the story, along with her charming personality, would help win her the assistance and talent of the teaching staff in the Art Department. And it did, or at least something did, which was lucky for her because her backup plan was to seduce one of the teachers, and she really didn't want to have to go there.

The two teachers she talked to seemed fairly naive, and gladly accepted the challenge. It only took a couple of weeks for the metal shop and wood shop teachers, working together, to recreate the bracelet, down to the symbol and lettering that were burned, almost branded, along the center of the bracelet. They even aged the snap to make it appear old and rusted. It was quite remarkable workmanship, and she thanked them profusely, with tears in her eyes, and false promises that she would register in their classes the following semester.

"You can cut the act Victoria." It was the older of the two teachers, Mr. Knowles, the metal shop instructor.

"Excuse me?"

"At first, I was curious to know if you really were as naïve as you were acting, or if you had known all along what you were asking for. Now, I just want to know why, and what you actually plan to do with it."

"It's for my brother, to remember our father by."

"No. That it is for your brother I believe, but not that it is a mere keepsake."

"Franklin, maybe she really doesn't know." Ms. Pickett nudged him.

"She knows, Sarah."

"I'm not sure what you're talking about," Victoria said, as she slowly backed toward the door with the band clenched tightly in her hand.

"That's fine. You can leave, but don't think of us as your enemy. When you are ready to talk, we will listen. We can help. Just know that you are not alone, you have allies." They watched her leave and the door slowly shut behind her.

Later that evening, when Victoria got home, she called Damian up to the attic. The attic had become *their* secret place, instead of only his. Although they no longer had to hide what they knew from their mother in terms of reading their father's journal and learning about what it meant to be a lycanthrope, their mother did not know of their plans to go to the Underground, or to seek out the man who had killed their father. Damian and Victoria both knew well enough that they needed to keep those minor details hidden from their mother, because she would never have approved.

Victoria tossed the new leather band to Damian, and he scrambled to catch it. "Check it out! Now we have a matching pair." Her smile lit up her face.

Shocked wasn't a strong enough word to describe Damian's expression when he saw the new band. "I can't believe you actually did it." Side by side, the two bands were identical. Even he couldn't tell them apart. From the worn and faded leather to the old rusted snaps it was virtually impossible to distinguish between them.

"You owe me ten bucks." There had never been a wager placed, but Victoria was proud of her accomplishment, and the fact that she had done something her brother had thought impossible.

"I owe you more than that." He couldn't stop turning the bracelets round and round in his hands. He was looking for any indication that might give the new one away as a replica, but there was nothing.

"So, want to go get some coffee?" Victoria smirked, and quickly wiggled her eyebrows.

"Coffee, huh?" Damian only knew of two doors to the Underground: the Town Hall Records, and the Java Jolt. Being so late in the day on a Friday, the Java Jolt did seem like their best option. "Yeah, we can do that, but V, it's dangerous down there. You know that, right?"

"I know, but not with those!" She smiled as she nodded to the matching bands in his hand.

"I'm not so sure about that." But even as he said it he knew he still wanted to go. "Trust me, it is—." Then looking down at his workout pants and old t-shirt he began to rethink his wardrobe. "I think we should—."

"—Change first? I couldn't agree more. You look like you just got out of gym class or something." She headed for the stairs, snatching one of the leather bands out of his hand, and snapping it around her wrist.

Damian called out to her as she approached the stairs. "Wear black!"

That stopped her in mid step. She slowly turned to face Damian as her brown eyes narrowed. "I think brown is more my color." Then with a wink, and a wicked smile, her clothes dropped to the ground in the place where she had been standing, and a beautiful chocolate brown wolf leapt through the air at Damian. She wasn't trying to hurt him, it was only playing, and he joined right in without even a second's hesitation. Before she had a chance to land, Damian had thrown himself off to the side, rolling, as he transformed into a snowy white wolf, slightly larger in size and stature. He shot up, meeting her in mid-air before she landed, and they wrestled on the floor like two dogs playing in the grass. Their claws scratched at each other's fur as they exchanged blows. The floor shook beneath them as they crashed into things left and right. Their mock display of force didn't last very long before it was sharply interrupted.

"What are you two doing?" Karen screamed, as she appeared through the attic entry. Both Damian and Victoria were startled by their mother's sudden appearance. Victoria hurriedly found the cover of a blanket and was back to herself, scrambling to get dressed.

Damian too transformed, but not back into his human form as his sister had. When he heard his mother's voice, he quickly pulled away from Victoria, ending the game they had been playing, and without a second's thought leapt into the air toward the open window. Halfway out the window he shed his fur and replaced it with the feathers of a hawk. He flew higher and higher, circling the house from far above.

Victoria stood in stunned surprise while Karen ran to the window. "Damian, get in this house this instant!" She was angry, and called to him like a mother calls a child who needs to be scolded. She then stepped back away from the window, arms crossed, and eyes narrow and focused. A gust of wind shut the window, but only after Damian had flown through. He landed gracefully on the floor between his mother and his sister. With a wingspan of well over six feet he was massive in size, intimidating and yet beautiful.

"Victoria, please go downstairs."

"But, Mom—."

"No buts—go!"

Victoria huffed as she gathered the rest of her clothes from the floor and started down the stairs as slowly as she could, trying to listen in on what her mother was about to say.

Karen just waited. Finally she tossed another blanket over Damian's body. "Change back now. Get dressed and meet me downstairs." When she was certain he had transformed back into his human form she left him alone to get dressed. Shaking her head, she turned toward the stairs, where she noticed the leather band that Victoria had carelessly left behind. Karen took the band with her into the living room, and waited patiently for Damian and Victoria to join her.

Damian was hesitant to speak, but they had been sitting in silence for almost five minutes already. "Mom—."

"No. Don't talk." Karen was gripping the telephone receiver tightly in her hands, willing her tears to subside.

Damian hated to see his mother cry, and knowing that he was the cause was even worse. He rushed to her side, falling to the floor at her feet. "Mom, we're sorry. We were only playing around." She didn't answer, or even look up at him. "Mom—I am so sorry. What can I do to fix it? Please don't cry." Victoria just watched. She couldn't shake the image of her brother, the wolf, leaping out of the window and instantly transforming into a hawk of equal size—if not bigger.

Karen brushed the hair out of her son's eyes and quietly, almost whispering, spoke to them both. "You don't have to apologize. You are who you are because of your father and me. Be proud of who you have become." Her words were comforting, but the tears rolling down her face didn't put their hearts at ease, only made them more concerned. "My intentions were to talk, and try to work this out, but—I've called your grandparents—." She wasn't even looking them in the eyes anymore. "I just don't think I am what you need right now."

"What?" Damian and Victoria understood at once what she was saying, and immediately started fighting back.

"You can't send us away. Our school is here. Our friends are here. You're our mother!" Victoria was grasping at straws, but the only thing that mattered to Damian was his family.

"Which grandparents did you call?" His voice was monotone, flat, and broken. He had visions of Granny Margie and Grandpa Phil trying to teach and guide him and his sister, but he knew all too well that their methods would be too passive—too docile. Then he imagined how his mother's family would most likely bind their powers, impeding them from learning anything at all. "You know what, it's not important. We're not going anywhere." When his mother looked up and their eyes met she started to protest, but she didn't get as much as a single word out. "Victoria is right, you are our mother, and anything we need to know you can teach us. Otherwise, we will learn it together. But you're not shipping us off like you're tired of us."

"I'm with Damian. I don't want to go anywhere either." Victoria sounded like a little child who had just been told her favorite doll was being taken away, and she was ready to fight to get it back.

They sat in silence for a while longer, until Karen finally spoke up. "All right, I won't send you to your grandparents. But, from this point forward you follow my rules, and you keep no secrets from me, no matter what. Do you understand?"

Damian glanced at Victoria, who quickly nodded her head, then back at their mother, who was waiting calmly. "We understand." He had been twisting the leather band around his wrist, as a nervous reaction. Damian knew that if they agreed to their mother's conditions then they were obligated to tell her what they were up to, and risk her saying no. But the alternative, being shipped off to who knows where to live with their grandparents, didn't seem all that much better.

Karen got up and crossed toward the kitchen. "Then be ready for dinner in twenty minutes. We will be eating as a family tonight. And if there is anything else you think you should tell me that will be the time." She disappeared into the kitchen, and Damian and Victoria could hear the sounds of cupboards opening and closing, and pots and pans being moved around as she began to prepare dinner.

"You know we have to tell her." He was whispering, but Victoria still heard him.

There was panic in Victoria's eyes as she nodded, "I know."

"What's wrong?"

"I think she might already know."

"What? How?" Victoria just lifted the sleeve of her shirt and revealed her bare wrist. "Oh my god, V. What did you do?"

"I don't know. I guess I dropped it upstairs or something. She might not know. Right? Maybe it's still up there."

"You should check. But either way we have to tell her tonight, at dinner. We can act like we don't know she already knows. Otherwise, she'll only think we're telling her because we know she knows." He looked at the band around his wrist and felt somehow encouraged, even optimistic. "Besides, it could be a good thing. Maybe tomorrow we can go get coffee. Who knows, maybe Mom will want to come with us."

"Yeah, right!" Victoria knew better than to believe that their mother was ever going to agree to let them continue their quest to find the man who had killed their father. She hadn't even supported Victoria's attempted attack on a witch—a witch! Victoria didn't see any viable reason why their mother would be any more supportive of their doing something that might risk their exposure, not to mention their lives.

Karen was a decent cook—not extremely skilled in the culinary arts, but good enough to make Damian want seconds of his mom's stuffed baked chicken breast. "Is there any more?"

Karen took his plate to the stove to dish out a second helping. "Would you like some more, Victoria?"

"No thanks." With their mom busy at the stove, Victoria took the opportunity to try one last time to change Damian's mind. "Let's just wait a few more days." But Damian shook his head.

"We can't wait. You didn't find the band upstairs. That means she already knows. It's just a matter of time before she asks about it, and you know she'll be even madder if she has to ask instead of us just telling her."

"Fine!" She didn't like it, but she knew her brother was right.

"Mom, before you say no—."

She didn't even wait for him to finish his sentence before she stopped him. "No Damian."

"Oh come on Mom. You have to at least hear me out."

Karen just rolled her eyes and sat back down across from Damian at the kitchen table. "I don't have to do anything, but I will. What did you want to say?"

All of a sudden Damian's mouth went dry, and he was at a loss for words. He looked to Victoria for help, but there was no way she was going to speak up. She didn't want to tell their mother anyway. Clearing his throat he spoke up. "It's just that—Well I was wondering—. Did Dad ever go to the Underground?"

"I thought I told you I didn't want you going down there. It isn't safe."

"Yes, I get it, you said that already. All I'm asking is if you ever knew Dad to go." His mother was staring at him with burning eyes.

"You get it, huh? Then why do you keep bringing it up? Why did I find this upstairs?" She pulled the leather band out of her pocket and tossed it on the table in front of Damian.

Victoria quickly snatched it up without thinking. "That's mine."

"Yours?" Karen asked a little surprised.

"Mom—."

"Wait." Damian quickly cut his sister off before she could say something she might regret. "Don't get mad at her. I'm the one—."

"I'm not mad Damian." Karen took a deep breath. "I'm just concerned. I'm your mother, and I have a right to be concerned even if you don't understand why." To Damian she didn't just sound concerned, she sounded downright scared. "Do either of you realize what that is?"

"I do. I think." Damian put his fork down and lifted his sleeve revealing that he too was wearing an identical band.

"Oh, God." Karen sank back in her chair, defeated and drained. Shock and fear was the only way to describe her expression. "Where? How did you get these?"

"I um—."

"How? Why?"

"Please don't be mad Mom. Damian just found one—and I—I had this one made. I'm sorry, we just needed some answers, and—."

"Did you find them?"

"Not yet, but—."

"You're only seventeen—you're not old enough to face the dangers of—these will only get you killed down there! The minute you step foot down there, this," she waved the band in the air, "will tell everyone what you are. That is if they don't smell it on you first. The only thing this will bring you is death. Not answers—death." The gears in her head where turning, Damian and Victoria could both tell she was thinking about something, but they didn't know what. Unfortunately they could only communicate telepathically with each other, not their mother. "I was ten. It was the last time I went to the Underground. Back then, shifters were seen as protectors—guardians—. That's why we wore the bands proudly! It wasn't shameful or disgraceful to be a shifter, or to be seen with a shifter. We were respected and held in high esteem within the community. My parents took the whole family to the annual Founders' Celebration that used to be held in the grand ballroom in the basement of the town hall building. For all I know they still do, but my invitations stopped coming a long time ago.

"I remember sitting at a table near the center of the room, waiting for the festivities to begin. They always started with the Mayor giving a speech, thanking those present for their generous donations to the community and town above.

But that year it was different." Her eyes started to well up with tears. "The sound of the doors slamming shut and locking all around us echoed throughout the ballroom. I remember that the first thing I noticed was the Mayor's eyes. They were no longer the gentle sapphire blue they had always been. They burned crimson red like the flames of a fire. When he opened his mouth to speak, we didn't hear the compassionate words of our leader, but instead the call to his followers: 'Take part in the feast I have prepared for you. Take part, as we reclaim our rightful place in the world.'" Karen swallowed back her tears.

"Mom?"

She closed her eyes, remembering it just as if it had happened yesterday, and held her hand up to quiet Damian before he could say anything else. "It started as individual screams at first, and then suddenly the room was filled with piercing, earsplitting cries from every direction.

"My father, mother, and I made it out alive, although not without remarkable injuries." She turned around, lifting the back of her shirt just enough to show the scar that spanned her entire back. "My little brother Billy wasn't so lucky. They grabbed him just as Dad was trying to pull him out through an open window. My parents couldn't live with his death, and from that point on they broke off all contact with the Underground, and that life."

Karen wiped at her tears with the inside of her sleeve, and started to clear the kitchen table. "Your grandfather uprooted the family, and we lived as mere humans, pretending to be something we never really could be. He found a coven of witches that was willing to cast a binding spell so that we wouldn't be able to shift, and so that no one else would ever be able to find out who or what we really are."

"Why did you move back?"

"I didn't know what else to do. Your grandfather had never been willing to move back, but he also was never able to convince your grandmother to sell their house. My mom is quite stubborn when she wants to be. So, when your father died I just couldn't stay in our house any longer. There were too many memories, too much history. You were not doing well with school and everything else. When my parents offered me this house it just seemed like the right place to go."

Victoria and Damian just sat there not knowing what, if anything, they should say.

"These leather bands symbolize everything my family used to believe in. But that place, that society, no longer exists. Things have changed so much since those days. I wish they hadn't, but they have."

Damian could see the pain in his mother's eyes, and wanted desperately to help. "Then we need to change things back. We need to fight for our place."

Karen just closed her eyes and shook her head. "Damian, one young boy cannot change an entire community of faithful followers. We no longer have any power to make a change like that, not without help. Those bracelets will only get you hurt, if not killed."

"Damian's right though Mom, we either fight for what we deserve in life, or we sit back and let life pass us by. I'm not going to just be a spectator in life. That isn't how you raised me." Both Damian and Karen looked at Victoria with amazement. That was probably the most profound thing she had ever said, and Karen was a little proud. "Besides, I can't imagine that it's what Dad would want either."

"No it's not." She sat there staring at her children, scared for their safety and in awe of their fearlessness. "How did you two get so smart?" Karen pulled Damian and Victoria close and hugged them tightly, not wanting to let go. "Maybe you're right, I don't know. Either way, I can't let you do it on your own."

"There have to be other people who feel the same way we do." Damian was grasping at straws. "Are any of the shifters who lived here when you were a child still around?"

"A lot of them didn't stay. Most of the people who survived didn't stay in town. The ones who did, well, I'm not even sure I would remember who they were. I was young." She looked down at the table, playing with the food on her plate. "I might know someone who would be willing to help us." The tension that Damian didn't even realize he had been hanging onto seemed to instantly evaporate, and Karen could see his muscles relax. "I can't make any promises though."

"I understand."

"Can I see those?" She pointed to the bands around Damian's and Victoria's wrists. She examined them with the same scrutiny that a jeweler uses to examine a diamond to ensure that it is genuine. "They're good. I can't even tell which one is real and which one isn't. But, two won't be enough. Can you get more?"

Victoria nodded and a smile spread across her face. "Of course. How many do you think we need?"

"I don't know, but if you're really serious about taking back the Underground, then we're going to need an army. When we make our move, having these will show how serious we are. It will send a message."

15

It was already mid-October, and the school year seemed to be flying by. Alee was comfortable in her daily routine of school, wiccan studies, and what she liked to call father-daughter bonding time. Referring to it that way made Kyle a little more comfortable—not entirely, but a little. He had grown used to her drinking blood, as long as she kept it in covered bottles and he wasn't forced to look at it, but the idea of her going out to hunt and "feed" still sent chills down his spine.

School was good, and getting better every day. Jathan, although strange, had grown on her and she found herself drawn to him in many of the same ways that she was drawn to Kyle, although she tried not to think about that. There was just something about Jathan that excited her. Got her blood boiling—in a good way. She had invited him to have lunch with her and Kyle a few times, but he never accepted. He always had an excuse: I have to study, I've got a project due next period, I'm meeting some other friends, and the list went on.

Whenever Alee mentioned Jathan around Kyle or Kyle around Jathan they each seemed to just zone out. She couldn't understand why they wouldn't at least give each other a chance. The two of them had never even met. She recognized that they were very different in many ways, but also could see that they were very similar in a lot of ways too. She had thought that they could actually become friends if they would only try, but she was beginning to give up on that idea.

It had been a few weeks since Damian had invited Alee and Kyle to lunch, and basically interrogated her for a half hour straight, and Alee had figured that she must not have made the right impression because the invite was never extended again. That is, until Victoria surprised her a few weeks later. Alee had been gathering books from her locker before school one day, when Victoria walked over. "You got lunch plans?"

"I'm sorry?"

"No need to apologize, but I'll accept it anyway."

"What?"

"I asked if you have plans for lunch, today."

"Um, I suppose I'll just be seeing Kyle, like always." Trying to look comfortable, but most likely failing, Alee had just watched as Victoria studied her. "Why?"

"You should join us, at lunch. You know the table, right?"

"Yeah, but—."

"We'll see you then." Victoria had turned to walk away, but stopped herself. "And, I'm sorry. About last time. We shouldn't have been so hard on you. You seem nice, and I would really like to get to know you." Then she was gone.

Alee had just stood there as the bell rang and the hallway cleared out around her.

Now, by mid-October, things seemed to be getting back to normal. Alee's lunch hour was spent with Dani, Tyler, Damian, Victoria, and of course Kyle, on a daily basis. She never did understand where Jathan had disappeared to, or why he wouldn't join them. They would all huddle together at the back table of the cafeteria just like old times. Kyle and Alee were finally able to have an open relationship in front of their friends without anyone mentioning "Alee", or staring at them in disgust. Alee saw it as a huge step forward, but still wondered if she would ever be able to fully repair her relationship with Dani.

One afternoon, Alee had just gotten her food and was making her way to the back of the cafeteria to claim her usual seat, when she started feeling flushed and claustrophobic—hyper-aware of being surrounded by so many people. She couldn't explain it but she wanted, no, *needed*, to leave the cafeteria. She wasn't upset, scared, or anything like that. It was just a sudden need to not be in the middle of so many people, and underneath that was a pull to be somewhere else. However, it wasn't at all clear where she needed to go. She didn't know where she would feel better. Not knowing why she felt that way she decided to be stubborn, and fight it. She decided to just go sit down and ignore the impulse, but it didn't go away.

"Hey, are you OK?" Kyle's hand felt warm as it rested on Alee's.

"Yeah, I'm fine. I just—." Her breathing was fast and shallow, and she kept looking across the room at the main entrance to the cafeteria. Kyle and Alee had been the first of their group to arrive at lunch that day, and although she could see Dani and Tyler snuggling up in line together, *I guess they're back together—again,* she had no idea where Damian and Victoria were.

"Aleerah?"

"I'm sorry. I'll be right back" Alee pulled away from him and quickly got up and walked out of the cafeteria. Kyle had gotten used to her sometimes-rather-odd behavior, such as often running off without any explanation. So she understood why he didn't follow after her. He knew she would be back when she was ready.

When Alee made her way through the crowd of students and into the hallway outside the cafeteria Jathan was standing just down the hall. He was leaning up against her locker as if he had been waiting for her to show up. "Hey."

Her breathing had slowed down, and she wasn't feeling as restless any more. "Hey." There was no one else in the hall.

"It took you long enough."

"What do you mean? Did we—?" She looked around the hallway. "What are you doing out here?" She didn't remember making plans to meet him.

He just smiled, and took her hand, something that had become all too natural for them. "There's something I need you to see." Jathan led Alee down the hall and out into the back courtyard in the center of the three campus buildings.

"Jathan, stop." He did as he was told and turned toward her, but stopping so abruptly caused her to bump right into him. He quickly wrapped his arm around her waist and raised his eyebrows in a way that asked, *"Right here, really?"* Then he gave her his famous smile that always seemed to shatter her concentration, but it didn't work, not this time. She stood her ground. "Jathan, you can't just smile and get me to do whatever you want. It doesn't work like that." But she could already feel the tension she had been hanging onto melting away.

"I'm sorry, I only—"

"Jathan, I like you. I do. But I have a boyfriend. I can't just run off with you every time you—you—." She looked behind her toward the door that led back into the school, then turned back to Jathan. "What did you do? Why did I come out here in the first place? Did you make me leave the cafeteria?"

He considered telling her the truth, but then changed his mind. "Honestly, Aleerah, I don't know what you're thinking, but I only wanted to show you something. If you won't let me show you, then you need to go see it on your own."

"On my own? Then you weren't just trying—." Instantly she could feel the heat of embarrassment warming her cheeks.

He smirked in a wickedly exciting way. "No, I wasn't, but if you'd rather—"

"NO!"

"Hmmm. I believe the lady doth protest too much."

"Go where? Where do you want me to go? Alone!"

Jathan's laugh filled the courtyard and echoed around her. When he finally pulled himself together Alee was standing with her arms crossed, glaring at him.

"If you want me to go then you should tell me now. Lunch will be over soon and I'm not going to be late for class."

"Go to the Arts Building. You need to look in the metal shop lab. There's something you need to find, and you will. But, if you won't go with me then take Kyle with you—please." His voice seemed to be fading away, even though he was standing right there in front of her. "You're not supposed to be in there if you aren't taking the class, but I'm sure you can find a way to hide if anyone comes in. Just do what you have to do."

Do what I have to do? What does that mean? She heard a door shutting behind them and quickly looked back but no one was there. "What do I look for?"

'You'll know it when you see it—.' When she turned back he was already gone.

"Aleerah—. Who are you talking to?" Kyle was laughing, as he whispered in her ear.

"Huh." Alee turned to find Kyle standing right behind her. "Where—. When did you get out here?"

Kyle and Alee were both worried, but for completely different reasons. "You OK?"

"Yeah, better now that you're here." She smiled up at him and wrapped her arms around his waist, snuggling into the warmth of his neck.

'Aleerah, you need to hurry!' It was Jathan's voice in her head pushing her, and even though she didn't want to listen she knew that if she wanted to get in and out before the teachers started coming back from lunch, she had to go now. She just wasn't really sure she wanted to.

"I need to do something—will you come with me?"

"Uh, sure." Taking Kyle's hand in hers she started for the Arts Building. "So, um—where exactly are we going?"

She just shook her head. "I don't know." Once they were safely through the doors of the Arts Building she turned back and admitted, with a shaky voice. "That's a lie, I do know. I just don't know why."

"OK—."

She didn't let him say anything else before she cut him off. "Kyle, I know my life is pretty crazy, and I've told you and shown you some really weird things, but the thing is—."

He was getting more worried by the second. "What's going on? What's wrong?" Alee was looking around as if she thought someone might be following them, but no one was there. Jathan's warning to hurry had her feeling paranoid, and she didn't even know why she was going in the first place. "Aleerah, what happened?"

"We can't stay here. Come on." She pulled him farther down the hall, whispering, "It's Jathan."

"Who is Jathan?"

"Oh my GOD Kyle—"

"Don't you mean goddess?"

"Kyle! I've been telling you about Jathan for weeks now. I get that you don't want to meet him. I don't know why, but whatever."

"I never said—"

"The thing is I don't care about your jealousy issues right now." As the words were spilling out of her mouth like word vomit she was praying she could take them back, but that's the thing, you can never take back what's already been said.

Kyle pulled away and continued down the hall not saying a word.

"I'm sorry. I didn't mean—." She was running after him.

"It's fine. Where are we going?"

"Kyle."

"I said its fine. What about Jathan? Why are we here?"

Alee didn't know what to say or what to do at that point. She had never seen Kyle so upset, mad. It wasn't like him to get emotional about stuff, but his lack of contact and lack of response clearly wasn't the norm. "He um—. He's in my head, and I can't seem to—."

"You mean you—what? You like him?"

"What?" She stopped dead in her tracks. "No! No, it's just that—every now and then it's like he's here, but he's not." She was even confusing herself.

"You're daydreaming about him?" Kyle stepped back letting go of her hand.

"No, Kyle NO! OK—five minutes ago I was in the courtyard talking to him, not you. We were standing there, and he told me I needed to go to the metal shop classroom to find something, but he didn't say what, only that I would know it when I see it."

"Aleerah, that's crazy."

"That's not the crazy part. When I asked him what I was looking for I turned around and it was you standing there with me, not him."

"When I came out to the courtyard you were alone. You weren't talking with anyone. Actually, you were talking to yourself." He took a step back. He was obviously a little upset, but so was she. "Who knows, maybe you ran off to the courtyard to meet up with some guy, maybe you just wanted to get away from me—"

Alee was getting irritated, and actually raised her voice. "Seriously Kyle, give me a break. If I wanted to meet up with some random guy, why would I tell you who I was with? Why would I tell you about it at all?" Alee noticed two girls, *probably freshman* Alee thought to herself, watching from around the corner. Alee could feel her cheeks turning red, and the palms of her hands beginning to sweat. She was already upset and getting angrier by the minute and couldn't help herself when she finally pounced. "What are you looking at?" The girls ran down the hall and out the main door into the courtyard.

Kyle just stood there staring at her. This was not the Alee he knew and loved.

"I'm sorry. It's just—I'm kind of scared. This isn't the first time this has happened, and I didn't know who else to go to. You're my boyfriend—you're supposed to help me when I'm scared."

Seeing Aleerah so vulnerable always got to Kyle. He reached out, and took her hand in his. "It's OK. I'm sorry. You were right, I got jealous, and I shouldn't have. I should have just trusted you." He pulled her in close for a hug and, resting his chin on her head, whispered. "So, metal shop huh?" She nodded, her face nuzzled in his chest. "Want to go check it out?"

"Yes please." Together they made their way down the hall.

"You know—. I took metal shop last year." He was smiling, all proud of himself.

She couldn't help but giggle. "Yeah, I remember. You almost cut the tip of your finger off during the second week of school, so they made you drop the class and take gym instead."

"Yeah, well—that's two weeks longer than Damian or that Jathan guy would last!"

"It's not a competition Kyle! You already won."

Kyle led the way through the building with Alee timidly following. "You know, *you're* the one with super human strength. Shouldn't you be protecting me and not the other way around?" She smacked him on the back but grabbed his arm even tighter. He just laughed. The idea of her needing him to protect her was something he liked, even if in reality it wasn't really true.

The metal shop door was unlocked and opened easily as he pushed it, and there was no one inside. "So—what do you think we're supposed to be looking for?"

"Shhhh. I don't know." She whispered as they split up and wandered around the room opening drawers and cabinets as they picked through things lying about.

Kyle held up a poorly made metal box with a hinged lid opening and closing the lid as if it were a mouth. "Check it out. Chomp—Chomp—." Laughing he set it back down.

Alee couldn't help but to smile at how playful and silly he was being, even after being so upset only moments before. It never ceased to amaze her how he could find the positive of every situation, and make her see it too. She played along. "If that's all they do in here, I should sign up next term. Talk about an easy A."

"Easy A? Um, hello—tip of my finger almost gone!"

She grabbed his hand and squeezed. "But it isn't—." Before she could finish the thought she heard footsteps from down the hall. "Shhhh. Someone's coming."

"I don't hear anything."

"Seriously Kyle, be quiet." It wasn't only that she could hear their footsteps on the hard linoleum floors; she could hear their hushed whispers, their racing hearts. She could even smell them: it was the smell of nervous sweat. She heard them more clearly now.

"Something's not right."

"He said they'd be ready today. Let's just go see if he's there." Victoria was coming down the hall, and, even though she was speaking softly, Alee was able to hear her loud and clear. Kyle and Alee just stood frozen, staring at each other.

Kyle's eyes were wide. "What do we do?"

"Do you think they're coming here?" Before Kyle could answer the door started to push open, and without thinking he pulled Alee down behind a large workbench.

"I don't know if we should be here. Why didn't he just bring them to you?" Damian sounded hesitant.

"Well, let me think about that Damian—. He's a teacher, using his work hours and equipment to make something for a student. How do you think that would look if anyone found out?"

Closing her eyes, Alee focused on the sounds in the room. She could hear that only Victoria's light soled footsteps continued into the room. The door never closed behind them, so she assumed that Damian must still be standing at the door keeping watch. Turning to Kyle, she motioned for him to move around to the far end of the workbench, and she followed as quietly as she could. She was worried that as Victoria continued into the room past the first set of tables she was sure to see them.

Victoria rummaged around on a couple of the tables. "Check out these boxes, this class is so lame!" Putting the metal box back on the worktable she headed for the teacher's station in the center of the room. She opened a couple of drawers before pulling out a thick legal-sized envelope. "Here it is." Victoria sounded excited. "See—in an envelope with my name on it and everything. It really does pay to be pretty."

"Right, pretty. So how did you really get him to do it? Because after what you told me about the first time I figured you'd have to spill our whole life history to him and then blackmail him into doing it."

"Um, no."

"Um, no? V, what did you do?"

"Nothing, I didn't do anything. Besides this isn't the place to talk about this. Just know that they're on our side."

"They? You said it was only Mr. Knowles helping you."

"I never said 'only.'"

Unable to stop himself, Kyle let out a quiet snicker. Alee clasped her hand tightly over his mouth and they held their breath, expecting Victoria to walk right around the table and confront them.

"Did you hear that?"

"You're paranoid Damian. It was nothing." Crossing the room back toward the door she waved the envelope in the air, not realizing that it was open, and one of the leather bands fell out onto the floor behind her.

"How many did he make?"

"I asked for ten, which gives us twelve altogether."

"Is that enough?"

"For now, but we can always have him make more later on if we need them. I told him it was a possibility, and he was fine with it."

"Did he ask why you needed them?"

"I told you, he's on our side."

"Wait, you mean he's—?"

"Yes! Now, let's go before we're seen." Their voices trailed away as they got further down the hall.

Aleerah and Kyle waited, listening, as Damian and Victoria mumbled their way down the hall and out of earshot before either one of them was willing to utter a sound.

"What do you think they were doing?"

"I don't know, but I heard something fall on the floor right before she left. Maybe she dropped something." Alee peeked around the corner of the workbench and the coast was clear. She scanned the floor where Victoria had been standing and sure enough—there was a dark brown leather band, like a masculine bracelet, on the floor next to the teacher's station. She picked it up, and instantly her mouth went dry and her heart started pounding in her chest. "Kyle—. Come here."

She pulled her necklace out of her shirt so that Kyle could see both her charm and the bracelet at the same time. The infinity symbol was identical on both. "Guardian," he said, reading the word that was burned across the band as he ran his finger across the aged leather. "Hmmm. This looks so familiar."

"What do you mean?"

"I'm not sure, but I think I've seen it before."

"What would Victoria want with this, let alone twelve of them?"

Alee just shook her head. "I don't know, but I'm going to find out. Let's go."

Hand in hand they made their way back out into the courtyard and back to the Classroom Building. They were both still a little on edge as they turned the corner into the main hallway. Jathan was there waiting for Alee, leaning against the lockers, with his arms crossed and a big smile on his face. "You ready for the Psych test today?" It was like he had been waiting for her, but then again that seemed to be a pretty common thing.

"Crap!"

"What's wrong now?" Kyle asked confused.

"I forgot all about my Psych test today." She looked up at Kyle with sad puppy dog eyes, asking for forgiveness for what she was about to do. "I'm sorry. Do you mind if I go study?" He didn't want her to go, but couldn't stop her either. He squeezed her hand tightly in his, then shook his head. She stood on her tiptoes and kissed him softly, then whispered, "Don't worry, I'll see you after class." Then as she turned the corner with Jathan following behind she stopped and grabbed his hand and dragged him off toward their fourth period classroom. She was gone before Kyle could even say goodbye.

"Quick," Alee whispered to Jathan, "what do I need to know?" This was the first time that *she* had initiated the hand holding, and although it wasn't as soft and comforting as when Jathan did it she still liked it!

Once they were alone, settled in their seats with their psych books open in front of them, Alee started thinking about how Jathan had just disappeared while she was talking to him in the courtyard. Then she remembered the weird dream she had had that first week of school when she thought she was chasing him through the woods, only to wake up in the front seat of her cousin's car. "Hey, Jathan—can I ask you something?"

"Of course, what is it?" He was always so calm. She felt stupid for even thinking the dream could have been something more than it was. However, lately, it seemed like that was happening a lot, and she needed to know for sure.

"How long have you lived in Atlanta?" She watched his eyes, listened to his heartbeat, looked for any signs that might tell her something he wouldn't come out and say.

"Um—." He thought about it for a few seconds. "Not long. I moved here this past summer, just before school started. Why?" There was nothing. If he was lying she couldn't tell.

She knew it was a farfetched idea, but she scribbled an infinity symbol on her notebook paper and turned it around so he could see it. "Do you know what this is by any chance?" She was grasping at straws here.

"Yeah, it's an eight—." She looked down confused.

"No, not like that." She turned the paper sideways. "Like this."

He traced drawing with his fingertip. "It's an infinity symbol." He looked up at her and his eyes were empty. "Why?"

"Um, no reason. Never mind. It's silly really, just a town history thing." But then it happened. As she took the paper back her hand brushed his, and she realized his body temperature had dropped significantly. "Are you OK?"

"Yeah, I'm fine. Are we going to study or what?" But, he wasn't fine and Alee knew it. Something about him was different. He wasn't smiling, and he seemed almost annoyed. Jathan never got annoyed with Alee. He was always smiling at her and trying to get her attention, almost flirting.

Oh God, does Jathan—. He can't like me!? Alee had thought the threat of Jathan liking her was long since past, after she had avoided his attempts to talk to her in private so many times. She thought she had made it pretty clear that she wasn't interested.

Luckily for her, class was about to start, so she only had to sit in the awkward state of awareness for a few more minutes before students started to fill the room. The rest of the day went pretty smoothly. When she got to her locker after school Damian was standing there with Kyle, waiting for her. She reached into her pocket, feeling for the small wooden talisman that she had started carrying with her a while back. *Still there.* Then with a deep breath she nuzzled herself under Kyle's arm. "Hey Damian, what's going on?"

"Not much, it's Thursday, so five dollar pizzas down at the *Pizza Pit*. We're all going, and—." Taking in a deep breath he continued. "—we just wanted to know if you guys wanted to come along." Kyle couldn't see how hard it was for Damian to ask them to hang out outside of the sixty minute lunch hour—outside of the safety net of the school walls—but Alee could, and it was a hard cold reminder that she still wasn't really part of the group.

Kyle tightened his arm around her shoulder, a gentle hug. "That sounds great. We'd love—"

"I can't." She looked up at Kyle, again batting her big blue eyes at him. "I have plans remember? But you should go." She turned to Damian and rolled her eyes. "Family stuff, sorry—I wish I could come. I'm sure you'll be having a lot more fun than me."

"No problem, maybe next time." To Alee's surprise, Damian actually sounded a little disappointed.

"I'd like that." She turned and opened her locker, but froze as Damian's next question completely caught her off guard.

"You live at that black arts shop just outside of town, right?"

She could feel every muscle in her body tense at the words 'black arts.' She didn't know if she should be afraid or just pissed off. Her throat began to burn, and she could feel her fangs exposed pressing into her lower lip. Her body had chosen for her, and she was pissed off instead of afraid. She didn't want to turn around, but knew she couldn't face her locker forever. She reached up and grabbed her pills off the top shelf and popping two into her mouth she turned and was eye to eye with Damian. "It's called The Black Onyx, but it's not a black arts shop. My family sells a lot of stuff, including herbs for holistic healing. There are even doctors who come into the shop to get stuff." Damian just smirked. She was keeping it together a lot better than she had expected, but deep down she was getting very uncomfortable. "Admittedly it's not for everyone, but I don't push my beliefs on anyone else, so—."

They stood there in silence for a while as Alee worked to control a mix of emotions that were flowing inside of her. But what she found the most interesting was what she could feel coming from Damian. He was worked up. His heart was racing in his chest, as if it was trying to escape. He was sweating more than usual, and to her surprise he smelled sweet, almost too sweet. But she liked sweet and to her he smelled good. His breathing was shallow and fast, like an animal that knows it's being hunted. When he finally spoke, his speech was hurried and short. "Right, well, I was just going to say it must be cool and all—. But, whatever. I guess I should get going. You think you'll make it tonight Kyle?" He was talking to Kyle, but he never took his eyes off Alee.

"I'll be there. What, in about an hour?"

"Yeah."

"Cool, see you then." With that Damian was gone. Kyle turned to Alee and her hands were shaking, and there were tears in her eyes.

"That's not what he was going to say, and you know it," she blurted. She was squeezing Kyle's hand so tightly his fingertips were turning white. "He was never comfortable with Dani, Victoria and me doing spells and stuff." Her grip got even tighter until Kyle was actually on his knees pulling his hand away. When she realized what she had done she fell to the floor next to him. "Oh no! Did I hurt you? I'm so sorry." Tears were pouring down her cheeks. "I'm so sorry."

Kyle, trying to be the tough guy that he liked to portray, just shook it off. "I'm fine—really. Don't worry about it." But, Alee could see that he was in a lot more pain than he was willing to admit. "Are you OK?" That was so Kyle—thinking about her at a time like this. She just shook her head. Kyle was confused. "Are you sure you don't want to come? OK, stupid questions. If you don't want me to go, I won't."

"No, you should go. They're your friends and you should go hang out with them."

"Are you sure?"

"Yeah, I'm sure. Go, it'll be fun."

"Do you want me to drive you home?"

"Yes please."

"Let's go." He grabbed her bag and flung it over his shoulder and led her out into the parking lot. The sky was cloudy and it smelled like rain was coming, but that wasn't what caught her attention as they crossed the parking lot. It was Jathan standing under the shade of an old oak tree, watching from a distance. She looked up at Kyle, but he hadn't noticed.

"Hey, I think I might walk home."

"Walk home? It's not like you live just around the block."

"No, but it's also not like I can't run faster than you can drive."

"Point made, but seriously? Are you sure? I don't mind taking you—just the two of us, alone in my truck. Huh? You know you wanna!" He nudged her shoulder and winked in an overly cartoonish kind of way.

She couldn't help but laugh. "I do, but I think I need the fresh air."

He bent down and kissed her softly, then leaned in close to her ear and she could feel the heat of his breath down her neck. "Go, but I want to see you tonight."

"OK" her voice was breathy as she leaned into him, pressing their bodies together. She could feel his body reacting to hers, and she knew that if she decided to take him up on this offer to drive her home he would never make it to pizza.

"You feel so warm." His lips brushed hers as he spoke.

She closed the small gap that remained between them and pressed her lips to his, taking his lower lip between her teeth. "You taste so—." She pulled away. "Wait, I can't do this." She looked around at the last few students headed toward their cars. "Not here—later, OK?"

"Later, but we still need to talk about earlier."

"We will, I promise. I just need some air." With that she was gone, deep into the woods in the direction Jathan had been standing. She left Kyle alone in the parking lot still carrying her bag.

Kyle stood there watching for a while, but once the distraction of Alee being around was gone the throbbing pain in his hand started to take over his focus. He had intended to head home to change before meeting everyone for pizza, but ended up in the emergency room at the Atlanta Hospital instead.

He waited for over two hours before they finally took him back, not because they were busy, but because they just didn't really care. If you ever had a real emergency, Atlanta Hospital was not the place you wanted to end up.

After the doctor examined him and took a series of x-rays he left with a temporary soft cast, which was really more like an ace bandage with a splint underneath it than anything else— from just above his wrist down to his fingers. She had broken three bones in his left hand, and fractured two others. Coming up with a story for the doctor as to how it happened wasn't easy either. All he could think of was that he had fallen down the stairs at school when he was running to catch up with his ride home. It wasn't a very good story since he had driven his own truck to the hospital. All it did was cause the doctor to order a whole new series of x-rays and neurological exams thinking there might be a more serious underlying cause. He couldn't exactly tell them that his super human half-vampire half-witch girlfriend crushed his hand because she got upset.

As he was heading down the hall to leave the hospital he spotted Petra walking toward him. "Hey, what are you doing here?"

She glanced over her shoulder then stopped just inches in front of him. "You didn't see me here tonight, OK?" It wasn't really a question—at least Kyle didn't take it that way.

"Um, OK, but first you have to tell me what you're doing." He was checking out her stealthy all-black attire.

"I'm working. That's all you need to know!"

"You're work—. You work at the—." She was gone before he could even finish.

When he finally made it back to his truck he was starving. He called Damian, who told him that everyone was still hanging out at the Pizza Pit downtown. As hungry as he was, it didn't take much convincing before he decided to join them.

All eyes were on Kyle when he walked in with his arm all wrapped up. "What happened?" Victoria was at his side in seconds. "Are you OK?"

"Yeah, I'm fine. It's just a couple of broken bones, nothing serious." He tried to laugh it off, which wasn't too hard at that point because they had put him on some pretty strong painkillers at the hospital and the effects hadn't fully worn off yet.

Tyler and Dani slid further into the booth they had been sitting in to allow room for Kyle to sit with them, which he gladly did. "So, how'd it happen?" Tyler and Kyle had hung out a lot before Alee died. With their girlfriends being best friends, they spent a lot of time together. But ever since Aleerah had come into the picture Dani had turned distant, and Tyler just followed suit.

"It's stupid really. I was running to catch up with Aleerah at school, and turned the corner too fast—fell down the stairs. Guess I caught myself wrong."

Damian just watched him. "Hmmm, was that after I saw you?"

"Yeah, yeah it was." OK, so Kyle knew he was busted. He wouldn't have had any reason to go back upstairs at the end of the day only to run back down to Alee who he had already been standing next to.

"Wow, well that really sucks man. How long do you have to wear that thing?" Damian smacked the brace from across the table with a huge smile on his face.

The pain shot through Kyle's hand like a dull knife being forced in between the bones. "You know, I think I liked you more when you couldn't talk."

"Yeah well, times have changed I guess."

It was eight o'clock before Kyle left the Pizza Pit. Tyler and Dani had already headed out at least thirty minutes earlier. Kyle had every intention of going to see Alee, but he was just too tired. Besides his hand was starting to hurt again, and he really just wanted to take his pain medication and go to bed; hopefully the meds would knock him out. He texted a quick goodnight to Alee as he headed out for his truck, but he only made it halfway through the parking lot before Victoria stopped him. "You want me to drive you home? It doesn't look like you're in much shape to drive."

"No, I got it, but thanks."

She snatched the keys out of his hand. "I insist, Damian can follow us to your place and take me home, right Damian?" She was yelling across the parking lot and Damian just nodded in return as he climbed into the driver's seat of his black Mustang. "This way you don't have to worry about your hand."

"Um—sure, thanks." Kyle wasn't really comfortable with anyone other than himself driving his truck and, except for a few times he had let Alee drive it, no one else had ever even sat behind the wheel besides him. "Just go slow, OK?"

She smiled as she hopped in and pulled on her seat belt. "Oh I plan to. Don't worry." Then with a little giggle she revved the engine. Later, he could remember pulling out of the parking lot, but after that everything got a little hazy.

16

     Kyle woke up lying on his bed still fully dressed from the night before. His mom was banging on his bedroom door, which was a pretty common morning routine for her. "Kyle, wake up. You're going to be late for school, and that girl Aleerah has already called twice this morning." He sat up, pushing himself out of bed. Unfortunately, he had forgotten about his hand, and the instant he put pressure on it he screamed in pain. "Kyle, are you OK?" His mom ran into the room. "What happened?" She was practically hyperventilating at the thought of her son being hurt.

     Oh crap. "It's nothing. I just broke a couple of bones in my hand, but I'm all right really."

     "What do you mean you broke a couple of bones? Doing what? Why didn't the hospital call me?" She was holding his hand up, inspecting the wrap the doctor had used, as if by some miracle she would be able to see through it and figure out how to fix it.

     "Mom, it's nothing really. They didn't call because it's not really a big deal."

"Not a big deal? Not a big deal! My baby boy—."

As soon as she called him her 'baby boy' he cut her off. She had been doing it since he was a baby, and that was fine, but now that he was older, it had really started to bother him. "Mom, calm down. You gave me my insurance card, I gave it to them—and so they had no reason to bother you."

"But you're my baby—."

"I'm seventeen, Mom!"

"Fine, my seventeen-year-old son breaks his arm, and no one thinks it's important enough to tell me?"

"I'm seventeen, Mom not seven. Listen to yourself. There are some things I have to be able to handle on my own." She just sat there listening, but he could tell she wasn't really hearing what he was saying. "I'm a senior this year. Next year I'll be off to college. You have to give me room to breathe. I'm not a little kid anymore." He stood up, and waved his arm in the air showing her it wasn't really a big deal. "Besides, it's just my hand, not my whole arm."

She just shook her head, and a single tear escaped her eye. "OK, fine." She brushed her hand across her son's check. "I just don't know when you got so grown up." Then, turning to leave, she called back over her shoulder. "Get ready for school. Breakfast is on the table already." Kyle could feel it; something had changed between them in that moment. How much had changed he didn't know, but things were different, for better or worse.

As the door shut behind her Kyle bolted into the bathroom shoving his right hand in his pockets searching for the pain pills the doctor had prescribed the night before. He didn't even bother with a glass he just stuck his mouth under the faucet and gulped down water as he swallowed two of the large white pills. He was in serious pain, even if he didn't want his mother to see it, and he prayed the medicine would kick in soon.

It took longer than usual to get ready. Doing things with only one hand was proving to be more difficult than he had expected. He managed to shower with one arm stuck outside of the curtain, and he pulled his clothes on with minimal discomfort, but he wasn't able to tie his shoes on his own. Instead of asking his mom for help after his independence tirade, he decided to slip on a pair of sandals. Downstairs, his mom was at the ready with a juice box and two pieces of cinnamon toast in a napkin. She gave him a quick kiss and he headed out into the cool October morning, pretending that his feet weren't cold.

Kyle tried calling Alee a few times on his way to school, but only got her voicemail. Making it there with time to spare, even after a quick stop at his locker, Kyle ran straight to the library hoping to find Alee in her usual corner, reading and sipping on her favorite coffee, but she wasn't there. As he was leaving the library he stopped by the librarian's desk. "Excuse me."

"Yes?" When she turned around Kyle realized it wasn't the usual librarian. It was Ms. Thatcher, the woman who worked in the front office.

"Um, Ms. Thatcher."

"Yes Mr. Fields, what can I do for you dear?"

"Have you seen Miss Wenham this morning? She usually sits back there—." He pointed to Alee's favorite chair. "—reading, before first period."

"No, I'm sorry. Her mother called. Apparently she won't be coming in to school today."

"What? OK, thank you." *Why isn't Alee coming to school?* A thought entered his mind, but quickly faded as he walked into the empty hallway. The lights were still off and no one was around. When he turned back to look into the library the lights were off in there too, and there was no sign of Ms. Thatcher either.

"If you're worried dear, you can call her."

"What?" Kyle whipped around, and Ms. Thatcher was standing just inches away, holding out a cell phone for Kyle to take.

Kyle took the phone, cautiously. He stared at the phone before asking, "Is this, my phone?" But, when he looked up she was gone and the phone had started to ring.

Startled, Kyle bolted upright in bed. He was still wearing the same clothes from the day before, his wrist and hand were still wrapped up with the hard splint preventing him from bending his wrist, and his cell phone was ringing on his bedside table. He grabbed it timidly, still confused about what had just happened. "Hello?"

"Kyle, it's me." Alee sounded tired, as if she hadn't slept all night. "I'm not going to be at school today. I need to—it's a long story. Can you just pick up Phoebe's and my assignments and bring them by tonight? My mom already called to let Ms. Thatcher know we'd be out, and to send everything with you."

"Are you OK?"

"I'm fine. It's just—." She didn't know how to explain. She wasn't even sure she believed it all herself, and the last thing she wanted was for Kyle to think she was crazy, or any crazier than he must already think she was.

"It's just what? Seriously Alee—Aleerah—whatever—after everything we've been through together, you should know by now that I'm the last person you need to hide things from." It was true. They had been through a lot together, more than most people.

"You're right, I'm sorry. I guess I'm just tired. It's been a really long night. You know that leather band we found yesterday?"

"Umm, yeah, the one that said 'Guardian' on it."

"Let's just say that I think Damian and Victoria have gotten themselves mixed up with the wrong crowd, and to top it off I've lost the band. I had it yesterday after school, but I must have dropped it on my way home, and I really need to find it." Alee took a deep breath, both to wake up and to stall. "Is it OK if we just leave it at that, at least for now? I promise to explain more when you get here tonight."

"I guess, but you know that isn't really fair." He kind of chuckled into the phone. "How am I supposed to focus at school all day with that hanging over me? I mean, honestly, now that I know that vampires and witches exist, and now you say something like 'the wrong crowd,' you got me thinking zombies."

She couldn't help but laugh. "It's not zombies. I promise." Kyle was perfect at lightening the mood and putting a smile on Alee's face. "I love you."

"I love you more." They hung up and Kyle got out of his bed just as his mother started knocking on the door.

"Kyle, wake up. You're going to be late for school, and that girl Aleerah has already called twice this morning."

OK, that's weird. "I'm already up, and I just talked to her on my cell."

Before his mom could even mention breakfast Kyle popped his head out the door, keeping his wrist hidden behind him. "I know, breakfast is on the table." She turned back with a quizzical look. "It smells great. Thanks Mom, you're the best. I love you."

She just looked at him and smiled. Then, gently rubbing the side of his face with the back of her hand, "I don't know when you got all grown up."

Déjà vu! It was like he knew everything that was about to happen before it actually happened. If he could just keep her from seeing his wrist he wouldn't have to worry about her reaction.

After his mom was down the hall and out of view he quickly shut the door and pulled the pill bottle out of his pocket, popping two into his mouth and swallowing them without any water. "Whoa—what's going on?" Although he was speaking out loud he wasn't really expecting an answer, let alone for some guy to actually be standing in the doorway to his bathroom when he turned around. "What the hell. Who the hell are you and how did you get in here?" OK, so he didn't see that one coming.

"My name's—Jathan, I'm new in town, but don't worry I'm not a threat. I go to your school, kind of. I'm a friend of a friend if you will." Jathan's hands were up in front of him as if to show Kyle he wasn't armed. "Cool room though, looks a lot like mine." Jathan just smirked. Then noticing Kyle's wrist, "Dude, what the hell did you do to my—your wrist?"

"Broke a couple bones, but it's—wait, you're Jathan. What the hell are you doing here?"

"I'm not really here."

On top of the pain Kyle was already feeling in his hand, he was starting to get a headache. "What do you mean you're not here? I'm looking at you, you're right there! How did you get in here?"

"That's not important." Jathan moved into the room and sat on a chair at the desk in front of Kyle's bedroom window.

"The hell it isn't." Kyle didn't really feel threatened by Jathan. In a fight there was no question in his mind that he would win, but the idea that the guy had gotten in his room without him knowing did kind of creep him out.

"Kyle, seriously, just listen for a minute. That medicine is going to kick in and you're going to be useless to me unless you listen now. I need you to deliver a message for me, and the only way you can do it is if you get out of school today." He was waiting for a response as if he had asked Kyle a question, but Kyle had no idea what the question was.

"What kind of message?"

Not the response Jathan was going for. "Again, not really important. Besides, you don't need to know what the message is. You just need to deliver it." He pulled a folded envelope out of his back pocket and held it out for Kyle to take. "Take this to Alee's family."

"Which one?" Like word vomit it just came out, and the instant he said it he knew he shouldn't have. Then it hit him, the guy hadn't said *Aleerah's family*, he had said *Alee's family*. *How does Jathan know about Alee—he wasn't even around last year!*

Jathan's eyebrows went up as if intrigued, or maybe to say *Ha! Busted!!!* Then with that same wicked smirk he was so good at, "Whatever do you mean Kyle? Aleerah only has one family."

Aleerah? Did he say Aleerah the first time? Crap, I can't think.

"You're not looking so good. I should be going. Just give it to her mom, her dad, her Grandma Edith, whoever. Just make sure they get it this morning. They need to move fast if they're going to do anything about it this time." Now it was Jathan who was looking guilty, as if he had spoken too quickly. "So, can you do it?"

"What's in—?"

Jathan was getting frustrated. Cutting him off before he could finish, he snapped, "Nothing is in it for you, except your life. Now, can you do it or not?"

"I was going to say, what's in it? As in, what's in the package?"

Jathan looked away to gather his thoughts, before saying something else he might regret. "Of course you were. It's just something she lost last night on her way home. Now, run along, and make sure they get it within the hour. Oh, and do try to stay out of things when she tells you to. It's for your own good."

"What?"

"You'll see soon enough."

"But, I—. How do you—?" Kyle had only looked down at the envelope for a second but when he looked up Jathan was already gone. He stood there, frozen in place, staring at the empty doorframe, and wondering if he should open the envelope. In the end he decided against it. Besides, he already had a good idea what was in it. The only thing he didn't know was how Jathan had gotten it, and where Alee had run off to after school yesterday.

17

With Kyle's kiss still warm on her lips she took off for the woods, for the spot where Jathan had been standing. Although she would probably tell Kyle about chasing Jathan later, she was glad he hadn't noticed him right then. She didn't want another argument, not right at that moment. Like the last time, Jathan's trail wasn't hard to follow, but he was still always a turn ahead of her, just out of reach. She knew these woods pretty well by now, having hunted them regularly for the previous few months with Eric. She felt comfortable in the woods, and she had already developed strong tracking skills.

Jathan's trail led her along the ridgeline for about two miles, and then turned and took her deep into the valley for at least three more miles. Alee was continually amazed at her pure physical strength and endurance. Having been 'sick' for so long, her body's capabilities never ceased to amaze her.

Atlanta had always been a small town in terms of population, but in land acreage it was actually quite large. The people living there had fought hard to protect the trees and the wildlife. As a child, Alee had thought it was just a way of life in Atlanta—fighting for what you believed in, or fighting to keep what was rightfully yours—but she was quickly learning that there was so much more to it than that. It was more a means of survival than anything else. Keeping Atlanta small, surrounded by vast acres of land, was a way to protect the town and its residents. She hadn't really figured out, though, whether it was more to keep unwanted guests *out* or to keep people *in*. Thoughts began to pour into her head as she ran, and she had to try hard to focus on what she was doing to keep them from distracting her from her objective.

She focused on Jathan's trail, reminding herself that this time, when she found him, she wouldn't let him go until she got some answers. She wasn't about to go all that way only to leave unsure of why he had led her into the woods—again.

She came to a stop when she found herself standing before what looked like the opening to a cave in the side of a hill. She couldn't remember having seen it before, but then again it did blend into the hillside rather easily, with wisps of greenery hanging loosely over the opening. The only reason she noticed it now was because there was a light wind blowing the greenery to the sides, causing the mouth of the cave to be exposed. Otherwise she might have just run right past it without a second glance, as she had probably done a hundred times before.

Alee took a step closer to the mouth of the cave. She brushed the plants aside as she squinted, trying to see into the dark space beyond the entrance, but it was no use. The sunlight didn't even so much as peek into the cave. Closing her eyes she took a small step forward, a leap of faith, into the mouth of the cave, and let the greenery fall down behind her, blocking out the world outside. When she opened her eyes they had already begun to adjust to the light, or lack thereof, and she was able to see shadows formed by the rocks that lined the cave walls. A few minutes longer and her vision would be almost as good inside the cave as it was outside the cave—just another little perk of being part vampire.

Alee ran her hand along the wall of the cave as she slowly moved deeper inside, and she could feel the cool moisture that covered the rocks. It was at least twenty degrees cooler in the cavern than outside, but Alee didn't really notice. It wasn't the cold that sent a chill down her spine, but the rustling sound of rocks being kicked against the cave wall just up ahead. She tried to focus, to see what it was, but she didn't see anything.

"Looking for me?"

She turned in a flash at the sound of his voice, and right behind her, standing just inside the cave entrance, was Jathan. He wasn't winded or tired. He didn't look as if he had just run ten feet let alone miles. He almost glowed as he smiled and held out his hand.

Oh no, it's happening again. It's all just a dream. "You're not real." She was so certain when she said it that it must be true, but then hearing his voice she began to second-guess herself again.

"I assure you, I am real." Again he held out his hand. "Take my hand, and I'll show you."

"You'll just disappear." She almost sounded more disappointed than matter of fact, and she could tell Jathan had heard it too.

"I promise I won't disappear, not yet." She took his hand and let him lead her deeper into the cave. Her eyes had already adjusted and she could now see that the cave walls were covered in what looked like clear shiny crystals, and thousands of stalactites in all different sizes hung from above. "Have you ever wondered why you're the only ones?"

She was focused on the beautiful crystals all around her and barely heard his question, let alone understood it. "What do you mean?"

"You and your father, have you ever wondered why you're the only vampires in Atlanta?"

"I'm not a—"

"Yes you are, but I get it, you just haven't accepted it yet. Don't worry, you will."

With that her heart literally stopped beating. If she were a mere human she would have been dead, but the vampire in her forced her to hang on. "I um—I don't know what you're talking about." Her voice cracked as she spoke, but he ignored it.

"Do you really think your secret is still safe inside that pretty little head of yours? This isn't the first time you've let me in, and it won't be the last." He turned to face her, and, sliding his left arm around her waist, he pulled her close and ran his right hand along her jaw line. Again chills ran down her spine, but it was no longer from fear. This time it was equal parts anger and excitement. Instinct kicked in as she leered at him, exposing her pearly white fangs. He lifted a single finger to her lips, unafraid, "Shhhh, it's all right. I'm not going to hurt you, and you won't hurt me."

"Stay away from me," she warned him as she tried to back away—but then found herself up against the wall of the cave and unable to move.

"You're not the only ones. Your father knows it and I think you deserve to know—."

"I do know. I'm not stupid. I know about the Underground, and that Atlanta was founded by vampires. The real question is, how do you know?"

"Of course you know." Jathan stepped back looking confused and concerned, mumbling to himself. "By now you would have already been getting ready. But, you haven't told me—him yet." He looked into her eyes and shook his head. "I should have listened to them. I should never have come back." He physically shook himself, trying to get back the control and focus he had lost. "You might know some things, but how much have they told you? They obviously told you there are others just like you." A smile crossed his face and he let out a soft chuckle. "Well, not *just* like you. You're special aren't you? Delicate and vicious all at the same time. You have powers you haven't even discovered yet. No, there is no one else quite like you—anywhere—despite what anyone tells you. But vampires, oh, their numbers are too high to even imagine."

She slid herself away from the wall and from Jathan, but the only way to go was deeper into the cave instead of toward the sliver of light that she could now see in the distance as the wind outside began to blow the greenery back and forth across the cave entrance. "Please, just let me go. I need—." She was struggling inside. Being so close to him, her thirst had begun to burn in her throat, but she desperately wanted to control it. She longed to get outside where she could hunt. She wanted very much to be free from him, but even more she desired to taste the warm blood she imagined flowing through his veins.

Jathan took a step back, giving her plenty of room to move. "I'm not keeping you here. You're free to go any time you wish." Alee pushed away from the rocks, and took a step toward the distant light, away from the warm touch of his flesh and his sweet scent, unlike anything else she had ever smelled. "But, don't forget, you came to me. There must be something here you—desire?" The way he said it was almost as if he was asking for something.

Before he could even react she turned and pinned him against the wall of the cave. With his back against the cold hard stone wall she held him still with one hand around his throat. "Is that what you want? Do you want for me to desire you—to drain you? Why are you tempting me? You know what I am, but do you not understand what I can do?"

He didn't look afraid, or even surprised. "It is you who does not understand. Can you not see how I feel about you?" Again she thrust him against the cave wall, scraping his back along jagged rocks and crystals. She licked her lips fighting back the urge to drink. "I can't spell it out for you, I'm sorry. Can you really not feel it?"

At that moment she felt little other than the hunger pulling at her soul. But then she felt his hand once again around her waist, pulling her closer to him, not pushing her away. As their bodies collided she lost her hold on his throat, but instead of running he held her—tightly—in his embrace. He ran his fingers through her hair and pulled her face to his. Their lips met with a sense of urgency and need. It was different than the gentle touches of Kyle, or even the desperate yet brief embraces she had shared with Damian, once upon a time.

She trembled as Jathan kissed her—as she kissed him. Closing her eyes she tried to focus on reality, knowing that at any moment she was going to wake up in Kyle's truck halfway home. She could picture herself there, sitting close to him with her head on his shoulder as he drove down the old dirt roads listening to music and drumming his thumbs on the steering wheel the whole way, but then it all slipped away, and she was back in Jathan's embrace with the taste of his lips on hers, the warmth of his touch all over her, and her legs wrapped tightly around his waist as he held her off the ground and closer to his body than she had ever been to anyone else.

Breathless, he pulled away, just a little. "I wish you could see yourself the way I do." She could see how desperate he was to hold on to her, but, fighting his own desires, he pulled away even more, and she unwrapped her legs as he set her back on her feet. "What lies ahead for you is so much greater than you can even imagine. They are keeping things from you, but it is time you see for yourself. Its time you demand answers. It's the only chance you have to survive what's coming, and I couldn't bear to know I came back just to watch you—." He wiped away a tear before it had the chance to get all the way down his cheek. "Take what you've found, and I pray your family will know what to do with it this time."

She could feel his desperation and without even thinking she balled her fists into the front of his shirt and pulled him to her. Their bodies fit together like puzzle pieces and their lips were once again on each other before he had a chance to object. Not that he would have objected if he had been given the chance.

A moan escaped her lips, and she wanted so much more from him.

Their lips still pressed together and their tongues explored each other's mouths, but he was still able to respond, "Oh, Alee."

"Alee?" *Did he just say Alee?* Her eyes flew open, but Jathan wasn't there. She was standing alone in the dark cave, surrounded only by the silence. In her hand she gripped the leather band that she had found earlier that day in the metal shop classroom. How it had gotten in her hand, she wasn't sure, but she suspected Jathan had something to do with it.

"Jathan? Hello?" She desperately called out into the hollow of the cave, but only her voice echoed back. A gust of wind pushed at her back as if guiding her farther into the darkness. She stood there waiting for a sign to turn around, but nothing came. "I am not afraid," Alee whispered to herself as she edged deeper into the cave. "I am not afraid. I am not afraid." over and over again.

She saw what looked like a large door up ahead, and she began to think that maybe this all really was just another dream. She knew it wasn't reasonable that there would actually be a door that far down into a cave. So, following what she thought was her imagination, she continued walking, waiting for the moment she would eventually wake up in Kyle's truck.

When she finally reached the door Alee took note of the infinity symbol carved into its center. *The pentagram is the symbol of our coven, but the infinity symbol represents the Underground, and lets others know that you are a protected member.* The words of her grandmother ran through her head.

"The Underground." She let out a breath she hadn't even known she had been holding. Grabbing hold of the large metal door-handle she pulled as hard as she could. The door opened with a loud rusty screeching sound that made the hairs on the back of her neck stand up. When she stepped beyond the threshold she found herself in what looked like a hallway in an old abandoned building. The door shut behind her, and when she tried to open it again, it was locked.

She couldn't tell where she was by the random doors she passed. They were all labeled with numbers that reminded her of the numbers you would find on the doors of hotel rooms or apartment doors By the looks of the place, though, there was no way anyone had lived here in years. The cobwebs and scurrying rodents made it clear that the hallway hadn't been cleaned in over a decade. She couldn't go back, so she began to make her way quietly through the maze of hallways. When she came to a dead end, she pushed open another door and—stepped out into a sea of people quickly passing by. She was startled at the unexpected change, and it wasn't long before people started to notice her too. She was a visitor, after all, and she quickly became the center of attention.

A crowd started to gather as a rather tall man in his late forties with a shaved head and a tattoo of a scull covering his face forced his way through the crowd to stand less than six inches from Alee's face. "I don't recognize you. It seems you've stumbled where you don't belong, child." He was standing even closer now, and sniffing at her neck as if he was a dog deciding whether or not to eat what had been placed before him. "Where is your master?"

"My master?"

The tunnel filled with laughter all around her. "Surely you didn't come here alone. Someone as delicate as yourself must have protection with you." Then he turned to the crowd, calling out as if she were a piece of meat. "Does anyone here claim this girl? Is there anyone willing to protect her? Anyone, anyone at all?" It was obvious that no one was going to jump to her defense. Instead they all just stood around as if enjoying a performance, smiling and laughing.

"I guess you're on your own." Then she saw them, the fangs, at least an inch long—much longer than her own. "Pity for your sake, but I can't say I'm all that disappointed."

These weren't ordinary people, and this was far from an ordinary threat. They were vampires, and they were moving toward her, preparing to attack. There was no way she could take them. She wasn't strong enough, and, without thinking, she closed her eyes tightly and raised her arms, crossing them in front of her face to shield herself from what she knew was coming.

But nothing happened.

When she opened her eyes again, their numbers had multiplied as she had feared, but instead of attacking her they were all standing back in shock, whispering back and forth. When she lifted her arms, the sleeve of her shirt had fallen back to reveal the tattoo on her forearm, which had begun once again to glow. They couldn't seem to take their eyes off of it.

"You're her." It was a girl in the crowd. It was a face Alee had never seen before. Then it started—the riot. People were yelling at one another from every direction. Some were pushing themselves forward in the crowd, trying to get to Alee, while others were backing away as if they had just seen a ghost. She didn't even notice Petra, dressed in all black and looking particularly Goth, pushing her way through the swarm until she had grabbed Alee's arm and began to pull her away from the ever-growing mob.

"Aleerah? Aleerah, what are you doing here? How did you even find this place?"

"I don't—."

"You shouldn't be here. Not on your own."

As soon as they were free from the grasping hands of the mob, Petra pulled Alee down another less crowded hallway. Nestled in a quiet doorway where no one else could see them, Petra quickly pulled off her black jacket and wrapped it around Alee, pulling the hood tight over her head. "When we get home, you're going to have some explaining to do."

Alee felt like a child being scolded for not doing her homework. "You're not my mother."

"No I'm not, and you should feel lucky that it was me who found you and *not* your mother, much less your father. He would do much worse than either your mother or I could even imagine." Then she pulled her out of the security of the doorway shadow, and back into the main hallway. "Stay close, do not let go of my hand, and above all do not make eye contact with anyone."

As Petra pulled her down hallway after hallway, Alee noticed more and more of the details of this underground world around her. Signs over the doors stated places like *Atlanta Hospital, Courthouse, Java Jolt, and Atlanta High School.* "Oh wow, it's the high school." She said all too excitedly, as she pointed up toward the sign. As they passed door after door, she started to realize that the tunnels were actually an underground mirror image of the city. You could go virtually anywhere you wanted in Atlanta simply by following the signs. And, not only did the tunnels give you access to the city above, they also housed an entire underground city. There were restaurants, bars, and all kinds of shops up and down the tunnel. The only thing different between this place and the above ground city was the lack of sunlight.

Lack of sunlight, oh my God. "They're all vampires aren't they?" Alee's heartbeat was racing, and her palms were starting to sweat.

Pulling her quickly through the crowd Petra realized that Alee was about to start to panic, which would only cause them more trouble. Trying to be quiet, Petra whispered under her breath, "Not all of them, no, but I can't explain that now. You have to calm down, and you have to do it now. If we don't get you out of here, and fast, I may not be able to get you out at all. I'm nowhere near powerful enough to protect you."

~ 251 ~

"But, I—."

"You're attracting attention. That's what you're doing. Now keep your head down, and hurry up." Alee did as she was told. She held Petra's hand as tightly as she could without crushing it, kept her eyes on the floor, and quickly followed step-by-step behind her.

They stopped only when they had arrived at a door labeled, The Black Onyx.

It shouldn't have come as a surprise to her, but seeing the sign above the door made it even more real. "Oh, my God."

"Shhhh, not until we're inside." Petra quickly looked around making sure they hadn't been followed before sliding her key in the lock and slowly turning the knob. Before stepping in she peeked inside. There was no one in the hall. She didn't want to get caught in the tunnels by the vampires, but she also didn't want Alee's parents to catch them sneaking in, neither ending would have been pretty.

Since the hall was clear she pushed Alee in first, then she followed, and shut and locked the door behind them. "Your room. Now!" She pointed down the hall but Alee didn't move. "Aleerah *please*, I will explain if you let me, but I can't do it out here." The look on Petra's face wasn't one of anger or even frustration, but one of fear. It was a look that made Alee quickly re-think her attitude.

Once they were safe inside Alee's bedroom with the door secured behind them Petra made her way to the bathroom and turned on the shower to drown out their voices. "What were you doing in the tunnels?"

"I don't—. I was just—."

"Aleerah, the tunnels aren't safe for you, at least not yet. Not until you know what you're doing, have your powers under control, and, most importantly, you know where you're going. You were in vampire territory, and the cute little tattoo trick you can do wasn't going to amuse them for long. Eventually they would have torn you apart as if you were just a light snack before dinner."

The thought of being someone's snack made her stomach churn. "But, I'm—one of them." It was the first time she had placed herself in that category willingly and, although it was hard to admit, she knew it was the truth.

"No you're not. You might be part vampire, but you are far from one of them. Aside from the pills, you feed primarily on the blood of animals. They wouldn't feed on an animal unless their lives literally depended on it."

"Then what do they—?" Petra shot her a look that answered her question before it was even out of her mouth. "Oh, never mind." Then it hit her, what Petra had said. "What do you mean 'aside from the pills I feed *primarily* on the blood of animals'?"

Petra had said too much, and she knew it. She quickly tried to change the subject. "It's true you're a vampire, but they don't even know that. Think about it Aleerah, your heart still beats. So to them you're just another unsuspecting human. Even if you did manage to show your fangs most of them would just see you as a half-breed, if they even believed they were real. Believe me, there are not a lot of people out there who really believe you even exist, or are any more than a witch trying to break into the vampire community. Most of them see you as a phony at best." She grabbed Alee's wrist and turned it out. "This symbol will protect you, as a coven member. Your necklace will show them you're allowed to be there, but only if they see it, and only if you follow the rules. You have yet to even begin to learn the rules."

"Then teach me." She waited for Petra to say something but she never did. "Mom is teaching me potions and spells. Dad—he teaches me to hunt, and, I'll admit, some pretty cool vamp stuff. But you—you can teach me to blend in. That's the most important thing, right? Teach me to be like you—teach me to survive." She waved her hand at Petra's entirely black outfit. "The whole package, scary Goth chick and all."

"Scary Goth chick?"

"You know what I mean. Teach me to be strong, like you."

"Strong, I'll take that." Petra did see her point. "OK, but Phoebe helps, and you do whatever we say, deal?"

"Deal!" Alee was excited and nervous all at once.

Petra on the other hand was ready to jump right in. She made herself comfortable, on Alee's bed, leaning back against the pillows. "Then start by telling me how you got to the tunnels in the first place."

Alee was hesitant, but she knew she was going to have to start trusting someone—why not Petra? "It's kind of a weird story, and I know I'm going to sound crazy, but it all started with this guy at school, Jathan. He was in the new student orientation with me, so I figured he must be new to Atlanta." She sat on the bed next to Petra. "There's something different about him. I think maybe he's a witch, like us. Is that even possible?"

"Of course it's possible. You didn't think we were the only ones did you?" Alee didn't answer. "OK—so you did think we were the only ones. Well, we're not. The thing is, Atlanta is full of witches—vampires—all kinds of different cultures—or societies, if you will. But, unless you're born into that community you will never hear about it. And there are still quite a few families who have no ties to our world." Alee was confused, and Petra could tell. "It's like this, we can't just run around using magic in public, and vampires can't just run around feeding in the streets. That type of behavior would attract global media coverage, and it wouldn't be tolerated by the Founders, or by any of the thousands of underground societies around the world. Once word got out, others would come to eliminate the threat of exposure. It wouldn't be long before Atlanta was completely wiped out."

Alee was about to overreact. She was bothered by this information, and rightfully so. Anyone in their right mind would be upset. "You're telling me that all my life I've been surrounded by—."

"Yes, and I'll stop you right there before you say something you regret."

"I'm supposed to be one of you, right? So why didn't anyone, including my parents, bother to bring this up!" She stood up. "I'm not a child. I'd rather know this stuff than be left in the dark."

"Well, like I said, there are rules. Outsiders aren't allowed to just be brought into the Underground. You have to follow procedures, and that means that someone like you has to be invited. It's stupid really, but it's the rule. Besides, I guess we all kind of thought you would put two and two together and figure it all out yourself. Why in the world would you think we were the only witches in town? Next you're going to tell me you thought you and your dad were the only vampires." She didn't say anything as Alee tried to hide her embarrassment.

"Fine, whatever, maybe I'm naïve, but I'm not an outsider! I was born into this society, and I wasn't the one who decided to leave. I was given away! How is that fair?" She crossed to the bathroom, and slammed the door shut behind her.

Petra quietly sat waiting for her to come back out, but
after a few minutes she started to wonder if there was a
window in the bathroom that she didn't know about.
"Aleerah, are you all right?" She started knocking on the
door. "Aleerah, please, I don't mean it like that. You're right,
it isn't fair, and I'm sorry. Come back out so we can talk
about it, please." Just as she was about to knock even harder
on the door Alee opened it.

"No more secrets!" Alee looked her in the eye. She
wasn't giving Petra a way out.

"OK, no more secrets."

She moved back into her room, sat down in the big
reading chair in the corner, and wrapped herself in a warm
blanket. "So, what exactly is the Underground?"

Petra couldn't help but laugh. "The tunnels. You
know that symbol on your necklace? Well, as you've already
been told, it's the official symbol of the Underground. It can
protect you while you're down there. It basically works like a
form of identity, or membership. It shows the officials that
you're allowed to be there."

"Then what was the big deal about me being down
there?"

"Let's just say today you got lucky because I was
there. The thing is, when someone is born into our world, our
society, we have to be registered into the official
membership. But, your parents didn't do that. They were
afraid, because of what you are—a dhampir—and they
decided not to report you. Instead, they moved away. Some
would say they made a bad decision, others might understand
that they did it for your safety. I really don't know. But what I
do know is this, because of the decision they made you aren't
seen as a true member. That means that until you're officially
invited you're not even supposed to know about the symbol,

let alone be wearing it. Your father kinda broke the rules giving that necklace to you when you were little, even if you didn't know what it meant. And Grams should never have let Phoebe give you the family mark until you were registered. Believe me, the security down there is thick. They know everyone who's allowed in and they know when someone who's not welcome is down there. That means—they know about you now." She lowered her voice even more. "I wouldn't be surprised if they've already started looking for you, and, considering that you were seen with me, it won't take them long to find you. I'm just glad they didn't come to me to track you down. I'd be obligated to turn you in, and that could start a lot of problems in the family."

"Why would they ask you to track me down and why would you be obligated to turn me in?"

"I can't really explain that. It's kind of like a job, but that's all I can say for now." Petra started to pace the room. "For now let's just worry about keeping you hidden, OK?"

"Great. Hide and go seek, my favorite game." Alee was laughing, but Petra wasn't in the mood. Besides, although she was trying to make a joke, she still wasn't really able to cover the growing terror that had begun to take over her.

"This isn't a laughing matter. This is serious. You may be in real danger."

Alee stopped joking around and took a deep breath. "What kind of danger? What can they do to me?"

"I don't know, but you should be safe here. I think. Besides, our family is pretty powerful. They can protect you."

"So, if what I need to be protected is to be registered, or invited, how do I make that happen?"

Petra shook her head. "No, what you need to be protected is to not go back down there. You aren't ready.

Besides, I've already answered a question for you. Now it's your turn to answer a question for me. Give and take, that's how this is going to work. Remember?"

Then it hit her. "Wait! You said I need an invitation—you mean like the one I received for the Founders' Celebration?"

"What?" Petra was stunned, and Alee knew she was right.

Trying to regain her composure Petra ignored the question. "Give and take Aleerah, tell me about Jathan." Without realizing it Alee started to blush. "Aaahhh, you like him."

"What?! No! He's just a guy I met at new student orientation. I mean, I guess we're kind of like friends, but that is all, nothing more!" She was a little too eager to convince Petra, or maybe herself.

"Have you kissed him yet?"

"No—well—."

"Wow, defensive. I know what that means." She couldn't contain her laugher anymore. "Have you kissed him yet?"

"No—I—He—."

"Aleerah!"

"You can't tell anyone, please. I didn't mean to."

"What about Kyle?"

"I love Kyle, the kiss meant nothing, honest. Please don't tell anyone. Please."

"No worries. I don't really care who you kiss anyway."

"Thanks, I think" Alee hung her head down staring at the floor as if she was preparing for the embarrassing walk of shame.

"OK, his first name is Jathan. Do you know his last name?"

Alee thought about it for a while and was surprised that she actually had no idea what his last name was. "No, actually I don't."

"Well, I haven't heard of any Jathan, but that could be because he's new in town. Tell me what makes you think he's a witch, and I'll tell you more about the Underground."

It sounded like a good deal. "It's hard to explain. You know when you have a dream that feels so real you would swear it really happened? He's like that."

"He's the man of your dreams?"

"No, that isn't what I said. It's just that these things keep happening, and he's always there. When it's over I never know if it really happened or not."

"OK—example?"

"Um, at school earlier today I was standing in the courtyard talking to him and he told me I needed to go to the metal shop classroom, but then all of a sudden Kyle was standing behind me, and Jathan was nowhere around. It was like I had dreamt it, but it wasn't a dream. Kyle said when he came out to the courtyard I was alone, talking to myself." Petra was just staring at her like she was crazy. "I took Kyle with me to check out the metal shop class, just in case there was something to it. It turns out we found something, a leather band, a bracelet."

"Wow, a bracelet—school projects are getting pretty weird these days." The sarcasm was oozing out of her. "And what, you think this means something?"

Alee practically jumped at her with her words, "I know it does. The infinity symbol was burned into the band. You can't tell me that is just a coincidence. It means something—I just don't know what."

That little tidbit of information got Petra's attention. "Wait, are you sure it was the same symbol?"

"I'm positive. It's not like an infinity symbol is all that hard to recognize. I'm not an idiot." She started searching her pockets, but couldn't find it anywhere.

"So, where is it now?"

Alee just stood there shaking her head. "I just had it. I was holding it when—." She realized she must have dropped it somewhere in the tunnels. She knew she had had it in her hand after Jathan disappeared in the cave, but she couldn't remember having it after Petra showed up. "I must have dropped it somewhere in the tunnels, maybe when I got scared. I don't know."

"Can you tell me exactly what it looked like?"

"Brown leather, a snap on the back, it was pretty simple. Why?"

Petra quickly got up and grabbed Alee's hand, pulling her behind her and out the door. "Do you think you would recognize it if you saw a picture?" She sounded excited and scared all at once.

"Yeah, of course, it's not like it was years ago—it was just this morning." Alee followed as Petra led her down the hall and into the family library, where she proceeded to search through book after book with no success.

"Was there anything else on the band?" Petra was probing for information, but she wasn't giving any clues or indication as to what it was she wanted to know.

"Um, the symbol, oh, and a word—."

"What was it?"

"Um, 'Protector'—'Keeper'—? No, that isn't right." She was shaking her head trying to remember.

"Think Aleerah, what did it say?"

"'Guardian!' It said 'Guardian,' right in the center of the band." Alee was proud of herself for remembering but it didn't last long, because Petra quickly grabbed her arms and pulled her down the hallway and into the front shop where she continued her search.

Petra scanned the book titles on shelf after shelf, until she finally pulled out a small book with a brown leather cover. The title was burned into the spine, and simply read 'The Guardians.' She flipped through a few pages then turned the book around for Alee to see. Sure enough a black and white sketch of the band was there in the book. It had the same symbol and even the same style of lettering for the word 'Guardian' next to the symbol.

"Hey, that's it." Alee smiled.

"Aleerah, are you a hundred percent sure this is what you found?" It was as if she had become a lawyer and Alee was the witness she was cross-examining on the stand in court, and Alee didn't understand why she was so serious.

"I'm positive. Why?" But Petra didn't answer—she just headed for the door. She left Alee standing there stunned and confused, and ran to the kitchen in search of anyone—everyone. Alee was soon in pursuit. "OK!" she called after Petra, "What is it?" Everything was just happening too fast.

By the time Alee got to the kitchen Petra was standing outside, talking with Jacinda and great grandmother Estelle. Just as Alee was deciding to turn back and go to her room, Estelle called out to her. She would have to bite the bullet and go face them all, not even knowing what it was she had found.

"Come here please, dear." Estelle wasn't the crone of the family, and the years had not been all that kind to her. She had severe kyphosis, also known as hunchback syndrome, and her eyesight had started to go, but that didn't seem to slow her down. Maybe what they say about your other senses kicking in when others start to fail you is true.

Alee took her great grandmother's hand in her own. "Yes, Granny Estelle?"

"Dear, Petra tells me you have found a Guardian band. Is this true?"

"I really don't know what it was. It just looked like a leather bracelet to me. Like the one in that book." She gestured to the book Petra was still holding, and Estelle's grip on her hand tightened. "What exactly is a Guardian band anyway?"

"In order to understand the Guardians, you need to know that witches and vampires are not the only members of the Underground. At one time lycanthropes were also active members. They were actually in power for many years."

"Lycanthropes? What is that?"

Estelle just smiled at Alee's innocent face and patted the back of her hand. "You have so much to learn dear." She didn't mean it in a rude way, and she wasn't talking down to her. It was simply a fact. "Lycanthropes are shape shifters. Your father has told you about them, yes?" Estelle guided her into the house, and sat her down at the kitchen table.

"Yes, a little, like werewolves, right?" A slight giggle escaped her lips as she said that word werewolves, but she regretted it the second it came out.

"Exactly like werewolves. Only lycanthropes don't all shift into wolves." She shook her head. "Your father really should have explained this in more detail by now. Lycanthropes can take on many animal forms. Some are wolves, others are lions, panthers, even hawks."

The blood drained from Alee's face, and her sun-kissed skin started to look like dead flesh. It's one thing to watch Hollywood movies about this stuff, but to know it's real is a whole other thing.

Petra grabbed a bottle out of the refrigerator and handed it to Alee, who quickly downed the contents without coming up for air. "Thank you." Petra just nodded. "So, the shape shifters, are they the Guardians?"

"They were, but that was a long time ago. When the power shifted, the remaining town founders took charge." There was that word again—founders. "They disbanded the Guardians, removing them from the Underground permanently."

"Why?"

"They were seen as a threat. While in power, the Guardians had tried to set laws regulating other members in ways many of us disagreed with. Finally we banded together, and helped the founding members take back the town. It wasn't the first shift in power, but it was the most recent, and we have hoped that it would be the last."

Loraline, Eric, and a number of other Wenham family members had gathered at the kitchen door. Shocked by what she was hearing, Loraline interrupted. "What is going on here? Granny, why are you talking about the Guardians?"

"There is a chance, not yet confirmed, that one of the Guardian bands has been seen—recently." Surprise and alarm filled the faces of everyone in the room.

"That's not possible." Loraline said, looking back at Eric.

They spent the rest of the night with the whole family crammed in the study off the shop. They sat around like it was movie night, eating snacks and sipping on sodas. Only they weren't watching television—they were listening to story after story about the Underground—vampires, witches, fairies, shape shifters, even dream walkers. "So you think that's what he is, a dream walker?" Alee was speaking of Jathan.

"Everyone thought their race had died out, but I suppose it's possible. It's the only explanation I can think of. From the way you describe him, I can't see him being anything but a dream walker." Elizabeth almost sounded like she doubted her own opinion. "I couldn't be certain without meeting him. Do you think you can get him here? Maybe invite him over?"

"Elizabeth!" Edith snapped. "That is unacceptable. You know that dream walkers are dangerous. They always have a motive, and we don't know what he wants from the girl."

"There is no proof that they are dangerous. All we know is what we've read in books. None of us have any real experience with a dream walker. I'm only suggesting—."

"No, it's out of the question." Edith stood up, and crossed the room. Before leaving she turned back to the others, who were still sitting patiently, waiting to hear more stories, and not wanting the evening to end. "I will not change my mind about this." The door shut behind her, and the room stood silent for a while.

Phoebe finally spoke up. "You know what I don't understand?" Everyone just looked at her. Phoebe had a way with the random thoughts, and it was well known that if you gave her a second she would answer her own questions. "I don't get why the Guardian band would have been at the school in the first place. How'd it even get there? I thought they were all destroyed."

"They were—" It was the first thing Eric had said all night, and he sounded not only angry but also defensive, as if someone had personally attacked his integrity or honor. "— for the most part. During the power shift the bands were taken away from every remaining Guardian—forty-three in all. Most of the bands were destroyed, but a few remained in order to preserve Atlanta's history. They were locked up where only the founding members and their families would have access to them." He could feel everyone's eyes on him.

"The founding members you say?" It was Ellen who spoke up this time. Ellen was Edith's oldest daughter, and had it not been for an illness that had forced her to move down South she would have been the next in line for the coven crone position. With her health as it was, she was unable to live in Atlanta during the winter months, and so moving down South had been her only option. She had flown in just a few days ago in order to prepare for the coming solstice. "Are you not on that list, Eric?" Ellen already knew the answer before she asked the question. Her words were pointed and accusatory; she had never liked Eric. Even Loraline could hear the insinuation in Ellen's tone, and she moved to stand next to Eric, ready to defend him if Ellen even for one second implied that he had anything to do with the Guardian bands getting out.

"You know I am, as are so many others." Alee's eyes went straight to Eric in shock. "But we have taken numerous measures to ensure that the records cannot be released." Then he turned to Loraline, because in reality her opinion was the only one he cared about. "And you have my word—" He spoke to all in the room, but his focus was still on his wife. "—I will find out who the band belonged to."

Alee raised her hand like a school child waiting for the teacher to call on her, "I can answer that."

All eyes were on her in an instant. "What? Who?" Eric spoke as if he was interrogating her, but she understood. His reputation was at stake, and he wanted answers.

"Um—I'm sure they have no idea what the band is, or what it stands for." She was regretting saying anything, and trying desperately to backpedal to protect her friends.

"They who, Aleerah?" Eric snapped almost furiously.

She scanned the faces around the room, and everyone seemed eager for her to answer, which made it only harder. Damian and Victoria had been her friends for so long, and even though they weren't very close any more she still felt a sense of loyalty to them. Besides, she was positive they had nothing to do with the Underground. They weren't even from Atlanta. However, she didn't understand why they had had the band, let alone twelve of them. "It belongs to two of my friends from school, Damian and Victoria. But they aren't even from Atlanta. They moved here from—" She tried to remember, but the name of the town had slipped her memory. "—I don't remember, but they only moved here a couple of years ago. There's no way they would have anything to do with any of this." Then she started to laugh out loud. "Actually, I think Victoria might faint if she even knew that any of this stuff—witches, vampires, all of it—really exists."

Phoebe had to agree, throwing her two cents in. "She *is* kind of a snob."

"That's not really what I said, but yeah, kind of."

"Aleerah—" Jacinda's voice was soft and thoughtful. "—was Victoria with you the day you first came to The Black Onyx?"

"Yes, why?"

Jacinda was closing her eyes, recalling the memory of that day. "Tall, with long brown hair, and eyes the color of chocolate. Is that right?"

Alee could feel the room getting colder around her. "That's right."

When Jacinda finally opened her eyes she was looking intently at her sister Loraline. "She's the one I told you about, the one who dropped the black tourmaline."

"That doesn't mean anything," Loraline said. "We can't just assume—."

Disappointed at her sister's reaction, Jacinda just shook her head. "Then we don't assume, but we do have to look into it."

Simultaneously, Eric and Alee turned toward the hallway door. "Are you expecting a visitor, Aleerah?" Eric's voice was low in his throat, and resonated throughout the room.

"No." Alee was well aware that all eyes in the room were on her.

"Eric? What's happening?" Loraline was worried.

"Nothing. I'll take care of it." Alee made a quick exit, and headed down the hallway to the shop where, seconds later, the doorbell rang just as she was reaching for the doorknob. She shouldn't have been surprised or startled. She had known that he was coming, of course, but still she stopped just inches away from the door and pulled her hand back.

It was only seconds before he was banging on the door and shouting, "Aleerah?! Aleerah, are you in there?"

She opened the door and reached out, grabbing him by the shirt and pulling him in, and slamming the door shut behind him. Then she locked the door, deadbolt and all, and turned to face him eye to eye. "You shouldn't be here. I told you not to come until later this evening." But even before she could finish talking she was melting into his arms. She felt safe in the warmth of his embrace, and she would have stayed there forever if she could. But she knew that just down the hall her entire family was plotting something against her friends, and it was all her fault. She wasn't sure what she could do to stop them, or if she even should. The only thing she did know was that she could at least protect Kyle by getting him away from all of this.

He pushed her back, and held her at arm's length. He could see the tears in her eyes, and he told her, in a tone that brooked no objection, "I'm not leaving."

"But——." That was when she noticed the bandage around his hand and wrist.

"I'm not leaving." He took her hand, and started leading her toward the back room. "Like I said before, I'm in this."

"What happened to you?" She held his hand up in horror.

"It's nothing, I'm fine." He lifted her chin so she would focus on him and not the bandage. "I'm fine, really." She briefly remembered bringing him to his knees the day before at school.

"Oh no, did I——?"

"Don't be silly. Besides, there are more important things to think about than my hand. Jathan sent me."

"What?" She turned to face him and stopped. "What do you mean, Jathan sent you?"

"Honestly, I don't know. I mean, up until this morning I thought you were just making him up to make me jealous. And then he paid me a visit in my bedroom. It was actually kind of creepy. How did he even know where I live?"

"I don't know." Alee glanced back toward the hallway, "What did he say?"

"He asked me to deliver a message to your family." He started to pull the envelope out of his back pocket but stopped before it was all the way out. "Aleerah, I need to tell you something." Kyle didn't know how to say it, and, worse, he hated the idea that she might believe that Jathan had found out from him. But keeping her identity a secret was important, and if it was no longer still a secret then she needed to know.

"Kyle, what is it? You're scaring me." She was looking into his eyes, but she sensed that his mind was somewhere else.

He took a deep breath and decided that it was like taking off a Band-Aid—it would hurt less if he just did it. "Jathan knows who you are."

"Um, yeah we've met before, remember? I've actually been telling you about him for months."

"No, Alee. He *knows* who you are!"

She didn't say anything for a long time, and Kyle could feel her hands trembling in his. She was scared, more scared then Kyle had ever seen her. "I know," she answered.

"You know? How?"

"I can't explain it, not right now, but—."

"There's more. I don't think Jathan's—. I mean, you know how you were saying that he's in your head? Well, it's just that, I think you might be right. There's something off about him."

Alee was in a daze, but seemed to be slowly coming out of it. "That's an understatement," she agreed. Then, looking up at him with her ocean blue eyes, she decided, "Come with me." They walked hand-in-hand toward the back hall. "Wait, what was the message?" Kyle pulled the envelope out of his pocket and handed it to her. When she opened it and saw the leather Guardian band she was stunned. "*Jathan* gave this to you?"

"Yeah, did you figure out what it is?" She pulled the band out of the envelope and held it up.

"Yeah, I did. How did he—?" She grabbed Kyle's hand and started running back to the study where the rest of her family was still discussing what they were going to do if in fact the Guardian bands had been discovered.

Alee and Kyle burst through the door and all eyes were on them. She took the band directly to her father. "Here it is. Kyle brought it."

Eric took the leather band in his hand, fighting hard not to scream—or worse—attack the messenger. He turned it over and over in his hand, but couldn't tell if it was a fake or not. He wanted so badly to believe that it was, but he was unable to say for sure, and that bothered him more than anything. If it was a fake, then it was a very good one, and that meant that the real thing was out there somewhere, and most likely in the wrong hands. Besides with a fake this good, it didn't matter if it was real or not. It would have the same effect either way.

It took him a minute to react. "Where exactly did you find this—the first time?"

Alee and Kyle exchanged nervous glances, but Alee was the one to speak up first. "At school, like I told Granny Estelle, in the metal shop classroom."

"Why were you—?"

She cut him off before he could continue. "It's a long story. But, there's something else. I don't know how important it is, but—." Her hands were shaking and the words were getting caught in her throat. What she was afraid of she wasn't sure, but she continued. "—there are more of them."

Gasps were heard all around the room. "What? How do you know?" Eric demanded.

"I heard them say that they had ten made—," Alee explained.

Kyle interrupted, "Yeah, but they said that they have twelve, remember?" He was looking down at Alee.

"He's right." Alee nodded. "They did say they had twelve all together."

Elizabeth was standing with her arms wrapped around her daughters when Jacinda asked, "Why would anyone need so many, unless—."

"The Founders' Ceremony." Eric's voice was as calm as night. "It's the only thing that makes sense."

Eric stood there, silent, with all eyes on him. When he finally spoke his intentions were clear. "Kyle, take Aleerah to school. You're both late already."

"But, Mom already called the school, and told them Phoebe and I wouldn't be there today."

"You're going now, and Aleerah, bring your friends to dinner tonight where they can be watched!" He didn't say to invite them to dinner—he said to *bring* them. That didn't leave any room for Alee to fail and she knew it. "I need time to find the other bands without them getting in the way." He was out the door with Loraline, Jacinda, Estelle, Elizabeth, and all the others quickly following. The only ones who remained were Kyle, Alee, Petra, Phoebe, and Elizabeth's husband William.

"You kids have your work cut out for you today." William had been around this family for a long time, and he knew that it could be a little overwhelming if you weren't used to it. He turned to Alee and gave her a hug. It reminded her of her father—not Eric, but David—the man who had raised her. The man she still felt in her heart was her dad, and, standing there with William's arms around her she started to cry. "It's OK. You're going to be fine. Just breathe." He was calm, no matter the situation, and it made Alee feel like she really would be fine. She was surrounded by people who loved her, in their own way. When the hug finally ended she could see on her cousins' faces, and in Kyle's eyes, exactly what it had felt like to be hugged like that by her grandfather—love.

She was ready for the day. "Let's go!"

18

Petra and Phoebe followed Kyle and Alee to school, staying as close as possible the whole way. They arrived just after first period ended, and slipped pretty much unnoticed into the crowd of students who filled the hallways. Each of them knew their role in the plan, and they were ready, or at least as ready as they would ever be.

Alee held on tight to the wooden talisman in her pocket as she approached Damian's locker. He had been busy gathering his books into his backpack when she came up behind him. "Hey Damian, how are you?" Alee heard how his heart pounded rapidly with surprise, and then how it slowed to an unusually slow pace as soon as he turned around to see her standing there.

"Oh God, Aleerah, you scared me." He turned back to his locker and finished what he was doing before shutting the door and slinging his bag over his shoulder. "I'm fine. How about you? Did you need something?"

"Um, no, I was just wondering—I mean, Kyle and I have been getting pretty close, and since you're one of his best friends—."

"Was."

"What?"

"I *was* one of his best friends. Until—" He stopped himself, but Alee could tell there was something burning inside of him, just waiting for the right moment to get out, and she had a pretty good idea of what it was. "—you know what, it's not important. So, what were you going to say?"

"Well, I was just thinking, since you're close, it might be nice for all of us to get together and get to know each other, outside of the school cafeteria that is." Damian couldn't hide the fact that he wasn't really interested. It was written all over his face. "It's just dinner, and you can bring Victoria too, if you want."

"I don't know. It's just—."

"I don't know a lot of people." It just came out, like a plea for pity. "I'm new in town, and Kyle was the first person to really be nice to me. Sometimes I try too hard to make a good impression, and it backfires. I tend to talk too much, and I know my family can seem a little weird at times, but hey, whose isn't, right? They're actually pretty cool once you get to know them." She was starting to ramble, but it seemed to be working. "I'm not perfect, and I don't expect anyone else to be either. God knows I have my flaws. I tend to pop my gum. I ramble when I'm nervous. And I have the worst frizzy red hair—."

Danielle had joined them without Alee noticing it, and was standing right behind her. Her former best friend interrupted Alee's rant. "You have blonde hair!"

"What?" Alee was startled.

"You have blonde hair, not red," Danielle said, flatly.

Busted! Alee's hands flew out of her pockets to her hair. It only took that simple fumble for Alee to let down her guard. *Oh God what have I done?*

What did you—? It was Damian's voice in her head, and she quickly put up her metaphysical walls again, blocking him out.

"I dye it. I used to get called carrot top at my last school. I just wanted a fresh start here." Turning back to Damian, she tried to undo the damage. "Look, I know you guys lost a close friend recently. Kyle told me about her, and I don't want to take her place, I swear. I was just hoping that maybe there might be room for me in your group sometimes." Dani and Damian just stared at her not saying a word. "OK, I get it. I'm sorry I bothered you. I'll go."

Just as she was turning to leave, Danielle put a hand on her shoulder. "It takes a lot of courage to put yourself out there like you just did. I'm sorry if I've been—." She swallowed back her pride. "—rude. It's just that Alee was my best friend, and it just felt like Kyle was trying to replace her or something. It was just too soon."

Damian still hadn't said a word. He just stood there watching Alee's every expression—every move, through narrow, questioning eyes. When he finally did speak it wasn't at all what Alee would have expected. "Yeah, I can see you two being friends, in time anyway."

"What?" Alee and Danielle responded simultaneously, and then, as if on cue, they started to giggle.

Rolling his eyes at their very teenage girl giggly response, Damian turned back to Alee with a newfound confidence he hadn't had before. "So, dinner. You were asking me out, right?" Alee's cheeks turned bright red, and she stood there not knowing where to go with this.

Damian took a step forward, backing Alee into the locker next to his. They were inches apart, and something inside of her desperately wanted to close the gap. "I'm only kidding, but just for the record, I wouldn't have said no." The corners of his mouth turned up just a little as he leaned in those last two inches and planted a kiss on her lips. It wasn't chaste and innocent, but hard and urgent—almost like he would eat her piece by piece, starting with her mouth, if he could. When he pulled away Alee released a long shuddering breath she hadn't even known she was holding. Damian continued, "And about dinner, just let me know when and where. Victoria and I will come." He slid his left hand down her right arm, stopping for only a second to squeeze her hand. "Or if you'd rather it just be the two of us, I can leave my sister at home. Think about it." Then he turned to leave, and left Alee and Danielle standing there alone.

Alee shouted with a quivering voice, "Um, my place six o'clock—tonight." He just glanced over his shoulder and nodded. "Kyle can give you—." There was no need to finish because Damian was already gone, down another hallway. She turned around astonished, and looked at Dani. "Did he just—?"

Alee didn't even finish her question before Danielle was answering. "Oh yeah." It was just like old times, only Alee was the only one who actually knew it.

"Oh, my God!" Alee had never known Damian to be so self-confident or domineering. He had kissed her a couple of times, but it had been more of a plea then a show of dominance. This had been completely different. She wondered what their relationship would have been like if he had been more assertive back when she was Alee. She wondered if they would have still stayed only friends or if their friendship would have evolved into something more.

"Right?! Damian never hits on anyone. I don't even think he's ever been on a date." Danielle grabbed Alee's hand and starting pulling her down the hallway. "Come on, let's go."

"Where?"

"This is big news. Victoria has got to hear about it. She is going to be so shocked."

"Danielle, no please." She stopped, and Daniele turned to face her. "Victoria doesn't like me. I'm not sure what I did to her, but she doesn't. I just don't want to get off on another bad foot. You know what I mean?"

"It's Dani."

"What?"

"If we're going to try to be friends, other than the fake plastic friends you only talk to while you're at school—then you should call me Dani. And, if you really don't want me to say anything to Victoria then I won't. I just figured she might get a kick out of it. Her brother isn't really the social type. The only girl he has ever liked was Alee, and I don't think he ever so much as winked at her, let alone talked to her like that. Well, they kissed once—at least that's what Victoria said. Let's just say he waited till it was too late to tell anyone how he felt. So, it's kind of a step in the right direction, for him to be able to do and say what he just did. You know what I mean?"

Alee knew exactly what she meant, more than she could ever say. She also knew that there were times when Damian was able to show how he felt just fine, but she was already with Kyle, so even though she wasn't dead it was still too late. "I get it. It's just Kyle, you know? Their friendship has already been through so much, I don't want to mess it up even more." The bell rang, but Alee didn't seem to notice. "So now what?"

"Now we go to class because that was the bell, and I'm late for a bio quiz." Dani turned to leave. "See you at lunch?"

"Uh, yeah. OK." Dani was gone somewhere down the hall, and Alee was left standing in the hallway all by herself. She had hoped to get Damian and Victoria to come over for dinner, but she had never imagined that the invitation would lead to rebuilding her friendship with Dani. Her day had just gotten a thousand times better than she would ever have thought possible.

On her way to class Alee slipped into the girls' bathroom. Pulling her cell phone out of her pocket she quickly dialed Eric's number, but it was Loraline who answered. "Aleerah? Is everything OK?"

"Um, yeah—. Can I talk to Eri—to Dad, please?"

"I'm sorry, he's—."

"Not there?"

"No, he's here, but he can't—."

"You realize you're being weird right? Just tell me."

"Aleerah, I think this is something your father really should explain to you, not me. In short, it's the middle of the day, and although he is old, and can stay awake through most of the daylight hours, he does need his rest—about four or five hours a day, when the sun is at its peak."

"Oh." The silence on the line was so thick you could cut it with a knife. "But, I've seen him...I mean, I've been with him when he's been awake during the middle of the day."

"I understand that. Yes, if he needs to, he can do it. It just takes some extra feeding. Like I said this is really something your father should explain to you."

"Um, OK."

"You called for a reason. Can I help you?" Loraline had been struggling daily for Alee's attention, and had been feeling like she was getting nowhere. "Aleerah, can I do anything?"

"It actually wasn't a big deal. I just wanted to let him know that Damian and Victoria will be joining us for dinner tonight. I told them to be there at six o'clock. I hope that works."

"It does. Thank you."

"No problem, I'll see you after school. I gotta run." Alee hung up without saying goodbye. She wasn't trying to be rude; she was just being the teenager she was.

By the time third period was over sleep deprivation had started to take its toll on Alee. She hadn't slept at all the night before, and she was finding it hard to keep her eyes open. When Jathan walked up behind her and slid his hand around hers she barely even noticed. "Hey you, are you OK?" He sounded far away, and dreamy.

"I think I just need a little—." Alee passed out right there in his arms.

"Hmmm, so I *am* going to have to carry you all semester." He lifted her up, and carried her through the hallway all the way to the front office, and sat her down in one of the hard plastic chairs. Then he turned to Ms. Thatcher who was sitting quietly reading a book, and trying hard not to be bothered. "Ms. Thatcher, this is Aleerah Wenham. She's sick. She needs an excuse for her afternoon classes."

Ms. Thatcher didn't even look up from her book as she spoke to him. "Hmmm, she already knows the drill, but give this to her and make sure she has her parents sign it before she comes back tomorrow morning."

"OK, fine." He snatched the paper out of her hand then turned back to Alee, who was slowly coming around.

"I'll be right back. I'm going to go get you some water. Don't go anywhere OK?" She just nodded before he took off for the cafeteria. He grabbed a bottle of water, but before he left he stopped by the table at the back of the room.

"—I really thought she'd be here," Dani was saying, sounding almost disappointed.

Kyle tried to fix things up. "I'm sure she's coming. She probably just got caught up in class." He was saying the right things, but he just didn't sound all that convincing. Damian and Victoria were nowhere around, and out of the corner of his eye Kyle could see Phoebe pacing the back cafeteria entrance. He couldn't help but wonder what had sparked Dani's sudden interest in Alee anyway. "What the?" Kyle's hands flew to the sides of his head as a sharp pain pierced his temples.

"Are you OK?" Dani was up and at his side in seconds.

"I don't know. I have the worst headache all of a—."

"Sorry to interrupt. Hey Kyle."

Kyle didn't look up but he knew the voice instantly. "Jathan!" Kyle didn't trust Jathan. They had only met once, in his bedroom, under the most bizarre circumstances.

Jathan leaned over so that only Kyle was able to hear his words. "I just wanted to let you know that Aleerah got sick during Art class. She's in the nurse's office." Kyle started to stand, but Jathan stopped him. "She's talking with Nurse Johnson, but she wanted me to tell you that she's OK—just a little dehydrated." He held up the bottle of water, almost like it was the solution to everything. Kyle didn't notice. He was too busy trying not to vomit—the headache that had come on so suddenly was turning into a full-blown migraine. Jathan stood up, watching Kyle struggle, "You know, you don't look so good yourself. Maybe Dani here can get you some water."

"Yeah" was pretty much all he could get out at the time, and Dani jumped up and headed toward the line.

"I think Nurse Johnson's going to drive Aleerah home," Jathan said. Then he pulled a piece of folded paper out of his pocket and handed it to Kyle. "Aleerah asked me to give this to you. She said you'd know what to do."

"I'm sure she did." As Jathan turned to leave Kyle called back, "Oh, hey, did she talk to you about dinner tonight?"

Jathan smiled. "Yeah, sounds great. I'll be there. Her parent's place, right?" Kyle nodded. "It should be fun." When he turned back toward the table Dani was there with a water bottle, staring wide-eyed at him.

"So, what was all that about? Who is that guy anyway? I don't think I've seen him before." She handed him the water and he quickly downed half without even blinking.

"His name's Jathan. He's a friend of Aleerah's."

"Oh." She nodded toward the paper in his hand. "What's that?"

"I don't know." He unfolded the paper and started reading the letter out loud so Dani could hear it too. "Kyle, I'm not feeling well. I think I just need a little sleep. I've been thinking, and I'm not sure you should come over tonight." He read the rest to himself as Dani just watched. *"I just don't know what my family has planned, and it could get dangerous. I hope you understand."* At the bottom of the page she had signed, *Love, Alee.* Kyle quickly crumpled the note into a ball and shoved it deep into his pocket.

Dani didn't seem to notice him trying to hide the paper, maybe because she was still focused on the fact that

Aleerah had told him not to come to her house, and Dani knew that she had invited Damian to dinner. "Are you OK?"

"Yeah, sure. Why wouldn't I be?" Kyle was trying, and failing, to pretend that he didn't care.

"I don't know, maybe because your girlfriend told you not to come over, or maybe because she invited Damian to dinner, and not you."

"It's cool. Aleerah just wants to get to know my friends better, you know? Maybe she feels like she can do that easier just one on one."

"Yeah, no I was there when she asked him. I'm sure she does want to get to know him better, one on one. It was plastered all over her face, right after he backed her into the locker and kissed her."

"He what?" Kyle was taking long deep breaths, trying not to lose it right there in the cafeteria.

"Oh, she didn't tell you? I wonder why, I really thought she would have."

"Look, I gotta run. I need to grab some Excedrin from the nurse. Besides, I want to check on Aleerah before she heads home." He stood up and grabbed his tray so quickly he almost dumped it all over Tyler who was walking up behind him.

"Hey man, what's up?"

"Nothing really. Dani can fill you in."

"Cool," he murmured. As Kyle left, he could see out of the corner of his eye as Tyler lifted Dani out of her chair, wrapped his arms around her, and planted a kiss on her lips. "Hey baby."

"Hey yourself."

Kyle made his way out of the crowded cafeteria and down the hall to Alee's locker, hoping to catch up with her before she left, but she wasn't there. When he opened it up everything was cleared out. "What the—."

"What's going on?" Phoebe was standing right behind him as he slammed the locker door shut.

"Jesus, Phoebe, you don't *always* have to sneak up on people." He leaned against the locker. "Apparently Aleerah got sick during art class, and the school nurse is going to take her home. I needed to talk to her first, but—."

"But what?"

Something didn't feel right, but he couldn't pinpoint what it was exactly. "I don't know. Jathan told me she was going to go home, but that was only a couple of minutes ago. Then I get here and her locker is cleared out—completely. That's not like her at all."

"Do you trust Jathan?"

He just shook his head. "I can't say that I do, no."

"Well, don't overreact." Phoebe laughed. "Let's just go check with Nurse Green and see what's going on."

"Nurse Green? Jathan said she was with Nurse Johnson." With that they started running down the hall to the nurse's office. When they got there the lights were off and the door was locked. Kyle didn't hesitate. He turned and ran back to the front office, with Phoebe following close behind, only stopping when he literally ran into the counter. "Ms. Thatcher, is Nurse Johnson here today?"

"Young man, Nurse Johnson hasn't worked here in over a year, and Nurse Green has the day off, so if you don't feel well you'll just have to suffer through today, or request a slip to be released for the rest of the day."

"No, it's not me. Aleerah Wenham is sick—."

"Yes, I already know. You brought her in only five minutes ago." She rolled her eyes as she looked up at Kyle's worried eyes. "I'll tell you this, that girl gets sick more often than anyone I have ever met. Well, maybe not anyone." There was a glint in her eye that said she knew something that they didn't, but then her attention went straight back to the book she was reading as if Kyle didn't really matter. "Ms. Wenham has already left. You'll just have to wait until after school to see if she's OK."

"Ms. Thatcher I didn't bring Aleerah to the office."

"Well, I may be old but I'm not *that* old. I don't know what kind of game you're playing, but it isn't going to work. Now go run along and get back to lunch."

Phoebe bolted from the office and pulled her cell phone out of her pocket. She speed dialed her sister Petra. "Hey, supposedly Aleerah got sick in class and is being taken home by the school nurse, but the nurse she is supposed to be with doesn't work at the school any more. Ms. Thatcher said Kyle brought her into the office to be released for the day, but Kyle has been in the cafeteria. I'm thinking she's with Jathan. Any way you can make sure she makes it home OK?"

"When is she leaving?"

"She already left. You should have seen them come out a few minutes ago."

Petra was in the school parking lot with a great view of the main entrance, and a perfect view of the only parking lot exit. "Phoebe, I've been out here since I dropped you guys off this morning. If she had come out I would have seen her. No one has left the building."

The color drained out of Phoebe's face as if she had just seen a ghost. "If he's not driving her home, then maybe they used—." She swallowed hard. "Petra, where's the door?"

Kyle could hear Petra yelling through the phone. "No Phoebe. You can't go down there alone."

"Just tell me where the door is."

"No."

They were arguing, and people were starting to stare, more than usual, as they passed Phoebe in the hallway. "I'll take Kyle with me, OK? You go home and let everyone know what's going on. But, first you have to tell me where the door is before they get too far."

19

Atlanta High was a rather large school building, what with all of the recent renovations, but most students had no idea how large it really was. Phoebe held her cell phone to her ear, and with her other hand she gripped Kyle's hand, leading him down hallway after hallway. When they finally stopped they were in the science wing in front of an unmarked door at the end of the hall. She opened it to find a dark stairwell. "Well, here goes nothing." She and Kyle went down the stairs, hand in hand. On the phone, she whispered to Petra, "We're at the bottom of the stairs. Just tell me one more time where we're going. Hello?" After a few seconds of silence she looked at the phone—no signal. She shoved the phone into her pocket. "I guess we're on our own now." She looked back over her shoulder and up the stairs they had just descended. "It shouldn't be far from here." Then, looking around, she led him down the hall to the right. After making a few turns, and backtracking a couple of times, they finally stopped in front of a large wooden door. "This is it," Phoebe said.

"Phoebe, are you sure this is a good idea? I mean, what's behind that door anyway?"

"Listen Kyle, you've seen a lot, and I'm actually impressed that we haven't scared you away yet. So, if you don't want to go you don't have to, but I do." She was about to break every rule in the book by taking a human into the Underground without permission, but if her gut instinct was right, she was going to need his help to get Alee back. "Behind this door is the Underground. It's where members of our society—witches, vampires, fairies, basically everyone who isn't merely mortal—can live free without fear of exposure. What you see behind this door you must never speak of. Do you understand?"

Kyle only nodded.

"While we're in there, you keep hold of my hand. You don't speak unless I tell you to. They must all think that you're my—pet." Phoebe almost choked on the word, and when his eyes snapped up to meet hers she could feel his anger. "I'm sorry. That's just the way it is down there. If you want to stay alive you'll play along." Again Kyle just nodded, but she could tell he wasn't happy about it.

She opened the door, and grabbed his hand. "Ahhhh! Crap, Phoebe, the other hand please."

"Oh, yeah sorry." Grabbing his other hand she led him into a darkened hallway as the door closed slowly behind them.

"I'm sorry, did you say fairies?" Everything was sinking in.

"Yeah, but don't let them fool you, they aren't the Disney kind with pixie dust to make you fly when you think happy thoughts." She laughed out loud, and he squeezed her hand tighter in his. "Sorry. It's just that fairies kind of have a bad reputation, but some of them are actually pretty cool, so

I'm told. Don't tell anyone, but when I was a kid I used wish I was a fairy. I mean, they get to read minds, and some even have the power of invisibility. How cool is that?! But as I get older, I'm glad I'm not one. I think the *eating babies* part kind of ruins it all for me."

"Um. Yeah, OK." Kyle was too nervous to think about anything other than the dark hallway, and the fact that Alee was somewhere lost down there. The hallway seemed to get lighter the farther they walked. "Where do you think they are?"

"I don't know, but if we keep going this way we should reach the main strip in a few minutes. From there you can pretty much get anywhere in Atlanta." She gestured toward a light at the far end of the hall. "We need to go through the door down that way. Once we're on the main strip you need to keep your eyes on the floor. I'll have to ask around to see if anyone has seen her, but leave the talking to me."

"If that's what it takes." He wasn't happy about it, but he knew he was walking into unfamiliar territory, and it was pretty clear that he didn't have the upper hand.

They were weaving in and out of people in no time, negotiating their way down the main strip. Kyle didn't look up, but he could feel everyone's eyes burning into his flesh. Phoebe stopped a couple of people to ask directions, and to inquire whether or not anyone had seen a slender young man around seventeen or eighteen with wavy black hair, with a girl around seventeen with golden blonde hair, come through the tunnels recently. No one would even look at her let alone give her any information. After questioning at least ten people and getting the same lack of a response every time, she knew she was going in the right direction. Sometimes no answer at all is your answer. The Underground isn't that much different than the world above. When there's danger, or even the perception of danger, most people tend to keep their mouths shut and look the other way, trying their best not to get noticed. "Come on. This way." She pulled Kyle to follow her deeper into the tunnels, but eventually the trail went cold.

They searched for over an hour without so much as a clue as to where they might have gone. When they finally stopped their search they were standing in front of the Underground entrance to The Black Onyx. Kyle looked up, reading the sign to himself, baffled by the fact that they had come that far in such a short time. Defeated, Phoebe unlocked and opened the door, and they made their way into the back hallways of the shop, stopping only when they reached the door to Alee's bedroom. Kyle knocked. It was wishful thinking, but he still couldn't help himself. When she didn't respond he tried the doorknob, it was unlocked. He slowly pushed the door open, and poked his head around the door. There, sleeping on the bed, was Alee, wrapped in a blanket and sleeping peacefully.

Meanwhile, up in the kitchen, literally *everyone* was planning what to do next in their family effort to find her. Petra had made it home in less than twenty minutes, and they had started working right away. The men had left to search and secure the shop and the surrounding land. Loraline and Jacinda were hovered over a map, scrying, in an effort to pinpoint Alee's location but having little success. Elaine, Elizabeth and Estelle were busy mixing a potion that they planned to use in a ritual only as a last resort if the scrying didn't work, and Elaine's daughters Melissa and Michelle sat with a crystal ball between them as they searched the Underground. Edith, the only one not busy, sat silently in a corner, meditating. Everyone had their jobs, and they were all so focused that when Phoebe and Kyle walked in with Alee, who was still barely awake and stumbling behind them, no one even noticed.

"Have you already started cooking?" Alee was shocked to find so many people working on a dinner that was only meant for her and a few of her friends.

The room went quiet instantly, and all eyes turned to Alee. Loraline ran to her, turning her around and around, examining every inch of her. "Are you hurt? What did he do to you? Do you feel all right?"

Alee pushed away from Loraline's probing hands. "I'm fine." She scanned the faces around the room. For the most part everyone seemed worried, but a few seemed genuinely scared, and Alee didn't understand why. "I told him when he brought me home that I just needed a little sleep. I feel much better now."

"When who brought you home sweetheart?" Loraline held Alee's hand in her own.

"Kyle."

"I—?" Kyle looked at Phoebe for help. "First Ms. Thatcher and now her? Why?" Phoebe knew that Kyle hadn't brought Alee home from school, but why would Alee think he had?

"Kyle's been with me." Phoebe jumped in explaining, for what it was worth.

Edith knew instantly what had happened, "It's what they do. It's the only way a dream walker has any power. He must have gotten into the child's head, and altered her memory. That means he's already been here." She moved through the room and out into the shop gathering a number of large crystals.

Loraline stood in shock, not wanting to let go of her daughter, and she didn't have to. Jacinda followed her grandmother's lead, as did the others. "We'll need to secure the shop to keep him out.

Alee was trying to catch up, but was still having trouble understanding everything that was going on around her. "Keep who out?"

"The dream walker—the young boy from your school, Aleerah." Edith said it almost as if annoyed by the fact that she had to explain herself.

Eyes wide, Alee asked, "You mean Jathan?"

"Fine, Jathan yes, he mustn't be allowed to return. He has gotten too close to you already."

Kyle sat Alee down at the table before explaining. "But Jathan is coming here tonight for dinner." Kyle was shocked that he was the only one who was thinking clearly.

Shaking her head, Alee tugged on the sleeve of Kyle's shirt to get his attention. "I didn't invite him." Alee's voice was no more than a whisper.

Kyle turned to her suddenly. "What do you mean you didn't invite him? When I talked to him he said you had already told him about dinner this evening. He said he'd be here."

"But I didn't."

Kyle pulled the crumpled letter out of his pocket. "He gave me this, said it was from you."

Alee read the note and shook her head. "I didn't write this Kyle. This isn't even my handwriting."

Kyle looked at the letter again. "Wait. It can't be."
"What?"

"It looks like my—nothing, never mind."

"Kyle, I invited Damian and Victoria. I wouldn't have invited Jathan tonight. I don't know how he found out."

"Next you're going to tell me you didn't kiss Damian either?" Alee didn't speak, didn't move, and didn't even breathe.

"Silence!" Something had changed in Edith. Her eyes went black and her skin turned cold as ice. "It doesn't matter who invited him!" She wasn't yelling—she didn't have to—but Alee and everyone else in the room could see an anger inside of her that was almost unnatural. "He is not welcome in my house!"

Alee tried to right things. "Kyle's right, Granny. He's already been invited, and besides, Eric, I mean Dad, said to—."

Edith snapped back with a bite that made Alee's eyes begin to water. "Your father said nothing of the sort. He told you to bring your friends to dinner. He never mentioned the dream walker."

"But he's my—" Everyone's eyes were already on her and Edith, but now they went to her. "—my friend."

Edith took a step back and a deep breath in. "You may *think* he is your friend, but dream walkers never do anything without a plan that benefits their own agenda. If he has led you to believe he is a friend then his plan must involve you specifically. To what end, I am not sure, but I can promise you it isn't going to be good." Then, turning her back on Alee, she stood before her family with sadness in her eyes, but power in her heart. "We have never welcomed a dream walker into our home. They are vindictive by nature, and will do anything in their power to get what they want, whatever that may be. I do not know what he is after, but we must be prepared for anything. We won't be able to keep him out, but we may be able to shield our minds from him, and protect our family.

20

Shortly before everyone was scheduled to arrive, the phone rang. It was Damian. "Is Aleerah there please?"

Melissa, Loraline's cousin, had answered the phone while everyone else was fussing about, preparing not only dinner but also potions, crystals, and talismans to be used as protective devices. "One moment please." With her hand covering the mouthpiece of the phone she called out to Alee who was on the other side of the room sitting with Kyle, working on homework they had gotten earlier that day and trying not to worry about everything else. "Aleerah, it's your friend Damian."

Alee jumped up immediately. She had no idea what to expect. She had been nervous all day about this, and just wanted the evening to be over. She knew that the Guardian bands were of importance to her father, and that there was more to the story that her family wasn't telling her, but right now it didn't matter. She had to support her family's wishes, and that meant going through with this dinner even if she wasn't really sure what her father had in store for her friends.

"Hello?"

"Aleerah?"

"Hi Damian, what's up?" Her voice was shaking, but she couldn't stop it.

"Um, who answered the phone?"

Alee looked around the room and realized that not a single person was moving or talking or even breathing perceptibly. They were all looking at her, waiting to find out what was happening at the other end of the phone line. "Oh, that was my mom's cousin Melissa. Why?"

There was only silence on the other end of the line. "Damian?"

"How did she know my name?"

"What?"

"I didn't tell her my name, but I heard her telling you. So how did she know who was calling?"

Alee didn't know what to say. Her mind was completely blank, but then it came to her. Duh! "You're calling from your cell phone right? Caller ID, silly." It was such an Alee thing to say that it almost felt unnatural now. She knew that Melissa hadn't actually seen his name on the caller ID. They didn't actually have caller ID, which until just then hadn't seemed weird. How she knew it was him, Alee had no idea, but she was starting to realize that her family members had a lot more powers, or talents, as they liked to call them, than any of them came right out and said.

"Oh, right." Damian's voice cracked. "That makes sense. Sorry."

"No big deal. So, are you and Victoria lost? It can be a little confusing trying to get here during the day, let alone in the dark. I can get my mom to give you directions if you—."

"No." He interrupted her before she could even finish. "I mean, no we're not lost. We actually can't—. My mom said I can't go out tonight. I failed a history test, so—. Besides, Victoria isn't feeling well. It's probably best she doesn't come either."

"Oh, OK, so um, maybe another time?" Alee was a little relieved inside, but also a little hurt. Hurt because Damian and Victoria had no idea that her family was planning anything, and it was clear they just chose not to come. Damian was a history buff, and aced every history project, paper, exam, and test. There was no way he had failed a history test, so the only explanation was that they had chosen not to come. If he had said science, maybe she would have believed him, but not history.

There was a click on the other end of the phone without so much as a goodbye. Alee slowly hung up the phone and walked back to where Kyle was eagerly waiting. "They're not coming."

"What? Why?"

Alee rolled her eyes and half laughed out of shear frustration. "Damian says his mom won't let them come. Supposedly Victoria isn't feeling well, and Damian said he failed a history test."

"Give me a break. Damian doesn't fail at anything. Well maybe science. Something about dissecting a dead frog last year really got to him."

"Yeah well, he either failed or he's lying so he doesn't have to come over."

Kyle took her in his arms and hugged her tightly against his chest. "Don't worry. Everything will be fine."

Meanwhile, Edith was gathering her daughters and granddaughters around her. "The shifters may not be coming, but I'm sure the walker will still make an appearance."

At that point all Alee wanted to do was go back to her room and lose herself in her dreams. She didn't want to think about Jathan coming over or the fact that Damian had lied to her.

Edith crossed the room and stood before Aleerah. "Well then, you kids should go get dressed, and you too Phoebe. We'll finish cleaning up here and when your friend arrives we'll call you."

As Phoebe, Aleerah, and Kyle left the kitchen, Edith turned back to the rest of her family and started divvying out the real assignments. "With the shifters no longer under our watch here, we're going to need more protection for Eric and the others. Melissa and Michelle, you'll go with Eric. You're the best at cloaking spells. Make sure he gets in and out undetected.

"Can't he just do that shadow thing he does?" Melissa and Michelle asked simultaneously.

"Vampire parlor tricks aren't going to work very well if he comes across shifters other than the children. He needs to be protected, now go." Turning to her granddaughter, she said, "Jacinda, you and Petra will need to prepare a second exit plan in case something goes wrong."

Down the hall behind the closed door of Alee's bedroom Kyle sat patiently waiting for Alee to come out of the bathroom where she was busily changing her clothes and primping herself for the evening. When the door finally opened and Kyle looked up he couldn't believe his eyes; Alee stood there in a flowing black satin dress that fit her curves perfectly and ended just above her knees. Her hair was pulled back in a loose ponytail with a few loose tendrils framing her face. Her smoky eye shadow and sparkling lip gloss were the icing on the cake.

Kyle was stunned.

She stood in the doorway waiting, but his lack of a response was better than anything he could have said. "I figure there's no reason we can't still enjoy tonight," Alee whispered. Kyle just smiled back at her and nodded.

Just as she was about to run into his arms there was a knock at the door. "Aleerah, open the door. It's Petra."

Alee hesitated, but crossed to the door with Kyle following quickly behind. As soon as she opened the door Alee noticed that Petra had changed clothes, but not into something for a fancy dinner party with friends. She was wearing heavy black military boots, black leather pants, and a skintight long-sleeve shirt, also black. Her hair was pulled back into a sleek ponytail. She was clearly ready to kick some butt if necessary, but Alee wasn't sure who Petra's primary target was, and the way she stepped into the room Alee was just praying it wasn't her.

"Do you own anything that isn't black?" Kyle was checking out her rather scary outfit.

"What would you rather me wear, Kyle, a pink mini-skirt with a floral print blouse?" She turned to Alee. "Granny said dinner's ready. No sign of—*Oh my God Aleerah, you look amazing!*"

Alee couldn't help but blush. "Thanks, so now what?"

"Well, for now, the two of you and Phoebe are going to start dinner and act like everything is normal. If Jathan shows up, which I personally don't think will happen, just invite him in to join you." She might look tough on the outside, but what Alee was most aware of was Petra's pounding heartbeat and the scent of perspiration that always accompanies fear.

"What makes you so sure he won't show up?" Alee asked.

"Honestly, I don't know. I just think that if he were planning something he would have done it by now. Besides, if it was you he wanted why even bring you back earlier today? Why not just keep you?" Petra did have a point.

Before heading up to dinner Kyle wrapped his arm around Alee's waist and they started toward the door. "So, what are you going to be doing tonight while we're enjoying dinner?"

"Protecting your butts of course," Petra laughed. "No, but seriously—. I'll be with my mom—recon stuff that you really shouldn't be worried about. Your dad has the search under control, and your mom has just about everything upstairs taken care of too." She laughed, but still Alee could sense an underlying tension and nervousness.

Out in the hallway they parted ways, Alee and Kyle going back toward the kitchen and Petra going deeper down the hall toward the mysterious wooden door that led to the Underground tunnels. "Be careful, OK?"

"Always am!" Then with a smile she was gone—disappeared into the dark hallway.

Dinner started out a little awkwardly, as the three of them stared at their food, waiting for the doorbell to ring. Everyone seemed on edge, and the fact that Alee's mother kept coming in every two minutes to check on them and let them know that Jathan wasn't there yet didn't help. But it didn't take long for them to forget all about Jathan and the others. Phoebe told Alee stories about her childhood and growing up in the Wenham family. Alee told stories about her childhood and how, somehow, dealing with so many doctors, hospitals, and the threat of death for so long kinda made being part vampire easier to handle.

Who would have thought that while they were home having such a great time, something so awful was happening only miles away?

It was true that Damian and Victoria had passed on Alee's dinner invitation because their mom had refused to give them permission. It wasn't because Damian had failed some history test, though. Karen had insisted that it was just too dangerous. She had already banned them from the place when she learned about Victoria's previous experience there. Victoria still had a small scar on her palm where the stone had burned her, and they had no way to defend themselves against that type of magic—let alone anything else the Wenhams decided to throw their way. And Damian and Victoria were staying true to their promise to keep their mom informed of their actual whereabouts at all times.

Damian had been looking forward to the opportunity to look around The Black Onyx for more information on the witches and maybe even his own family, but he realized that trying to do that in a family dinner setting just didn't seem like the best plan. So, when his mom put her foot down, he settled for "picnicking" with Victoria in their own attic, and research the materials their mother had stored there. They had everything set up—sandwiches and chips, and a bag of popcorn for later—and Damian ran downstairs to get their drinks. As he passed the living room he heard the front door lock click. Karen was working late and shouldn't be home for at least another three hours. Damian pressed his back against the wall just around the corner from the front door and listened as the door opened, but when he looked around the corner there was no one there.

"Mom? Mom, are you home?" Cautiously, Damian made his way to the front door, and poked his head out to scan the porch and front yard. *Hmmm, she must have left it ajar.* He pushed the door shut and locked both the doorknob and the deadbolt. Shaking off the uneasy feeling, he headed into the kitchen and grabbed two cokes out of the refrigerator and headed back up to the attic, looking back over his shoulder only once.

After Damian had pulled up the ladder, closing off the attic entrance, Michelle and Melissa shimmered into view. They released the cloaking spell to reveal Eric sitting silently, his back against the hallway wall. His cold, clammy skin was even paler than usual. "Eric, are you all right?" Michelle asked, and Melissa knelt down beside him, with her hand on his shoulder. But Eric gave no response—no indication that he had heard her at all.

If he had still been alive his heart would have been beating a thousand beats per minute: not from fear, not from anger, and not from lust—but from shame and guilt. When he met Loraline so many years ago his world had changed, turned upside down. He had fallen madly in love with her from the second he saw her. It was like nothing he had ever felt in the hundreds of years he had existed. From that moment, he had vowed to himself, and later promised her, never to drink human blood again. And he hadn't—as long as he had Loraline at his side. He had learned to survive solely on the blood of animals, even considering the strong bitter taste.

But that all changed the night he found her lying on their bedroom floor, bleeding to death. When the nurse told him that Loraline was "no longer with us" Eric had vowed to seek revenge.

Revenge didn't come quickly, but it did come. When he finally arrived at the home of his wife's killer it was late, and most of the lights were already out, save for the dim glow of the television. He had entered through the front door— locks mean nothing when you have the strength of a vampire.. And since it was the house of a shape shifter Eric didn't have to worry about being invited in. The rule was pretty simple:

any home occupied by anyone other than a human—vampires, shape shifters, fairies, etc.—was free game. He wasn't concerned about making noise. He wasn't planning to leave any witnesses behind. He found his target half asleep on the couch and was almost disappointed that it was going to be so easy.

He approached from behind, fangs exposed. "Did you really think you could kill my wife, and get away with it?" he hissed. Just as Eric moved to attack, James reached out and grabbed him by the collar of his trench coat, lifted him up, and flung him across the room, straight into the entertainment center. The noise must have woken up James' son because Eric saw a young boy on the stairs, taking in the unexpected scene with confusion and alarm. James leapt up from the couch in one smooth move, transforming into a massive sleek black panther before he landed, crouching, in front of the intruder.

Eric heard a gasp escape the little boy—a sound he would never be able to erase from his memory. But the battle had begun, and the presence of a child wasn't going to change the fact that Eric's wife was dead, and that the man—the animal—here before him had killed her. The fight didn't last long. James had noticed his son, who was still standing on the stairs, and the distraction gave Eric the upper hand, and the ability to rip at James' throat with his teeth. The blood was sweet on his tongue and he longed to drain his prey, but the presence of the child stopped him. His self-control was failing him little by little each day, and the promise he had made to Loraline was of little importance to him without her there, but he wouldn't feed in front of a child. That he still couldn't do.

Just before leaving he looked up into the silent grey eyes of the young boy, and knew he would never forget the fear and pain he saw there. Now, sitting on the floor of this house, it all came rushing back. It wasn't the same house. It wasn't even the same town. But they were the same eyes—Damian's eyes! Grey like the sky before the thunder and lightning is about to start—grey like the fog that rolls in off the lake in the early fall mornings. Here in Damian's home, Eric had just seen that those eyes, still to this day, reflected the fear and pain from so many years ago, and, what was more—they reflected years of anger. No wonder Damian had the Guardian bands if anyone deserved to seek revenge it was Damian, and Eric couldn't blame him for wanting that, but he also didn't regret what he had done. Given the chance he would do it all over again. He would have done anything to protect, or avenge, Loraline, even if that meant killing. Somehow Eric had to find a way to stop Damian from doing whatever he was planning, but that wasn't going to happen tonight.

Sound of movement coming from the attic prompted Michelle to whisper urgently, "Eric, we need to hurry." Eric pulled himself out of the daze and, groggily, pulled himself off the floor. Michelle and Melissa walked close behind him to ensure that their cloaking spell maintained its power. Eric was able to manipulate shadows in order to stay hidden, but he had chosen to have Michelle and Melissa there because their spells were powerful enough to hide him not only visually but also to hide his scent. He knew that if Damian and Victoria were in fact the shape shifters they were looking for, then they would be able to smell him coming—if they knew what they were doing.

Eric searched the ground floor of the house, then moved upstairs to the bedrooms. He stayed in Damian's room the longest—not because he had found anything useful there, but because of the picture on the dresser. It was the young Damian sitting on his father's shoulders. Father and son were both smiling, both happy. There was no doubt that Damian's father was the man Eric had so brutally murdered so many years ago. He was the 'kill' that had tipped the scale, and led Eric on a ten-year downslide before he picked himself back up and forced himself back onto animal blood. He knew he would have to do it—not for himself, but for his daughter who would soon be coming of age.

As the three 'visitors' were leaving Damian's room the overhead entrance to the attic dropped open. The three backed themselves tightly against the wall, breathing as little as necessary. Damian and Victoria both came down the stairs, closed up the attic, and headed for Victoria's room.

Eric followed, staying slightly behind, but when he hit a creak in the hardwood floor both Damian and Victoria turned to look. The cloaking spell was still working, and Damian turned and walked away, but Victoria wasn't as convinced. She went back to where Eric had stopped, sniffed around him and even reached out into the air, just missing his face by inches. "Do you smell that?" She stayed there for a good thirty seconds before turning to follow her brother into her room. "You know Damian, if Mom's plan works we're going to need more bands."

"Like I said, V, I'm not so concerned about getting more—that shouldn't be hard. What I want to know is whether we're missing a band, or if he only made nine. If one is missing then we need to find that first."

Victoria just rolled her eyes. "Yeah, but Damian, the Founders' Celebration is only three weeks away. It took that long to get the nine we have. If mom needs us to get another ten, or even more, we need to request them right away. The missing band isn't going to matter a whole lot after the Celebration is over."

"And how do you plan on explaining that we need more? Hell, I don't even know how you convinced him to do the last set. You had told him the first one was for me, right?"

"Yeah, but like I told you before, Mr. Knowles and Ms. Pickett are on our side. He told me, 'don't think of us as your enemy. When you are ready to talk, we will listen. You're not alone.' Blah—blah—blah, something about allies." Victoria just laughed. "That's why I told Mom about him. She wanted to see a picture of him, and as soon as she saw his photo in the teacher section of the yearbook she remembered him. Apparently their families used to be close, before Grandpa went all crazy."

"Grandpa didn't go crazy, the vampires did. If they hadn't massacred everyone and kicked us out of the Underground none of this would even be necessary." Damian turned away and continued into the bedroom.

"Yeah, I get that D." Victoria followed behind "But Grandpa didn't have to bind everyone's abilities. What was the point of that?"

Then Eric saw it. As Victoria walked away she reached up to pull her hair into a ponytail. The sleeve of her shirt slid just low enough to reveal the dark brown leather band that fit loosely around her wrist.

Convinced that the remaining bands must be hidden somewhere in the attic he ended the search. He led Melissa and Michelle back downstairs and out into the front yard. "We'll have to come back later when they're both at school. We need to get into that attic." The girls nodded in agreement and Eric tossed his truck keys to Melissa and disappeared down the road.

Back at The Black Onyx Michelle and Melissa contemplated whether or not to tell Loraline about Eric's strange behavior upon seeing the photo of the boy and his father. They didn't know what it meant and weren't sure if it was their place to bring it up or not. In the end they decided that it wasn't significant and they kept it to themselves. They gave Loraline a basic account of the 'visit,' and explained that they would have to go back again to check out the attic. They added that Eric had gone off into the woods for a while, and would be back a little later. Then they left Loraline alone, sitting in front of the fireplace waiting for Eric to return. Around three o'clock in the morning she was woken up by a soft whisper in her ear. "I love you."

"I love you more."

"Not possible."

When she opened her eyes he was kneeling before her, eyes bloodshot from tears that wouldn't come. "Are you OK?" She had never seen Eric this way in all the years she had known him, and she was truly concerned.

"I will be."

She took his hand in her own, and kissed his palm. "Are you hungry?" Eric just nodded, and she was up and out of the room in seconds. She returned with a sports bottle from the kitchen, and he gladly took it.

They spent the rest of the night in front of the fire. They talked about Damian and Victoria, and they brainstormed all the possibilities of what they could be planning. "She said it was their mother's plan."

"What's their mother's name?" Loraline was trying to figure out why someone so new to town would have a grudge against the Founders.

"I don't think that matters. Obviously they know what the bands are, and if they're planning to get more it means there must be a lot of them." Eric sat back, just staring into the fire. He was considering whether to tell Loraline about what had happened on that night so long ago. It had been five years after her 'death,' and in his heart he had finally avenged her murder—and the fact that he later discovered that she was still alive didn't really change that. In the end he decided that there were more important things to be thinking about right now. The Founders' Celebration was only weeks away, and, with what little information he had, Eric wasn't confident that he would be able to stop whatever might be coming.

For the next few weeks until the Celebration, Eric, although seemingly absent, was keeping a close eye on The Black Onyx. After the discovery of the Guardian bands, he and the other founding members of Atlanta were working day and night to ensure that nothing could go wrong during the annual event.

They had gone to great lengths to protect their members, and make sure that no one not on the list could gain access to the ballroom prior to the event. Although Eric hadn't been able to find the bands, he was confident of the precautions that were being taken, and that no matter what Damian and his family were planning, there was no way they would succeed.

21

Call it cliché, trite, tired, or unoriginal—call it what you will. But the Atlanta Founders' Celebration has always been on the evening of the wiccan Festival of Darkness, also known as Samhain, or, to mere humans, as Halloween. That particular date had been selected because a majority of the original town founders were of wiccan faith, and even though the sole remaining founders were all vampires, the tradition continued in their honor.

Samhain is one of two different spirit-nights of the year, the other being Beltane, which is celebrated at the beginning of May. Those of wiccan faith believe that during the spirit-nights the veil between the worlds is lifted, briefly. It is a time to commune with long lost ancestors, and to spiritually move between the worlds. It is also a time to honor the crone within a wiccan coven.

Many cultures also see the Festival of Darkness as a time to guide the lost souls of the deceased to their final destination, or a time to help lost family members through their journey home. They do this by leaving a single candle burning in a window, with offerings such as apples, nuts, gourds, and mulled wines out on the porch for their arrival.

The Wenham coven had always been firm believers in tradition, and they always began their Samhain preparations weeks in advance. This year was no different.

On the morning of Friday, October twenty-ninth, life went along as usual. Alee and Phoebe went to school as usual and, not surprisingly, since it was the last school day before Halloween, they were greeted by the sight of students in every imaginable costume—from hippies and cheerleaders to horror film monsters and witches. The stereotypical witch costumes were not only ridiculous but they were also downright offensive. As they walked through the parking lot to the main campus Phoebe pointed out a group of students sitting at a nearby picnic table and whispered, "You'll be seeing a couple of them on Sunday night."

"Why?" Alee didn't know who they were, but she realized that they were among the few students who were not dressed up for Halloween. "Wait, you mean at the—?"

"Yup." Then she nodded toward another small group of senior girls gathered by the main entrance. "They'll be there too. Today will be a real treat for you. Like a peek behind a curtain."

"What do you mean?"

"Well, look around. What do you see?" They scanned the school lawn as students meandered through the parking lot, and stood around with friends, waiting for the first bell to ring. "Members of the Underground aren't going to trivialize the true meaning of Samhain by dressing in costumes. Samhain is a time to show respect for our ancestors, and to celebrate our culture."

Alee looked around at all the costumes, all the students, and wondered how she could have ever been so blind. "So, everyone not in costume—?"

"No, of course not, there will be some people who just decided not to dress up, for no other reason than they just didn't want to. But, today will give you a good idea of who here at Atlanta High are among the birthright members, and Sunday—. Well, let's just say after Sunday night you'll have no doubt as to who is and who isn't a member, at least those of age." Phoebe chuckled under her breath. "Come on let's get inside." She pulled Alee through the halls where it seemed like every guy in school was dressed in a gory mask of some sort, and trying to scare the girls.

They turned the corner to find Kyle leaning against Alee's locker, waiting patiently. He was dressed normally. *Thank God*, Alee thought to herself. She didn't want to have to defend him to Phoebe if he had done something stupid or offensive like dressing up like a—.

"WaaaHaaaHaaaHaaa—. I want—to suck—your blood!" It was a horrible Transylvanian accent, and the fake acrylic fangs he was wearing weren't even remotely believable. Alee was breathless, not knowing what to say or do, until Phoebe burst out in laughter.

"You're such an idiot." She was still laughing as she said the words and slapped Kyle on the arm. Then she turned to Alee, and whispered. "Hey, now you're a matching set. Maybe he'd like a sip of your coffee." She nodded down toward the large travel mug Alee was holding, then left them alone as she walked off toward her locker, still giggling to herself.

Kyle stood there smiling, proud of himself for his two-dollar costume.

"I can't believe you did that." She wanted to sound annoyed, but the smile gave her away.

"What? You can't say it isn't funny."

"It is, but—."

"But what?" He pulled her close and hugged her. "Come on—. I didn't mean to offend you. I'm only trying to have a little fun." He lifted her chin and kissed her softly on the nose. "OK?"

"OK." She was pouting, but only so he would kiss her again, and he did. This time with more passion, and only stopping when one of the teachers walked into the hallway and noticed their inappropriate public display of affection.

"Break it up you too, hands to yourselves. You know the school rules." She was dressed in a long black gown with a pointy black hat with little purple bats made of felt glued to the sides. Kyle quickly showed his fangs and hissed at her. "Don't make me force you apart young man." She was waving her fake wand at him, and smiling. Kyle did as she said, and moved away from Alee, but he didn't let go of her hand. The teacher nodded and headed off down the hall.

Alee just shook her head. "Wow—. I am a witch, and I wouldn't be caught dead in that outfit!" She and Kyle both started laughing, as he put his arm back around her waist and they headed off in the direction of Alee's first class.

The rest of the morning was pretty much pointless in terms of classes. There wasn't a single teacher who was under the delusion that any real schoolwork was going to get done, and after the lunch hour there was a schoolwide assembly in the gymnasium. The drama department put on a thirty minute Halloween-themed performance that was dismal at best, awards were given to the best, most creative, and most unique costumes. The cheerleaders led the crowd in the familiar school spirit activities, and the principal dismissed everyone from school an hour and a half early. That was the only time everyone in the building actually seemed to cheer at the same time, and in minutes the room was completely empty. That was, except for Alee and Kyle, who were still sitting together, cuddling, on the bleachers.

They sat there for a while, hand in hand, not even talking. The silence surrounded them and it was nice to just be alone without any fear or worry. Alee could feel her arm slowly start to warm up, and when she pulled up the sleeve of her shirt she noticed that her tattoo had begun to glow. When she looked around she didn't see anyone else in the room, and all the doors were shut. "Hey, watch this." She smiled as she nodded for Kyle to look at the basketballs lying on the floor not far from the net.

She stared for a while then raised her left hand and pointed to one of the balls. She moved her finger up and down, slowly at first, and then more rapidly as the ball started to bounce in place. Then with a flip of her wrist the ball flew higher into the air, and landed directly in the center of the net, and then fell back to the floor among the other balls.

Kyle's eyes were wide with amazement, and they laughed together again.. "I bet you can't do it again." He was egging her on and she kind of liked it.

"You're on!" This time it was easier—she bounced the ball a couple of times, then flicked her wrist toward the basket and the ball flew up and landed directly in the center of the hoop, and then fell back to the floor.

"If my hand wasn't broken I'd take you on. Even with all your witchy ways I still think I could beat you at a game of horse."

"Oh yeah, you think so?"

"Yes, yes I do."

As they were laughing, a sudden sharp pain shot through Kyle's temples. "Oh *God*." his hands flew up to the sides of his head.

"What's wrong?"

"It's just a headache. I keep getting this stupid pain, I don't know."

Just then, Jathan stepped out from the side of the bleachers, clapping in a slow one-man standing ovation kind of way. "Wow—great shot, very nice."

Both Alee and Kyle sat there in shock. "I don't know what you mean." The words just tumbled out of her mouth.

"Right—. OK." Then, turning to leave, he looked back over his shoulder. "Well, I guess I'll just see you Sunday night." Then he was gone.

"What does he mean Sunday night?" Kyle had no idea what he was talking about. "I thought you were doing some family holiday thing on Sunday?"

"We are." She stared off in the direction Jathan had gone. "I mean, I am." She had no idea how Jathan could have known about the Founders' Celebration—*unless?*

She was still not ready to tell Kyle about the Celebration. She didn't want him to get upset that she hadn't invited him. It wasn't that she didn't want to invite him, of course. It was the rule: her parents had been very clear about that. In all the years since Atlanta had been founded there had never been a human in attendance at an Underground event, and there was no way her family was going to allow Kyle to be the first, no matter how or why the goddesses had marked him. Nor did Alee want to put him in any kind of danger.

"What is it Aleerah? What aren't you telling me?"

"Sunday is the wiccan Festival of Darkness—" He just waited. "—and there's an annual festival or celebration type event that I have to go to with my parents."

"Like a party?" He was looking at her, almost jealous, or hurt.

She quickly tried to backtrack. "Yes, but no, it's not like that really. It's hosted by Atlanta's Founders. It's an Underground thing—trust me, I would have asked you to come, but it wouldn't be safe, or even allowed." She stopped him before he was able to object. "Only members of the Underground are allowed to attend, and even then only if they're invited. Most of my family isn't even going." She leaned in and kissed him on the cheek. "I honestly have no idea why Jathan would be going. You know as much about him as I do. As far as my grandmother knows, his kind is extinct. So there is no way he would have gotten an invite."

"Well, maybe since he didn't take you up on your dinner invite he figures he can crash the Halloween party."

"I didn't invite him to dinner. I already told you that. And it isn't a Halloween party."

"Yeah, OK."

Alee stood up, "Are you seriously upset about this?" Kyle just looked at her. "We should get going, who knows if Jathan in still around listening." She was hoping that would be the end of the conversation, and it was, for the five minutes it took to walk through the courtyard, and back through the hallways of the Classroom Building.

"How did you get invited?" Kyle just wasn't ready to let it go.

"Invited to what?"

"The celebration on Sunday. You said only members of the Underground were allowed to go. So, how did you get invited?"

"I don't know. I mean, you know my dad is a founding member, maybe he—." She had allowed herself to relax a little and was looking down at her feet as she walked, not really focusing on anything that was going on around her. "I think maybe it's because of the power share—." Kyle squeezed her hand, and she stopped talking as she looked up to see Damian and Victoria standing about thirty feet away. They quickly shut a locker door when they noticed Alee and Kyle approaching, then started walking in their direction.

The twins slowed down and nodded to Alee and Kyle as they passed, and Damian's hand slightly brushed against Alee's. "Have a happy Halloween—" He winked at Alee as he said it. "—in case I don't see you Sunday night."

Alee was a little taken aback. Turning to Kyle, she asked, "Did you see that? Did he just—?"

"What?" Kyle hadn't noticed.

"Oh. Nothing, sorry, it was nothing." There was no reason to upset Kyle any more—not after she had basically just told him that she was on her way to the party of the year, and that he wasn't allowed to attend. But, glancing over her shoulder as she opened her locker, she could see Damian still watching her, until he and Victoria turned the corner. Turning back to her locker it dawned on her that neither Damian nor Victoria had a locker anywhere near Alee's and Kyle's. Yet Alee had clearly seen them closing a locker when she and Kyle were walking up. "Kyle, could you tell what locker they were in?" The only explanation she could think of was that they had gotten into *her* locker somehow, but for what reason she didn't know.

"No, why? Wait, you don't think they would—?"

"Yeah I do." She quickly began searching her locker to see what might be missing or to find what they may have left behind, but there was nothing obvious, at least not until she opened her backpack to load up her books for the weekend. In her backpack was a book about dreams and their meanings that Alee recognized instantly: it was the one that

Victoria had purchased at The Black Onyx when she, Dani, and Alee had gone on their road trip so many months before. But why Victoria would hide it in Alee's locker now she had no idea, unless Victoria was trying to send her a message. When she opened the cover she saw the words, '*Beware of the Guardians*' scribbled on the first page. "Oh, God!"

They gathered their things and ran straight to the parking lot. Kyle drove her right home, and Alee took the book directly to her mother, who decided that the message was clearly a warning: '*We know who you are!*' But, Alee wasn't convinced. She felt that it was a little less specific than that, more like '*We know* what *you are.*' Who and what are two completely different things, and Alee was hoping she was right about this one.

22

While Alee was at school, Eric was at the Ward house. He had gotten there early and watched from a distance as Damian and Victoria left for school and then as their mother left for work. It didn't take him long to get in.

He started in Damian's room—not because he thought he would find anything, but because he wanted, no, *needed* to see that picture again. He had been certain that Damian's father had been the one who had attacked and, as Eric had believed, killed Loraline. But now something was eating at him. He couldn't get the thought out of his mind that maybe, just maybe, he had made a mistake. He ignored his instincts and pushed those thoughts away as he left Damian's room and made his way down the hall to Victoria's.

Victoria's room was your typical teenage girl's room. She had makeup scattered out across her dresser, a closet full of clothes, and a bed covered in throw pillows and stuffed animals. It almost seemed too normal—too girly for what Eric knew she was. His search was unsuccessful. There was nothing in either of their rooms. But the real purpose of his visit was the attic.

In the hallway he reached up and pulled at the rope hanging from the ceiling. The ladder came down without a sound and he quickly climbed up. It wasn't what he had expected. The whole space, already small, was crammed with boxes from wall to wall. He followed the thin trail through the boxes to a small clearing that Damian and Victoria had been using, and he sat down. He could still smell them there, and knew that they had just been there that morning.

"What were you looking at?" He asked aloud, to no one at all, as he scanned the boxes around him. Then he saw it, an old crate with a lock hanging open. The dust on top of the crate had been disturbed and there were slide marks on the floor from where they had moved it closer and then pushed it back into place time and time again.

When he pulled open the lid there was just a bunch of old newspaper clippings, but as he moved them out of the way he saw a stack of files. They were thick, and each had the name 'WARD' typed onto the tab. The front of each file had the Atlanta city seal on it, and Eric knew right away that they had been taken from the Records Department. He pulled out the files and scanned through them one at a time: marriage certificates, birth certificates, death certificates, and finally, at the end, a letter from the Founders, written to James Ward, expelling him from the Underground and informing him that collection of all Guardian Bands was mandatory. He continued the search of the files, knowing that what he should have found next was either a certificate indicating that his band had been properly destroyed or a sealed envelope with the Guardian band inside, but neither were there. There was however, a three by five notecard

indicating that the band had been retrieved, and, on the
bottom of the card was the Founders' seal.

"At least I know how they got it, but why?" He closed
up the crate, trying to make it look undisturbed then made his
way back downstairs. The only thing he took with him was
the letter from the Founders, the one expelling James from
the Underground. He stood in the hallway just below the attic
door and stared at the letter trying to decide what to do next.
He went back into Damian's room and placed the letter on the
pillows of his neatly made bed. "I hope you get the message,"
he whispered. Then he was down the stairs and out the front
door as if he had never been there.

The next day and a half were spent preparing for the Celebration on Sunday evening, and, although he wasn't able to attend the festivities, Kyle was there with Alee and her family the whole weekend, helping with the preparations. When Sunday night finally arrived, and Alee came out of her room all dressed and ready to go, Kyle and her father just stood there in awe of how beautiful she looked. Loraline had bought her a shimmering silver satin sheath of an evening gown that fit her perfectly, flowing to the ground and hugging her curves delicately as she glided through the doorway and into the hall, almost floating on air.

"Does it look all right?" Alee still wasn't used to getting the kind of attention that was inspired by her looks, even though Kyle had been looking at her that way for months now.

"No." She caught her breath when Kyle said it. "It looks so much better than all right." OK, he truly was amazing. "You are stunning."

"He's right you know." Eric wrapped his arms around Loraline when she came out from behind Alee and into the hallway.

When they finally said their goodbyes for the night, Kyle didn't want to let Alee go. He stood back with Phoebe and the others who wouldn't be attending the Celebration and watched as Loraline, Eric, Alee, Jacinda, Petra, Edith, and Estelle loaded into a long black limousine and drove off down the road.

"Why aren't you going?" Kyle was looking down at Phoebe as she stood there with wishful eyes.

She just shrugged her shoulders. "Can't. No one under seventeen is allowed. Besides even after you turn seventeen it's rare to be invited. You have to have some special power or something—. Who knows! I'm sure it's stupid anyway." It was obvious that she was a little jealous or maybe bitter, but she tried to hide it as she turned away and walked back toward the shop entrance.

Kyle followed quickly behind. "Hey Phoebe, wait up." She turned back to see him only a few steps behind. "What kind of special power does Petra have?"

"What doesn't she have?!" Phoebe just rolled her eyes. "Sorry. It's just that I so hate being compared to her. Petra came into her powers early, she mastered them quickly, and now to top it all off, she's a tracker, and a warrior."

"I'm sorry, a what?" Kyle looked a little shocked. "What is a tracker, and what do you mean by warrior? Like a fighter or something?"

"Exactly, Petra's talent or power is tracking. It just comes natural to her. But even beyond that she's an amazing fighter. That's why she's always running around here in all black, and looking like G.I. Jane gone Goth. She patrols down in the Underground, and when someone is down there who isn't supposed to be, she is one of the members who tracks them down and, well, eliminates them."

Kyle was a little taken aback by this new information, and he couldn't really picture little Petra eliminating anyone, but he didn't question it either. "So, what if you *could* go, to the Celebration I mean. Would you want to?" He was whispering, and no one else seemed to notice as they passed by, making their way back inside.

"It's not allowed."

"Yeah, I know, but what if no one else would know?"

She grabbed his hand and pulled him through the shop and down into the lower level library. Peeking in, she could see that no one was inside so she quickly shut the door behind them. "What's your plan?"

Meanwhile, Alee and Petra sat, silently staring out the window, as Edith, Estelle, Jacinda and Loraline whispered together.

"Is this your first time?" Alee finally asked Petra, who just nodded and turned back toward the window. "OK," Alee pursued it. "I like your dress." She smiled, trying to break the tension.

Petra was wearing a white lace ritual gown that she had worn numerous times before, and it was completely unlike her usual tough sexy girl attire. "Thanks." Then glancing back at Alee she added, "I really like yours too." Petra wasn't really very good at small talk. She was much better when she had a purpose other than just random chit chat. "My mom said I wasn't allowed to get a new dress tonight." She sneered in her mother's direction. "She said traditional is better. Humph."

The rest of the ride was spent in silence. As they drove up to the courthouse in the center of downtown Atlanta, Alee saw cars lining both sides of the road. On street after street, people her age and others well into their seventies and eighties were making their way up the courthouse steps They were dressed in everything from tuxedos and evening gowns to more traditional suits with capes, and dresses with lace-up corsets.

The driver took them down into an underground parking structure that Alee hadn't even known existed. When the car finally came to a stop and the door opened she was helped out by her father on one side, and her mother on the other. They walked down a red carpet in the center of the parking structure toward a private elevator. The attendant took Eric's coat and the ladies' wraps before guiding them into the elevator and selecting a floor that appeared to be two floors—down.

As she stood in the elevator surrounded by her family, Alee began to feel a little nervous. "Everything's going to be just fine." Eric had his hand on her shoulder, and was leaning in close to her ear.

"But what about—." Alee couldn't help but think about the Guardian bands that Damian and Victoria had gotten their hands on. She still didn't know what they were planning, and Eric had been extremely vague about what he had found during his search.

"Don't worry about the shifters. Even if they wanted to get in, there would be no way." Eric kissed her gently on the forehead and then led Loraline, with Alee following behind, off the elevator into the entryway of the Grand Ballroom.

To call it a Grand Ballroom didn't even do it justice. As they stepped off the elevator onto the elaborate tile floor the room opened up in front of them. Directly in front of the elevator entrance was a beautiful marble fountain adorned with gold inlay and a statue of the three wiccan goddesses:

the maiden, the mother, and the crone. Looking up, Alee
noticed that the cathedral ceiling was at least two stories high,
with large crystal chandeliers hanging throughout the room.
Large round tables were decorated with black tablecloths,
silver napkins, tall candelabras and rose petals scattered
about.

Alee noticed that there were only two entrances: the
elevator they had come in on, and the other at the far end of
the room directly off to the side of the head table. The two
walls off to the left and right had what appeared to be
archways that most likely had, at one time, held doorways.
However, now they were sealed off, floor to ceiling, with
bricks. It didn't look natural, but it didn't look bad either.

People had already started to find their seats, and
small groups were clustered throughout the room, catching up
with people they hadn't seen in a while. At the head table
Alee noticed that there were place settings for twenty people,
but so far there were only six people gathered there. She
couldn't see their faces because they were huddled talking
quietly among themselves. "Who sits up there?"

Loraline was glad to be there for Alee's first
experience at the Celebration. "That's where the founding
members sit." With that, Eric leaned in and kissed his wife
goodbye and left to take his own place at the head table.
"Your father and the other six you see there are the last
surviving founding members."

"Then who else sits up there?"

"No one. The remaining place settings are for the
members they have lost over the years. It's a way to honor
and remember them by welcoming their spirits here with us."
OK, that's a little creepy. Loraline just laughed, "Don't
worry, chances are you won't see any ghosts tonight."

"Chances are? What, is it like a fifty-fifty chance?"

"No dear, there won't be any other-than-corporeal-beings here tonight."

"Great," Alee replied, looking suspiciously around the room, "so nothing without a body. That *so* doesn't put my mind at ease."

"Come on, let's find our seats."

Petra and the others had already taken their seats at a large round table near the middle of the ballroom. Alee and Loraline hurried to join them and quickly sat down as the lights started to dim. Alee noticed that except for the head table, every table was full. There had to be at least two hundred people there, if not more. She searched the faces nearest her, trying to see if she recognized anyone, but it wasn't bright enough to see. When a spotlight on the head table came on, everyone's attention went immediately to Eric who stood before them.

"We are here tonight to celebrate one hundred and thirty years together." The room exploded with thunderous applause. "It doesn't seem so long ago that I was sitting here with so many more of my close, dear friends—" He indicated the empty seats around him. "—celebrating our very first anniversary, and now to be here before so many new young faces it excites me to know that Atlanta is flourishing and growing still today." Again the crowd showed their approval—their excitement—by cheering out loud. "With that said, I welcome you to the annual Atlanta Founders' Celebration. Tonight is a time to celebrate those we have lost, and welcome those newly awakened members of our society." Maybe it was just Alee's imagination, but she could have sworn that he had looked at her and smiled when he said it.

Eric took his seat as waiters and waitresses, dressed in traditional black suits with white shirts, scurried through the room refilling wine glasses, and setting out the first course for the guests. As the staff was completing this task and leaving the room a tall slender man at the head table stood up. Even without a microphone he could easily be heard throughout room. First he turned to Eric, "Thank you Ermanes, my brother, my son."

"Ermanes" Alee whispered looking at Loraline.

"Your father's birth name."

"My father?" Then she remembered hearing Damian talk about Ermanes son of Chalkeus. "Oh my God, it's him."

"Who's him dear?"

"Eric—Dad—I heard Damian talking. He was looking for an 'Ermanes.' What if—?"

"Nothing is going to happen." Loraline cut her off, but even she didn't sound like she was sure of what she was saying. She turned back to the head table and tried, unsuccessfully to get her husband's attention.

The speaker turned back to address the rest of the room. "He is a great man among us. As he was lost to us for so many years, we now welcome him back into the fold with open arms and rejoice this night, not only for our successes, but also for the return of one of our own. Sisters and brothers, I stand before you in awe of what we, together, have created."

Leaning over to Petra, Alee whispered in her ear. "Oh my God, that's Principal Greg." Petra just nodded. "Is he a—?"

"Yes, he's a vampire. He's one of the oldest, even older than your father," Petra whispered back, confirming Alee's suspicions.

"Wow." Alee sat there feeling uneasy, staring up at him as he spoke.

"Atlanta is thriving, and it is because of each and every one of you. Tonight, celebrate! Celebrate everything we have accomplished together—celebrate the lives we have built here, and the strength we have created within our community." Then, lifting his glass up high he toasted each and every one of them. "A toast to the night walkers among us, a toast to our wiccan sisters, a toast to our fairy friends, a toast to the dream walkers if there be any, a toast to the sirens, a toast to the arachnes, and of course a toast to the reapers we hope never to face—" Jacinda and Loraline exchanged looks of concern and trepidation. "—to those among us, and to those we have lost." Then, as he and everyone else in the room were about to tip their glasses back, both the elevator door and the door behind the head table opened simultaneously. In flooded a mass of men, women, and beasts. It would be simple to have called them animals, but these lions, panthers, wolves, and even bears were not mere animals. The rage and hunger in their eyes was more pronounced than any animals in the wild. These beasts were there with a purpose, and they meant nothing but harm. They scattered throughout the room like wild fire before anyone had a chance to react.

Among the humans Alee immediately recognized Ms. Thatcher, the older woman who worked in the school office, Nurse Johnson who had worked at the high school the previous school year and Karen, Damian's mother. It was Karen who led the pack. She stepped up onto the head table as a large lion threw its weight straight into Principal Greg's chest, forcing him to the floor. "A toast to those you have lost? What about those you have banished—those you have murdered for no other reason than your pleasure? You may have thought you tamed those of us who still remained, but we are not your pets any longer. The Guardians have returned and we plan to reclaim our rightful place among you, even if that means with your blood on our hands." Principal Greg had regained his footing and, fangs exposed, was ready to attack, when she leapt into the air toward the tables, instantly transforming into a fierce mountain lion, and attacked the first person she could sink her teeth into. She tore into the flesh of a young girl, and the screams of others throughout the room echoed through the air.

Eric started around the table headed toward his family in the center of the room, but he was blocked by a large white wolf with razor-sharp teeth. The wolf snarled, and slowly backed Eric into the corner, step by step. Eric showed his fangs, and hissed back at the wolf trying to scare it away, but it had no effect. *'I'm not afraid of you.'*

Eric could hear the voice in his head, but didn't put two and two together, that it was the wolf communicating with him, until—. *'You killed my father! Now I will kill you, or die trying.'* Damian's heart was racing with fear and excitement. He could see into the eyes of this man—this vampire—this demon—and he knew that twelve years of waiting had prepared him for this day. He was no longer afraid to confront his father's killer—he knew in his heart that he was ready.

"Damian, you don't want to do that." Eric knew what this boy meant to his daughter, and although his instincts told him to rip him to shreds for the filthy lycanthrope he was, he knew better. "This will not end well for you—."

'It will not end well for you!' Damian leapt into the air, and landed with his front paws square on Eric's chest, and his teeth mere inches from Eric's throat. But Eric was too strong for him, and it was only a matter of seconds before Damian was on the floor, struggling against Eric's grip. A quick bite to Damian's throat, a small amount of venom from Eric's fangs, and Damian was useless against him. The venom would only last a short while, but it should give Eric

the time he needed to get to Loraline's table and get his family to safety before he had to worry about a second attack.

Eric quickly moved through the room, taking down at least five other lycanthropes on his way to his family's table. In the huge ballroom, there wasn't a single person not fighting, screaming, or running in fear.

Breathless, Alee looked around for help. Petra, who had been sitting next to her, was now up and fighting. Alee watched in awe as Petra moved with such grace and ease. She took down attacker after attacker, without even breaking a sweat. Finally, when there was a brief pause in the action, Alee grabbed Petra's arm and, not really knowing where they should go, she turned to pull her toward one of the far walls. And somehow, there beside her was her mother, Loraline, calm as always, and commanding. "Aleerah, Petra, come with me!" Everyone was scrambling to find an exit, but both exits were blocked by guards more vicious than she had ever seen. Loraline led the girls toward the side wall, where Alee could see that Edith and Estelle were already gathered, along with a few others.

They were almost there, and suddenly Jathan was also there, standing next to Edith. His hand was high on the wall, and the brick began to shimmer as they approached it. Suddenly, the entire wall started to fade away, almost as if it had been an illusion, and was replaced with—nothing. Alee, Petra, and Loraline were almost to the opening when Petra was grabbed and dragged away by a large black bear. The bear was just too big, and much stronger than Petra. Jacinda screamed and ran toward her daughter, but as she launched her attack on the bear, she was attacked herself. Karen bit into the calf of her leg, ripping the muscle out, and sending her to the floor screaming in pain. Tears streaming down her face,

Loraline forced Alee forward toward the now-nonexistent wall.

"Alllleeeeraaaahhhhh!" The scream came from somewhere far behind her, but she knew exactly who it was. She turned and saw Kyle on the other side of the room, dressed like one of the waiters, trying to get to her through the crowd. Alee pushed away from her mother to run to him.

"Aleerah, NO!" Loraline and Jathan yelled it at the same time.

Loraline tried pulling her back, but couldn't keep a hold on her arm. Eric had caught up to them and was standing directly behind Loraline forcing her toward the portal that Jathan had created. She was fighting him with all she had, and just before she slipped out of his grasp Alee turned back, threw her arm up, and with a force she couldn't explain, sent a wave of energy toward her mother that pushed her, tumbling, through the opening.

Then, turning back toward Kyle, her natural instincts kicked in and she fought her way through the crowd. A large white wolf sprang up from behind a table and tackled Kyle to the ground. She could see the pain in his eyes as he fell to the floor.

As utter fear and rage swept over her she stopped and screamed across the room. "RELEASE HIM!" Her voice echoed above all others in the room, the lights flashed, and in that instant her blonde hair was a blazing auburn red, her sun-kissed skin faded to pale porcelain, and her eyes were as black and hollow as a black hole.

The wolf froze, and stared at her with smoky grey eyes, and, in an instant a transformed Damian stood naked, just a few yards away from Alee, covered in Kyle's blood. "Alee?" Tears poured out of his eyes as he looked down at Kyle's lifeless body and then back at Alee, realizing what he had just done. He ran to her, leaping from table to table, reaching out with both hands. "NOOOOOO—!" His scream was cut short as Alee was hit from behind and thrown to the floor. She could feel the flesh of her back being ripped from her body. In the distance she could hear the cries and screams of so many other victims being brutally torn apart.

Lying there on the floor, in a pool of her own blood mixing with the blood of so many others, she watched the scurrying feet of terrified victims and vicious prey. The pain started to subside and she felt lightheaded as she drifted in and out of awareness. Then the screams faded and her heart calmed, and there was nothing but black.

The End for Now

Keep reading for an exciting preview of

The final installment of
the Blood Angel Series
by Nina Soden

http://www.ninasoden.wordpress.com
http://www.facebook.com/BloodAngelSeries
http://www.twitter.com/Nina_Soden

1

The lights dimly flickered in the abandoned ballroom. No movement could be seen. No breath could be heard. And everywhere you looked, bodies lay piled about in pools of blood, amidst broken glass and tables, and fallen chandeliers. There was no way to know which side had lost more lives that night. One thing was clear, though: great tragedy had been suffered by all.

The founders had had reason to suspect an intrusion at this year's annual Celebration, and had taken great care in planning the event, to ensure the safety of everyone in attendance. Checks and double checks had been put in place to prevent the entry of anyone without the official invitation. Twice the usual number of guards had been stationed inside and outside the ballroom. But it was all for naught. The lycanthropes' swift and vicious attack had not been avoided.

As soon as the first drop of blood was spilt, Gregory Davis, the principal of Atlanta High and the oldest vampire still residing in Atlanta, had activated a silent alarm beneath the founders' table, alerting the security office three stories up, and protocol had been followed. Their orders were to evacuate as many members and founders as possible. If evacuation was impossible, containment was the only option. They were to block the two exits immediately and ignite an explosion in the elevator shaft that would eliminate the risk of the threat expanding into the city.

Years ago, for security purposes, the six underground tunnel routes that led to the ballroom had been bricked up and sealed. Few people outside of the founding members even knew they had existed at all. As far as most members knew, the only ways in, or out, were the elevator shaft entrance and the back stairwell behind the founders' table.

Knowing what security procedures were going to be taken, Eric's focus had gone straight to getting his family out at any cost necessary. He knew that the primary exits would be sealed within minutes, but was confident that if he could get them to one of the bricked up underground tunnels he, with the help of others, should be able to break through, and get them out. He hadn't expected to be the direct target of any of the attackers, but Damian had zeroed in on him in seconds, before he could take a single step away from the founders' table toward his family across the room. *'I'm not afraid of you.'* The great wolf form snarled, baring enormous teeth, and growled, but Eric could hear its human voice clearly in his head, almost as if he was thinking the words himself. *'You killed my father! Now I will kill you, or die trying.'* Damian now knew who and what Eric was, and was fully prepared to fight to the death.

The great wolf leapt into the air, and landed with its front paws square on Eric's chest, its teeth only inches from Eric's throat. Eric was too strong for it though, and in mere moments it was on the floor struggling against Eric's grip. Eric gave the creature's throat a quick bite, releasing a small amount of venom from his fangs, and it, Damian, was powerless against him—at least for the short time it would take Eric to get his family to safety.

Eric ignored the chaos before him, looking only for Loraline. He wasn't going to lose her again. Not after just getting her back. He was relieved that when he did spot her she was already nearing the tunnel entrance that they had previously agreed upon as their escape route in the case of just such a catastrophe.

Loraline had Alee and Petra in tow, and Edith, Estelle, and a few others were already gathered at the wall with a young slender boy with dark hair. Eric didn't recognize the boy, but didn't take time to puzzle over it.

However, even over the sounds of screaming and fighting, Eric was able to zero in on Edith's voice as she spoke to the young man, "Your name?"

"Jathan ma'am."

Edith stepped back an arm's length. She wasn't scared. Concerned? Maybe a little. "You're not a dream walker!"

It wasn't a question, but he answered anyway. "No ma'am. I'm not even sure what that is."

Eric would have heard more, but a deafening scream—"Alllleeeeraaaahhhhh!"—from somewhere on the other side of the room interrupted his concentration. He heard it clearly and knew that it was Kyle. Eric had just started moving toward Loraline, and he saw Alee turn and pull away from her mother, and run in Kyle's direction. Why Kyle was there was a mystery to Eric, but as he searched the far end of the room he saw that Kyle was dressed like one of the waiters and was trying to push himself through the crowd. *Typical stubborn boy,* Eric thought to himself.

"Aleerah, NO!" Loraline had lost her hold on Alee's hand, and was grasping at the air trying to catch her, to pull her back before she was lost in the crowd. Eric was already behind Loraline, forcing her toward the wall where the rest of the family stood waiting as a portal was opening under Jathan's hand, which he held high against the brick wall.

A foggy mist billowed around Jathan as Edith glared at him. "You have to tell her. She deserves to know."

"I—."

"You don't know how much time you have left. Tell her, before it's too late."

Loraline was struggling against Eric's grasp, intent upon saving her daughter, but as she twisted and slipped free, Alee turned back, threw her arm up, and with a force that neither Eric nor Loraline would later be able to explain, she sent a wave of energy toward her mother that pushed her, tumbling, across the room and through the black hole that Jathan had created. Satisfied that her mother was safe, Alee re-focused on getting across the battlefield to Kyle, with Eric in quick pursuit. Eric didn't have time to worry about where the black hole would take his family. He just took comfort in knowing they wouldn't be here for the massacre that had already begun.

Eric lost sight of Alee in the pandemonium around him. Only about forty lycanthropes had attacked, but they had the element of surprise on their side, and, with about three-fourths of the guests in attendance being witches, fairies, and other such beings, there were a lot of easy targets. A few witches were casting basic defensive spells, but no one had brought any tools that could have helped with that. Only a few of the fairies engaged in the fights, but those who did tore into their attackers with such fierce hunger it was like watching a starving dog attack a steak. When you live with constant suppression of so much of yourself, it's hard to control your natural instincts when you finally do let go.

The vampires were clearly fighting back. Fear and panic suffused their victims' last breaths, but there was nothing more fearsome than Alee's scream, echoing above all others in the room. "RELEASE HIM!" The lights flashed, the ground shook, and in that instant her blonde hair was a blazing auburn red, her sun-kissed skin faded to pale porcelain, and her eyes were as black and hollow as the black hole into which her family had just disappeared.

Everyone in the room froze in shock—fear—and awe. She was more beautiful than any angel in heaven, and more malicious, at that moment, than any demon in hell. She leapt across the remaining distance of chaos, and was face to face with a huge white wolf with smoky grey eyes. Its muscles were taut beneath its thick fur and its lips pulled back to reveal enormous teeth. It growled a warning.

Eric heard whispers spread through the crowd as people began to recognize who had issued the screaming command and now stood facing the wolf. Rumors had spread throughout the Underground of a dhampir returning to Atlanta, but no one had really believed it. Even those who had seen her glowing tattoo only weeks before weren't truly convinced. Now they all knew that the rumors were true, and, if the legends passed down from generation to generation about the powers a dhampir can hold were also true they all had reason to fear.

A subtle shift in the wolf's posture revealed his recognition as well. Only he didn't know her as the mysterious dhampir. He knew her as Alee, his first and only love, even if she didn't know this herself. Recognition brought instant transformation, and the human Damian stood naked and vulnerable, just a few yards away from Alee, covered in Kyle's blood.

"Alee?" Tears poured down his cheeks as he looked down at Kyle's lifeless body and then back at Alee, realizing what had happened—what he had just done. The pause in the fighting was only momentary, but to Eric the room seemed to be moving in slow motion as fights resumed all around him. His focus was on Alee, and he raced to her, leaping on and over tables, debris, and bodies, aware of no one else. As he closed the distance, he reached out to her with both hands.

"NOOOOOO!" Eric heard Damian's scream, but it was too late. Alee had been hit from behind and thrown to the floor by a huge brown wolf with deep chocolate eyes.

The attack was swift and ferocious, and the wolf disappeared into the crowd. Damian carefully scooped Alee up into his arms and held her close in anguish. "What have I done?"

Eric was fast approaching, and Damian knew that if he was still there when Eric got to him, he too would be lying dead on the floor. Reluctantly he lay Alee down, wrapped himself in a bloodstained tablecloth, and dodged his way past continuing battles and bodies in search of an exit.

Eric ignored Damian's retreat as he finally reached Alee's side. The skin and muscle of her back had been ripped off, down to the bone, and she was drowning in a pool of blood. He pulled her into his lap and held her to his chest, weeping at the loss of his child. The screams and growls and crashing sounds around him slowly faded away and eventually, not knowing how much time had passed, he realized he was alone—alone with his dead daughter and so many other brutally mutilated victims.

Eric remained there with his daughter in the deepening silence, unable to leave her there in that bricked up

tomb with death surrounding her. He knew the emergency
plan, having masterminded it himself, but there was no room
in his mind or his heart to consider the fact that by now he
himself might have no escape route.

The longer he sat, empty and aching, the more he
became vaguely aware that he wasn't alone. It wasn't the
rapid sound of a human heart that tipped him off. In fact he
didn't hear a heartbeat at all. It wasn't the sweet scent of fresh
blood that triggered his senses. As he turned toward the wall,
he could smell nothing but the warm blood, already starting
to congeal, that covered the floor all around him. What he
sensed was a sudden chill, as if a cool breeze had just drifted
through the room—as if death itself were watching over him.

A dimly flickering chandelier on the far end of the
room slowly swayed from side to side. Through a thickening
fog, Eric caught glimpses of the tall, slender, dark-haired boy
standing with his back against the wall, almost completely
hidden from sight. Eric had never met Jathan, but he
recognized him at once. He lay Alee on the ground and with
lightning-fast speed he was face to face, and toe to toe with
the boy.

"Did you do this?" His voice was a deep guttural
growl and there was no question as to the insinuation in his
words.

"No. I came only to help—to try and stop it. I'm
sorry. I failed." With that, he put his palm against the brick,
ignoring Eric's exposed fangs and flaming eyes, and
proceeded to open another portal. Eric could see the genuine
pain in Jathan's eyes and, going against his true nature, he
didn't push the boy for more.

"What is that?" he asked, gesturing toward the portal.

Reaching toward Eric with an open hand, the boy
replied simply, "It's your way home."

Eric looked back around the darkened ballroom with disbelief and sorrow. "I can't leave her."

"Neither could—." Jathan shook his head. "Neither can I, but we must."

Hesitantly, Eric took Jathan's hand and stepped through the portal with him. Vampires have a heightened sense of sight. Like cats, their night vision is just as good as their daylight vision. However, stepping into that portal was like nothing Eric had ever experienced—darkness so black he couldn't even see his own hand two inches in front of his face. It didn't last long. In seconds they were stepping through to the other side.

As his eyes adjusted he looked around, realizing he was standing in the kitchen at The Black Onyx. It truly had been his way home. Jathan, however, was gone.

Loraline sat at the table, her head in her hands. When she saw Eric step through, she rushed to his side, throwing herself into his arms and wrapping her arms around his neck. He felt solid under her fragile hands and yet she knew before he spoke that something wasn't right.

He drew back, and their eyes met—and she realized what that uneasy feeling was. Alee wasn't with him. Not only was she not there, but Loraline knew, with all her heart, that her little girl hadn't made it out alive.

Eric silently shook his head, confirming her fears. Loraline crumbled to her knees still holding onto him as she wept.

Much later, exhausted, her eyes red and swollen, she let Eric help her slowly to her feet. They gazed at one another in misery. "We will get through this," Eric said, with more conviction than he felt.

His own eyes were burning red from tears that he was incapable of shedding, but his voice was steady and she could feel his strength. It wasn't a mind trick. He never used those on Loraline—a promise he had made her long ago—but just then he wished he could. He wished he could make her forget—make the pain go away. It would be so easy, and she wouldn't have to suffer any longer, but he knew it wasn't right. He knew that she would never forgive him and he couldn't stand to lose her too.

"How did—?"

"No." He cut her off. He knew she couldn't handle knowing what had happened. He himself could barely stand to think about his little girl lying there in a pool of her own blood—limp, lifeless, and alone, surrounded by so much death and destruction.

She didn't push him. Maybe deep down she knew she didn't want the answer, or maybe deep down she felt she already knew the answer. Either way, she dropped it, for now at least.

Eric suddenly realized that the kitchen was empty, when normally it would be bustling with life. "Where is everyone?"

She didn't answer. So much had happened, so much sadness. She just dropped her eyes to the ground in silence.

"Loraline, what happened?"

When the words finally came out they were abrasive and raw. "Granny Estelle." The tears started again. "She didn't make it—." Then, as if a plug had been released, everything came flooding out of her. "My sis—sister, she's dead, and Petra, I couldn't—I couldn't save her. Then, when you didn't come through, I thought I had lost you too—. Phoebe and Kyle are gone, and we can't find them anywhere—and Granny Edith—she isn't doing well. My whole family is falling apart. They're dying all around me and I can't stop it."

Everything was happening so quickly, and he was trying to catch up. He already knew about Kyle, and with the loss of so many others he thought it best not to bring him up just yet. He knew he would have to deal with Kyle's family eventually, but right now he wanted to focus on his own. "One at a time—what do you mean Granny Edith isn't doing well?"

"The boy—Jathan—he opened a portal to bring us back here. Granny insisted on being the last one through. She said it was her job to protect us. As she was coming through—she was attacked." She was staring across the room as if she were watching it happen all over again. "I saw her, she almost made it, and then she was thrown to the ground. I grabbed her arms and Tom and I were able to pull her the rest of the way through, but not without injuries."

"Take me to her."

She took a deep breath, and led him out of the kitchen and down the hall to the study. "Mom is with her now. I don't know how much longer she has."

Entering the study, he realized that everyone who was left in their family had gathered here together as if it were the only safe place in the world. Maybe it was. Everyone turned to Eric and Loraline with hopeful eyes—as if maybe he would be able to save Edith. He could have, if she would only let him, but she was old and stubborn and he wasn't going to force her if she didn't want his help.

She was losing blood at an alarming rate, and was dropping in and out of consciousness. "Edith, can you hear me?" She didn't respond. Knowing that the only way to help her would be for her to drink some of his blood, he quickly sliced a small cut across his wrist. As the first drop of blood touched her lips, she slapped his arm away.

"Edith, your family needs you and, therefore, you need me." The blood of a vampire has enormous healing powers, and if she allowed him to help her she would recover within days. Without his blood, however, she would probably be dead within hours.

Edith coughed up blood as she tried to speak. "If it's my time to die then it's my time." Then, looking deep into his eyes, she pulled Eric close. "You're a vampire. I accept that. Loraline loves you, and I accept that too. I'm sorry it has taken me so long to see you as the man you are. A good man. A strong man. And I see the love you have for my granddaughter. Thank you, for wanting—." She coughed again, and this time it shook her whole body. "Thank you, for wanting to save me, but it has to be this way. I'm old, and I'm allowed to be set in my ways."

Eric smiled, although her heartfelt admission was not lost on him. "Yes, I suppose you are."

"You can't help me now." She looked out through tear-filled eyes as her family gathered more closely around her. "You help them, and let me go home to my husband—to the one who loves me as much as you love Loraline. That is what you can do for me." He wanted to respect her wishes, and he did, but it wasn't easy. It wasn't only about not wanting to disappoint his wife or the rest of her family—he wasn't ready to let her go either. He wasn't ready to lose yet another important person in his life.

"No! Granny, you can't just give up!" Loraline was kneeling at her side. "You can't let her give up. You have to do something."

Eric just pulled Loraline into his lap and held her like a child. "I can't make that decision for her. I'm so sorry, sweetheart." He kissed her forehead and held her as she cried.

"No," Loraline cried, "she can't die. Not yet, not after we've lost so many." Neither Eric nor anyone else had an answer to that. Eric just continued to hold her. Nearby, Elizabeth and William were comforting their son-in-law, Tom, Jacinda's husband.

A little while later, Eric noticed that the grief in that room seemed to be materializing into a thickening fog. He gently removed himself from his wife's embrace and went to inspect the fog. He went toward the far wall of the study that seemed to be its source. From close up he could see that the fog was coming through the brick wall, and increasing in density at an alarming rate.

Then, in the center of the fog, a large black hole formed and Jathan stepped through, holding Phoebe in his arms. "She's not hurt, only sleeping," he quickly announced as everyone who could jumped to their feet and hurried to him.

Tom carefully lifted his daughter out of Jathan's arms, thanking him over and over again for bringing her home. Then, without warning, Jathan stepped back into the fog and disappeared back into the black hole.

After the commotion of Jathan's short visit was over, the family's attention went back to Edith, who was holding a shaking hand out to Loraline.

"What is it Granny? What?"

She whispered so softly that Loraline had to lean down, with her ear just above Edith's lips. "She will return, but do not underestimate the devastation that will follow in her wake." Then, she closed her eyes and took her last breath. No one knew what to do or say. Bewildered, they all sat there in silence not wanting, or willing, to accept that she was really gone.

want to read more?

~ book 3 ~
the Blood Angel Series
by Nina Soden

Available on Amazon.com September 2014

Want your copy autographed? Order directly from the
Author at http://ninasoden.wordpress.com

Made in the USA
Charleston, SC
20 February 2016